Willa Anderson (1890–1970) studied classics at the University of St Andrews where she took a first class honours degree in 1910. She studied Educational Psychology and moved to London to become a lecturer and Vice-Principal of Gipsy Hill Training College for teachers. She met Edwin Muir during a visit to Glasgow in September 1918 and they were married within a year. Working as a costing clerk for a Renfew shipbuilding firm at the time, Muir was making a reputation by writing criticism for *The New Age*, but was deeply unhappy with his life and the Glasgow environment. Spurred by his wife's confidence (he later said that meeting her was 'the most fortunate event in my life'), Muir moved south in 1919 to begin his career as a full-time writer, and later, again with Willa's unfailing encouragement, as a poet. The couple travelled about Europe in the early twenties, living in Prague, Germany, Italy, and Austria. They collaborated in the translation of modern writers, most notably plays and novels by Lion Feuchtwanger, Kafka's *The Castle*, and Hermann Broch's *Sleepwalkers* trilogy.

Willa Muir's only two novels were *Imagined Corners* (1931) followed by *Mrs Ritchie* in 1933. *Mrs Grundy in Scotland* (1936) is a cultural essay, while *Living with Ballads* (1965) offers an extended study of oral poetry from children's singing games to the great Scottish ballads. *Belonging* (1968) is a memoir of her years with Edwin Muir from their first encounter until his death in 1959.

Willa Muir

IMAGINED CORNERS

Introduced by J. B. Pick

CANONGATE
CLASSICS
I

First published in 1935 by Martin Secker
First published as a Canongate Classic in 1987
by Canongate Publishing Limited
17 Jeffrey Street
Edinburgh EH1 1DR

British Library Cataloguing in Publication Data
Muir, Willa
Imagined corners.—(Canongate classics).
I. Title
823'.912 F   PR6025.U633

ISBN 0-86241-140-8

The publishers gratefully acknowledge
general subsidy from the Scottish Arts Council
towards the Canongate Classics series
and a specific grant towards the
publication of this title.

Set in 10 pt Plantin
by Alan Sutton Publishing Ltd, Gloucester
Cover printed by Wood Westworth, St Helens
Printed and bound in Great Britain
by Cox and Wyman Ltd, Reading

Contents

Introduction

If I were to say that Willa Muir's *Imagined Corners* deals with the confining moral conventions of a small town in Scotland you might well expect another *House with the Green Shutters*. But nothing could be farther from the truth. *The House with the Green Shutters* was written in bitter reaction to the sentimentality of the kailyard school, and its attitude is blacker than that of the blackest Calvinist. The effect of this extravagance is to turn the book into melodrama with a plot as unreal as that of *The Lilac Sunbonnet*. There is neither melodrama nor sentimentality in Willa Muir. Indeed, the particular value of *Imagined Corners* is the mature balance she achieves between light and dark.

She was a woman who combined intellectual clarity with emotional vigour to a formidable degree. A friend of the Muirs confessed, 'I was fond of Edwin, but Willa frightened me a bit,' adding, 'though when she got older she was very warm and grandmotherly.' Other witnesses describe her variously as gay, caustic, brave, forthright, intellectual and 'fun to be with'. The quality of her mind is quickly shown in this fresh, sprightly account of Edwin written for their American publisher (quoted by P.H. Butter in *Edwin Muir: Man and Poet*):

> Has an enormous forehead, like a sperm whale's: a fastidious, fleering and critical nose: an impish and sensuous mouth, a detached, aloof, cold eye. Witty when at his ease: elegant when he can afford it: sensitive and considerate: horribly shy and silent before strangers, and positively scared by social functions. Among friends, however, becomes completely daft, and dances Scottish reels with fervour.

That is the work of a natural writer with a feeling for

words, an ear for rhythm and a keen eye for character –
someone, in fact, to whom the novel form would be entirely
congenial.

Wilhemina Anderson's family came from Unst in Shetland, but Willa was born (in 1890) and brought up in
Montrose. She went to St Andrews on a bursary, gained a
First in Classics, but refused a job offered on the strength of
it because she did not want to be parted from a favourite
rugby footballer. She soon lost interest in the rugby footballer, and when she met Edwin Muir – then a tormented,
Nietzschean young writer from Orkney living in Glasgow –
she was vice-principal of a London teachers' training college.
She lost her job because of her marriage (in 1919) and
devoted herself to restoring Edwin's balance and encour-
aging him to write. She worked only to keep the wolf from
the door – running courses for shop workers, teaching in
schools, and so on. The wolf never left the neighbourhood
for long, and when they left the neighbourhood themselves it
followed them about. Willa and Edwin travelled, in fact, all
over Europe, and together translated more than forty books,
the majority from the German. Willa, the better linguist, did
the bulk of the work. They were most settled and happy
while Edwin worked for the British Council in Edinburgh
during the Second World War and in Rome after it, and later
when he acted as Warden of Newbattle Abbey, a college of
adult education in the Borders.

Willa's own two essays in fiction were written not to make
a name for herself but to buy bread and butter, and it was
because they did not buy enough that she abandoned the
novel. Yet *Imagined Corners* has a psychological percep-
tiveness, a philosophical realism and a sharp, affectionate
detachment which seem to me a major contribution to that
tradition of wisdom which has been so unaccountably
ignored in Scottish fiction.

Willa was over forty when she wrote the novel (published
in 1931), and that may explain its remarkable assurance.
Soon after it was issued she wrote to Neil Gunn:

> One thing I have learned from publishing a novel is that
> reviewers are apparently mostly half-wits, stupid both
> in praising and blaming . . . nobody, for instance, has

seen that the dreams I give my characters are meant to be at least as important as their waking actions: that William Murray is another version of Elizabeth in different circumstances: that opinions put into the mouths of my characters are not necessarily mine: and that I was trying to illumine life, not to reform it; to follow my own light, not deliberately to explore blind-alleys in Scotland; although, being Scottish, my approach to any universal problem is bound to be by way of Scottish characters . . .

She says, too, in *Belonging*, her memoir of life with Edwin, 'we females were strong natural forces deserving a free status of our own as free citizens.' Accordingly, *Imagined Corners* asks the question: How can a sensitive and intelligent woman avoid being crushed or stultified by the narrow conventions of a small Scottish town?

Willa knows well enough that conventions are necessary and laws inevitable; what concerns her is their effect upon those in the community with the greatest potential for creative feeling. She herself explained in *Belonging* that the origin of the book was to imagine what might have happened had she married her rugby footballer and settled in Montrose. The story of Hector and Elizabeth is her answer, although Elizabeth Shand is by no means Willa Muir.

Each character in *Imagined Corners* needs freedom to follow personal insights and to test their validity; if they refuse these insights they refuse life itself. The book is a plea for integrity of spirit in the face of moral blindness. William Murray cannot help his demented brother Ned because he cannot gain his own balance; he hides in hell-fire dogmatism. Hector, the clan warrior lost in modern life, hides in drink. John Shand, the romantic, hides in business respectability. The only two characters in a rich complexity of intertwining relationships who prove capable of facing life honestly are Lizzie and Elizabeth Shand. When the unconventional Lizzie returns to Scotland each comes to recognize the value of her opposite. As Lizzie says, 'You and I . . . would make one damned fine woman between us.' The understanding they reach is an understanding between sceptical intellect and mystical intuition. Whereas Lizzie believes that people can never really help one another, only themselves, Elizabeth replies that, on the contrary, people are necessarily part of one another, 'only separate like waves rising out of the sea'. There is a sense in which both propositions are true.

Throughout the book Willa's feminism is confident without being aggressive. There is always a healthy clarity about her view of things: 'The sexual instinct has such complicated emotional effects on men and women that its masquerade as a simple appetite ought not to be condoned.'

It might be held that the message of *Imagined Corners* is simple – the one way to deal with Scotland is to leave it. But what the story of Elizabeth and Lizzie seems to me to tell us is more universal: that the way to deal with life is to take risks, go deep, make your own discoveries and live by them. This may not be the last word in philosophy, but it is the view of a strong, intelligent woman. And there is much more in the novel than any message which can be derived from it. There is acute and painful observation of the ways in which men and women limit themselves and defend themselves from one another.

The book has a certain technical panache, and a high degree of calculation. There are deliberate shifts in character between the first part and the second, prompting a question whether such changes can be credible. For me, at least, the answer is yes. In all of us there are potentialities which different circumstances and relationships may bring out. A novelist's job is to make circumstances and relationships authentic.

Willa wrote in *Belonging* that there was 'sufficient material in *Imagined Corners* for two novels', which she was 'too amateurish to realise at the time'. She certainly gave herself problems in running simultaneously the stories of five sets of characters, but she seems to relish the challenge and due balance is kept without violence being done to a realistic view of people. If the book lacks tension it is because Willa is too detached to 'let herself go'. This is at once a virtue and a limitation. On the whole Edwin's words – written about Neil Gunn's *The Serpent* – apply equally well to *Imagined Corners*: 'The effect of imaginative maturity is to make you feel that everything you are shown is in its proper place and on its true scale.'

We may regret that Willa did not write more – only the sociological *Mrs Grundy in Scotland*, the grim and powerful *Mrs Ritchie*, and after Edwin's death *Belonging*, *Living with Ballads*, and a slim book of genuinely amateurish poems. But Willa herself regretted nothing. She concluded *Belonging* with an expression of faith:

> That was the end of our Story. It was not the end of the Fable, which never stops, so it was not the end of Edwin's poetry, or of my belief in true love.

It was not the end of Willa's novels, either. *Imagined Corners* is the work of a mind of high quality which is at home in the world. And that is rare.

J.B. Pick

Calderwick 1912

I

That obliquity of the earth with reference to the sun which makes twilight linger both at dawn and dusk in northern latitudes prolongs summer and winter with the same uncertainty in a dawdling autumn and a tardy spring. Indeed, the arguable uncertainty of the sun's gradual approach and withdrawal in these regions may have first sharpened the discrimination of the natives to that acuteness for which they are renowned, so that it would be a keen-minded Scot who could, without fear of contradiction, say to his fellows: 'the day has now fully dawned,' or 'the summer has now definitely departed.' Early one September there was a day in Calderwick on which the hardiest Scot would not have ventured so positive a statement, for it could still have passed for what the inhabitants of Calderwick take to be summer. Over the links and sandy dunes stretching between the town and the sea larks were rising from every tussock of grass, twitching up into the air as if depending from invisible strings, followed more slowly by the heavy, oily fragrance of gorse blossom and the occasional sharpness of thyme bruised by a golfer's heel. The warmth of the sea-water was well over sixty degrees and the half-dozen bathing coaches had not yet been drawn creaking into retirement by a municipal cart-horse.

All this late summer peace and fragrance belonged to the municipality. The burgh of Calderwick owned its golf and its bathing, its sand and its gorse. The larks nested in municipal grass, the crows waddled on municipal turf. But few of the citizens of Calderwick followed their example. The season for summer visitors was over, although summer still lingered, and the burgh of Calderwick was busy about its jute mills, its grain mills, its shipping, schools, shops, offices and dwelling-houses. The larks, the crows and the gulls, after all, were not ratepayers. It is doubtful whether they even knew that they were domiciled in Scotland.

The town of Calderwick turned its back on the sea and the links, clinging, with that instinct for the highest which distinguishes so many ancient burghs, to a ridge well above sea-level along the back of which the High Street lay like a spine, with ribs running down on either side. It was not a large enough town to have trams, and at this time, the Motor Age being comparatively infantile, there was not even a bus connecting it with outlying villages: but the main railway line from Edinburgh to Aberdeen ran through it, and it had an extra branch line of its own. In short, Calderwick was an important, self-respecting trading community, with a fair harbour and fertile agricultural land behind it.

On this clear, sunny day in early September – a good day on which to become acquainted with Calderwick – a bride and a bridegroom were due to arrive in the town, the bridgroom a native, born and brought up in Calderwick, the bride a stranger. Human life is so intricate in its relationships that newcomers, whether native or not, cannot be dropped into a town like glass balls into plain water; there are too many elements already suspended in the liquid, and new-comers are at least partly soluble. What they may precipitate remains to be seen.

II

Of the various people who were to be affected by the precipitation, Sarah Murray was one of the most uncon-scious. She had her own problems, but these did not include any reference to the newly married couple. At half-past six she was still asleep, but the alarm clock beside her bed was set for a quarter to seven.

She woke up five minutes before the alarm clock was due to go off, and stretched out her hand to put on the silencer, as she did every morning. By a quarter past seven she was on her way downstairs to the kitchen, stepping softly to avoid disturbing the minister, whose door she had to pass. If a celestial journalist, notebook in hand, had asked her what kind of a woman she was she would have replied, with some surprise, that she was a minister's sister. Throughout the week she was mistress of his house, and on Sundays, sitting in the manse pew, she was haunted by a sense of being mistress of the House of God as well.

She found Teenie, the maid, watching a tiny kettle set on the newly lit kitchen range.

'Put that damper in a bit, Teenie,' she said, 'you'll have us burnt out of coal.'

Teenie turned round and burst into tears.

'I canna thole it, Miss Murray,' she sobbed, smudging her face with a black-leaded hand. 'I'll have to give notice. Tramp, tramp, tramp half the night, up and down, up and down, and him roaring and speaking to himself; I havena sleepit a wink. I canna thole it.'

Sarah lit the gas-ring and transferred the kettle to it.

'You're needing a cup of tea, and so am I. Whisht now, Teenie; whisht, lassie. You must have slept a wee bit, for he was quiet by half-past three.'

'It's no' just the sleeping, Miss Murray, it's the feel of it. I canna thole it any longer; I just canna thole it.'

Teenie's voice wavered and the sobs rose again in her throat. Her eyes had deep black rings under them.

'The kettle's boiling. Get down the cups, Teenie.'

Sarah's voice was firm. They sat down on either side of the table and drank the tea in silence. Together they lifted their cups and set them down, and whether it was the sympathy arising from common action that brought Teenie more into line with her mistress, or whether the strong warm tea comforted her, she was much calmer when the teapot was empty.

'Don't give me notice this morning, Teenie,' said Sarah abruptly. 'It's not easy, I know, but if we can hold out a bit longer. . . . And I don't want a strange lassie in the house while he's like that. He knows you, Teenie, and you get on well enough with him, don't you?'

'Oh ay,' said Teenie. 'When he's himsel'. But whenever it begins to grow dark, Miss Murray, I canna explain it, but it just comes over me, and I'm feared to go upstairs when he's in his room. And his feet go ding-ding-dinging right through me. And it's the whole night through, every night the same, and I canna sleep a wink, not even after he's quiet.'

'You'll go to your bed this very afternoon. . . . I'll see to that. . . . I'll get the minister to take him out. And, shall we say, try it for another week and see what you think? I don't want to lose you, Teenie, after two years.'

Teenie flushed.

'I ken you have it worse than me. But I canna thole it for much longer.'

'Another week?'

'We'll try it,' said Teenie, getting up.

'We'll try it,' echoed in Sarah's mind. She had never yet admitted that there was anything she could not stand up to; she believed that persistent attention, hard work and method could disentangle the most complicated problem, and she despised people who did not apply themselves. Her brother the minister, the Reverend William, she could not despise, for he was unremitting in his duty, although his duty seemed to her at times a queerly unpractical business. Still, all men were queer and unaccountable. But even the worst and wildest of them were not so unaccountable as her younger brother Ned, whose conduct was driving Teenie into hysterics and forcing Sarah herself to realize that human energy is not inexhaustible. She was tired, her head ached, and the mere thought of Ned exasperated her. Besides the way he carried on during the day he was wasting the gas every night in a sinful manner, and even after he was in bed she could not go to sleep until she had peeped through the crack of his door to see that the gas was turned off. William's salary could not stand it. It was all so unreasonable. What made him do it? What on earth made him do it?

But from this question, against which she had battered herself in vain for months, her mind now turned resolutely away. If there was any meaning at all in life Ned was bound to come to his senses again. Of course.

'We'll give it another week, then, Teenie. Mr Ned's bound to get better. I must say I don't see how he could get any worse.'

Sarah smiled wryly, and even the effort of smiling strengthened her returning faith in the reasonableness of life.

She gave herself a shake and set about the business of the day.

On the first floor the Reverend William Murray, awakening slowly as he always did, was also strengthened by faith, but not by faith in the reasonableness of life. His faith grew out of the peace which surrounded him in that half-suspended state between sleeping and waking wherein his spirit lingered every morning, freed from the blankness of sleep and not yet limited by the checks and obstacles of perception. His eyes were shut, and his vision was not prejudiced by the straight lines of roof and walls; his ears were shut, and in their convulsions there reverberated only the vibrations of that remote sea on which he had been cradled, unstirred by desire or regret, at one with his God. Slowly, almost reluctantly, his spirit returned to inform his body, ebbing and shrinking into the confines of consciousness. He lay still, scarcely breathing, trying to prolong the transitory sense of communion with the infinite; but his awareness spread out in concentric rings around him, and he knew himself as William Murray, lying in bed in the manse of St James's United Free Church, Calderwick. Even then he did not open his eyes. His thoughts would presently follow him and rise into their place, the first thoughts of the morning which were sent to him as a guidance for the day.

During the past fortnight his first thoughts had been more and more conditioned by the existence of his brother Ned, and on this morning too it was with an indefinite but pervading sense of reference to Ned that the thought came to him: yonder there is no forgiveness, for there is no sin. It was an immediate crystallization of experience, and he felt its truth. In that other world forgiveness was superfluous, for there was no sin. There was neither good nor evil. . . . That startled his newly awakened consciousness. He opened his eyes and got up.

The thought persisted, however, as he shaved. No sin; that was the state he was striving to attain, a life wholly within the peace of God. But neither good nor evil? That meant the suspension of all judgment as well as of all passion. Yet he was uplifted by the mere idea that the peace of God was neither good nor evil. . . . To know all is to forgive all, someone had said. He stared at his own reflection in the

mirror. How much better simply to accept without forgiveness! Could he meet Ned on that plane perhaps he could
cure the boy's sick spirit. . . .

'Ned's still asleep,' said Sarah, as she poured out tea, this
time China tea from the silver teapot. 'I'm going to leave him
till he wakens. It was half-past three when he put out the gas.'

William said nothing. He looked so absent and so pleased
that Sarah could not resist giving him a tug.

'Teenie's threatened to go, William, if this lasts much
longer. It's got on her nerves.'

'Teenie? Oh, surely not. Tell her to keep her heart up; I
don't think it'll last much longer. I think . . . '

He paused. It was difficult to explain to Sarah.

'I have an idea,' he went on, 'but I haven't quite thought it
out. Still, I believe . . .'

Sarah felt so irritated by the way his spoon was wandering
round and round in his teacup that she knew her nerves were
sorely stretched as well as Teenie's.

'William, it mustn't go on!' she said. 'In the first place,
we'll be ruined. What with the gas, and a fire on all day in his
room – we can't do it much longer. If he doesn't come to his
senses soon we'll have to – to send him away.'

Her words were indefinite, but as she and William looked
at each other neither doubted what was meant. William
stopped stirring his tea. With unexpected force he said in a
loud tone: 'No! That would be inhuman. That would be
unchristian. What can you be thinking of, Sarah?'

Sarah covered her eyes with her hands.

'I'm so tired! You don't hear him at night, but he's just
over my head, and the tramping up and down, up and down'
(unconsciously she echoed Teenie's words) 'drives through
and through me.'

William rose from the table to bend awkwardly over her.

'My poor Sarah, my poor lassie. Of course you're tired. but
bear up just a little longer; we'll do it yet. He's our own
brother; he's bound to be all right.'

God never forsakes his people, he was thinking to himself.

Sarah dropped a tear on his hand and looked up.

'Could you take him for a walk this afternoon? I've
promised Teenie an afternoon in bed, and I think I could do

with a rest myself.'

'I'll take him out this afternoon,' William's voice was confident. 'It's only Friday, I can finish my sermon to-morrow. But can't you take a rest now?'

'No; I have to get flannelette and stuff for the Ladies' Work Party, from Mary Watson's.'

Teenie could give Ned his breakfast when he came down, she was thinking. He was nicer to Teenie than to his own sister. . . .

Before letting herself out Sarah mentally rehearsed her various errands and the number of yards of flannelette she needed. She never simply went out on impulse, nor did she expect to be surprised by anything in the streets. She could have predicted what was to be seen at any hour of the day. It was now ten o'clock, and as if noting the answer to a sum she observed that the baker's van was precisely at the head of the street and that the buckets of house-refuse were still waiting by twos and threes at the kerb for the dust-cart. She would have been disturbed had things been otherwise. It was a satisfaction to her that everything had its time and place; that streets were paved and gardens contained within iron railings, that children were in school, infants in their peram-bulators, and hundreds of shopkeepers waiting behind clean counters for the thousands of housewives who like herself were shopping. The orderly life of Calderwick was keeping pace with the ordered march of the sun. She could hear the prolonged whistle of the express from King's Cross as it pulled out of the station. Punctual to the minute.

III

At about the same time, in the same town of Calderwick, and only round the corner from the manse, young Mrs John Shand was buttoning her gloves and tilting her head to study, in the long mirror, the hang of her new coat. It had a perfect line, she decided; most women, of course, wouldn't have the shoulders for it. Whatever Hector's wife had on, bride or no bride, she would be put in the shade by such elegance.

Mabel Shand smiled to her own reflection, an approving smile. Her teeth were strong, white and even; her skin was naturally fresh and finely textured. She bent her knee slightly and admired the fall of her garments; most women's thighs were too short, but she had a long and graceful curve from the hip to the knee. She felt that she was marked out for superiority, unlike the majority of the Calderwick women, botched and clumsy creatures who should be thankful for anything they could get.

Her gloves were buttoned. While she was still at school she had read in a magazine that no lady ever left the buttoning of her gloves to be done on the stairs or in the hall or, horror of horrors, outside the front door. Mabel had never forgotten that, and in her marriage she had her reward. From a farm in the village of Invercalder she had, two years ago, hooked the biggest fish in the town of Calderwick, John Shand, the head of an old-established firm of grain merchants and flour millers.

Sarah Murray, too, had been born in Invercalder, where her father was the village schoolmaster, and like Mabel had been promoted to Calderwick, so that, geographically at least, their worlds were the same. But either because the grey stone schoolhouse stood bleakly on a hill at the west end of the village and the farm lay snug in a hollow at the east end, or because a schoolmaster's time-table is ruled by will while a farmer's is governed by capricious seasons, life in the schoolhouse was hard, angular and rigid, whereas in the farm it was kindly and easy-going. Mabel accordingly was left to form herself, but Sarah was rigorously formed by her father, and the process had been so thorough that she had no inkling of it. From the kindling of the first fire in the morning to the blotting out of the last light before going to bed she found the whole justification of life in the fulfilment of daily routine. That routine Mabel Shand ignored, in so far as a Calderwick woman could ignore it. In the same way she ignored the orderly activities of the municipality; it gave her no thrill of satisfaction to know that her bread was regularly delivered and her dustbins emptied daily. Sarah, if she had pictured a web of the world, might have regarded herself as one of many flies caught in it by God, her sole consolation being the presence of the other flies and the impartial symmetry of the web, but Mabel lived at the heart of her own spider's web, and every thread from the outside world led directly to herself.

Mrs John Shand came down the steps of number seven Balfour Terrace just as Sarah Murray rounded the corner. She might as well walk up with Sarah, she thought. Poor old thing, what a frump!

Sarah paused and looked round. 'Are you going up my way, Mabel, to the High Street?'

'Yes; to the new house, you know. Hector and his wife are coming home this morning.'

'Oh, I'd forgotten they were coming to-day. They've been up Deeside, haven't they? I've never seen Mrs Hector; what's she like?'

Mabel nearly shrugged her shoulders.

'You'll see her in church on Sunday, I suppose. She's considered clever.'

You won't like that, thought Sarah, but checked the thought immediately. Even though she had known Mabel from childhood she tried to be charitable towards the wife of her brother's leading elder.

Mabel's face twinkled for a moment as she recalled the first occasion on which she had seen the present Mrs Hector Shand. Hector had whirled her up to the University to meet the girl, and Elizabeth had turned up for tea in a cheap, striped cotton frock and sand-shoes. Sand-shoes!

'That's a nice coat, Mabel.' Sarah was trying to atone for her uncharitable thoughts. 'New, isn't it?'

'First time on to-day. Latest fashion, my dear. John likes it immensely.'

'No doubt.'

In spite of herself Sarah's tone was blighting. It was long since she had had a new coat, and what with one thing and another, Ned's gas and coal and keep, it would be a long time before she got one.

She always dries up when I mention John, said Mabel to herself. And John would never have looked at her in any case.

'How's Ned?' she asked.

'Not any better, I'm afraid.' Sarah's voice lost its edge. 'Mabel, I simply don't know what to do. What *can* we do?'

Mabel felt a vague discomfort.

'Ned's always very nice to *me* whenever I see him.' It sounded almost like self-defence.

'That's just it,' burst out Sarah. 'He's nice to everybody except to me and William. It doesn't matter what we do. Yesterday it was a newspaper he said I'd deliberately hidden from him because there was a job in it he meant to apply for. He said I was always interfering with his happiness. It's so unjust, Mabel; it's so unreasonable: the more I think of it the more desperate I feel. I've tried everything; I've coaxed him and scolded him and ignored him, and he just gets worse and worse. I told William this morning that if—'

She stopped herself. When Ned came again to his senses it would never do for Mabel to be in a position to tell him that Sarah had even thought of sending him away.

'You've known Ned all his life,' she went on. 'Was he ever like this when he was going to school?'

'He was always shy.' Mabel's discomfort was increasing. 'It wasn't easy to know what he was thinking.'

'But you used to bicycle in to school with him every day, Mabel. Surely you would have noticed if there was anything? I've racked my brains and racked my brains and I can't think of an explanation. He was so brilliant at school and at the University, and he was always as quiet as a mouse when he came home. Even when he had that breakdown in his finals he wasn't like this.'

Mable's uneasiness was now tinged with excitement. It seemed natural to her that she should be the centre of the world to others as well as to herself, and she had always suspected that what had unsettled Ned in the beginning was her marriage to John Shand. It wasn't her fault, was it? She had flirted a little with the boy, but then she had flirted with so many boys. A kiss or two meant nothing when one was sixteen. It wasn't her fault. But it must have left an impression on Ned. She could wager that no other girl had ever kissed him. Half rueful and half pleased she glanced sideways at Sarah. Of course Sarah wouldn't understand.

'He'll get over it,' she announced confidently. Then on a sudden impulse she added: 'I'll help him to get over it if you like. Let him come out to golf with me this afternoon.'

Sarah's excessive surprise and gratitude might have betrayed her to a less indifferent observer.

'Oh, that's nothing,' said Mabel. 'Tell him to come round for me at two o'clock.'

Sarah hesitated.

'It's so good of you that I don't like to suggest – but do you think you could possibly come round for him? It's so difficult to get him to do anything.'

Mabel raised her eyebrows. However, the occasion was an extraordinary one.

'Very well,' she said.

Even though her relief was tempered by self-reproach Sarah turned down the High Street with a lighter heart after parting from Mabel. She felt confusedly that William's Christian charity towards all the world was on a higher level than her own suspicious judgments, but she found it difficult to believe in Divine grace without concrete instances. This morning, however, she had had a lesson. Let that be a lesson to you, she told herself sharply, emerging from her depression into the imperative mood which she mistook for God.

That was a common mistake in and around Calderwick, and Sarah's father, who had passed it on to her, was not its originator. Even her brother William could not eliminate the imperative mood from his speculations, although his use of it was quite opposed to Sarah's. 'God's in His heaven, therefore all must be well with the world,' was his version, while Sarah's, as she made her way towards Mary Watson's shop, could have been expressed as: 'All's well with the world – or nearly so – therefore God must be in His heaven.'

Mary Watson's shop was another stronghold of the imperative mood. Miss Watson felt it her duty to see that all was well with the world around her, in case God should be jeopardized in His heaven by aberrant humanity. Her father had been an elder in St James's United Free Church, and although she had inherited his business as a draper she had not been allowed to inherit his eldership, which was perhaps the reason why her moral vigilance, unremitting in general, was especially relentless towards the minister and elders of that church. It was the boast of the town that Mary Watson had driven three ministers away from St James's in as many years. Even William Murray's mildness had not disarmed the doughty woman; she dubbed him 'Milk-and-water Willie,' and told him to his face that he would never win grown folk from their sins.

Usually, on entering Mary's shop in the High Street, Sarah felt that she had interrupted a tirade against her brother. The over-loud tones of a customer saying hastily, 'Aweel, I'll just take these, Miss Watson,' never failed to make her bristle. On this occasion, however, she found the shop empty, and, still remembering her lesson, even smiled pleasantly in Mary's face, saying: 'Lovely weather for September, isn't it?'

'No' sae bad,' admitted Mary, 'But a'thing's very dry.'

Things were not drier than her tone. Her attitude said plainly: 'I don't take it as a favour that you come into my shop: it's only your duty to support a member of your own congregation.'

As the bales of material were unrolled with a thump and measured off on a yardstick Mary's tongue was as active as her hands.

'I suppose you've heard that the Town Council has granted a licence to the braw new Golf Club? That's a fine state o' things, Miss Murray. There's mair pubs than kirks in the town already. I hope the minister is to do something about it? The Town Council should be weel rappit ower the knuckles.'

Sarah was well aware that Mary regarded the minister as incapable of rapping anyone over the knuckles. His failure to rap the Town Council would only become another grievance.

'You should stand for the Town Council and do it yourself, Miss Watson.' This was a hastily improvised defence, but its effect was unexpected. Mary bridled.

'Me, Miss Murray! What would put that into your head now?'

'I'm sure the minister would agree with me.'

'Aweel, I'm no' saying. If you and he think it's my *duty*—'

Mary's face was impassive again.

'Of course it's your duty.'

'Ay, now, I never thought o' that.'

Mary slowly folded up the stuff and made it into a neat parcel.

'I'll see what my sister says till't.'

Then, as if conscious of weakness, she added in her sharpest voice:

'And you might tell the minister that he hasna darkened our door for mair than twa months. My sister's a poor bedridden woman, and even if he wasna the minister it wad only be decent of him to give her a look-in in the by-going.'

IV

Number twenty-six High Street, which was being prepared for its new master and mistress, was approved by Mabel. Like every house in the old High Street, of course, it had to be entered from a 'close', but once the narrow close entrance was left behind a fair-sized paved courtyard opened out, framed by two respectable Georgian houses, pillared and porticoed, with clipped box-trees set in green tubs before the doors. Dr Scrymgeour's name shone resplendently on one door, and on the other a smaller and more modest brass plate read 'H. Shand'. Mabel's eye fell on that as usual with a slight sense of shock; she could never think of Hector as H. Shand, a householder. She became very much Mrs John Shand as she looked at it; she stiffened a little and examined the big brass bell-knob on its square plate and the whitened doorstep. Both were speckless. That maid wasn't going to be so bad.

The said maid was breathless when she opened the door, and her eyes were shining.

'Miss Shand's here,' she said. 'An' everything's like a new pin.'

'You must never answer the door in a kitchen apron. You must always change into a clean one to open the door, Mary Ann!'

'But that would keep folk waiting.'

'Better to let them wait. Better still to keep a clean apron under the dirty one, and then all you have to do is to slip it off. Try to remember that.'

Mrs John Shand sailed into the hall.

'Are you there, Aunt Janet?' she called in a clear voice.

'Here, my dear,' came the answer in a deeper more muffled tone. 'Up here in their bedroom.'

Mabel mounted the stairs, still armoured in dignity. It was her sole defence against the thought of her husband's young half-brother, who annoyed her by making her feel like a schoolgirl. He was the only young man who had ever kissed her with indifference. But she was Mrs John Shand now.

Aunt Janet appeared in the doorway.

'How are you, my dear?' She pecked Mabel's cheek and went on without a pause: 'I think everything's all right now; the sheets are airing and the kitchen's in apple-pie order.'

'I had to check Mary Ann for coming to the door in a dirty apron,' said Mrs John Shand. 'Do you think she'll be all right?'

'Oh, she's strong and willing, and, you know, my dear, we can give Elizabeth a few hints, perhaps, now and then, you know.'

Between them there vibrated a mutual though unspoken opinion that Elizabeth would need those hints.

Aunt Janet drew Mabel into the bedroom and lowered her voice.

'It's a good thing I came up here. Do you know, that girl had set out the chambers *under the beds*.'

Mabel could not resist the reflection that Hector had survived more shameless facts than unconcealed chamber-pots. Nor was Elizabeth likely to be a stickler for propriety.

The flicker of mirth in her face did not escape Aunt Janet, who became almost voluminous as she enfolded young Mrs John in benevolence.

'I know you'll do your very best for Elizabeth, my dear. She hasn't as much social experience as you, but she's a dear girl – a dear girl. And she's so clever you know; she has done very well at the University.'

'Clever she must be,' admitted Mabel, trying to shake off her aunt-in-law, 'or she would never have got Hector to marry her. She's the only woman who has ever managed that.'

If there was any personal feeling in these words Aunt Janet did not notice it; she observed only an aspersion on her beloved nephew.

'Hector may be thoughtless, but he's not so bad as you and John think. I assure you he's not. And he's so conscious of

Elizabeth's goodness in marrying him. "She'll keep me straight, Aunt Janet," he said. "I promise you I'll go straight." Poor boy, he has so much against him.'

She absentmindedly patted the eiderdown on the nearest of the twin beds.

'Oh, Elizabeth will keep him in order,' said Mabel, walking to the window and staring out of the garden. Aunt Janet was too irritating.

'A dear girl. A dear girl.' Aunt Janet furtively wiped her eyes. 'I'm sure they'll be happy.'

In the kitchen Mary Ann was singing to herself. 'Isn't it fine,' she was thinking, 'a bride comin' hame to her ain hoose? My certy! they'll be here in half-an-'oor. Where's that clean apron?'

William Murray stood looking out of the window, his hands clasped behind his back, while Sarah piled the dirty dinner-dishes on a tray. Now that Ned was actually out of the house she felt exhausted; the exertion of lifting the tray was almost too much for her. She would be thankful when she got into bed. So precisely regulated was her scheme of life, however, that she thought it rather a disgraceful weakness to lie down during the day, and for the same reason it did not occur to her that William, being stronger and less tired, might carry the tray into the kitchen.

Nor did it occur to William. He had not quite escaped the influence of his father, who had ruled his house, as he had ruled his school, on the assumption that the female sex was devised by God for the lower grades of work and knowledge, and that it was beneath the dignity of a man to stoop to female tasks. But although this assumption lay at the back of William's mind it appeared so natural that he had never recognized it; if Sarah had asked him to carry the tray he would have taken it willingly; the assumption merely hindered him from thinking of such an action. So he gazed out of the window, meditating on his sermon and on Ned.

'Judge not, and ye shall not be judged: condemn not, and ye shall not be condemned: forgive, and ye shall be forgiven.' That was his text. The thought which had arisen in his mind that morning had given it a new aspect; he was looking at it from a longer perspective. Instead of being an absolute virtue forgiveness was merely a second-best, a concession to ordinary flesh and blood which was too imperfect to enter at once into the full peace of God. That blessed state, he thought, could not be conveyed in words alone to those who had never experienced it; but perhaps it could be transmitted by contagion. . . . It was a state of fearless trust in the love of God, a fearless acceptance of the universe, acceptance without criticism, without fear of criticism, without self-consciousness. But most of us, he thought, live on the defensive; we live as if under a jealous and critical eye. 'Thou God seest me.' For such timid creatures the leap into the infinite space of God's love is too great; small fears must first be cast out, small encouragements given. That was the purport of his text: to cast out people's fear of each other, as a step on the way to boundless trust in God.

Ned was clearly an extreme instance of human mistrust. He filled the world with the shapes of his fear. Every act, every word, every inflection of other people's voices he construed as hostile; kind words appeared as hypocrisy, kindly services as specious intrigue. His fears were so monstrous that mere persuasion could not dispel them; he must be cured by the greater force, the more absolute revelation. The text was not enough for Ned.

'Did you notice,' said Sarah, 'how Ned flared up at me when I told him Mabel wanted him to golf with her? And the things he said about her! But when she came he went off as meekly as a lamb. . . . I don't understand it. It seems as if we brought out the very worst in him.'

Ned's tirade was still rankling in Sarah's heart.

'You think I don't see through you!' he had shouted when she mentioned the proposed golf match. 'Low, sneaking cunning,' he had reiterated. Women were snakes in the grass. All alike. Not one better than another. . . . On the whole, it was a comfort to Sarah that he had abused Mabel too. But when Mabel appeared, gay and pretty, asking him if he cared to golf, he had become even excessively complaisant. It tortured Sarah to think that Mabel could succeed where she had failed.

'No, no,' said William, turning round. 'We don't bring out the worst in him. He fears us less than other people, that's all. Other people impose a constraint on him. Don't let such ideas discourage you. Go to bed now and sleep a little.'

'What are you going to do?' Sarah still lingered as if there were something left unsaid. She did not herself know what it was.

'I shall visit Ann Watson,' said the minister. 'Go to bed now.'

Reluctantly Sarah withdrew, reminding herself again that she ought to feel grateful to Mabel.

William walked slowly by unfrequented by-roads towards the house where Ann Watson lay in bed. The sand-scoured, windswept little streets were filled with clear light; everything was sharply focussed as if seen through a reducing lens; above the plain grey-stone houses the sky was pale and remote. Clear and thin and sharp as the air were the voices of the passers-by, for the Calderwick dialect is born in the teeth of an east wind that keeps mouths from opening wide enough to give resonance to speech. The shrill almost falsetto tones pierced the minister's meditations; he ceased to think about the peace of God, and remembered the querulous voice of Ann Watson. In spite of himself, his heart sank a little at the thought of the close-lipped, tight-fisted old woman. He turned a corner into a cobbled lane, at the end of which the Watsons' house stood at right angles to the others, enclosed by a fence and presenting a blank wall to the street. Here Ann and Mary Watson had been born, and here they would die. Here as children they had played among the cobbles, like the children playing there that day. The minister paused to watch half-a-dozen little girls who were rushing, with screams of simulated terror, towards another girl standing by herself in the middle of the lane.

'Mither! Mither!' they shrieked. 'I'm feared!'

'Tits!' said the 'mother', 'it's just yer faither's breeks. Away ye go!'

Back they all rushed pell-mell to the Watsons' gateway.

'What are you playing at?' inquired William, laughing.

The girls crowded together shyly and looked at him.

'Bogey in the press,' one of them suddenly spoke up.

'And is this the press?' he pointed to the gate.

They nodded, giggling.

'Oh, well,' said William, 'I don't mind the bogey. I'm going right into the press; look at this.'

He opened the gate and went into the garden, followed by an outburst of disconcerting childish laughter.

My bogey is just as much of a fabrication as theirs, thought William, walking along the narrow paved path to the front door. Why did children like to frighten themselves?

He lifted the big knocker and rapped it firmly before he noticed that the door was ajar. A shrill scream sounded within the house, and he took it as a command to come in. He pushed the door open and saw across the kitchen another open door leading into Ann's bedroom. She was half sitting up in bed, so that she had a clear view of the kitchen.

'Oh, it's you, minister! Come away in. Have you seen that lassie o' mine?'

The minister looked round the kitchen as if the lassie might be hiding somewhere.

'She's awa' oot half-an-hour syne to go to the baker's; set her up with her gallivanting,' said Ann, still stretching her neck towards the kitchen. 'I'll give her a flea in her lug – Oh, there you are, you good-for-nothing jaud!'

A sulky-looking girl bounced in past the minister, and set two loaves of bread on the dresser.

'Dinna leave the bread there!' screamed Ann. 'Put it in the bread crock. And see that you put the lid on right.'

The minister advanced and sat down on a horse-hair chair beside the bed.

'You wouldna believe it,' went on Ann in the same high scream, 'what I have to suffer. Folk just take a pleasure in spiting me. I canna trust that lassie to do a thing right.'

A loud rattling from the kitchen fireplace answered her.

'What are you doing there?' cried Ann.

The minister got up and shut the bedroom door.

'I don't like to see you worried, Miss Watson,' he said. 'Never mind the lassie. It's you I've come to see.'

'It's all very well to say never mind the lassie,' grumbled Ann; 'if I didna keep an eye on her she would have everything going to rack and ruin. And she puts things where I canna bear them to be, just to spite me. And my sister Mary's every bit as bad. You wouldna believe it, but yestreen she changed every stick o' furniture in the kitchen, till I was nearly blue in the face. I kept that kitchen for years,

and I kept father's auld chair in its right place beside the
dresser, but last night nothing wad please her but to have it
out at the cheek o' the fire for her to sit in. I tell you, I've
made Teenie put it back beside the dresser, and there it'll
bide. We'll see what my lady has to say till't when she comes
hame.'

'But if Miss Mary wants to sit in it—'

'She'll no' sit in it! Na, she'll no' sit in it! The shop's hers,
but the house is mine, and I'll no' put up with interference.
Day in, day out, I've had to mind the house while she was
fleein' all over the town enjoying herself; she needna think
she's to have everything her own way here as well as outside. I
may be bedridden, but I'm no' done for yet.'

Ann nodded her head vehemently, and drew down her
upper lip. She had forgotten the minister and was carrying
on an inaudible quarrel with an invisible opponent. William
Murray found himself looking at her as if for the first time.
Her long, hard face must have been handsome once. And
once she must have been a little girl playing outside on the
cobbles. He felt a sudden sympathy for her; it was touching
to see a human soul journeying from one infinity to another
in such a narrow cage.

She was still nodding her head, but her lips had ceased to
move. So he addressed her again:

'How did you come to stay at home while Miss Mary took
over the shop?'

Ann, without knowing it, might have been affected by
the sympathy in his voice; at any rate she now answered him
simply and directly:

'Because I aye had to keep the house, you see. Mother
was like me, helpless wi' rheumatism for years an' years,
and I was the handiest in the house. She couldna bear to see
Mary flinging the things aboot, so I bude to bide, and Mary
gaed to help father in the shop. And she just stayed on
there. I never got a chance to do anything else. I've just
been buried alive here – buried alive.'

Her high voice quavered.

'I dare say,' said the minister, 'you didn't feel like that
while your father was at home? He must have liked you to
keep house for him?'

'I aye got on fine wi' father,' said Ann. 'I aye got on fine wi' father. . . . But Mary wadna let me in the shop. An' I'll no' let her in father's chair. Na, I'll no'.'

'And yet,' said the minister, 'she and you are all that's left on this earth of your father.' He put his hand on hers. 'You were bairns together,' he said.

Ann's mouth opened in amazement. But what she was going to say remained unspoken as her eye met the minister's.

'We're all bairns together,' he went on: 'bairns frightened to believe in the love that's behind everything, the love of our Heavenly Father. There's a lot of love in you, Miss Ann, that has never had a chance.'

The Reverend William Murray walked down the lane much more briskly than he had come. Ann had suffered him to read 'a chapter', and had even asked him to put up 'a bit prayer'. Instinctively his eye sought the pale sky, now veiled with insubstantial clouds through which the light of the declining sun was softly diffused. The firmament, he said to himself, with a new realization of the word. A firm basis. An enduring reality. It did not even enter his mind that there were people in the world who might regard his firmament as a mere illusion of beauty woven of light and air. The Reverend William Murray did not doubt the universal validity of his personal experiences.

THREE

I

Mr and Mrs John Shand, as was fitting, gave a dinner in the evening to welcome the bride and bridegroom, a family function, the only other guest being Miss Janet Shand.

The dinner itself was a success. Mabel had studied even more intensively than usual her stock of ladies' magazines, and the table decorations, the glass, the silver, the modish little mats recommended instead of an enveloping tablecloth by Lady Fanny of *The Ladies' Fashionmonger*, had all attained the high standard set by that arbiter of refinement. And had knocked Elizabeth flat, decided Mabel.

Such a satisfactory conclusion ought to have made her happy. But a hostess, a figure who carries the main burden of civilization, whose difficult task it is to invent a progressive notation for mankind's faith in the ability of the human spirit to surpass itself, cannot ignore the more rarefied ingredients of a dinner-party, the blending of temperaments, the flavour of conversation, the pleasant aroma of expanding minds. A dinner-party that provokes quarrels is like a bouquet containing nettles, and it was undeniable that all three of them now remaining by the fireside, Mabel, John and Aunt Janet, were nettled.

John was standing with his back to the fire. He was a tall, bulky man with reddish fair hair; his features were large but harmonious, and the beard he wore dignified his appearance. In spite of the beard, however, there was something simple and childlike in his face; perhaps it was the candid expression of his blue eyes which had no eyebrows to give them depth.

'She's much too good for him,' he said.

Aunt Janet laid down her knitting again. It was a custom

that she should spend the night with John and Mabel after dining there.

'You have always misjudged Hector,' she objected.

'I think his wife has misjudged him. A quiet, sensible girl like that: what induced her to marry him I can't think.'

Great lump that she is, said Mabel to herself, with irritation.

A hostess is only human, and Mabel had had a trying afternoon before her dinner-party began. Ned Murray had not proved amenable. She did not mind so much his absent answers to her questions – although it is annoying to have someone answer 'Yes, yes,' to everything one says – but she could not stand his behaviour to the other people on the links. She would never been seen in public with him again. A man who scowls at people and mutters and turns round to glare at them is a compromising partner. And on top of that Hector had been almost rude to her.

'Hector has a most affectionate and loving nature, and nobody is more unhappy than he is when he does wrong, poor boy,' said Aunt Janet.

John tut-tutted. 'He has no moral sense. And his loving nature is too promiscuous for my taste.'

'He's too sensitive, John, that's all. Girls simply throw themselves at his head. He can't help being so attractive to women.'

'Tut!' said John again; 'he uses women to feed his vanity. You're not going to tell me that that poor girl he ruined – Duncan, wasn't she called? – threw herself at his head whenever he bought a cigarette from her? Much he cared for her! His sensitive heart didn't keep him from clearing out to Canada when he was given the chance.'

'But he confessed the whole story to me, John, with tears in his eyes.'

'That was just another way of getting rid of it. A few tears are an easy price to pay. You're too soft with him.'

Janet Shand's short-sighted eyes filled with tears.

'I know him, John, as well as if I were his mother.'

'Well, well.' John stroked his beard. 'Let us hope his wife will take a stronger line with him.'

Aunt Janet picked up her knitting with a sigh.

'Elizabeth is very young, of course.'

Elizabeth, she felt, was not quite the right kind of wife. There was something about Elizabeth that made one uncertain. . . .

'Four years younger than Hector, isn't she?'

'Yes, John; only twenty-two.'

'Well,' said John, 'Mabel's only twenty-three, and she has sense enough.'

'Too much sense to marry Hector,' said Mabel, preparing to go upstairs.

'I think Hector's insufferable,' she burst out as she was brushing her hair. 'I wish he'd go and live somewhere else. Must you take him into the mill, John?'

'I can't very well keep him out. He's a Shand, after all.'

'He's a bad Shand.'

'I didn't know you disliked him so much.'

'I *detest* him,' said Mabel, brushing her long hair furiously.

'I haven't much use for him myself. . . . But I passed my word that if he settled down I'd take him on. . . . You needn't see much of him, you know; and Elizabeth's a sensible girl, don't you think?'

'I think,' said Mabel, and bit the words short.

'I'm sorry for *her*,' she added. But she deserves what she'll get, her thoughts ran on, as she brushed and brushed the long strands of her bright brown hair.

After he turned out the lights and got into bed John made one more reference to Elizabeth:

'It's funny to think that there's another Elizabeth Shand now, isn't it?'

'Why – of course,' said Mabel. 'They're not like each other, are they?'

John chuckled.

'About as like each other as fire and water. I'd give anything to see Lizzie dealing with Hector.'

'What would she do?'

'If she's still what she used to be she'd have him deflated within ten minutes. There wouldn't be much left of him.'

'I wish she'd come and do it,' murmured Mabel.

All through the evening the phantom of the other Elizabeth Shand, his sister, had haunted John, and now that he was safely under the bedclothes he allowed himself the indulgence of thinking about her. He had tried for so many years to forget her that even now, when anger had died away, he felt his persistent affection for her as a weakness to be indulged only when his head was under the blankets, when the respectable citizen of the daytime had merged into the boy of five-and-twenty years ago. He was startled by the painful leap his heart gave when Mabel murmured: 'I wish she'd come and do it.' He had not known how greatly he desired to see Lizzie again. Twenty years it was since he saw her last. She must be thirty-nine now, three years younger than himself. But that was absurd; he could not picture Lizzie as a mature woman. A wild thing she had been, always in hot water. What a day that was when their father had married again! She was three miles down the coast when he found her, hatless and coatless; she made him miss the wedding too, and she must have been at least twelve then; yes, Hector was born a year later, thirteen years' difference between them. . . . What an extraordinary thing affection is, John reflected. Aunt Janet was always down on Lizzie; she couldn't stand Lizzie; and yet, there she was, sticking up for Hector who wasn't fit to black Lizzie's boots. Lizzie was a wild creature, but not a selfish one. On the other hand, his own affection for Lizzie was just as unreasonable as Aunt Janet's for Hector. Lizzie had behaved scandalously; she had outraged everything he stood for; he had been ill with rage when she ran off with that foreign fellow. Yet that was in keeping with Lizzie's character; she was always dashing into adventures. It had been she who had discovered the disused pottery miles from home where they set up house for so many weeks one summer. He could remember the tumbledown shed, with a low bench covered with dust and fragments of baked clay, fluted moulds broken and crumbling, whorls and handles lying in careless heaps. With closed eyes John re-traversed the road that led there through a hot summer's afternoon, with Lizzie, like an elf, darting from one hedgerow to the other, until she discovered the overgrown side-path, and set off down it at a run. She would never keep on the main road, not Lizzie. Nobody knew what it meant to him when she ran off with that German. He nearly threw up everything to go after her. But even if he had tracked her down, how could he have brought her back to be a perpetual reminder of disgrace? A drunken father was bad enough without a dishonoured sister; no family could have lived them both down. Yet though he could justify his anger and his estrangement from her the long companionship of their childhood was still alive and seeking fulfilment. Twenty years. She was nineteen then. But when he dreamed of her, as he did now and then, she was always a slip of girl. . . . He drifted into sleep with the vague idea that he was stumbling through a dark forest of lofty trees, pursuing a brilliant butterfly that would dart off at a tangent and would not keep to the path.

Mabel Shand had never seen her sister-in-law, and, like everybody else, was unaware of John's passionate regret for her. Like everybody else, too, she knew the facts of the scandal; Elizabeth Shand had run away with a married man, a foreigner, the head of the modern languages department in the Calderwick Academy. Mabel also had the benefit of Aunt Janet's comments, including the information that John could not bear to have his sister's name mentioned; but she had been surprised shortly after their marriage to hear John say lightly: 'You remind me of my sister Lizzie; she was a gay young thing something like you.' He had added hastily, 'But you have more sense,' and Mabel realized that the comparison was intended as a compliment. Of course she had more sense; she knew too well the value of social prestige. Her position as John Shand's wife was more worth while than any fly-by-night nonsense of true love. Mabel had no intention of falling in love. She preferred to see others in love with her. She had fancied Hector, but that was when she was a mere child, and now, lying in bed beside John, she was convinced that she hated Hector. The thought flashed through her mind with savage suddenness: 'I wish I had him here; I'd *smack* him!'

Her body quivered with the intensity of her feeling. Smack him, good and hard, she would.

II

About the same time Sarah Murray was sitting in her bedroom with a rug over her knees and a shawl round her shoulders darning stockings, as she listened to the irregular tramp of Ned's feet overhead. He would stand for a long time on one part of the floor and then stride up and down speaking to himself with increasing vehemence in high tones of exasperation, only to fall silent again, standing motionless on some other spot. He had come in from his golf match taciturn and sullen, but at tea he had brightened up when William asked him how many he had gone round in; his one nasty remark had been made quite jokingly, that the links were all right if it weren't for the people on them who infested the grass; they should be combed out like fleas. After that he had opened the piano, which he hadn't done for months, and played beautifully for a long time until she asked him for something out of the *Messiah* and then he brought his hands down with a crash and stamped out of the room, saying: 'O God!'

He had refused to come in to supper until she and William were finished; since then he had been walking up and down in his own room at the top of the house. Sarah looked at her watch; it was now midnight. Three hours he had been going at it, and might go on for three hours more. What could it be that was troubling him? What could it be that kept him turning and turning round it like an insect on a pin? He had crumpled up the local weekly and thrown it across the room; she had smoothed it out later and looked it over to find what cause for offence he had discovered in it. But there was nothing. Nothing in particular. The usual records of sudden deaths and police cases; local appointments, farmers' dinners, auction sales, and the movements of prominent citizens. She had noticed, for instance, the arrival of Mr and Mrs Hector Shand at their house in the High Street. But how could any of it conceivably enrage a sane person? Insanity? Sarah's hand shook as she darned. The footsteps upstairs seemed also, with furious persistence, to be darning an invisible hole across the room.

'I can't stand it,' said Sarah aloud. 'I must do someting or I'll go crazy.'

She stuck her needle into the stocking and got up. She tiptoed upstairs, although she feared that Teenie was not asleep, and listened at Ned's door.

'Security!' she heard him cry, half sobbing. 'Surely that's not much to ask for? Security's all I want.' His voice died away into mutterings; then it rose again. 'Good God! They have to do it at somebody's expense, but why me, me? Couldn't they work it off on somebody else? It's incredible, logically and mathematically incredible—' He came to a dead stop on the floor, continuing the argument with his voice rising hysterically at the end of every statement. 'With hundreds of millions in the world to practise on they make a dead set at me. All I ask is peace and security and they all climb by kicking me down. Are all the low, sneaking, cunning imbeciles to enjoy a home and a job at my expense? Just because I'm not so low and cunning as they are? Good God!'

He was silent again as well as motionless. Sarah's heart was pounding wildly against her ribs. This was sheer raving. It was no use merely to listen; she must go in and bring him back to a sense of proportion. She opened the door. Ned started. 'Get out!' he screamed. 'Can't I have peace even here?' Sarah spoke mildly, to her own astonishment, for she was shaking. 'I've only come in to see that you haven't let your fire out, Ned. You always forget to put coal on.' The fire was actually half dead. Sarah went firmly towards it and made it up in silence. She could feel Ned's eyes burning into her back.

'That's all right now,' she said, rising from her knees and dusting her hands. 'You won't catch cold now. Are you working on your mathematics?'

'Why? What sneaking cunning is at the back of your mind now?'

'I though you were swotting for your examinations?'

'That's it! That's the conspiracy again! Nobody would believe what I have to put up with!'

'I don't see why an examination is a conspiracy.'

In spite of her fears Sarah said this in the voice of one who is convinced of being reasonable and a little coldly superior to the unreasonableness of the other party.

Ned advanced upon her as if we would strike her. She stood her ground.

'Everybody has to pass examinations. You're not the only one,' she said.

'Oh, I'm not, am I not?' he sneered. 'Does everybody have to sit an examination twice, tell me that? Is everybody compelled to do things over and over again – and *why* I should be persecuted, God knows! What good does it do you? Anybody would think you'd be glad to see me in a job instead of sneaking behind my back —'

'Nonsense! I didn't make you fail in your examination —'

'I didn't fail in my examination!' screamed Ned. 'It's a lie. It's a lie. Liars and hypocrites! Am I to be downed because you are liars and hypocrites?'

'Calling me a liar won't change the facts,' said Sarah. 'You failed because you were ill; that's no disgrace.'

'Ill, was I? What are you going to saddle me with next?'

Ned's voice was less bellicose, and Sarah pressed her advantage.

'No disgrace at all to be ill. But it will be a disgrace if you deliberately leave yourself unprepared for the next time. And you can't pass examinations if you don't go to bed. You know very well what Dr Scrymgeour said.'

'To hell with Dr Scrymgeour! To hell with you, too! Get out of my room!'

Sarah got steadily enough to the door, and turned round for a parting shot before shutting it:

'And if you don't believe you were ill, just go and ask him. Good-night.'

She managed to get downstairs to her room without stumbling. She was shaken, but in some queer way triumphant.

The footsteps above did not worry her so much. She lay in bed listening.

'I wonder if he's forgotten all about it,' she said to herself, 'and can't account for it?'

For the first time since Ned's unreason had bewildered her she saw a glimmering of reasonableness in it.

Ned was apparently walking more aimlessly; there was not so much hammering of his feet on the floor-boards and he stopped more frequently.

Finally she heard him fling himself on the bed, and dragged herself upstairs again to make sure that the gas was turned out.

All was quiet and in darkness.

The Glass is Shaken

I

The sentiment of family reunion that rises in flood over Britain towards the end of every year had always carried John Shand with it, but this year, to his own astonishment, he found himself deliberately surrendering to it long before Christmas. Even in his office he caught himself day-dreaming that Lizzie was in Calderwick for Christmas and the New Year. Instead of attending to the papers before him he was conducting Lizzie all over the mill, and she compli-mented and teased him about the success he had\made of it. She stayed with him in the house at Balfour Terrace; they laughed together at breakfast and were still laughing in the evening. They reminded each other, for instance, how they had climbed over their own garden wall and plundered a pear-tree, leading a band of young brigands into their own territory. And finally had to bury half the pears beneath a mound of ivy leaves, after all, although the six of them had eaten and eaten, throwing away larger and larger cores as their appetites began to fail. Not one of the six was left in Calderwick but himself. . . . On another autumn day they had gathered all the red and yellow leaves they could find because Lizzie swore that she could brew a magic potion out of them. They had brewed it in a silver coffee-pot in the wash-house. She was a little monkey.

He went up one evening to an attic merely to look at an old rocking-chair on which they had once played waves and mermaids, with their legs buttoned into coats and tied up with shawls to resemble fish-tails. The old rocking-chair could still rock valiantly. But Lizzie was – where was she?

Twenty years ago he had torn up her letter and thrown it in the fire. He had sent her a communication through his solicitor, assuring her that an allowance of one hundred and fifty pounds would be paid to her yearly but that her brother wished never to see her again. That allowance had been paid scrupulously, even when he could ill afford it; nobody knew anything about it, not even Mabel. He had insisted on letting Lizzie understand that the money was hers by right, her patrimony, for if she had guessed it was a gift she might have refused it. But she had accepted it. Tom Mitchell sent it to her every quarter. Tom Mitchell must have her address, of course.

He rose from his desk almost in agitation. There was nothing to prevent his writing and inviting Lizzie to come home for Christmas. Nothing, except his own bitter words of twenty years ago, which were vanishing like grains of dust, blown away by the wind of Lizzie's presence in his imagination.

For an irritable moment or two he caught himself regretting that he had a wife and other responsibilities. How could he explain to Mabel and Aunt Janet that he was going to invite Lizzie? It would set tongues wagging in the town, he knew; and for the first time in his life he wished that he was a vagabond. Could he not shake himself free and set off alone? His imagination, however, which was definite and clear when it played around the familiar scenes of Calderwick, faltered in confusion before the uncertainty of such a journey and the faint suggestion of dishonesty surrounding it. For he would have to pretend that he was going away on business.

His conflicting selves tormented him. But the anguish which contracted his heart when the idea occurrred to him that Lizzie might refuse to see him, or refuse to come, overwhelmed his hesitations. He must see her again; that was all. And he must see her in the most honourable manner, without subterfuge. He would invite her home to Calderwick, let gossip say what it liked, and he would write to her in such a way that if she still cared for him she would not refuse.

He shut himself up in his study for several evenings writing and rewriting the letter: *My dear Lizzie. Twenty years ago we were both fools.* . . . That would make her smile; that would make her feel indulgent. But was it not possible that it would only infuriate her? If she had bitterly resented his silence a light and easy attempt to resume their relationship would undoubtedly infuriate her. She might have suffered during these years; she must have suffered; one cannot do wrong with impunity. *My dear, dear Lizzie. Will you ever forgive me?* But that wouldn't do; he had been quite right in his attitude; she must have recognized that. Even now he was braving public opinion in asking her home; and his position in Calderwick was now unimpeachable. How impossible it would have been to bring her back twenty years ago! After all, it was she who had been in the wrong, flagrantly in the wrong.

He wished that he knew at least what kind of woman she had become. A hundred and fifty a year must have kept her from sinking into the very gutter, he thought grimly. That, indeed, was why he had settled it upon her. Still, human nature being what it was, as she had taken one wrong step she might have taken many. A woman of ungoverned passions, nearly forty, a coarse licentious figure, his common sense told him, the female counterpart of their father, and, being a woman, ten times worse than their father, that was what he might reasonably expect to find.

He leaned his head on his hands, shutting his eyes. And once again the delight of Lizzie's presence enveloped him; he could have sworn that she was somewhere in the house, and that they were going to have a vivacious evening together. While his eyes were shut he felt it impossible that Lizzie should have become anything but just Lizzie.

He suddenly realized that her address would be some kind of a clue to her circumstances, and decided to ask Tom Mitchell for the address before writing the letter. This decision somewhat restored his cheerfulness and carried him to the lawyer's office early next day.

Tom Mitchell had never seen the big man so embarrassed. The childlike look in his eyes was more evident than ever. He stood behind the chair offered to him, refusing to sit down, as if he feared to be drawn into explanations. The lawyer, a small rosy-cheeked old man who was a walking graveyard of family secrets, pulled out a drawer.

'Ay, weel,' he said, in an affectedly broad accent, 'it just happens that Miss Lizzie sent me a letter for you some months syne, with positive instructions that it was not to be given to you unless you speired after her. Man, she must have jaloused that you were going to do it. Or else you must have jaloused that the letter was here. There's queerer things happens than that.'

John Shand made a step forward.

'Bide a wee, bide a wee; I'll find it in a minute. Here we are. To John Shand, Esquire.'

He held out a thin bluish envelope, larger than those usually seen in Calderwick. The same handwriting, said John to himself, as he eagerly snatched the letter. Lizzie always printed her capitals instead of writing them.

'When did this come, Tom?' he asked in a casual voice.

'Nineteenth of July.'

'And where is she now?'

'South of France. The address will be inside. Sit down, man, and read it.'

John put the letter in his pocket. As jealous as if it were from his lass, Tom Mitchell remarked to himself. He could feel it there all the way down the street. Dear, dear Lizzie. He had been an unconscionably long time in jalousing the message. Nineteenth of July. And this was the twenty-eighth of November. She might have been in great trouble; it might even be too late now.

He stopped on the pavement, his heart in his mouth, plucked the letter out of the envelope, and read it, standing on the kerb.

'My dear John, – This is to let you know that I am now made an honest woman of – much against my will, but the man is dying and wouldn't take no. It's not Fritz, by the way; I shed Fritz long ago; but it's another German, a friend of mine for years. I am now Frau Doktor Mütze, which is to say Mrs Doctor Bonnet, so you see although I threw my bonnet over the mill it has come back like a boomerang. I don't think he can live for more than a month or so. We did it last week. I can't explain it all now, but I feel that I ought at least to tell you, for I know how much importance you attach to getting married and things like that. But I don't want you to think I'm proud of it. I don't want to tell you either, unless you are feeling friendly towards me, so I'll instruct Tom Mitchell accordingly. Anyhow, there it is. Love from Lizzie. Villa Soleil, Menton.'

John laughed as he crammed the letter back into his pocket without folding it. Mrs Doctor Bonnet. Love from Lizzie. The same old sixpence, he said to himself in glee; the same old sixpence!

In his first exuberance he wrote her the letter of invitation and gummed down the flap of the envelope before he rememberd that her new-made husband might be dead by this time. He checked himself. It was indecent to be so overjoyed if Lizzie were a widow. Yet he could not feel grief-stricken; her being a widow was the best thing that could happen; it would set her free to come home. He tore up that letter, however, and wrote another. When that was in its envelope he took it out at the last minute and added as a postscript: 'Do come.' Then he went out to post it himself. Before he slid it into the letterbox he looked again at the superscription, 'Frau Doktor Mütze', and grinned like a boy.

Now that the letter was posted he realized how much of himself had gone into it. His heart had not stirred in such secret delight since Lizzie's disappearance – not even on his wedding-day. Something hidden very deep seemed to have come alive again. He felt like whistling, and he had not whistled for fifteen years, he dared say, yes, fifteen years at least.

I must have been growing old, thought John. That was what growing old meant, saving up one's energy, no whistling or running or jumping. There was a flight of stone steps leading up to his own front door; he took them in two strides and paused at the top to reflect that Lizzie would certainly push him down again if she were there. What were steps for!

II

Mabel was feeling pettish. For days John had been mooning about as if bewitched, shutting himself up all evening and either looking at her as if she were not there or evading her irritably whenever he came out of the study. One might as well be married to a log. It was a pity John was so old.

Their marital relationship had been well regulated during the two years of their marriage. After John's first ardours were over she had escaped his embraces except on Sunday mornings when they lay longer in bed. These Sunday-morning embraces now had the sanction of tradition, and Mabel sometimes wondered if John kept them up because they were a tradition. It was a pity John was so old. A woman so well made as she was should have a husband to match her.

She looked up resentfully from her magazine as John came in.

'Are you going to change?' she asked.

'Won't take me a minute,' said John, balancing himself on his toes before the fire.

He would break it to her after dinner, he was thinking.

'You're growing fat, John. Must do something to take down your tummy.'

'Am I?' John looked down at his waistcoat and fingered his beard. Mabel noted with satisfaction that he seemed dashed.

'Do I look very old, Mabel?' he asked in a surprisingly humble tone. Mabel's possessiveness reasserted itself.

'No, you don't, darling; you look very dignified, but not old. A little less on the tummy would be an improvement, though.'

'I'll do exercises every morning,' decided John. He still lingered, however, and then brought out the question which had been troubling him.

'Should I shave my beard off, Mabel, do you think?'

Mabel was astounded. She had never seen him without a beard.

'I don't know what you'd look like without it!' she cried. 'Oh *no*, darling. It gives you such a distinguished look.'

John went upstairs to change and as he looked in the glass he could hear Lizzie saying: 'Saves you washing your neck, doesn't it?'

He laughed out loud.

If he took off his beard, Mabel was thinking downstairs, I might as well be married to anybody.

She gazed idly at an illustration to the story she was

reading. The hero and heroine were standing clasped in each other's arms, a typical magazine embrace, with the woman swaying backwards and the man masterfully overtopping her. She had a hand on each of his shoulders, pushing him away; when the inevitable kiss came she would enjoy it with a good conscience because of this show of resistance. Mabel's eye lingered on the picture. It came into her mind that the hero's shoulders were like Hector's, and although startled, even shocked, she felt for an infinitesimal space of time that it would be thrilling to stem her hands against Hector's broad shoulders and push him away with all her strength.

During dinner and afterwards John and Mabel were more talkative than usual. Perhaps they were each trying to atone to the other for a secret feeling of guilt. John found it easy, at any rate, to confess all, or nearly all, of what was in his heart. Mabel, apparently, had nothing to confess.

TWO

On looking at them one could never have told that Hector and John Shand were half-brothers. John resembled his Highland mother; with his big frame and his reddish fair beard he might have been a viking from the Western Isles. Hector was like the Shands; his wrists and ankles were small and sinewy, his hands and feet small and beautifully shaped; he had a swarthy skin, black hair and dark hazel eyes, so quick in movement and expression that he seemed to be always on the watch. For his size he had uncommonly broad shoulders, and whether it was the shoulders or the nervous hands or the quick, ready eye that endeared him to women he was, at any rate, extremely attractive to them.

His mother, a delicate, submissive woman, had died shortly after he was born, and he was brought up by Janet Shand, who expended upon him in double measure the affection she felt for his father, sharpened at times to a keen edge of anxiety lest he should grow up to resemble his father morally as well as physically. Janet could never rid herself of the knowledge that the Shand men were sexually unbridled; even her own brother had given her a queer feeling; she could not look at him without remembering how often he was reported to lie with women in the town. It was indeed difficult to think of anything but bodily appetites when one met Charlie Shand.

Thus the atmosphere in which Hector Shand grew up was, one might say, heavily charged with sex between the two poles of Janet's anxious abhorrence of the subject and Charlie Shand's open devotion to it. Before the boy was twelve his father had become so dissolute that he was a byword in the town. Shamed to the soul, young Hector found little comfort in the thought of his mother, for his

Aunt Janet always spoke of her with contemptuous pity as of a poor spiritless thing, who was no wife for Charlie. Hector became convinced that his heredity was tainted; he became fatalistic about it; he persuaded himself that John had escaped the curse only because he had a different kind of mother, and he resented his half-brother's robust superiority.

Nor did school help him to escape from his fatalistic preoccupation. Examinations made his stomach queasy with nervousness. Everything that he knew ebbed out of his mind when he was ordered to set it down, and his increasing nervous tension in the ordeal invariably discharged itself in a way which made him miserable and strengthened his sense of inborn guilt. In every bodily activity, in every game he played, he had a lightning correspondence between his body and his brain, but the mere sight of ink and paper was enough to paralyse it. A problem in arithmetic, which, given real bricks, he would have solved, became a torturing muddle of cubic feet; rules of grammar, which unconsciously in speaking he adhered to, changed into malignant mnemonics which he could never retain; and the simple recording of facts, even facts that he knew well, such as how best to guddle for trout, was subject to a mysterious standard of appraisal called 'style' which was never defined, and for which, apparently, he had no natural gift. He took it for granted that books and all that they stood for were beyond his capacity, and sustained himself against humiliation by his prowess in games, and, in later years, by his success with women. He had found nothing else in life.

Every morning on entering the office of John Shand & Sons he felt a faint recurrence of the old nausea. He would add a column of figures five, six or even seven times before assuming that his answer was correct, and even then he convinced himself only by totting the whole up on his fingers.

'Is that how you count, man?' said John, one day. 'That's how they used to do it in the Stone Age.'

'Is there nothing else you can give me to do?' burst out Hector in a rage. 'I can't stick at these damned figures all the time.'

John wheeled round. His manner was curt; he had been

irritable for some days past, for he had not yet solved his own problem with Lizzie.

'I want to see whether you can stick to anything at all once you've begun it,' he said, and went away without waiting for an answer, being in a hurry to get to Tom Mitchell's.

Hector turned white. John always roused him to defiance. John was always expecting him to make a mistake of some kind, and not only expecting it but waiting for a chance to say: 'I thought as much.' By setting his teeth Hector could only just cope with that; here, however, was a new obstacle to overcome, the deadly suggestion that even if he could master anything he lacked steadiness enough to stick to it. It was a deadly suggestion, because in his own experience of himself Hector found nothing to rebut it.

He gritted his teeth, but the figures swam before his gaze. The office window looked into the deep well of the yard, where horses were backing and carts unloading. In spite of the sick distaste he had for the office Hector liked the rest of the mill; even the men who worked in it were better than the clerks, he thought, who were all elderly dried-up machines like John himself.

'Hell and damnation!' He clapped the ledger to. In the outer office he paused and said to the head clerk who peered at him enviously over steel-rimmed spectacles: 'If Mr John asks where I am, Mason, you can tell him I'm taking a turn through the mill.'

He had a child's delight in watching belts whiz and wheels go round. The impalpable flour that floated in the air sifted over his head and shoulders as he lounged from one corner to another, edging his way between piles of full sacks. He liked the smell of the mill, a compound of machine grease and the fragrance of grain; he liked the regular thud thud of the big dynamo which shook the whole building as if a giant were trying to kick the walls out. He watched the fat golden grains of wheat go sliding down the chute in a lazy mass, and turned up his sleeve to plunge his arm among them.

'That's good wheat,' he yelled to the man in charge.

'Mains of Invercalder,' the man yelled back. 'Best wheat in the haill countryside.'

That was Mabel's father's wheat. I should know good wheat when I see it, thought Hector, bitterness overcoming him again. A whole year and a half on that damned Alberta farm. What he didn't know about wheat wasn't worth knowing. Horse-feed, too, he knew something about that.

'Damnation!' he swore again, emerging into the yard. John's last remark was still active. He hadn't been able to stick to farming anyhow. Could he stick to anything?

He nodded to the carters tramping over the mud of the yard with bits of dirty sacking laid over their shoulders. Probably that was the kind of job John thought him fit for. 'Wouldn't that jar you?' he found himself sneering; the Canadian phrase had not occurred to him for a long time. Hell, what a life it had been!

He leaned against a doorway and watched the horses; their haunches were wrinkling, and their great bearded feet were braced against the cobbles. On his farm he had felt something like that, like a brute in blinkers between two shafts. He rememberd his disgust and forlornness at the plough-tail; he had even kicked at the ploughshare with his heavy boots in a senseless frenzy of rage, and sent long imploring letters to Aunt Janet. What maddened him most was the feeling that he had been turned down by the whole lot of them, even by Aunt Janet. And then Aunt Janet had assured him that all was forgotten and forgiven, and on that assurance he had sold up his farm and come home to make good.

It was more than a year since he had come back, but he was still angry when he remembered how John had so high-and-mightily washed his hands of him. It was the affair with Bell Duncan that did it; everybody turned against him when that came out. And what was there in that? The girl was asking for it. Fellows had done much worse than that. His own father had been a damned sight worse. And he was only a boy when the affair began; he was heartily sick of the girl by the time she started slandering him right and left. Glad enough he had been to clear out when they offered him the chance. But in any decent family the whole history of the affair would have been different. As it was, they merely clapped blinkers on him and stuck him between two shafts, the shafts of a plough.

It was a raw afternoon, and to the dull rage he felt was added the discomfort of cold. With an abrupt jerk he turned and marched up to the office again, hurled a ledger on the floor and put on his coat, hat and muffler. Without thinking he then went out through the main gateway facing the dock. It was high tide; the dock-gates were open, and a dirty-looking steamer was warping her way in. A rope came curling on the quay beside him, and was knotted in a trice round an iron post rooted among the worn granite setts that surrounded the little square of deep water. Foreign-looking chaps, thought Hector, as he glanced at the crew leaning over the side, and he strolled away to see where they had come from. *Elsa*. Kjobenhavn. Copenhagen. Strange, clipped syllables were tossed along the deck, and he listened to them with a vague pleasure in the strangeness. Calderwick wasn't the only place on God's earth after all.

He wandered round the dock, peering into the water. One corner, the corner nearest to Dock Street, which led into the heart of the town, always used to be foul with straw and floating rubbish, he remembered, a nasty, stagnant corner which would be damned unpleasant to fall into. It was still as dirty and foul as ever. On a dark night, he reflected, it would be easy to come down to Dock Street and walk right over the edge into that scum. When he was a child that corner had always given him the creeps. He gazed into the murky water. Better to drown in the open sea than in that stagnant muck.

He shivered and turned up his coat collar. Damn it all, he would get even with John yet. There was Elizabeth to back him up. Elizabeth swore that it took a higher kind of courage to come back from Canada than to stick on out there. So he hadn't been a quitter when he left the farm. He had come back with more money than he started with. Nobody could say he was a quitter. Damn it all, if he was an out-and-out rotter Elizabeth would never have married him, and there was precious little about himself he hadn't told her.

Elizabeth made a fellow feel he had some guts in him. He would go home and shake it all off. Elizabeth was a wonder, he thought, striding up the street with the sea-wind behind him. Queer that none of the other chaps had had the nerve to make love to her. Of course, she said herself she was too brotherly for them. But she had fallen for him all right, all right.

At the moment he was filled with passionate gratitude towards her. She was the biggest success he had ever had. She was one of those superior people who understood books, and yet she hadn't turned him down. Far from it. He was the first man she had ever fallen for.

He studied the figure of a girl coming towards him, her head down against the wind. Showed up a girl, that did. Elizabeth was as well made as any of them. God, he was glad to be well out of the time when he couldn't look at a girl without thinking there was only a skirt between him and her. Elizabeth had saved him from that.

Not consciously in words, not even in half-glimpsed images did he recognize Elizabeth as anything like an anchorage or a haven for his storm-driven life, but the feeling which was swelling his heart as he neared home would have engendered such a conception in a more articulate person. He was only aware that he had never felt like that before about any girl. As he fitted his latchkey in the door he was excited because he was to see his wife immediately, and his disappointment was all the more overwhelming when he found the drawing-room empty. The mistress, said Mary Ann, rushing from the kitchen, had left word she was sorry but she had to go out for tea. 'With Mrs Doctor Scrimmager,' added Mary Ann of her own accord; 'at least they gaed out thegither.'

'I'll mak' you a fly cup for yoursel',' she offered.

'No, no, Mary Ann; you'll never get a man if you offer him nothing but tea,' said Hector. 'Tell the mistress if she comes back before me that I'm away to the Club for something better than tea.'

Mary Ann giggled. A heartsome young man, the master, and with a wee spark of the devil in his eye; just what a man should have.

The wee spark of the devil in Hector's eye was occasioned by a curious blend of emotions. Because Elizabeth had gone out he was not only disappointed, he was resentful with the same kind of resentment a child feels when it has hurt itself and its mother does not pick it up. He was also irritated because it was Mrs Scrymgeour whose company Elizabeth had preferred to his; he disliked Mrs Scrymgeour and wished that his wife were less intimate with the woman. At the same time he was conscious that he was a man, a swaggering, independent creature, and he was pleased to have an excellent excuse for flourishing his masculinity in despite of Elizabeth. He would go to the Club and have a high old time with the fellows. He was popular in the Club. He might, in fact, make a night of it. It would serve Elizabeth right.

On his way to the Golf Club he passed close by the lighted windows of number seven Balfour Terrace, where Mabel was sitting alone at tea, turning over the new magazine the perusal of which was to lead her imagination to startling conclusions a little later in the evening.

Next day the wind had increased to a storm; the thunder of the breaking grey sea could be heard in the High Street, and a relentless rain stung the faces of the goodwives as they scuttled from one snug shop to another doing their shopping.

Mrs Hector Shand was standing at her drawing-room window gazing at the low clouds racing behind the few leafless trees of her garden. The prospect was bleak, but Elizabeth, being accustomed to unkind weather, was not depressed. She was planning to take a run on the links, for when a strong wind blew she could not help taking to her heels and following it.

But the front-door bell rang, and almost immediately Mary Ann's voice cried: 'The mistress is in here, Miss Shand.'

Aunt Janet was breathless; she tumbled rather than walked in, clutching a sodden umbrella and a brown-paper parcel.

'Oh, my dear!' she exclaimed. 'Oh, my dear!'

'She's heard about it,' said Elizabeth to herself, feeling trapped.

Aunt Janet was brimming over with solicitude; she had obviously come to comfort and to exhort, to investigate and bewail the scandal.

'What a terrible thing!' she cried, endeavouring to seize Elizabeth's hands at the same time as Elizabeth tried to take the parcel and umbrella from her. 'What a dreadful thing! Oh, I'm *so* upset. Where is he?'

'Come and sit by the fire,' said Elizabeth; 'let me get your wet things off.'

'I was sure I should find you in. I said to myself: "The poor child will be mourning her heart out." Is Hector upstairs?'

No, he's gone out to the football match.'

'But, my dear Elizabeth!'

'It's dreadful weather for standing about, I know. *I* shouldn't spend a wet afternoon like that —'

Aunt Janet's visibly increasing distress broke off Elizabeth's sentence.

'That's not what I meant at all – not at all.'

Janet put a hand on the younger woman's knee.

'My dear, how do you know he won't go and get drunk again? Why did you let him go? I heard all about this dreadful affair of last night —'

'How did you hear about it?'

'But, Elizabeth, it's the talk of the town. I heard about it from at least three different sources.'

'Oh, I suppose so. I didn't think.'

'And now you say he's at a *football match*.'

'He won't be tackling people there,' said Elizabeth, laughing. 'And he won't get drunk, Aunt Janet, for he promised me—'

'I was sure of it. I was sure you would lead the poor boy in the right direction.'

'Besides, it wasn't so bad, not so very bad, from what I can make out. They were all rather well on, and Hector was practising Rugger tackles. It was quite an accident that Hutcheon got his collar-bone broken.'

'But, my dear, I heard that young Hutcheon was brought home in a dreadful state, simply covered with mud and blood.'

'Then they must have been scrumming in the street. Still, I'm sure it was only a lark. It's easy to break a man's collar-bone when you pitch him over; I've seen Hector do it before.'

'Hector doesn't know his own strength. Well, my dear, it's a mercy you can take it so calmly; but really, my dear, I am *so* distressed. I was told that they were swearing and blaspheming in the street in the most dreadful manner, wakening people out of their beds.'

Elizabeth repressed a smile.

'I don't believe it'll happen again,' she said. 'Hector's terribly ashamed of himself.'

'It mustn't happen again, Elizabeth. You must do all you can to prevent it.'

'Well, last time I told Hector I would go down to the Club and drag him out by the hair of the head if he did it again, and this time I have threatened to go down and get drunk beside him—'

'But, my dear Elizabeth! I know you're only joking, but really!'

'Why, what else could I do?'

Aunt Janet was genuinely shocked.

'My dear, I don't think you quite realize . . . Hector isn't like other young men who can take a drink or leave it. His father literally died of drink, and Hector is so like him. In every way. Whisky is dangerous for him.

'Aunt Janet,' said Elizabeth, becoming earnest, 'I do know all that. Hector has told me everything about himself.' (Things he wouldn't tell you, she added silently.) 'But surely I'm not a kind of policeman keeping guard over him, am I? He's so ashamed of himself that it wouldn't be fair to take advantage of him and tie him down with promises. I don't want to say to him: "You mustn't do this, or that." Why should I? It was of his own accord he promised me he wouldn't get drunk again; I didn't ask him to promise anything. And that's much the best way, I'm sure.'

Aunt Janet shook her head. 'I hope, my dear, I only hope you're right, but I'm afraid you're not. We all hoped that marriage would settle Hector, but I know John isn't at all pleased with his work, and this is the second time already that Hector has been violently drunk since you were married.'

Is it my fault? thought Elizabeth, her temper rising.

'Hector likes excitement,' she objected. 'Perhaps he needs it. He hasn't been accustomed to office work, and there isn't much excitement to be got in this town. As for me, I can go for long walks and read, but Hector —'

Nonsense! said Janet Shand to herself angrily. She was angry with Hector too, but Elizabeth had no right to be so slack with him. She had no sense of her duties to her husband.

But her anger lessened as she peered at the girl's face. In spite of her casual, cheerful air Elizabeth was looking worn. Aunt Janet recovered herself.

'Well, well, you look as if you hadn't slept,' she said as kindly as she could. 'When did Hector come home, my dear?'

'Not so very late – about one o'clock. But we didn't get to sleep till after five.'

Elizabeth stared into the fire and suddenly smiled, reminiscently, it seemed to the watching old woman. She felt a pang of jealousy. Hector had been used to confess his sins and seek absolution in her lap; but now he was in the power of this strange girl.

'You have a great influence over him, my dear Elizabeth,' she said solemnly. 'You must try to use it properly.'

'He has a great influence over me, Aunt Janet.'

Janet Shand asked the question she had been longing to ask for months:

'Why did you marry him, Elizabeth?'

Elizabeth's blush mounted as usual till her ears were burning. She hated it; she wished she could control her blood.

'Because I was madly in love with him – and I still am, and I shall be always.'

Her answer was almost defiant.

The short winter afternoon was rapidly waning, and Elizabeth still stared into the glow of the fire, the shadows darkening around her. She saw there the glow in her own heart.

'I know what you mean,' she added in an abrupt voice. 'Lots of people have said it to me. I'm supposed to have brains, and Hector has none, not the academic kind, at any rate. I have the knack of passing examinations; Hector hasn't. I like to read all kinds of books; Hector never opens a book if he can help it. What can we have in common, people wonder. That's the superficial point of view. What do these things matter? They're all second-hand. What we read or don't read makes no difference to ourselves. The real *me*,' she struck her bosom, 'is made of the same stuff as Hector —'

She broke off as abruptly as she had begun. She could not explain it to Aunt Janet. They were both wild and passionate; they wanted the whole of life at one draught; they would sink or swim together. Images flowed through her mind: in the air or under the sea or rooted in the earth she saw herself and Hector living, growing, swimming, breasting the wind together. She thought of his wide shoulders, his strong neck, his swift and lovely feet. . . .

'What have brains to do with it?' she asked, looking up. 'It's a miracle, Aunt Janet; a miracle that sometimes takes my breath away. Whatever made him fall in love with me, I often wonder. . . .'

She smiled suddenly, and touched Aunt Janet.

'You can't explain away a miracle, can you? A miracle swept us off our feet, and we got married because we couldn't help it. That's the answer.'

Much of what Elizabeth had refrained from trying to express was none the less transmitted to the old woman on the other side of the fire. She had lived so long on vicarious emotion that it had become her one solace, and she was grateful to Elizabeth for the thrill she now experienced. Her gratitude submerged her resentment.

'I love him, too, Elizabeth,' she said, wiping her eyes. 'But you have the greater influence over him, I am sure. If you would only use it!'

'When you are driven by a strong wind you can't *use* it, Aunt Janet!

'But, my dear Elizabeth —'

A note of helplessness sounded in Aunt Janet's voice.

Elizabeth suddenly felt exasperated. She sprang to her feet.

'You don't believe in us! You don't believe it has any meaning! You're only thinking of the little things, like keeping house and coming home at ten o'clock —'

'But surely you want Hector to get on in the world,' protested Aunt Janet, whose head was whirling. 'I only want the best for both of you.' She was crying.

Elizabeth's emotion transformed itself again.

'My dear, my dear,' she coaxed, kneeling before Aunt Janet, 'don't worry, don't worry. We'll be all right. There's something in both of us.'

She petted the old woman for some minutes. Then, still, kneeling, she went on: 'To tell you the truth, I don't like Hector's getting drunk any more than you do. But I think I understand it. I might do the same myself, if I had been accustomed to it as he has. What good could it do to coerce him? He'd only be angry with me. It would destroy the unity between us. Give us time, that's all. We'll both grow in grace. Don't you see? I feel that so strongly that I know I must be right.'

She went on soothing Janet, who was wiping her eyes again.

They were both startled by the ringing of the front-door bell. It was now almost dark.

'Whoever can that be?' Elizabeth started to her feet.

Mary Ann, mindful of her manners before the minister, ceremoniously announced:

'Mr Murray.'

William Murray came in eagerly, carrying a small book, but hesitated when he found he could barely discern his hostess by the flickering light of the fire.

'Hello!' said Elizabeth. 'I'm afraid we're rather in the dark here. Wait a minute and I'll light the gas.'

'I hope I haven't disturbed you.' The minister hung back.

'Not a bit,' said Elizabeth, striking matches. 'I'm very glad to see you.'

The gaslight flooded the room with brightness, submerging along with the shadows Elizabeth's glowing sentiments. The minister sat down. Elizabeth looked gay.

'We've been having an argument. Should one coerce other people for their good? Which side do *you* take, Mr Murray?'

The minister smiled because Elizabeth was smiling at him. Mrs Hector stimulated him pleasantly.

'I should need to know something about the circumstances,' he said.

'Oh, Miss Shand says: yes, one should force other people

to do things, and I say: no, one shouldn't. Tell us what you think.'

'Well,' said the minister, 'do you know, I should never *force* anybody in anything. But surely one person can *influence* another? In fact, I think we all influence each other, whether we ought to or not, and perhaps whether we know it or not.'

'Ah, but that's a different thing' and 'That's just what I say' broke simultaneously from Elizabeth and Janet.

'To force ideas or conduct on another,' went on the minister, 'is egoism; but to influence another, if it's done in – in love,' he stumbled over the word, 'is surely the highest altruism?'

'Altruism my hat!' retorted Elizabeth, to Aunt Janet's horror. 'How can it be altruism if we influence other people without knowing it.'

'I should have said rather that we influence other people *more* than we know.'

'Then we can't take much credit for it, can we?'

'Perhaps there's something in that.' The minister was thoughtful. 'We all transmit rays of which we know very little. Or, rather, they are transmitted through us.'

'I agree with you there,' said Elizabeth unexpectedly. 'And that's just why we shouldn't interfere with them.'

'But if there were no interference, if we allowed the unknown influences free play, would you not agree that the world might be flooded with – with love?'

Again the minister stumbled over the word.

'In that case, I should look out for a Noah's Ark.'

Aunt Janet looked from one to the other in bewilderment. Elizabeth laughed.

'I feel contradictious,' she said. 'I think we might dilute our arguments with tea.'

She wondered, with an inward chuckle, as she pulled the old-fashioned handle which jangled a bell in the kitchen, whether the minister too had come to condole. But that wasn't like him, she decided; and in that she did him justice.

Mabel Shand, however, who was then on her way towards number twenty-six High Street, was coming expressly to gloat – which is another form of condolence. She thought

that Hector would certainly be at home, and that she would
have an opportunity to pay off old scores. She promised
herself she would not leave him a leg to stand on.

'Where's Hector?' was her first question when she was
shown in. She was surprised to see the minister; he seemed
to be very chummy with Elizabeth, she noted. Aunt Janet
there too, of course, waiting to enfold the sinner in her
benevolent arms. Elizabeth was almost indecently gay; she
did not seem to care a rap.

'Hector? Oh, he's out at the football match.'

'Is it safe, do you think, to let him go out to football
matches?'

'He won't scrag anybody, if that's what you mean.'

Mabel's dislike of Elizabeth was beginning to be returned.

'But that, it seems, is just what he does do,' murmured
Mabel.

'My husband nearly killed a man last night,' said
Elizabeth gravely addressing the minister. 'At least, that's
what people seem to think. Should I keep him forcibly in the
house to prevent him from committing murder in the high
streets?'

The minister was embarrassed. He recollected that Sarah
had spoken to him of some scandal concerning Hector
Shand. But Mrs Hector, for all her gravity, still had a
twinkle in her eye; she was obviously dangling bait in front
of him. Yet he could not rise to it with the lightheartedness
he had felt before Mrs John Shand came in.

He murmured something about his argument in favour of
influence.

Mabel laughed a little.

Elizabeth turned her back on her sister-in-law.

'I was only teasing,' she said. 'It's not so bad as that. Will
you have some more tea? Is that my Maeterlinck you've
brought back? What do you think of *Wisdom and Destiny*? I
had an idea it would appeal to you.'

'Yes, yes.' His embarrassment still persisted. 'I like some
of it very much.'

He could not discuss the book just then.

The real reason of his embarrassment was that the
presence of any lady member of his congregation reminded

him that he was the minister. In speaking to Elizabeth he quite forgot the minister in the man, an experience so unusual that he found it delightful. But his present constraint brought back his formal vocabulary and he said:

'I really came to ask you to take a stall at the Christmas sale of work, which is run by the ladies of the congregation.'

'What?' said Elizabeth, open-mouthed. 'Me?'

Mabel laughed again. 'You're one of the ladies of the congregation, Elizabeth, although you don't seem to know it.'

'Yes,' said the minister. 'Mrs John Shand is kindly taking over the sweet stall, and I thought – I imagined a gift-book stall would be very suitable for you.'

'That's the very thing for her, Mr Murray,' said Aunt Janet heartily. She was glad to see that Elizabeth's pertness had not offended the minister, and it pleased her to think of Hector's wife taking a dignified place at a church function.

'Oh, Aunt Janet,' interrupted Mabel, 'that reminds me, you'll give me some jam for my stall, won't you?'

Mabel and Janet began a lively exchange of confidences about jam and marzipan sweets, under cover of which Elizabeth said to the minister in a low tone:

'I couldn't possibly do it. I wish you wouldn't ask me. I'm no good at things of that kind.'

William Murray got up to put his teacup on the table, and remained standing beside her. His constraint vanished.

'I wish you would try,' he urged, bending down.

'I don't feel like a lady of the congregation.'

'It's not really in that sense that I ask you to come; it would be a great pleasure to me to have you there.'

The yearly sale of work made him feel nervous and distracted. Elizabeth's presence would in some way be a support to him. 'I'm no good at things of that kind either,' he added, 'and we should help each other out.'

Elizabeth smiled up to him as he bent confidentially nearer to make this confession.

'If you put it like that,' she said.

It was at this moment that Hector Shand, having let himself in, walked into the drawing-room.

In spite of the fresh air with which Calderwick was liberally supplied he did not feel much the better of his afternoon's outing. He was already dissatisfied with himself when he went out to the football match, and neither the weather nor the bad play of the local team had relieved his dissatisfaction.

At the close of play, mindful of his promise to Elizabeth, he had refused the invitation of several friends to 'have one' at the Clubhouse, and as the men of Calderwick were as self-conscious about their drinks as about their women there had been a considerable amount of chaffing when he said with attempted heartiness: 'No, I promised the wife.'

All the way home his grievances harassed him. John had jumped down his throat that morning. Calderwick was a one-horse town where a man couldn't enjoy himself without everybody kicking up a fuss. Damn it all, a fellow had to go on the loose sometimes. A fellow couldn't be mollycoddling about his own fireside all the time. All very well for Elizabeth; she had her books; but it gave him a pain in the neck when he tried to read a book.

His head ached and there was an evil taste on the back of his tongue. As his physical misery increased his dissatisfaction with himself, his sense of failure threatened to overwhelm him completely. The one thing he needed was to lay his head on Elizabeth's bosom, as he had done to his comfort in the small hours of the morning. He hurried on, and almost burst into the drawing-room.

His quick eye at once caught the picture of Elizabeth and the minister smiling intimately to each other, while Aunt Janet and Mabel were talking in a corner. Half of him seemed to rise inside and choke in his throat, while the other half sank clean through the pit of his stomach, leaving him hollow and sick. The figures in the room changed their positions like puppets while he stood there glaring.

The look in his eyes made Mabel forget her intention of teasing him. Better go at once, her social sense warned her. She hastily put on her furs.

'Glad to see you enjoying yourselves,' said Hector at last, removing his eye from Elizabeth but making no attempt to come farther into the room.

Elizabeth felt and looked bewildered.

'We're only having tea,' she said. 'Here's your cup.'

'I'm afraid I must go now,' put in Mabel quickly. 'Good-bye, Elizabeth; good-bye, everybody. It's good-afternoon and good-bye in the same breath to you, Hector, I'm sorry to say.'

Hector had moved his lips once or twice as if swallowing, and he now turned to Mabel with exaggerated *camaraderie*.

'Not a bit of it, Mabel. I only looked in to say I wasn't having any tea. I'll come with you.'

'Why, where are you going, Hector?' cried Elizabeth.

'To the Club,' said Hector, without looking at her. 'So long, Aunt Janet,' he went on. 'See you another time. Sorry I can't stop. Come along, Mabel.'

The door shut upon them. Elizabeth found herself filling a cup with hot water instead of tea.

'Oh, I'm sorry,' she said in a flat voice.

Then she suddenly burst into tears.

'Go away!' she sobbed. 'Go away! Both of you.'

With another sob she rose and rushed out of the room.

To his own amazement the minister's first impulse was to rush out after her. He was literally upset; everything within him felt topsy-turvy. Little enough had been said, but Elizabeth's agitation seemed to him natural and his own not less so. Something evil had struck into the very heart of the room like an invisible thunderbolt and had scattered the peace of all the people in it. Yet he was amazed to find himself involuntarily springing to the door.

Janet Shand caught him by the sleeve. Tears were streaming down her cheeks, but her voice was harsh and angry. 'Let her go!' she said. 'You can't do anything with her. Nobody can do anything with her. She'll be the ruin of him yet.'

William shook his arm free but stood irresolutely shifting his feet while Janet Shand sank into a chair crying: 'My poor boy! My poor, poor boy!'

William Murray could not bear to see anyone in tears; and it was not only because he was a minister that he felt obliged to comfort those in disress. On this occasion, however, his own distress was so immediate and unexpected that his instinctive attempt to comfort the old woman was awkward and perfunctory.

He found himself outside on the pavement with some confused idea in his head that Miss Shand had sent him out to find Hector and bring him back. He started off mechanically with long strides, but the street was so thickly crowded with Saturday-nighters that his impatience drove him into the roadway. He ejaculated irrelevant words as he walked. 'No, no,' he said, and 'Evil, evil.' The rain had stopped, but the storm was not yet spent; high above the blue arc-lamps of the High Street a wild scud of clouds was flying over the waning moon, and, as if driven by the same force, the minister flew along the street below.

Blindly he turned out of the High Street. He wanted to get hold of the man. Had Janet Shand asked him to catch Hector Shand, or had she not? Anything might happen, she had said, with Hector in that mood. His fists clenched and unclenched as they swung. His heart was pounding; little pulses hammered in his eyes. 'Evil, evil.'

In the side-street where he now was, a dark street indifferently lit by gas-lamps that flung yellow rings upon the wet pavement, the minister suddenly came to himself, and leaned against a wall. He was possessed by evil, his body was shaking with anger, his fists were thinking of hitting Hector Shand, of hitting him and hitting him until he crumpled up. The last time he had been so invaded by anger was as a boy of fourteen when he had seized a bully at the school and pounded his head against a window until the window smashed in. His remorse afterwards, and his terror of the murderous fury that had thrilled him, had converted him to that contemplation of the eternal love of God in which he had found serenity. Not until this day had the devil entered into him again.

He walked to and fro between the two gas-lamps, filled with an anguish of shame. He a minister of the Gospel, a servant of Christ! He stood on the edge of the pavement and stared at the wall, a high, well-built wall enclosing a garden. Its regularly cut stones were so smoothly fitted together that there was neither handhold nor foothold all the way up to the top, although the stones were greenish with age. The minister stared at it as if obsessed.

Smooth, blank, and yet frowning, the wall stared back at him. The minister shut his eyes as if the sight of the wall had become intolerable. 'O God,' he prayed, and again, and again: 'O God,' the simple incantation with which the soul seeks to recover a communion it has lost.

When he began to walk again it was at a more sober pace. He had sinned. He had met evil with evil. One should overcome evil with good. One should be sorry for a man like Hector Shand, not murderously angry with him. At any rate, he was in no fit state to pursue the man; he could do nothing spiritually effective; he felt spent.

But young Mrs Hector was sobbing her heart out. He shivered a little as the remembrance of her tears called up the scene again. It was dreadful to live with evil in one's own household. She had in her husband the same kind of problem that he had in Ned. They needed all their strength, both of them. . . . They must help each other. . . . And for her sake something ought to be done at once. Something had to be done if only to relieve the oppression round his own heart. . . . The minister decided to ask John Shand to go himself and fetch his brother home.

'Is Mr Shand in?' he asked the maid, wearily supporting himself by the iron railing. 'Can I see him privately for a few moments?'

The girl hesitated.

'Is it Mr John Shand or Mr Hector?' she said.

'Are they both here?'

'Yes, sir.'

The minister swayed a little.

'Oh, then it doesn't matter; it doesn't matter,' he mumbled, and turned down the steps again.

The sound of a gramophone followed him, as the astonished maid peered after him.

'Losh keep's a'!' she said to herself as she shut the door.

Sarah Murray observed her brother's dejection when he came into the sitting-room, where she was knitting by the fire.

'What's the matter, William? Didn't you see Mrs Hector?'

'Yes.'

'Is she going to take a stall, then?'

'I think so; yes, I believe she will.'

Sarah knitted on in silence. If William wouldn't tell her she wasn't going to ask.

'Supper's nearly ready,' she said finally.

'Was Ned all right at tea-time?' asked William, without lifting his head from his hand.

'Not so bad. That's to say, he never said a word.'

'He *is* better, Sarah, don't you think?'

Sarah scratched her head with a knitting-needle.

'You can't call it a way of living to lie in bed every day till dinner-time and sit up every night till two in the morning and never set a foot across the outside door,' she said sharply. 'The only difference I see is that I've got the upper hand of him now.'

'What makes you think that, Sarah?'

'I've *daured* him,' said Sarah. 'Ever since one night I went into his room and stood up to him. He knows now that I can stand up to him, and we've had less trouble ever since. There's no more word of Teenie giving notice, nor there won't be as long as I'm in the house, and Ned knows it. So I just let him lie in bed in the mornings; it keeps him out of the way. I believe, William, that it's yon breakdown of his he fashes himself about: I think he can't account for it. So I rub that into him between times. . . . It's just pure daftness to put up with him,' she added angrily. 'What kind of a life is it for a laddie of his age? He's just been pampered in this house. But you won't find strangers willing to do that. It might do him good to be living away from us. Except that I don't see what kind of a job he could possibly be any good at.'

'You're wrong there, Sarah; he's a very able fellow, Ned.'

'He is, is he? Pity his ability can't be turned in a more useful direction. . . . I must say I don't think much of intellect,' finished Sarah. 'People who can pass examinations often don't seem to be fit for anything else.'

If that was a furtive fling at Mrs Hector Shand it missed the mark; William seemed not to have heard it.

Sarah collected her knitting and went to see about supper.

Ned came down to supper and sat silently hunched over his plate. William was uncommonly silent too, and Sarah felt a little sulky as she filled the plates and passed them down. She could not help wishing for once that she had a sensible man like John Shand in the house. William was all right, of course; but he was in a queer mood. He had been having queer moods lately. And he was seeing a good deal too much of that young Mrs Hector. What had happened to-night, she wondered.

After supper, as Ned was sliding out of the door, William called: 'Ned!'

Ned paused suspiciously.

'Won't you play me a game of chess!'

'No, I'm busy.'

Ned pulled the door behind him with his usual force but the usual slam did not result, for William had caught hold of it.

'What are you busy at? Mathematics?'

Ned thrust his head in and jerked a thumb at Sarah.

'Needn't think you're going to copy *her*,' he said.

'I was only asking,' said William gently, 'because I'm interested. I know you're a wonder at mathematics.'

'*She* thinks she knows everything,' said Ned, still glaring at Sarah.

But he did not go.

'I'm not doing mathematics; I'm writing a story,' he shot out suddenly.

'A story?' William was pleased.

Sarah shrugged and began to collect the dishes.

'A story,' said Ned emphatically. 'About the world as it should be. Every house in all the towns empty. Nothing but cats and dogs. No *women*.'

His eye was still fixed on Sarah's back as she vanished into the kitchen. Then he looked doubtfully at his brother.

'I'd like to see it,' said William eagerly. 'May I come up?'

'What d'you want to see it for, all of a sudden?'

Ned's face was twisted with suspicion; his eyes had a dull, guarded look.

How thin the poor fellow's getting! thought William, and he put his hand on Ned's shoulder.

'My dear lad,' he said, 'my dear Ned, just because you're my brother.' He let his hand lie, endeavouring to convey his affection through the contact.

Ned shook it off furiously.

'Who do you think I am?' he shouted. 'Jesus Christ?'

He spat venomously in his brother's face and slammed the door.

THREE

Elizabeth was still lying on her bed when Hector came home.
She could see a patch of the night sky through the window.
She had long stopped sobbing, and in the centre of the black
cloud which encompassed her world a nucleus of calm
weather was forming. She stared at the patch of sky; there
was enough moonlight to illumine it faintly; clouds seemed
to be marching over it to an unheard processional music,
punctuated now and then by a star. What a fool she was, she
thought. The love between Hector and herself was as enduring as those stars behind the fugitive clouds.

Her heart leapt as she heard him come in. He had not
stayed at the Club, then; he had come back to her. She half
turned, listening; his feet seemed to be mounting the stairs
into her very bosom.

'Elizabeth!' he said, opening the door. His voice was
humble. She sat up and held out her arms in the darkness.

'My darling, my darling,' she said.

With inarticulate murmurs they caressed each other. The
bliss of relaxation began to steal over Elizabeth, the peace of
reunion, but Hector was still clutching her tight and pressing
his face against her. She stroked his cheek.

'How could you do it, my love?' she asked.

'I was just mad with jealousy,' said Hector, still clinging.
'Jealous of that damned snivelling sky-pilot. I couldn't help
it, Elizabeth; it just came over me, and I felt mad.'

She kissed him on the forehead.

'But you *know*, don't you, that you needn't feel jealous of
anybody?'

He shook his head vehemently.

'But you *do* know,' she insisted. 'You're a part of myself. I
simply couldn't fall in love with anybody else.'

61

'I'm always afraid of losing you,' said Hector, his voice muffled in her dress. 'I'm no highbrow; I can't talk about books and things; and some day you'll turn me down. . . . I deserve it,' he went on, lifting his head. 'When I think of all the girls I've turned down I feel that you're going to be my punishment for the lot.'

Elizabeth's spirits were rapidly rising; she shook him a little and said: 'Oh, you silly ass!' Then she kissed him full on the mouth. They lay for some time without speaking.

'All the same,' said Elizabeth at last, 'I'm glad you didn't stay at the Club drinking yourself dottier.'

'I didn't go to the Club,' said Hector, twisting and untwisting a piece of her hair. 'I – you won't forgive me if I tell you, but I must tell you.'

Elizabeth drew away a little. She had forgiven him; she didn't want confessions; she was beginning vaguely to dislike Hector's insistence on lengthy confessions.

'What does it matter?' she said. 'The only thing that matters is *this*.'

'It does matter.' Hector's voice was sombre. 'You don't know what an out-and-out rotter I can be. I went down the back lane with Mabel, and I was feeling so mad, and she was jawing at me about behaving myself better, and I knew what a little bitch she was, and her arm was always coming up against mine, and – well, I just took hold of her and kissed her as hard as I could.'

'What?' said Elizabeth incredulously. 'Mabel? Did she let you?'

'She liked it all right, you bet your life! She pretended she didn't. But I was — Oh, hell, when I'm in that state I *know*, I tell you, and I just knew she was itching for it.'

'Well,' said Elizabeth, 'is that all?'

Her voice was quite cool.

'That's about all,' said Hector.

He was beginning to feel relieved. Elizabeth wasn't going to cut up rough after all.

'I swore I'd paint the town sky-blue scarlet unless she asked me in for a drink, and I gave her a lot of slosh about her influence over me and all that, until she nearly purred. So I went in with her and had a drink, and we danced a bit —'

'Have you been there all this time?'

Hector stopped in surprise at the sudden sharpness of the question.

'It's not so very late,' he said. 'John —'

Elizabeth pushed him away and sat up sobbing:

'That's all you care, is it? That's all you care. You go out leaving me heart-broken, and then you go fooling with Mabel for hours and hours, leaving me – leaving me —'

All the rage and self-pity that had apparently vanished was closing over her again.

'I had to tell you, don't you see?' Hector kept on repeating. 'I *have* to be sure you won't turn me down.'

He felt rather helpless; he had not expected her to be quite so jealous. He said so.

'I'm not jealous!' shrieked Elizabeth. 'It would never come into my head to be jealous of anybody, let alone Mabel. I think jealousy is idiotic. I'm simply *angry*, because you could go out and enjoy yourself after hurting me so much.'

'The hell you are!' Hector began to feel angry too. Damned unreasonable, he thought.

Elizabeth slapped the hand he was trying to caress her with.

He got off the bed.

'I might as well go and get roaring drunk,' he said, making for the door.

Elizabeth sprang after him. 'If you do,' she said, 'I'll come and get drunk too.'

Her threat sounded like mere bravado even to herself. A sense of weakness came over her.

'Don't go,' she said. 'I can't do without you.'

The reconciliation made them very happy. It also blinded them to the real issue between them which had obtruded itself nakedly enough in their quarrel, and as they sat cheek by cheek agreeing together what fools they had been their unanimity was more apparent than real. Elizabeth meant that she had been a fool to be miserable at all, since their love could never die, while Hector meant that he had been a fool to be jealous of a half-man like the minister. Elizabeth was now ready to regard Hector's sojourn with Mabel merely as an attempt to distract himself from his unhappiness, and

Hector was ready to look on Elizabeth's friendliness to the minister as the polite amiability of a hostess; but they did not recognize that in so construing each other's actions they had each left out a good deal of the truth.

'We need a change of some kind,' said Elizabeth finally, after turning over in her mind the various circumstances preceding the outburst. She was glad to lay the blame of it on Calderwick. 'Let's take a day off to-morrow.'

But perhaps it was an obscure sense of some change in herself that prompted her to use these words, for in the small hours she awoke with an anguished feeling that she was lost and no longer knew who she was. She had been dreaming that she was at home, but now the window, faintly perceptible, was in the wrong place, and she knew without seeing it that she would collide with unfamiliar furniture were she to get out of bed. There was sweat on her brow and her heart was thumping; the world stretched out on all sides into dark impersonal nothingness and she herself was a terrifying anonymity. She took refuge in a device of her childhood. I'm me, she thought; me, me; here behind my eyes. Mechanically she moved her arm and crooked her little finger as she had often done before. It's me making the finger move; I am behind my eyes, but I'm in the finger too. . . . But the clue she was striving to grasp still eluded her, and if she could not seize it she would be lost for ever. When she was almost rigid with terror the name 'Elizabeth Ramsay' rose into her mind, and the nightmare vanished. Her body relaxed, but her mind with incredible swiftness rearranged the disordered puzzle of her identity. She was Elizabeth Ramsay but she was also Elizabeth Shand. Hector was there. She put out her hand and gently touched the mass of his body under the coverings on the neighbouring bed.

Elizabeth Ramsay she was, but also Elizabeth Shand, and the more years she traversed the more inalterably would she become Elizabeth Shand. Those years of the future stretched endlessly before her; with that queer lucidity which is seldom found in daytime thinking she could see them as a perspective of fields, each one separated by a fence from its neighbour. Over you go, said a voice, and over she went, then into the next and the next and the next. But this was no longer time or space, it was eternity; there was no end, no goal; perhaps a higher fence marked the boundary betwen life and death, but in the fields beyond it she was still Elizabeth Shand. She was beginning to be terrified again, and opened her eyes. Mrs Shand, she said to herself. It was appalling, and she had never realized it before.

Hector's quiet breathing rose and fell like an almost imperceptible ripple of sound. He was sunk beneath the waves of sleep, she thought, flying as usual from metaphor to metaphor; he was gathered up within himself like a tightly shut bud, remote, solitary, indifferent. He was stripped of everything that made companionship possible; he was now simply himself. You are a part of myself, she had told him, but was that true? When she had first emerged from sleep she had had no consciousness of him. In the ultimate resort she too was simply herself.

She was now wide awake, and she lay staring into the darkness seeing the separateness of all human beings. But as if they had gone round an immense circle her thoughts came back to the question of her own identity. Elizabeth Ramsay she was, but also Elizabeth Shand, and she herself, that essential self which awoke from sleep, had felt lost because she had forgotten that fact.

Elizabeth liked to find significance in facts, but she confused significance with mystery. The more mysterious anything appeared to her the more she was convinced of its significance. The change in her name which she had hitherto lightly accepted now seemed to her of overwhelming importance.

Hector, separate as he is, she argued, would not be sleeping so quietly if he and I were not in harmony. So even in sleep, that last refuge of the separate personality, there must be some communion between us. He rests in me and I in him. In a sense therefore it is true that we are part of each other.

She sat up in bed and bent half over him. He was curled up on his side, facing her, and she could just discern the outline of his cheek beneath the darker hair. A great tenderness towards him flowed through her. She could not live without him. She was not only herself: she was herself-and-Hector.

Their quarrel had ended, she remembered, when she had abandoned her pride and told him she could not do without him. Pride is the stalk, she said to herself, but love is the flower. Give up the old Elizabeth Ramsay, she told herself, emotion sweeping her away, and became Elizabeth Shand.

She lay down again. She must learn to be a wife. Was that what Aunt Janet was driving at?

It was a long time before she fell asleep. But she fell asleep smiling.

FOUR

On Sunday mornings in Calderwick the streets are hushed; no whistling of baker is heard or monotonous jangling of coal-bell; the very dogs, furtively let out for a run before church time, slink more quietly along the pavements, missing the smells and sounds of weekday traffic. On this Sunday morning both sky and earth were new washed and sparkling after the storm; the air was unseasonably mild, and the people of Calderwick, as they struggled into their Sunday clothes, felt that it was real Sabbath weather.

At a quarter to eleven the church bells began to ring. With an effort one could distinguish the various bells – the four United Free, the Congregational, the Wesleyan, the Baptist, the Roman Catholic and the Episcopal bells – but all were overborne by the peal from the Parish Kirk, which rang out irregularly, gaily and yet commandingly over the town. The Parish Kirk had the only peal of bells in Calderwick, including the great bell whose deep note rang curfew every night at ten o'clock: the single tones of the free-lance churches could not but sound tinny in comparison.

In response to the summons doors opened in every street, and streams of soberly clad people began to converge in the middle of the town, where the river of churchgoers flowed strongly down the High Street, overbearing with ease a small cross-current setting towards the Plymouth Brethren. Like other large rivers it divided again near the end of its journey, and drew off congregation by congregation, leaving the main wash of the flood to spend itself in the spacious dusk of the Parish Kirk.

St James's United Free Church, where Sarah Murray was already at her post in the manse pew, was a small building holding about six hundred souls. It was lined and seated with pine-wood in a cheerful shade of yellow; it had an organ with painted pipes, a canopy of stars shining on a blue sky above the pulpit, and windows filled with lozenges of transparent coloured glass, red, yellow, blue and an occasional purple, which combined into geometrical patterns if one looked at them long enough. High up on the wall immediately facing the pulpit was the large white dial of a clock. It was not true to say of William Murray, as Mary Watson did, that he preached with his eye on the clock, for although he gazed at the clock face he never noticed what hour it registered. He stared at the expressionless white circle because it helped him to forget the rustlings and coughings in the congregation below, and through a kind of self-hypnosis helped to lift him into a transcendental world favourable for sermons.

On this Sunday morning the minister was paler than usual, climbed very slowly up the pulpit steps, and seemed to have taken a vow not to look at his congregation. Once he cast a hasty glance at the Shand pew, then during the hymn he looked steadily again in the same direction; there were only three figures in the pew, however – John Shand, his wife and Miss Janet Shand, in her best toque. But he gave out his text in a firm voice: 'Matthew, chapter five, verse twenty-two: "Whosoever is angry with his brother without a cause shall be in danger of the judgment . . . but whosoever shall say, Thou fool, shall be in danger of hell fire."'

When the rustling of turning pages died down the congregation began to sit up. The way in which he had said 'hell fire' gave them a shock. Mary Watson twisted round to look at the clock, put a cinnamon lozenge into her mouth, and prepared to listen.

Because hell fire was not to be taken literally, said the minister, one dared not assume that it did not exist.

Mary began to nod her head emphatically, and kept on nodding it. This was something like. What had come over Milk-and-water Willie? His een were fair blazing.

'Cut off from the communion of God and cast into outer darkness,' said the minister. There was a desperateness in his voice which thrilled his hearers.

It was a pity that Elizabeth and Hector did not hear that sermon; he was never to preach another so good.

Hector and Elizabeth were escaping on bicycles, pedalling along the upland ridges to the north of Calderwick where wide fields sweep down in bare curves to the sea-cliffs and on the other side thick forests of pine run up to the flanks of the mountains. Rain never lingers on these sandy roads and winter takes little from the austere beauty of the landscape. Elizabeth and Hector tinkled their bells merrily as they ran down a slope towards a foaming brown torrent that was carrying its load of rain to the sea. Elizabeth gazed at Hector's broad shoulders receding in front of her. It pleased her to recognize that he was both stronger and heavier than she was. That helped her to be Mrs Hector Shand.

Next day she was still happy and humble. Her new mood of dedication led her after breakfast to darn Hector's socks 'exactly like a wife', as she said to herself. In the afternoon she avoided Emily Scrymgeour and went down to the sea.

The sand was firm and level; the sand-dunes had been curved by the wind as by a slicing knife into clean, exact curves; the long tawny grass above was matted and tufted like the sodden fell of a weary animal. The land was still and quiet, but the sea had not yet forgotten its rage. There was a deep swell, and the smooth backs of the rollers heaved to an incredible height before toppling and plunging in cataracts of foam. Elizabeth turned her back upon the land and revelled in the recklessness with which the walls of water hurled themselves headlong. Shock after shock of the plunging monsters vibrated through her until she was lashed to an equal excitement and hurled back again the charging passion of the sea. That was the way to live, she cried within herself. Hector and Elizabeth Shand together would transform the world.

Characteristically she did not remember that although she had turned her back on the land it was still there, quiet and unshaken.

After her orgy by the sea Elizabeth felt the need of making a large decisive gesture. She took the longer way home, which led past the manse of St James's, and pulled the bell loudly at the manse door. Teenie dumbly opened the sitting-room door for her and vanished. There was a figure in the dusk beside the window curtain, and Elizabeth, still panting for immediate action, rushed towards it crying:

'Oh, Mr Murray, I've come to apologize. . . .'

Ned stepped forward, and Elizabeth's ears burned. At the same time she felt that Ned's thin white face was pitiful, and her heart nearly died away when he said: 'So I'm not to be kicked in the gutter like a dog and left lying?'

'You?' said Elizabeth. 'No, never.'

They stared at each other.

'I saw you get the Dunlop Medal,' said Elizabeth suddenly, in a breathless voice. 'A lot of us went in to see the Math. show and I saw you get the Dunlop Medal.'

'Of course, I remember you,' said Ned. He waved an arm. 'Please take a chair. What are you doing here?' he went on. 'Got a job?'

'No, I'm not working.'

This answer seemed to please Ned.

'So I'm not the only one,' he said. 'I'm staying here with my brother; he's a minister, you know. I might have been a minister too, but they never let me take Hebrew. . . . There's always something.' He bent forward confidentially and tapped on the table. 'The thing to do is to keep dodging. Keep dodging, for they're cunning. They'll get you if they can —'

The door opened, and Ned's expression changed in a flash. His face, which, as Elizabeth noted with a sinking depression, was essentially handsomer than his brother's, twisted until it became mean and ugly, he contracted his shoulders as if ready to spring and snarled rather than said: 'Good God!'

William Murray came in quietly, as if nothing had happened. He greeted Elizabeth almost with coldness, and sat down. Ned was still glaring at his brother, and Elizabeth's mouth dried up as she looked at him. She could think of nothing to say.

William's voice said politely: 'This has been a lovely day, hasn't it?'

'Glorious,' she answered quickly. 'I've been down to the sea. It was – it was glorious.'

Ned rose and stood at the window with his back to them,

jerking his head round from time to time with an uneasy twist as if his collar irked him.

'When the sun began to set,' Elizabeth babbled on, 'the foam caught all the colour, first rose and then lavender. And the lip of each wave spilled over the sand was opalescent. And just beneath the top that curls over, you know, the light shone pure green through the water.'

Ned turned swiftly.

'Do you know what I saw in the paper this morning – this very morning?'

His voice was harsh. He came back and leaned over the table.

'A butcher found a little stray kitten in his shop and chopped off his front paws and threw it out. A little stray kitten. Chopped its paws off.'

'Oh no!' cried Elizabeth.

'I'll let you see it in the paper.'

Ned began to shake out a newspaper with exaggerated gestures.

'Mrs Shand doesn't want to hear about it,' said William.

Ned stiffened.

'Mrs Shand?' he said. 'Mrs *Shand*? That's not your name.'

'I've married Hector Shand,' said Elizabeth faintly, because even as she said it she felt that it should not be said.

Ned flung down the paper.

'Trickery!' he said. 'I knew it. The same low cunning! But too obvious, madam, too ob-vi-ous.'

He thrust his face into Elizabeth's with a sudden sneer, and then as suddenly marched out of the room with his head in the air, slamming the door.

The minister propped his elbows on the large table and covered his face with his hands.

Before Elizabeth could do anything Ned's head popped in again.

'The worst of the lot,' he said, 'is Hector Shand.'

He slammed the door, and reopened it immediately.

'He'll wait for you at a back door,' he said, 'and stick a knife into you!'

This time he could be heard tramping away from the door and up the stairs.

William Murray had not moved.

'Mr Murray!' said Elizabeth in a low voice sharpened a little with fear. 'Mr Murray!'

The minister removed his hands.

'You're not afraid of him, are you?'

'I shouldn't be, I know. Oh, it's not *him* I'm afraid of; its the state he gets into that frightens me. I mean, that a human being should be able to get into such a state. I thought at first it was pitiful, but it's more than that.'

She was twisting her fingers together.

'How can such a thing happen?' she said. 'What does it *mean*?'

'I am beginning to think,' said the minister with cold precision, looking at his hands, 'that it means hell fire. Ned is in hell.'

'You mustn't say that.' Elizabeth rose to her feet. 'That's what you mustn't say.'

The minister shrank; he looked weary

'What else?' he muttered.

'I don't know what else. . . . But that makes it seem hopeless. There *must* be some way. . . . You can see that he was meant to be different.'

'Did you know him at the University?'

It was Elizabeth's turn to shrink.

'Not exactly,' she stammered. 'I knew about him, of course. He was a nice boy.'

'And now this.' The minister looked up fiercely. 'The love of God has been withdrawn from my brother.'

Elizabeth sat down again. She felt suddenly both assured and eager.

'I'm not religious in the ordinary sense,' she began. 'I don't think I'm a Christian. I don't believe in your heaven and hell. I believe in something that flows through the universe. When I'm in touch with it I know at once; I feel happy; I feel I can do anything. You can call it God if you like. I have just found it again after losing it for months. It can be lost and found. It's not a permanent state like heaven or hell. Your brother has lost it and why should he not find it again?'

The minister covered his face again, and muttered something undistinguishable.

'It's not outside, it's *inside* oneself. And yet it comes suddenly, as if from outside. You must know what I mean, or you would not be a minister.'

William Murray stared at her.

'You are right,' he said. 'I would not be a minister if I did not know it.'

'It's what makes life worth living,' said Elizabeth, her face glowing.

It occurred to her on the way home that she had forgotten to apologize to the minister. The apology, however, no longer mattered. They had gone far beyond that.

FIVE

On the following Thursday Hector was surprised to find on his office desk a note from Aunt Janet asking him to come in to see her on his way home in the evening. When he saw the envelope he had a vaguely guilty feeling, but even after reading its contents he could not think what was in the wind. Probably nothing much. Perhaps she only wanted to talk over John's extraordinary invitation to Lizzie. Queer old card, John. Hector looked at him with the secret satisfaction he had felt all the week and reiterated to himself: 'I've kissed *your* wife, you old pi-jaw, and that's more than you can say to me!' He wondered for a second or two if Mabel had said anything to Aunt Janet, and even though he was sure that she was not such a fool he had an uneasy conscience when he met his aunt.

'Haven't seen you for a long time,' he said in a loud, affectionate voice. 'Been too busy all week being a good boy. Let me see, yes, Monday, at home canoodling the wife; Tuesday, pills at the Club and *no* drinks – home at ten o'clock; Wednesday, canoodling the wife again, and this is Thursday. See the wings beginning to sprout just where my back tickles?'

Aunt Janet patted him fondly. But he knew his aunt, and he knew that something was bothering her. He sat down and pulled his chair plump in front of her, then, taking her hands in his, he said: 'Cough it up, Mumsie. Anything you don't like about your little Hector?'

The pressure of Aunt Janet's fingers responded as he had expected to the name she liked best to hear him use, and which he never used before others.

'I want to talk to you about Elizabeth, Hector,' she said.

Hector's relief was as great as his astonishment.

74

'About Elizabeth? What's she been doing?'

'Oh, nothing – nothing that means anything at least. She's a dear girl, Hector, and I know she loves you, but she's just a little thoughtless. Thoughtless, that's all. She doesn't know how people look at things. And Mabel and I have agreed that perhaps a few hints from you would help her more than anything we could say.'

Hector's eyes darkened.

'Mabel's a little cat. I'd like to know what *she* can find to pick on in Elizabeth.'

'Yes, yes, I know, I know. Mabel has her faults, I don't deny it. But she has more *experience* than Elizabeth, dear. In some ways Elizabeth is very young for her age. For instance, at the University slang and student manners are all very well, but they don't do in a place like Calderwick, Hector.'

'Has she been saying damn or something like that?' Hector was grinning.

'It's much more serious than that, my dear. Although that's bad enough. You now what a position the Shands have in the town, and I will say this for Mabel, she keeps up her position wonderfully. But Eizabeth seems to be quite unconscious of it. It appears she has been quite rude to some of Mabel's friends – not unkind, you know, but thoughtlessly rude; and she goes about a great deal with that Mrs Scrymgeour. Mabel and I don't think Mrs Scrymgeour is a good influence for any young woman. Of course, Dr Scrymgeour is a good doctor, and Mrs Scrymgeour goes to church and all that, but the nice people in this town don't think very much of her, and Elizabeth is being tarred with the same brush. Little things, Hector, little things; like running about without gloves and saying damn, and screaming with laughter in the street like a mill-girl – all little things, Hector, but they count for a great deal. Mrs Scrymgeour is not the companion for Elizabeth. She spends all her time gossiping in shops, I hear. Well, Elizabeth's father was a small shop-keeper himself – I don't like to remind you of that, but —'

'Stuff and nonsense! Elizabeth has nothing to do with that. I'm damned lucky to have her for a wife, Aunt Janet.'

'I didn't mean that, Hector. It's so difficult. What I mean is that she doesn't *know*, she has no standards to tell her that gossiping with tradespeople isn't the right thing for a Shand. Not that she's a common girl, at all —'

'See here, Aunt Janet, you're backing the wrong horse. Elizabeth has more brains in her little finger than Mabel ever will have in her whole body.'

'But that's just why she needs guidance, Hector. If she weren't a very unusual girl it wouldn't matter so much. It's just because she doesn't think of the little things that somebody must do it for her. And it's not only Mrs Scrymgeour. . . . The town is beginning to talk about the way she's been going about with Mr Murray. Every day this week, Hector.'

'The town has a damned impudence!' Hector scowled.

'She's told me all about that,' he went on. 'The sky-pilot's in trouble, and Elizabeth is doing her best for him and his measly brother. I don't say they're worth it, but that's no reason for blackballing Elizabeth.'

'I know, I know; but then people are *like* that.'

Aunt Janet saw she would have to produce her trump card after all.

'And with my own eyes, Hector, I saw something I hoped I wouldn't have to mention. There was a meeting on Wednesday afternoon about the sale of work, which is on the 20th you know, and I saw Elizabeth sitting so close to Mr Murray at one point that one of her feet was between his. I know that others saw it too.'

Hector no longer grinned; he laughed, perhaps too loudly.

'Sure you weren't seeing double, Mumsie? Was it only tea you had at the meeting.'

'My dear Hector, you don't need to tell me that Elizabeth didn't intend it: I am sure she didn't even notice it. And that's just the point. She must be taught to notice these things.'

Aunt Janet was in her most earnest mood, but she failed to get a serious reply from her nephew. When he suggested chaining up Elizabeth with a padlock during his absence if John would do the same for Mabel she began to grow angry.

'These things may not matter very much among men, although I should have thought that no decent man would like to see his wife making a fool of herself, but they matter very much among women.'

Women be damned, thought Hector.

He was perturbed, both by Janet's disapproval of his wife and by her indignation. Her anger always made him feel uncomfortable, but when it was visited on his own head he could allay the storm by a confession and penitence which finally brought absolution. Her anger with Elizabeth merely confused him; he did not know what to do.

'What's more,' added Aunt Janet, 'this ridiculous idea of John's is going to bring Lizzie here, and Elizabeth will be exposed to *her* influence next. If you don't put Elizabeth on her guard – you don't know Lizzie, of course, but I do.'

Aunt Janet's shake of the head relegated Lizzie to unmentionable depths.

Hector, like all the other men of his acquaintance, accepted unthinkingly the suggestion that women were the guardians of decorum – good women, that is to say, women who could not be referred to as 'skirts'. Good women existed to keep in check men's sensual passions. A man, driven by physical desire, they argued, is mad and reckless, and his sole protection from himself is the decorum of women. They believed that any decent man would afterwards be grateful to a woman who had prevented him from seducing her. It is possible that 'the weaker sex' – a phrase constantly on their lips and in their minds – was an accusation against women for not being entirely exempt from frailty. At any rate, Lizzie Shand used to tell her friends that in Scotland man's chief end was to glorify God and woman's to see that he did it.

Hector's emotions, therefore, as he listened to Aunt Janet's strictures on Elizabeth's want of decorum were disquieting and profound. He felt much as the driver of a high-powered locomotive would feel on being assured at the top of a steep decline that his brakes were defective. His business was to drive the engine; the brakes were Elizabeth's concern, not his; but if she could not do her duty as a woman he would leave the rails and wreck himself fatally.

Hector Shand was not extraordinarily stupid. This apparently logical division of duties between the sexes seemed natural even to clever men in bigger towns than

Calderwick. Still more surprisingly it was accepted with pride by accomplished women, who devoted all their ingenuity to putting on the brakes as frequently and as smoothly as possible.

Because Hector's confusion was painful to himself, and because he felt that women knew their own affairs best, he repeated with increasing energy 'Women be damned!' as he made his way home. He had been struck, too, by Mumsie's reference to the approaching arrival of Lizzie. What could have come over John? He supposed that, after all, John had not wholly escaped the herditary weaknesses of the Shands, and that his weakness was coming out in queer spots, the old hypocrite!

But Elizabeth was so happy to see him that he began to feel resentful of Aunt Janet's insinuations. Elizabeth was all right.

'Been to see Aunt Janet,' he said carelessly. 'She's in an awful stew because Lizzie's coming.'

'Oh, Hector, I'm looking forward so much to seeing Lizzie!'

'Whatever for?'

'She sounds exciting. Besides, just think of meeting another Elizabeth Shand! Elizabeth Shand by birth and Elizabeth Shand by marriage – it gives me the queerest feeling. It's like seeing yourself in a mirror for the first time.'

'By God, I hope not! According to Aunt Janet, Lizzie's a worse Shand than I am. Aunt Janet hates her like poison. A sneering, godless bitch, that's what she is. Probably drinks like a fish. I shouldn't wonder. Lying about in the streets of Monte Carlo most likely and damned glad to come here for a decent meal. I wouldn't have believed it of John. Aunt Janet thinks he must have sent her money to come with. I wonder what his little game is?'

'You just swallow whatever Aunt Janet says. I don't believe a word of it. My opinion of John has gone up ever since he asked her.'

'I don't swallow everything Aunt Janet says. What have I been doing this last hour but contradicting her to her face?'

Elizabeth was amused.

'Have you been sticking up for yourself?'

'No, I've been sticking up for you.'

'For *me*?'

'It's all that little wretch Mabel,' said Hector hastily. 'She's been spinning yarns to Aunt Janet about you. I told her they were yarns.'

'What yarns, Hector?'

'Oh, yarns about you letting Mabel's dignity down in Calderwick.'

'I like that! Mabel!' Elizabeth's tone was scornful enough.

'And Aunt Janet was begging me to save you from the Scrymgeour female.'

'Oh, I know all about that,' said Elizabeth, her nose in the air. 'Mabel's set are always trying to have a dig at Emily Scrymgeour. I even heard Mrs Melville calling Emily vulgar because she nods and smiles to her own maid when she meets her in the street. And I said in a loud voice that I'd stop and pull my Mary Ann by the tail if she were to pass me without seeing me. They didn't like that.'

She added with a laugh: 'I'm glad you kissed Mabel. It makes me feel more equal to her.'

'Kiss her every day in the week to please you,' offered Hector.

Elizabeth settled herself on his knee and pulled his hair.

'I'm being a good wife this week, am I not?'

'A peach of a wife, I don't think! What about your scandalous goings-on with the sky-pilot? Aunt Janet was telling me about that too.'

'Why, what on earth could she have to tell?'

As lightly as possible Hector retailed the incident reported by Aunt Janet, exaggerating his aunt's horror. Its effect on his wife was not at all what he had expected.

Elizabeth was more of a prude than either of them realized. She had freed herself only partially from the prevailing suggestion that sex was shameful. If in the beginning she had not enjoyed Hector's first kiss so much that she was convinced of her great love for him she would have been ashamed to remember it. She had never been accustomed either to give or to receive caresses, and it was only with Hector, her lover and her husband, that she could feel unashamed of her body.

But because she set love above marriage she thought herself broadminded, and other people, including Hector, accepted her at her own valuation.

She was flaming with rage and shame.

'But Aunt Janet *knows* me!' she repeated. 'How could she ever think of such a thing?'

Hector followed her about.

'I told her it was all rot,' he kept saying.

'But that she should *think* it, Hector. What can one do with people who have such dirty minds. And she *knows* me; it isn't as if she didn't *know* me.'

That was the sore point for Elizabeth. She began to think that she must be vulgar without realizing it if other people could believe such things of her. Vulgarity was a word she despised, but it had the fascination of mystery. It made her feel woolly-headed, she used to say, because it was so meaningless. Did she lack something, she now asked herself, that everybody else possessed? Had she a blind spot?

With a fresh access of shame she remembered how less than a week ago she had opened her heart to Aunt Janet. Surely, she told herself, surely anybody who wasn't an utter fool would have realized then what kind of a woman Elizabeth Shand was. If one were to be misunderstood like that the only thing to do was to keep oneself to oneself. It was she who had been the fool to trust Aunt Janet so much.

She felt inclined to avoid everybody except Emily Scrymgeour. As for the minister – she had said already all she could say to him: one could not go on repeating oneself interminably.

'They can all go to the devil!' said Elizabeth to Hector. 'The Murrays too, for all I care. And I'm damned if ever I'll attend another Ladies' Work Party!'

The intensity of his wife's resentment assured Hector more than ever that Elizabeth was right. She wouldn't let him down.

SIX

Mabel was feeling restless. Calderwick was a dull little hole,
she reflected, as she stood at the window playing with the
cord of the blind. There had been rain all morning, and the
roadway was full of irregularly shaped puddles through
which there bumped an occasional tradesman's van. Drops
of rain were still starring the puddles from time to time, and
the laurustinus behind the railings was dripping. The room
behind her was dark in spite of a fire, but it was too early to
switch on the lights, and at any rate she was bored to death
with the room. She had read the last magazine; she knew by
heart all the bits of music on the piano; she was fed up with
the gramophone; it was too wet to play golf, and nobody was
likely to call. Apparently the only thing that attracted her
interest was the acorn-shaped wooden bob at the end of the
blind cord.

Mabel was not the kind of woman to escape from her
boredom by considering it as an objective phenomenon. Is it
a peculiarly human affliction? she might have asked herself.
Are cats ever bored? Would a child be bored if its parents left
it alone on a desert island? None of these questions occurred
to Mabel. It did not strike her that boredom was a remarkable state in a world full of things to smell, to touch, to taste,
to listen to, and to think about. She assumed – and she may
have been right – that the laurustinus was as bored as she
was, and that the patient grass in the park opposite was
bored by the rain.

She did not even wonder why she was bored. She knew.
John, her husband, was too dull and elderly for her. He went
to the office every day; he came home for meals; he went to
church on Sundays; he kissed her every morning and every
night; he gave her money when she asked for it. He wouldn't

dance; even the records he liked to hear on the gramophone were boring things without a decent tune; he wasn't interested in her friends, and, in general, he was just a bore. Mabel let go the acorn bob so that it hit the window-pane with a sharp rap.

The only person he was really interested in, she thought, was his precious sister. And he was getting grumpy because he hadn't heard yet whether she was coming or not. But if Lizzie Shand were in the south of France why on earth should she come to Calderwick in the middle of winter? Mabel had seen posters advertising the south of France, and as she gazed out of the window she noted that Calderwick was colourless – grey skies, grey pavements, grey people. She herself would become grey in the course of time. Sarah Murray, she thought with a flash of spitefulness and horror, was grey already, inside if not out, although she was only a little over thirty. Mabel looked down at the silken sleeve of her rose-coloured gown. Then she walked deliberately up to her bedroom, turned on the lights and drew the curtains.

Nearly an hour later she was standing with all the frocks she possessed scattered around her, hanging over chairs, and lying on the bed. Her hair was a little ruffled; her cheeks were glowing. She had tried the frocks on, every one, but she had now come to the last of them, and she did not know what to do next. She was no longer bored, however; she was pleased by her own prettiness, and with renewed self-confidence she began to approve of herself in other aspects also. For instance, she had conscientiously done her best for Hector.

Any other woman might have led him on after that sudden kiss in the back lane; it was nearly a whole week ago, but she still remembered the thrill that ran down her spine when he kissed her. A heartless woman would have made a fool of him; a prig would have told her husband; but she, Mabel, had magnanimously used her power over him to keep him out of temptation. Nor had she told Aunt Janet of her favourite's lapse; she had instead urged on Aunt Janet the necessity of making Elizabeth into a better wife for Hector. She and Janet between them, she had suggested, could turn Elizabeth into more of a lady and less of a vulgar lump. Hector should be grateful. Why not pay a call at number twenty-six, just to show Elizabeth that bygones were bygones? She hadn't seen either of them since that last Saturday. It was nearly half-past four now; Hector would be at home by five; they would all have tea together.

The last shreds of her boredom vanished into the wardrobe with her frocks. John could have tea by himself. She was going on an errand of mercy, as it were, and even wifely duty had to give way to larger issues, had it not? She put on her pearls.

The acorn bob hung listlessly at the window of the empty drawing-room.

Both Mr and Mrs Hector Shand were at home when Mabel was shown in. Elizabeth was coldly polite, but Mabel had expected that.

'Got up to kill, aren't you?' said Hector, almost savagely. She laid her coat over his arm almost as if she were laying herself, he thought, and seizing her hat he brutally clapped it on his own head. The plume of cock's feathers streamed out behind his ear.

'All I want are a few kiss-curls,' he said, his eyes glittering as he looked at Mabel, 'and then I could play the peacock as well as any of you women.'

Mabel gave a little scream of concern.

'You'll ruin my hat, Hector! Take it off.'

'You deserve to have it ruined.' Hector twirled the hat on his hand.

Elizabeth was still cold.

'Put Mabel's things on the sofa,' she said. 'And ring the bell for another cup, please.'

Hector sniffed loudly as he sat down again.

'Been drenching yourself with some kind of stink, haven't you? All the street-walkers do that. I thought you were a respectable married woman?'

He had reverted to his old habit of baiting Mabel, but he was doing it with more venom than before, thought Elizabeth. She began to think he was going too far in his merciless criticism of Mabel's clothes, voice, manner, and conventional standards. Mabel was showing more and more resentment. No wonder.

Mabel too was aware that there was a new undertone in

Hector's railing. It annoyed her, but it fluttered her with an excitement that was quite pleasurable. At any rate, Hector did not bore her as John did. . . . She was conscious of her own lithe figure under the rosy silk of her dress, and of her long, well-shaped legs.

'By the Lord!' said Hector, 'I'll have to thread pink ribbons through my pants, or something. If respectable married women can doll themselves up like that, I don't see why respectable married men shouldn't put up something of a show.'

Elizabeth smiled, but she was not amused by the duel.

Their voices got sharper and sharper. Mabel finally shed all her dignity and put out her tongue: and the more hoyden-ish she became the more quiet and detached was Elizabeth's attitude.

When Mabel rose to go Hector growled:

'I suppose you expect me to take you home in all this rain?'

'You forget, Hector, we're dining with the Scrymgeours to-night: there's no time to spare,' put in Elizabeth.

'Thank God for that,' said Hector. 'The *Scrymgeours*, Mabel, your particular friends, did you notice? We're having dinner with them.'

'You were awfully rude to her,' said Elizabeth, trying to laugh, when Mabel had departed, cock's feathers and all.

'She went off in a huff all right,' Hector's voice was complacent. 'She deserved every bit of it after the things she said about you to Aunt Janet.'

Mabel was annoyed at first as she picked her steps in the dark wet streets. It wouldn't have taken Hector a quarter of an hour to escort her. He was deteriorating. Aunt Janet was right in thinking that Elizabeth would be the ruin of him. Dining with the Scrymgeours were they? Indeed!

She was still smarting from the lash of his tongue. But, incomprehensibly, Hector's rudeness was less offensive than Elizabeth's stupid attempts to palliate it. A phrase from one of her magazines came into her mind as she noted the rustling of her own petticoats: 'the delicious *frou-frou* of femininity'. Elizabeth had none of that, not a particle of it. She perceived suddenly that Hector had been gibing at her femininity in order to save Elizabeth's face.

He's beginning to feel that Elizabeth is a great lump, she said to herself.

She felt younger, more alive, and, on reflection, pleased with the openness of Hector's tactics. He was hard and aggressive; she liked men to be hard and aggressive. She preferred people to be successful rather than sentimental. He was an unscrupulous brute, of course; but she had the whip-hand of him, no doubt of that. John would turn him out of the mill at a word from her. His boldness in the circumstances was not unpleasing.

'Well, little woman?' said John, beaming upon her and showing his strong teeth. 'Where have you been to in all this rain?'

John's contentment was soon explained. He had received by the evening mail a letter from his sister, who was coming on the thirteenth.

'Next Saturday,' said John, rubbing his hands. 'Thirteen was always Lizzie's lucky number, she used to say.'

Mabel curled her lip as she went upstairs. John was growing positively soft.

'I'm so tired,' he had said, yawning and stretching his arms. 'I'll be glad when the week's over and it's Sunday morning again.'

Thank goodness, thought Mabel, it's only Friday night.

Elizabeth was puzzled by the fact that she had felt like a wet blanket during Mabel's visit. She had actually discovered herself feeling outraged by the childishness of the other two, and she had never before regarded herself as definitely grown-up. Was this a part of the process of becoming a wife?

Surely I'm not going to turn into a walking Morality, she thought impatiently. I don't like disapprovers. But if she refused to disapprove, she could not deny that she was disquieted. In Hector's rudeness to Mabel there was something that she did not like.

'I don't know what came over you,' she said to him. 'You made me quite uncomfortable. Suppose I had been going on at John like that, how would you have felt?'

'Grand! I'd have backed you up for all I was worth.'

Elizabeth had to laugh.

'I dislike Mabel too much to chaff her,' she said. 'I suppose that's it. It was really comical how ladylike I felt!'

The Scrymgeours rarely gave dinners, partly because Dr Scrymgeour liked to be left alone at his own fireside and partly because his practice was so extensive that his presence at home could not be guaranteed. But Emily was longing to show off her husband to her new friend, and Elizabeth was now so intimate with Emily Scrymgeour that she felt almost a proprietary interest in the doctor. She was, in fact, identifying a part of herself with Emily, exactly as she had identified a part of herself with Hector. In consequence she thought it absurd of Hector to say he did not like Mrs Scrymgeour; he would like her well enough when he got to know her.

The doctor's wife was a small neatly made woman with large vivacious eyes of so dark a grey that they looked black. Her abundant black hair was glossy, her skin of a smooth pallor which remained impervious to the climatic effects of Calderwick, her quick hands short-fingered, nervous and capable. Her tongue was as quick as her hands, but she had a warm voice and the confiding manner of a child, although she was a good ten years older than Elizabeth.

She had comforted Elizabeth by assuring her that most of the other women in the town were dreadful sticks who hadn't two ideas among them.

'And they're all so frightfully pi,' said Mrs Scrymgeour, 'not like you and me.'

It was a relief to pour into Mrs Scrymgeour's ready ear a confession of inability to be interested in such topics as the winter underwear of husbands and how to keep darns from being scratchy. Mrs Scrymgeour agreed too that whist drives were awfully boring.

'I go to some of them, of course – good for my husband's practice. But they're glad when I stay away, if you know what I mean. I'm such a good player, and it sounds a dreadful thing to say, but most of them are terribly greedy for the prizes.'

Mrs Scrymgeour's method of rearing her child was sniffed at, it appeared, by the Calderwick ladies. She was suckling it herself.

'They think that's so vulgar,' she confided to Elizabeth.

It was also considered undignified for a doctor's lady to push her own perambulator, and no argument could have more effectively secured Elizabeth's constant attendance.

Her friend's manner in shops filled Elizabeth with envy. She had a special crony behind every counter on whom she lavished her bright smiles and who was rewarded for extra attentiveness by confidential gossip. Portly grocers carrying reserved baskets of large eggs came out in their aprons to admire the baby while Elizabeth held the perambulator, and even Mary Watson smiled, although she nodded her head vigorously and said: 'That bairn o' yours is far owre spoilt.'

The care bestowed on the upbringing of young Teddy surprised and fascinated Elizabeth. The doctor, it appeared, was always firing off new theories about the child's development, and these his wife retailed to Elizabeth with great vivacity. She was proud of her husband, and had a fine sense of showmanship.

'But he never screams!' Elizabeth had remarked one day. She had had a vague idea that babies screamed incessantly.

'Oh, doesn't he! He screams for his milk all right. You should hear him.'

'But he never screams while he's out,' persisted Elizabeth.

'Why should he? His little tummy's happy, and he trusts the whole world – even Mary Watson.'

'Da-da,' said the baby.

Mrs Scrymgeour remembered the doctor's latest discovery and expounded it. The baby was saying da-da at present because his teeth were beginning to push through, and his attention kept returning to that part of his mouth. Before that he said ba-ba and boo-boo because his attention was concentrated on putting his lips together, on sucking; and still earlier he said goo-goo, and gay-gay, and gi-gi.

Mrs Scrymgeour bent over to her baby with each new sound and the baby chuckled as if at a great joke.

'And he said that because he was attending to swallowing his milk, guggling it down, which must have been about the first thing he had to learn,' she concluded in triumph. 'Isn't he a nut, my Jim?'

To see a pattern suddenly emerge in life where no pattern was discernible before is one of the keenest of human pleasures, and Elizabeth was thrilled by this orderly explanation of a baby's random sounds. But Mrs Scrymgeour had not finished. She chuckled like her baby and glanced sideways at Elizabeth, saying: 'Of course, it wasn't only swallowing he had to learn in the beginning. When you take in food you have to let it out at the other end, too: and so Teddy used to attend to both ends; he used to grunt at both ends simultaneously.'

Their laughter rang out in the street and even passers-by smiled.

'And Jim swears that the only thing which keeps us from speaking with our tails as well as with our mouths is insuff – insufficient apparatus.'

They both held on to the perambulator, weak with laughter. The baby joined in.

It was simple and pleasant laughter, but Mrs John Shand had not thought so. She had wrinkled her pretty nose in disgust as she saw her sister-in-law making a spectacle of herself with the Scrymgeour woman, and crossed the street to avoid meeting them.

A vulgar creature, she said to herself. It would not be long till Hector's eyes were opened, for, in spite of his faults, he was, after all, a gentleman.

Elizabeth, however, had no misgivings as Hector sat down beside her vivacious friend. She turned expectantly to Dr Scrymgeour.

The doctor looked tall beside his wife, but small beside Hector. He had the slightly explosive manner of the shy man who is daily forced to overcome his shyness. His head was broad rather than long, with a wide forehead that was the first thing one noticed about him. Its width was accentuated by the parting in the middle of the fair hair above it, and it made the rest of his face at first sight insignificant. But his blue eyes were keen, Elizabeth discovered, and his lips, although thin, were beautifully cut. In repose they lay folded upon each other like the lips of a child, she thought.

The promise of that wide forehead attracted her, for she was naïve enought to believe in foreheads as an index to intelligence. She did not think it necessary to stumble over

preliminary nothings, for Emily, with her delightful
directness, had introduced her husband with these words:
'You can tell Elizabeth the worst, James. I've given you
away completely already.' Yet the doctor evaded her with
generalizations when she asked him point-blank for some
more of his theories about the upbringing of children. His
smile was nervous, it even verged on a giggle: he had false
teeth, too, and although she tried to be tolerant Elizabeth
disliked false teeth.

She felt balked.

Her identification with Emily made her feel humiliated as
well as balked. If he tells Emily why shouldn't he tell me?
she thought, and the only possible answer seemed to be that
he did not consider her to be sufficiently intelligent. Perhaps
he was afraid she would be shocked. For the first time it
occurred to Elizabeth that a capacity for being shocked
argued a lack of intelligence. This new idea excited her, as
new ideas always did, and she turned to the doctor, with an
imitation of his wife's most arch manner, crying: 'I believe
you are afraid of shocking me, but you know it's only stupid
people who are ever shocked! Besides I know all about
Teddy speaking at both ends—'

The corners of the doctor's mouth went up.

'Emily's too fond of that story,' he said.

'What story?' called Mrs Scrymgeour across the table.

Elizabeth answered her and Emily laughed heartily.
Elizabeth glanced at Hector to share her enjoyment with
him. To her surprise he looked almost sulky. He shot one
glance at her which she could not interpret and crumbled his
bread.

'Teddy is illuminating a great many phrases and attitudes
for me,' went on the doctor. He began to giggle again.

'Why do the ministers speak of the "milk of the Word"?'

'Do tell me.'

'Watch any baby sucking,' said the doctor with glee, 'and
you'll see it.'

'Oh do tell me!'

'When Teddy sucks he puts all his energy into it—'

'Hear, hear!' from Mrs Scrymgeour.

'And that makes him clench his fists and bend his arms in

and draw up his knees. Now the flexion of the arms brings
the fists close together. Turn him up endways in that position and he would be kneeling in prayer. Sucking the milk of
the Word. There you have it. Isn't it illuminating?'

'What a *lovely* idea!' Elizabeth forgot all about Hector.
'Drawing comfort from Heaven like a child at the breast.'

'There's the Milky Way up in the sky too,' added the
doctor. 'The first god must have been a mother-god. Yes,
yes.'

He was fingering his wine-glass.

'Bottle-feeding,' he fired out suddenly, with another giggle, 'will probably mean the end of religion.'

'James!' said Mrs Scrymgeour in delight. 'That's a new
one!'

'Well, your bottle-fed baby sees the milk going down in
the bottle until there's none left, and he knows that it's
empty. He can't have the same emotional satisfaction as a
child sucking at the breast, which is an apparently inexhaustible source of comfort. Communion with nature, you
know, and all that. Your bottle boy isn't likely to grow up a
mystic.'

'I shall put Teddy on a bottle to-morrow,' declared Emily.

'I wish I had some proof . . . statistics of bottle-fed infants. . . .'

The doctor shook his head in comical rue.

'Nobody draws up the kind of statistics I want. But if
religion knew its business the Pope would issue a Bull
forbidding feeding-bottles. On the other hand, you would
have the rationalists financing feeding-bottles.'

He broke off, chuckling, and drank his wine.

Mrs Scrymgeour was radiant. Her husband was going
through his paces very well, and Elizabeth looked as if she
were enjoying herself. The doctor relinquished his wine-
glass and applied himself to a highly decorative sweet which
Elizabeth was privately attempting to analyse and deciding
to acquire from Emily's book of recipes. Mrs Scrymgeour
turned the full broadside of her charms upon Hector.

But although Elizabeth was stimulated by the doctor's
remarks and preoccupied with the sweet, she was at the same
time trying to ignore a certain uneasiness in her spirit. There

was something in what had just been said that threatened danger to her inner life.

'Don't you believe in religion, then?' she asked.

The doctor seemed embarrassed again. . . . Apparently he did not like serious questions.

'Er–er a childish way of comforting oneself, don't you think?'

'But how can one live without it?'

Elizabeth was genuinely shocked at last, and since something she valued was in danger she did not stop to reflect upon stupidity and intelligence.

'Oh, well, one does, doesn't one?'

'I don't mean conventional religion, going to church, and that kind of thing. I mean precisely that capacity to draw comfort from the universe, that mystical communion you were speaking of. Don't you believe in that?'

'Er–no,' said the doctor.

He looked at Elizabeth, then he looked away.

'I believe many people feel such a communion,' he added, 'but it isn't what they think it is.'

'But if I don't believe what I feel,' burst out Elizabeth, 'what *am* I to believe?'

Dr Scrymgeour carefully spooned up the last of his sweet and said nothing.

'You take all the poetry out of life,' murmured Elizabeth.

The doctor brightened and laid down his spoon:

'I haven't a grain of poetry in me.'

Elizabeth stared at him, and saw again that his lips were cut like the petals of a flower. Her blank horror was invaded by a secret sense of superiority. He did not understand himself.

'Perhaps you have more poetry in you than you guess,' she returned, smiling, and for the rest of the evening she refrained from lapsing into seriousness.

'Well,' said Emily, whirling round upon her when she went upstairs for her wraps, 'well, what do you think of my husband?'

'I think he's a darling.'

'Isn't he clever?' said Emily, with satisfied triumph. She then handed Elizabeth a compliment: 'He's a shy creature, you know, and he doesn't usually trot out his pet ideas before company. He must have liked you.'

'Do you know,' said Elizabeth, flattered, 'he has such a lovely mouth that I couldn't keep my eyes off it.'

'Better not tell Mr Shand.'

It occurred to Elizabeth that she ought to return the lead and ask for a verdict on Hector, but Emily had already screwed down the gas. Elizabeth obediently went downstairs.

But when Hector was fumbling with the latch-key at their own door she was appalled to hear him say: 'Thank God, that's over!'

'What's the matter, Hector?' she called, pursuing him into the drawing-room, where he was striking matches. She thought that he was jealous, perhaps, and perhaps even a little excited with wine.

'I can't stand that woman,' retorted Hector, pitching his coat on a chair and unwinding his muffler. His nose was very high and haughty.

Elizabeth's eyes widened.

'She was very nice to you.'

'Nice to me! Huh! Expects every man she meets to eat out of her hand, doesn't she? Bloody bitch, that's what she is. Thinks everybody's going to fall for her. She makes me sick.'

Hector stuck his pipe between his teeth and reached for the tobacco-jar.

'But heaps of people like her.'

'You bet your boots they don't,' said Hector through his clenched teeth as he stuffed his pipe.

'Oh, nonsense, Hector; I know they do.'

'She only tells you they do. I tell you she would turn any decent fellow *sick*.'

'I can't see what's the matter with her.'

'The matter with her,' said Hector between puffs, 'is that she's all my eye. I'd like to smack her skinny little bottom good and hard.'

Elizabeth burst out laughing.

'Is that all you have against Emily, that she's too skinny for your taste?'

'No!' said Hector, with unexpected ferocity.

Elizabeth, however, went on laughing. Fresh from a new environment she had not yet accommodated herself to the familiar room and all that it connoted. At the moment she was not a wife.

'Oh, Hector, didn't you once tell me you couldn't look at a woman without thinking of going to bed with her? It's not really Emily's fault if you think she's too skinny.'

'If you must have it,' said Hector, rising and standing on the hearthrug; 'I don't think she's the kind of woman you should associate with.'

'Indeed!' Elizabeth sobered all at once. 'And why?'

'Look at the kind of talk she hands out. Tells me her baby's first sense of beauty comes from feeling her breasts. Feeling her breasts, she tells me! Might as well ask me to feel her bubs and be done with it. And her husband's no better.'

'Do you mean to tell me that you were shocked?'

'I should damn well think I was.'

'You've said many worse things to me.'

'Not before other people.'

'And you've done many worse things.'

'Damn it all, haven't I been sorry for them? What's that got to do with it?'

Hector too was defending something he valued that he felt to be in danger. He was particularly indignant that it should be threatened by a woman, since women were its natural defenders.

'You're a stupid fool!' cried Elizabeth, her eyes hard.

'Go on.' Hector was grim. 'Go on. Spit it all out.'

Elizabeth remembered her wifehood. She went up to him and locked her hands round his unyielding arm.

'Don't you see, Hector, don't you see, darling, that it's simply stupid to be shocked at things?'

'I may be stupid, but I don't see. I'm only thinking of you,' he went on less grimly. 'I don't want my wife to be an easy mark for other people to sneer at, and that's what will happen to you if you get into that woman's habits.'

Elizabeth unloosed her hands.

'The Scrymgeours are the only intelligent people I've met in Calderwick. I intend to go on being friendly with them.'

'Intelligent be damned! Don't come with that highbrow stuff to me.'

'I'm not going to stultify myself, not even for you. You can do what you like about it.'

'So that's that,' said Hector in a stifled voice. He did not know the meaning of the word that Elizabeth had brought out with such a grand air, and his ignorance made him savage.

'That,' responded Elizabeth, 'is that.'

She felt such a cold ferocity in herself that she was frightened. This was like none of their previous quarrels. There were tears in her eyes as she walked upstairs, but they were tears of mortified pride, not of wounded love. How dared he dictate to her what she was to think? Stupid, sulky fool. He was as bad as Aunt Janet. She grew hot again as she remembered how near she had been to asking Emily: 'And what do you think of *my* husband?'

Disjointed sentences started up in her mind. She walked about the bedroom saying, 'Oh, my God.' Then she flung herself on the bed and stared dry-eyed at the wall. She was terrified at herself. 'If I don't believe what I feel what *am* I to believe?' she had said to Dr Scrymgeour. And at the present moment what she felt was that she didn't give a damn for Hector.

Hector poured himself a glass of whisky and gulped it down. As he found himself biting on his pipe-stem so fiercely that he was afraid he would break it he emptied out his pipe and lit a cigarette. . . . The cigarettes and the glasses of whisky went on in an uninterrupted chain.

So that was that. She despised him for a stupid fool. Now he knew where he stood. Nothing more to expect.

Using words he didn't understand, by God! And all he asked for was a little decency.

Hard lines on a poor devil who was only trying to do the right thing. Trusting to his precious wife to help him not to make a bloody mess of his life and she turns round and sneers at him.

What the hell was the use of trying?

As the whisky diminished in the decanter Hector more and more savagely shook himself free from the entanglements he felt irritating him. His love for Elizabeth was one; it only put him in the power of a woman who despised him. His love for Aunt Janet was another; it only related him to a code of prohibitions which he could not observe unaided. Elizabeth and Aunt Janet stood on either side of him demanding what he did not have, for he had neither intellectual freedom nor moral constancy. His slighted vanity, his wounded love, and his morbid feeling of insufficiency filled him with pain and dull rage, and he turned that rage upon the two human beings who stood nearest to him.

Damn all women, he said to himself as he emptied the decanter. He had come to no other conclusion: he was very drunk and intensely miserable.

When he finally stumbled upstairs in his stockinged feet a reek of whisky came with him. Elizabeth was undressed and lying in her bed with her face to the wall. She was very rigid, but he was too drunk to suspect that she was awake. She could hear him disentangling himself from his trousers; he was obviously attempting to make no noise. Suddenly she did not know whether to laugh or cry. His physical presence had thawed that terrifying ice about her heart. Almost palpably she felt her love for him joining them together again. . . . Hector put out the light and crawled groaning into bed. Elizabeth turned round and stretched out a hand in the darkness as if across a gulf that could still be bridged.

Her hand touched him lightly. He shook it off, growling: 'Leave a fellow alone, can't you?'

She turned her face to the wall again and wept quietly, while Hector dreamed that he was dead, lying on a bier in a place that looked like a church, and that Elizabeth and Aunt Janet in deep mourning walked up the aisle to look at his body.

SEVEN

Saturday was Mary Watson's busiest day. Coats hadn't been going so well this winter as they should have done, but at last they were beginning to sell, and she was kept hard at it running upstairs to the mantle showroom.

'I'm fair run off my feet,' she complained, slumping on to a stool covered with black American cloth. 'That Mrs McLean is just like the side o' a hoose; there's not a coat in the whole of my stock that'll meet across her, and I've had every single outsize off the hangers. I'm fair worn out.'

Her first assistant made no comment. She got on very well with Mary chiefly because she was taciturn.

'There's Jeanie come back,' she said after a while, as the door opened with a rattle and a stumble of feet came down the steps.

'Ay,' said Mary dryly, 'Jeanie's a handless and footless creature. She'll come a clite on her head one of these days. . . . Is all the messages done? Has she ta'en Miss Reid's trimmings yet?'

'No' yet.'

'Jeanie, you've to take this down to Miss Reid the dressmaker. And on the way back ye'll speir at the manse for Mr Murray, and say that Miss Watson would like to see him at once. At once, mind ye.'

Mary allowed herself a few minutes more on her stool. She was indeed weary. But the chief cause of her weariness she was keeping to herself. No need to make a scandal in the town, although the scandal was bound to come unless a miracle happened, she thought bitterly. Well, she would try the minister first.

Jeanie's scared little voice piped its message at the manse door. When she stumbled down the shop steps again she elbowed through a throng of customers and hovered uneasily at the back until she could rid herself of the answer.

'Miss Murray said to say the minister was writin' his sermon and she couldna disturb him, but he would come as soon as she got at him.'

'Tchuk, tchuk,' said Mary.

Writing his sermon on a Saturday afternoon! When he had the whole week to do it in! She was indignant.

When, nearly an hour later, William Murray diffidently appeared Mary was more than tart.

'It's to be hoped the Lord answers prayer quicker than his ministers,' she said. 'I might have been dead by this time for all you kenned. But I've noticed that folk that hasna muckle to do take the whole week to do it in.'

The minister inquired what service he could render.

'I canna tell you here,' said Mary. 'Come into the storeroom. Na, ye're that late it's just on tea-time: I'll walk hame wi' ye mysel'.'

'Has anything happened to your sister?'

'You may weel ask, you that hasna been to see her for months and months.'

A ready answer, a bit of fencing, would have refreshed Mary, but the minister was in no condition to give battle. Since that terrible evening when Ned had spat in his face he had indeed driven the devil out of himself, but the house of his spirit although swept and garnished was still empty. God had forsaken him. Prayer had been unavailing; the sky was merely indifferent sky; he himself was nothing but a vessel of clay, a wretched body of flesh and blood that felt both night and morning as if it had swallowed an enormous cold grey stone.

This oppression in the region of your solar plexus, somebody might have told him, is only a derangement of your sympathetic or your parasympathetic nervous system, my dear fellow. You have had some emotional shock, that's all. It is a salutary experience if you face it frankly. Revise your hypotheses. Some of them must have been wrong, for the world is exactly the same as it was.

It is doubtful whether that would have comforted William Murray. Like Elizabeth, and, incidentally, like his own brother, he believed in the last resort only what he felt. But the interpretation he had put on his own feelings for so many years had lulled him into such security, had flooded his world with so much sunshine, that he was unfitted to discard it. Ask a man who has been capsized in a cold sea, apparently miles from land, to believe that he never had a boat and that he must have swum out there in a trance, and the task will not be less difficult than that of persuading William Murray that his personal assurance of God's support had been for nearly twenty years a delusion. Your swimmer will believe in the non-existence of a boat only if he awakens to discover, for instance, that he is not swimming, but really flying in the air, or pushing through a crowd; nothing less than the shock of a similar transposition, an awakening into a different kind of consciousness, could revise William Murray's conception of God.

As they walked through the darkening streets Mary told him her tale. It appeared that on Friday, the day before, she and Ann had quarrelled. They were aye quarrelling, that was nothing unusual, but this time Ann had taken some notion into her head and had locked the house, snibbed the windows, and refused to let Mary in at night. Mary had trailed back to the shop and slept in the mantle showroom, and cleared it up so that the lassies suspected nothing when they came at eight next morning. She had made an excuse to slip out for a bite or two in the forenoon, and she had eaten a dinner at the nearest baker's. But this was Saturday night; she couldna sleep in the shop and bide there all Sunday; and would the minister do something with Ann? 'She can hear you fine through the keyhole. I gave her some fleas in her lug, I can tell you. But not a word to anybody, Mr Murray; I dinna want this to be the clash of the town. I dinna want to have the door forced.'

'But surely,' said the minister (people who defend an indefensible position always begin with 'surely'), 'surely Miss Ann didn't do it deliberately? She may be lying helpless.'

'Preserve us a'!' said Mary slowly, nearly stopping. 'You've kent my sister Ann for twa years and yet you say that! You're a bigger fool than I took you for. . . . Dinna mind my tongue,' she went on quickly, 'I canna help laying it about me. But Ann! She's been a hard and cantankerous woman all her life, Mr Murray. The de'il kens who would have put up with her the way I've done. She plagued my mother to death when the poor woman was lying bedridden; mother didna dare to move a finger in her bed or Ann was at her like a wild cat for ravelling the bedclothes. She was the same when she was a lassie. . . . Many's the skelp across the face I've had from her, the ill-gettit wretch. Father widna have her in the shop; he said she would ruin his business in a week with her tantrums, and yet she was better to him than to anybody. And since father died she's led me the life of a dog, Mr Murray. I sometimes dinna ken how I've managed to keep going.'

It may have been the darkness of the small streets and the impersonality of a silent and only half-visible companion that encouraged Mary to be so confidential. She had never told so much about herself to anybody. Depressed as he was William Murray could not help feeling vaguely that after all there was much to be said for Mary Watson, and that the goodwill he liked to postulate in everybody was not lacking in her, but only hidden away. His mind was not clear enough to let him perceive that her aggressive attitude towards the world was a kind of self-defence, but he was sorry for her.

'I've aye tried to be respectable,' said Mary. 'I've done my duty; nobody can say I havena done my duty. But this last carry-on of Ann's fairly crowns a'. This is the first time I've had to ask help from a single living being, Mr Murray.'

William Murray was touched by this confession. It did not occur to him that Mary so fiercely resented the necessity of asking help that she might not be grateful afterwards to the helper.

'We all need help sometimes,' he said, to himself as much as to her. Perhaps in turning to God he had turned his back too much on his fellow-men. God must be present in all His creatures. . . . In Mary Watson, for instance, in Ann Watson . . . even when He gave no sign of His presence, even when the soul felt empty and forlorn. . . .

It was only one's consciousness of God that was intermittent. . . . Elizabeth Shand has said something like that. . . .

His mind kept returning to Elizabeth Shand, as if warming its numbed faculties at a fire. He had not seen her for some days: he hoped she would be in church to-morrow. God was not a mere person, she had insisted, not a limited creature with fits of bad temper who sulkily withdrew Himself from His children; the fault is in us, she had repeated, if we feel ourselves cut off from God, and that alone should keep a man from falling into despair, since faults can be discovered and corrected. That was one-half of what she had pressed so urgently upon him: it was the half from which he drew some comfort. The other half of her argument was a doctrine he would not admit, that God existed not in another world, but in this very material one. 'We shan't discover God anywhere if not in ourselves,' she had said. 'I don't believe in your separation of the body from the spirit. I can't think of my spirit without feeling that it's even in my little finger.'

No, no. William Murray knew that the body and the passions of the body could darken the vision of the spirit. In itself the body was nothing but darkness. That was what oppressed him so much.

'We all need help,' he repeated to Mary Watson, becoming aware that she had stopped speaking and was expecting an answer.

'Tits, man,' she retorted, 'you said that before. That'll no' get Ann to open the door to us.'

'I'm sorry,' said the minister. 'I was thinking of – I was thinking, Miss Mary – that—'

'What you are going to say to Ann?' demanded Mary.

The minister did not know what he was going to say to Ann. He had a confused hope that God would put the right words into his mouth.

'As I was saying,' said Mary, with marked emphasis, 'it's no' so easy to get her oot; I just canna bring the police, even if I wanted a scandal, for the hoose is hers, no' mine. The shop's mine, but the hoose is hers. She hasna a penny piece besides what I give her, but the hoose is hers. Father willed it like that. And what she wants is to make a scandal; just that, just that. She's waiting girning behind that door for me to break it open, and then she'll have the police on to me; I ken it fine. Brawly that. Ay sirs!'

'Surely she's not counting on that. . . .'

Mary snorted and turned up the lane towards the cottage. The nearer she got to the gate the more she ceased to believe that the minister would be of any use at all.

'It's the fear of God you have to put into her, mind you that,' she said, opening the gate and preceding him along the garden path.

The cottage was in darkness save for a feeble light shining through the blind of the kitchen window.

'She's in her bed,' said Mary in a loud whisper. 'That's the light from her bedroom shining through the kitchen. Chap at the front door as hard as you can.'

She pushed him past her, and stealthily pried at the lighted window.

'It's snibbed,' she whispered. 'A' the windows are snibbed. Chap at the door, man, I'm telling you.'

In the mirk of that winter night William Murray, as he rapped firmly with the cold iron knocker on the door of the little cottage, felt incongruously that he was making a last trial of his faith. It was not in a great arena that he was to be proved worthy or unworthy, not even in a despairing battle for his own brother's soul, it was in knocking at a door trying to persuade one bitter old woman to give shelter to another. The cottage itself reminded him of the text with which he had been wrestling all the week: 'But if thine eye be evil, thy whole body shall be full of darkness.' The kitchen window was a dim and evil eye; the cottage was, like himself, a body full of darkness. He rapped once more, and remembered again how Ned had spat in his face. A shrill scream followed his rapping, which he recognized although it was intercepted by the door, and he could make out slow and shuffling footsteps. Ann was not helpless, then: she was able to walk.

'Cry through the keyhole,' urged Mary, but the minister remained upright and silent as the footsteps became more audible.

There was a sound as of unlocking, and a scream: 'Wha's there?'

He nearly jumped: the voice came not from behind the

door but from the kitchen window to his right. Ann had
stopped there, unsnibbed the window and opened it a little
from the top. He could see her dark outline.

'It's me, Miss Ann: Mr Murray.'

'What were you wanting?'

'I want to talk to you.' The minister's voice was gentle,
but firm.

'Come back the morn then: I'm no' wanting anybody the
night.' The window shut with a bang.

'Eh, the obstinate wretch,' muttered Mary. 'Try her
again; chap on the window; go on, man; go on.'

The minister walked to the window and rapped on it. Ann
was barely discernible inside. His sympathy for her welled
up again.

'She shouldn't be shut up all alone like this,' he muttered,
and rapped more insistently than before.

Ann came closer to the window and peered through the
glass as if she were spying into the darkness behind his
shoulder. For a fleeting second William Murray thought of a
human soul in captivity, peering into the unknown through
the dim glass of its conciousness: Ann's situation was too
like his own not to disturb his emotions. He rapped harder
still, crying: 'Let me in.' Standing there in the loose soil of
the garden bed he felt an infinite pity for both of the sisters
and for himself.

Ann suddenly undid the window and thrust out her head.

Although her face was only a few inches from his she
screamed at the highest pitch of her voice: 'Come back the
morn, I tell you! I have to keep the hoose lockit – for a
purpose. I'm no' safe from my sister Mary if I open that door.'

Her remarks, like her glances, were fired into the
darkness behind him.

William Murray put up a hand and held the window down.

'Come, come, Miss Ann,' he said coaxingly, 'that's not
the kind of woman you really are. I know you better than
that.'

Ann seemed not to hear a word. She had no desire to
appear a saint, she merely wished to prove her sister a devil;
and she suddenly cut clean across the minister's cajoleries by
screaming: 'I see you! I see you, you jaud! Come oot frae

ahint the minister! Ye needna think I dinna see you. I'll let
the whole toon ken hoo you've treated me, so that I have to
lock myself up in my very hoose to be safe from you!'

'Nonsense, Miss Ann! No, no – you'll just injure yourself—'

The minister's voice was drowned by Mary's energetic
reply:

'Lock yersel' in then. Bide there. Not a penny piece will I
give you—'

'I'll let the whole toon ken it, then. On Monday I'll awa'
into the poorshoose, and what'll you have to say to that?
Better to live in the poorshoose by myself than to live wi'
you. Mary Watson's old sister in the poorshoose! They'll ken
you then for what you are, my leddy.'

Mary was tired, disappointed and angry.

'Ye cunning auld deevil,' she retorted, 'I'll set the police
on you, that's what I'll do. It'll be the police office and no'
the poorshoose for you, and that this very night, as sure as
my name's Mary Watson.'

'This is my hoose. The police canna take a body up for
locking her ain hoose door. Na, they canna!'

'They can take a woman up for keeping what's no hers.
You've a' my gear in there, and my fur coat and my —'

Ann had disappeared with a thin satirical chuckle. Mary
darted to the window and began to throw it up.

'You're a fushionless fool o' a creature, are ye no'?' she
said to the minister. 'Ye might at least help me through the
window.'

Before William Murray could move Mary was thrust back
by some large soft object which fell on the ground. Rapidly
after it came a succession of things, scattering in the
darkness.

'My fur coat, ye deevil!' he heard Mary cry, half sobbing,
and then he saw her clutching Ann by the hair and shaking
the older woman to and fro over the window-sill. Ann began
to scream. Instead of desisting for fear of scandal Mary
tugged the more furiously; she was as if transported out of
herself. The minister at first felt almost suffocated at the
sight of the two women worrying each other, and then the
inert mass in his bosom seemed to burst into flame.

'You call yourselves Christians,' he found himself crying, as he held Mary at arm's-length. 'I'll cut you both off from the communion of the Church – both of you, do you hear? I'll blot your names from the Church books. I'll expel you publicly from the congregation!'

He almost flung Mary away from the window.

'Open that door at once, Ann Watson,' he continued, 'or I shall proclaim you from the pulpit to-morrow.'

His own vehemence amazed him, even while he exulted in it. This time his anger gave him no sense of sin: it was like a clean flame burning up dross, and like a devouring flame it swept the two women before it.

Ann groaned as she shuffled to the door, but the key grated in the lock, and the minister stalked in.

'Let us have a light,' he said.

Ann's fingers were shaking, but the minister avoided looking at her.

'Go and put on a wrap,' he said, 'while I bring in your sister.'

Mary was sitting on the ground where he had left her. She was crying. She had not cried since the day of her father's funeral.

'Go inside,' said the minister coldly. 'I'll pick up your things.'

He groped in the flower-bed, which was now faintly illuminated by the paraffin lamp in the kitchen. A fur coat, a hat with hard jet ornaments, two black kid gloves, a flannel nightgown and, gleaming in the dark soil, a large gold watch with the glass smashed he collected one by one, shook the damp earth from them and took them into the cottage.

Mary was sitting at the table, her head supported on her hands. She had unpinned her hat. He noted that Ann was in her bedroom and that Mary had stopped crying. For the first time in his life he felt scornful of tears: his old susceptibility was gone. He noted simply that she had at least stopped crying.

'Get me a Bible,' he said, in the same cold, authoritative tone, laying his armful on the table.

Mary looked up and saw the watch.

'It's broken! Father's watch, and she's broken it! Fifteen

years I've had that watch —'

He silenced her. What were fifteen years compared to eternity?

The minister picked up the watch, and when Ann reluctantly appeared, in an ancient dressing-gown, he made it the text of his sermon.

On earth, he told them, what is broken can be repaired, but although mended it can never be unflawed again. A moment, a second, suffices to smash for ever what has for years been intact. How much more irrevocable is a break in one's relations with God! What is done can never be undone, never; even repentance cannot undo it. . . . The least of our actions is of eternal significance. . . .

The more he berated them the more they felt involuntarily drawn together. His insistence that they were both equally wicked exacerbated but united them. It was the threat of expulsion from the Church that had cowed them, and they now submitted to his exhortations from fear rather than from conviction.

Mary was the first to fidget.

'I have to get back to my shop, Mr Murray.'

'Your shop! You should be thinking of your immortal soul.'

'My shop canna wait.' The ban was lifting from Mary. Her immortal soul could wait till the morn, she was thinking, but Saturday was Saturday and *not* Sunday.

Ann exchanged a look with her sister, a look which said plainly: Get him out of here.

'I'll mak' you a cup o' tea before you go to the shop,' she offered.

'Aweel,' said Mary, rising, 'we've had it out, now, and I dinna think we'll flee at each other again for a while, Mr Murray. If Ann has ony mair o' her tantrums I'll let you ken.'

'Me! It's no' *me* has the tantrums—'

The minister rose quickly, clapped on his hat and marched out into the night without another word.

Half frightened the two sisters looked at each other.

'Na, he'll no',' said Ann abruptly. 'He's no' like us. It winna last.'

She hobbled to the fire and drew the simmering kettle on

to the middle of the range. In response to this generous action Mary cleared her things off the table, merely compressing her lips as she looked at the condition they were in, and shaking them out ostentatiously before taking them into her room. A tacit truce was thus concluded.

Common sense had triumphed over rage and tears.

We're queer folk, reflected Mary, as she went slowly back to her shop. Queer, dour folk, the Watsons.

That evening had brought her closer to her sister Ann. She actually felt the better for it.

The minister also was feeling the better for it. Although he had departed in impatience the heavy oppression which had weighed so long on his bosom had discharged itself like a gun with the flash and explosion of his attack on the two sisters. As if he had finally vaulted an obstacle he had balked at for years, William Murray was exhilarated and wondered at his previous foolishness. It now seemed to him that he had been faint-hearted all his life. He had made himself spiritually sick by evading the fact that God's anger was as real as God's love. The old ecstatic serenity was gone, but in its place he felt a tense determination to fight the battle of the Church. Instead of spreading himself anonymously into the universe, as if he were a quiet wave lapping into infinity, he recognized himself now as an individual with a definite place in the world; he was a minister, backed by that authority and prestige of the Church which, for the first time in his life, he had invoked, and invoked successfully. His appeal to the Church had been involuntary, almost unconscious; its very spontaneity convinced him that it had been prompted by God Himself.

Anger was at times good and necessary, he said to himself, as he walked home buoyantly. It was weakness to be too sympathetic. In his sick state he had sympathized too much with everybody: for instance, he had sympathized with both Mary and Ann Watson, first with one and then with the other, and yet they were both in the wrong – not to be sympathized with at all. Christ had driven the money-changers out of the Temple, and had spoken to devils as one having authority. That was the right way with those poss-essed of a devil.

He remembered suddenly how Sarah had said about Ned:
'I've *daured* him.' She was right. One could not create light
without dispelling darkness. For years he had shut his eyes
to the fact of evil; but now he had heard the word of God,
and he would deal faithfully with evil wherever he found it.
He had awakened out of his sleep. 'Wherever I find it,' he
said, opening his own front door.

The wall in front of William Murray was no longer
smooth, without handhold or foothold, no longer blank. It
now had both lights and shadows on its surface. He could
climb it.

EIGHT

When Elizabeth Shand awoke in the morning Hector was still asleep. He was facing her as he lay, but his head was half-buried in the pillow and little of him was visible save his tumbled hair and closed eyes. The terrible sensation Elizabeth had of having dropped down a bottomless chasm began gradually to fade before the reassuring familiarity of Hector asleep in the next bed. She could not see his face, but she knew that his body was the same body it had always been; behind those closed lids the same Hector must exist. If once she had been daunted by the aloofness of her sleeping husband she was now comforted by it. Asleep, he was still her sweetheart, unchanged by the conflicting storms of yesterday, sunk into the most profound part of himself, which, of course, was the essential Hector, the Hector who loved her and whom she loved. Their quarrel of the night before seemed irrelevant as she lay looking at him. She remembered how she had told the minister that she could not believe in the separation of the spirit from the body; and now she thought that it was when most completely sunk in the body, as in sleep, that the spirit was most itself.

Quietly she crept out of her own bed and crawled in beside Hector. Let him awaken to find her close to him, she thought. Surely there was some current of invisible force which flowed in an unbroken circuit around them as they lay motionless together, a healing current, she thought, which would bear away all their differences. She felt his eyelashes stir on her cheek, and pressed him to her in a passion of tenderness.

If Hector was surprised to be awakened in this fashion he did not show it. He rubbed his cheek on hers and kissed her tenderly enough. Even the reek of stale whisky did not annoy Elizabeth; she was both exalted and contrite, and she dismissed all scruples as unworthy. But Hector had a fiendish headache, a rotten headache; that damned whisky couldn't have been good stuff. Elizabeth got up and fetched him two aspirins in a glass of water.

'You're much too good to me, Elizabeth.'

Did this protest mean that Hector felt himself fettered by his obligations to her? She did not stop to wonder.

Her mood, persisting until next day, which was Sunday, inclined her towards going to church, and she was a little surprised and touched by Hector's ready acquiescence.

Whenever they went to church they sat in the Shand pew, and after the morning service all the Shands strolled home with Aunt Janet, and returned by way of Balfour Terrace, where John and Mabel took their leave and Elizabeth and Hector, waving good-byes, went back to the High Street alone.

John, being the senior Shand, sat at the outside end of the pew; Hector was next to him, then Elizabeth, Aunt Janet and Mabel. Elizabeth found it possible to smile on both the other women, but unconsciously, after the first silent greeting, she edged towards Hector and away from Aunt Janet. She found herself also regretting that she had cut off her intercourse with the minister merely because of Aunt Janet's scandalmongering, and she waited eagerly to catch his eye and send him a message of reassurance.

The minister walked up to the pulpit with his usual solemnity, with even more than his usual dignity. His glance crossed Elizabeth's once, but his blue eye flashed such a cold strange gleam that she felt snubbed. Perhaps he resented the way she had dropped him?

She forgot this personal question in her amazed disapproval of the sermon. She could not know that William Murray had sat up until far into the morning reshaping that sermon to fit his spiritual rebirth into the Church. Where was his sympathy, his tolerance? she asked herself. The man was thundering theology from the pulpit; splitting hairs, logic-chopping. Far above the heads of his congregation, anyhow, thought Elizabeth scornfully, looking round at the vacant or sleepy faces. He was now proving to them that the existence of good connoted the existence of evil; this world was a world of both good and evil, unlike the Kingdom of God, which, when it came, would be neither good nor evil, but equally beyond both, transcending both. Meanwhile, because on earth we had intuitions of good, we must admit also intuitions of evil.

'The metaphor of darkness, like all metaphors, misleads our childish minds,' said the minister. (Was that meant for her? thought Elizabeth.) 'We fold our hands passively and wait for the sun to dispel the darkness of evil, when we should be fighting it, driving it away, casting it out, as Christ cast out devils.'

In her mind's eye Elizabeth suddenly saw Ned's distorted face, and her heart grew heavy with a feeling of doom.

'The Church, as the visible body of Christ,' preached the minister, 'is an alliance against the powerful forces of evil. Alone, we cannot fight evil; it is too strong for the individual; we all need help in the struggle, and so we are banded together to form a Church. Who is not for us must be against us. . . .'

Elizabeth, more and more confounded, leaned forward in the pew and rested her chin on her hands. The man was actually talking about original sin. What had happened to him? What was he going to do to Ned?

'The body in itself is evil,' insisted the minister, 'until we deliberately consecrate it to God.'

Elizabeth sat back with such violence that she dislodged a Bible from the shelf in front of her and sent it clattering to the floor. She wished she had the courage to rise and contradict the minister on the spot. . . .

Aunt Janet was offering her a peppermint.

'Don't you feel well, Elizabeth?' she whispered.

'Me a peppermint too,' whispered Hector, grinning.

Aunt Janet rustled the little paper bag. Elizabeth turned fully round and looked at the clock to see how much of this apalling sermon was still to come.

She would not listen any more. The odour of peppermint and cinnamon, the incense of a Scottish Presbyterian church, floated around her. Sucking her hard peppermint, she stared at one of the windows, combining the little panes of glass into squares and diamonds of colour. Let him stew in his own juice, she thought angrily. Let him take a whip and beat the devil out of Ned if he chooses; it's none of my business.

The congregation stirred; the sermon was finished; everyone stood up to sing the final hymn. Elizabeth kept her mouth shut. She would never, never go to church again, let the Shands say what they liked. She wasn't going to have all that theological tapestry hung between her and the universe.

Slowly and sedately they moved out in the throng.

'Did you feel ill, Elizabeth?'

Aunt Janet was at her ear, solicitous.

'No, I was only angry.'

'Angry, my dear?'

'Angry with all the nonsense Mr Murray was talking.'

'I thought it was a very good sermon, I'm sure. Didn't you think so, John?'

'A very good sermon,' said John.

'Well,' Elizabeth laughed a little, 'I think it's awful to have to listen without being able to contradict. I wanted to answer back.'

She turned round, looking for Hector as usual, but was surprised to see him walking off with Mabel. It was extraordinary. He had never done that before.

She could not help watching the two figures in front. Mabel walked very well; she had an elastic step; her very back looked gay. She and Hector were laughing. It was queer, she commented to herself, that the sight of Mabel and Hector exchanging badinage should rouse in her the same feeling of disapproval that had invaded her the other day. She felt grown-up again, relegated to the background with the sober adults, as it were, while the children frolicked along in front. It puzzled her.

John seemed to be amused at something. Whatever it was, he checked himself from putting it into words. But the twinkle in his eye suddenly delighted Elizabeth as she caught it.

'Your beard twinkles when you smile, John,' she said, feeling audacious. 'The point of your nose twinkles, too. Look at it, Aunt Janet, doesn't it now?'

She had never before suspected that she could venture to chaff John, or that he would like it. Apparently he did like it, and her grown-up feeling vanished when she discovered that John was an excellent victim of teasing. She forgot that for a second or two she had resented being left to his society. Behind a cross-fire of personal remarks she escaped for the moment from her anger with the minister, her forebodings about Ned, and her uneasiness with regard to Mabel and Hector. In spite of his beard, and his size, John was not so very grown-up after all.

'I was afraid of you at first because of your beard,' she confessed, 'but now I see that you are only hiding behind it.'

When Aunt Janet was safely within her own front gate Elizabeth found herself still beside John.

'You know my sister is coming on Saturday?' he said suddenly.

'Oh yes,' cried Elizabeth. 'I'm looking forward *so* much to meeting her.'

'I think you'll like each other. I couldn't help laughing when I saw you fidget so much in church; she used to do exactly the same.'

'Did she want to answer back too?'

'She always did,' said John gleefully.

Elizabeth's heart leapt. 'Is she at all like me?'

'No, not at all. She's more like Hector, I must admit. But, although you may not care to hear me say so, she's much better-looking than Hector.'

'I'll let you say so as much as you please. When does she arrive on Saturday?'

'I think she's to travel overnight from London coming in here about ten o'clock. Hasn't Mabel invited you and Hector to come to dinner on Saturday night to meet her?'

'No, not yet —'

'She'll probably do it before you go home. We'll have a jolly evening.'

John actually hummed a little song to himself. That finally broke down the frail wall of Elizabeth's discretion.

'Do you know, I think I must have several blind spots,' she said, 'I'm only finding out now what you're really like.'

John smiled half-shyly.

'I've decided that your bark is worse than your bite, John.'

'How do you know that?'

Elizabeth laughed; her eyes sparkled.

'I'm learning sense. I used to judge people entirely by what they said; but now I know that it's the person behind the words that matters. When you like people it doesn't matter very much what they say.'

'I thought you liked Murray?'

'That's a shrewd hit,' said Elizabeth, with a rueful grin.

John grinned back. 'And yet you were nearly jumping out of the pew at him this morning.'

'I couldn't help it. But I'm sure it's because he himself has changed that what he said annoyed me. Something has changed him. I'm afraid of what he might do. . . .'

'How's that? I thought myself that he seemed to be coming to his senses. He's been mooning about for years in a kind of dream, quite off the earth; and this morning I thought he had wakened up.'

'I liked his dream better. . . . I don't want to be brought down with a thump on to solid earth. Besides it wasn't solid earth, John. It was only logic. It was husks for the prodigal sons and daughters, that's what it was; and who has a right to say that we are all prodigals and must be fed on husks?'

John did not answer at first. Then, with an appeareance of lightness, he said: 'Oh, well, after the husks comes the fatted calf, you know. We'll have that next Sunday.'

Elizabeth realized with a stricken feeling that he had applied the parable to himself and his sister.

'I'm for the fatted calf all the time,' she said as heartily as possible, and dropped the discussion, feeling clumsy and foolish.

When they all halted at number seven Balfour Terrace she could not resist slipping her arm inside Hector's, as if it were necessary to let Mabel see that Hector had been merely on loan. In this graceful position they both accepted Mabel's invitation for Saturday night to meet Lizzie.

As they turned home Hector disengaged his arm. Men and women in Calderwick certainly never walked arm-in-arm by daylight, but Elizabeth quite unreasonably felt chilled by his action.

'You ran away and left me,' she said.

'Oh, Mabel wanted to tell me about the car she's going to get. She screwed it out of John this morning.'

'A car! How lovely.'

'I'm going to teach her to drive it. We're going up to Aberdeen some time this week to buy it.'

'You know, John really is a dear,' said Elizabeth suddenly, apparently ignoring Hector's statement. 'I've only just found it out.'

'John? He's a swine.'

'No, he's not! How can you say such a thing?'

'I suppose you're going to call me a liar, are you?'

'What's the matter, Hector?'

'Oh, nothing. I suppose you think I've bloody well deserved all I've got from John?'

'I don't care whether you did or not. He's certainly different now.'

'Hell of a difference!'

'People *do* change, Hector. It's queer that they do. I suppose we all do. . . .'

'Well, I'm not going to *argue* about it.'

The tone of Hector's voice as he said 'argue' conveyed that he had had enough of argument with Elizabeth, and reminded her, with a shock, of their previous argument. All her uneasiness came back, and her thoughts congealed like a crust over her feelings, so that she did not venture to say another word. They walked on in a silence that grew more oppressive the longer it lasted, and it lasted until they got home.

The invisible barrier between them seemed to cut across the table as they sat at dinner. Elizabeth was scrupulously polite in offering more helpings, and Hector accepted them with equal politeness.

'What are you going to do this afternoon?' she asked. On Sunday afternoons they had always gone out together, but to-day she was determined to thrust no assumptions upon Hector.

'I think I'll run up and see Hutcheon.' Hector's tone was quite careless. 'He's got a small car – a beauty – and I'd like to have a shot at driving her somewhere this afternoon, to get my hand in.'

In other circumstances Elizabeth would have cried, 'I'm coming too!' but she only looked at her plate and filled her spoon with exaggerated care. In another moment her emotions would break their crust and come bubbling up. . . . Hector felt the imminence of the outburst, and he laid down his napkin.

'I'd better be getting along,' he said, 'or Hutcheon will be gone. Excuse me, please.'

Elizabeth had learned a few things that Sunday morning, and in the afternoon and evening she learned something more. Her first lesson was that in the absence of Hector her painful agitation subsided with incredible quickness. Half-an-hour after his departure she was able to sit down to a book by a philosopher called Bergson, whom she had discovered just before leaving the University and who excited her. The second lesson for the day was that the same agitation returned with the same incredible suddenness the minute Hector set foot again within the house. She seemed to have become two separate persons, one of whom was calm and confident in Hector, while the other was childishly, almost hysterically, affected by his presence.

All the understanding excuses she had found for him during the afternoon, all her quiet resolve to find a harmony which should include both her love for Hector and her good opinion of John, all her faith in the underlying permanence of that love, disappeared when he came in, as the clear reflection in a still pool disappears when the mud at the bottom is stirred up by a stick.

The whole of Elizabeth's world was in flux, although not exactly as Bergson had declared it to be, and instead of regarding the phenomenon with scientific interest she felt as if she were drowning in it.

NINE

Elizabeth, governed as she was by images, thought of herself and Hector as the terminals of an invisible and powerful current which ought to flow unimpeded from one to the other. Hitherto she had not imagined that a distortion of the current could distort the terminals also, but in the next week she grew more and more baffled by the effects of the distortion upon herself. Whenever Hector spoke to her a lump rose in her throat; his approach seemed to graze an intolerable wound; and the more grimly she told herself that this was absurd and petty the more she was bewildered by her own spurts of resentment. On the other hand, whenever he ignored her or turned away in impatient anger her resentment was lost in a self-pity that sometimes passed off in a fit of submissive tenderness towards her husband and sometimes drove her sobbing to her bedroom. She could never tell what she was going to do, and in none of her actions was she recognizable to herself except during Hector's absence. As soon as he left the house she would stop crying and say: This is not me! What *have* I been doing?

These more stable moments emerged like rocks once the waves of emotion were spent. They might have served Elizabeth as a basis for self-examination but, being young and indeterminate, she preferred to gaze with increasing bewilderment at the cross-currents of the sea. Elizabeth had a habit of turning her back on the land.

Hector was less bewildered because he was deliberately drifting, and in doing so he was perhaps subserving a deeper purpose. The ports we try to make by tacking may be less salutary for us than those to which we drift. There may be no such thing as chance in human conduct. Hector, at any rate, although unhappy, was less surprised by the estrangement than Elizabeth. It seemed to him now that he had foreseen it all along. It served him right, he thought, for marrying a woman supposed to be brainy; she was bound to despise him sooner or later. He could not forget her contempt; he kept worrying it like a dog at a bone. For a few hours on the day after their quarrel he had apparently forgotten it, but it had been only temporarily buried beneath a load of depression, and now he was turning it over so often that there was no chance of its disappearing. His persistence in dragging it to light was indeed so obstinate that there must have been some other motive at work which he did not surmise. In vain Elizabeth tried to assure him that she was sorry, that she hadn't meant it, that it was too absurd – he refused to be placated. It began to look as if he were clinging to an excuse. That was perhaps what bewildered Elizabeth most.

She was incapable of realizing that she had failed him in something essential, and he was too inarticulate to make it clear. Even when he said, 'You don't give a damn for decency, so why the hell should I?' she was merely angry.

So Hector drifted deliberately, even defiantly, as if he had argued the situation to some such conclusion as this: Elizabeth should have steered him on his course; she should have guided him into the haven of respectability; and if she refused, if she unshipped the rudder and flung it at his head, whose fault was it that he drifted?

Moreover the current that was bearing him away had been pulling at him ever since his marriage. In becoming estranged from his wife Hector was only doing what the whole of Calderwick expected of him. Wives, in Calderwick, were dull, domestic commodities, and husbands, it was understood, were unfaithful whenever they had the opportunity. Hector also had the reputation of being the wildest daredevil in the town, and in the Club, where every man liked to be thought a bit of a gay dog, his prestige was enormous. His prestige was now likely to increase still more, for he spent every night in the Club getting drunk. When he was not at the Club or in the office he was flirting with Mabel. Because of Elizabeth's inexplicable failure as a wife he could not hope to rival John as a respected citizen, and to captivate John's wife seemed an alternative way of getting even. Mabel was asking for it anyway, he told himself.

It is difficult to see what current could have carried Elizabeth away had she too been minded to drift. In Calderwick wives are not so well provided for as husbands. Wives in Calderwick, for instance, do not forgather in drunkenness, so Elizabeth was denied that relief. Nor could she count on support from Aunt Janet; she could not, indeed, count on any of the women she knew except Emily Scrymgeour. The only thing she could have done was to be unfaithful to her husband, but for a Calderwick woman to do that is not to drift: the whole social current sets the other way. Mabel was not drifting towards Hector, for instance; she had no intention of leaving the social current; she was only swimming a little against it to try her strength, to give herself something to do. There was no easy drift to which Elizabeth might commit herself except the traditional stream of respectable wifehood. Both as a member of society and as an individual she was more buffeted than Hector.

For the first day or two she took long, solitary walks, seeking an assurance from the sea, the grass, and the leafless trees in the little valleys that she was still the same Elizabeth. The house seemed to be agitated by stormy emotions, but out of doors, she thought, in the slower, larger rhythm of the non-human world, she would again find herself, and, in consequence, find Hector too. She laid her hand on the smooth trunk of a large beech and looked up through its rounded boughs at the grey sky. It was a wise old tree, she thought, sixty years old perhaps, maybe a hundred; she had watched its leaves change from green to russet, and now she could almost feel the warm life withdrawn into its trunk, which in spring would flow out again into a thousand buds. An old, old tree, but it would put out silky new leaves, with downy edges, leaves so young and tender that one would hesitate to touch them. . . . Sudden tears filled her eyes as she thought of the spring buds; it was an intolerable thought that such young things should bourgeon only to be burned in the fires of autumn and stripped from the boughs by savage winds. We are like the leaves, she thought, and when we flutter from the tree we think it is freedom, but it is death.

She stood there, with the palm of her hand pressed on the smooth grey bark, and stared at a world that was filled with death. Everything died. Everything *could* die. It was intolerable. How could she have been so unthinkingly happy in such a world?

She fled back to the town, where mortality crowded together and roofed itself in from the terrible emptiness of the sky. Men and women were incredibly pathetic, she thought, or incredibly courageous. But, in comparison with death, of what importance were their silly little notions of right and wrong? What did it matter if Hector thought the Scrymgeours indecent? How could she bother to be angry with him when he might die?

The thought of Hector dead haunted her all the rest of the afternoon. The physical presence of living people usually keeps us from inflating their images with sentimentality, but when the objects of our desire are removed from us in space or time their images can shrink or swell disproportionately; and as Elizabeth in her imagination was removing Hector to a point much farther away than the office, where he was presumably detained, his image became gigantic, filled with all the qualities her frustrated tenderness longed for. By five o'clock she was sitting at the tea-table waiting for him in a state of almost painful anticipation. At half-past five she made tea and drank it by herself; his absence had become a voluntary absence, and his image began to shrink; the sentiment which had sustained it flooded back upon her until she had to get rid of it in an outburst of tears, after which she lay on her bed in cold despair. Hector had dwindled into nothing; he was worse than dead to her, for there was no consoling image left. She felt as if it were she herself who was dead.

When Hector came in, some time after midnight, she turned her face to the wall. He was very drunk.

Next day she shrank from going out. But she could not settle; she wandered from the window to the bookcase, and from the bookcase to the window again, forgetting her book. The certainty of death made everything irrelevant and trivial. Born to die, she said to herself. She might equally well have said, Dying to be born, for what she was gazing at was the winter death of the garden, but her eye was prompted by the apparent deadness of her own heart, where no quickening movement promised new life. The end of Hector's love for her seemed like the end of the world.

Elizabeth was a victim of her upbringing as well as of her temperament. From her earliest years she had been subjected to the subtle pressure of the suggestion that a husband is the sole justification of a woman's existence, that a woman who cannot attract and keep a husband is a failure. That some such theory should emerge in a society which regarded the sexual act as sinful was inevitable; one cannot train women in chastity and then expect them to people the world unless the sinfulness of sex is counterbalanced by the desirability of marriage. In Elizabeth's case temperament had modified tradition so far as to set romantic love as well as marriage on the other end of the lever depressed by sex: marriage alone without love would not maintain the equilibrium. One might admit that the odds were heavily weighted against her.

Her restlessness was perhaps a symptom of vitality. At any rate, after walking round and round the drawing-room she went on an impulse into the kitchen, where the strong-armed and red-headed Mary Ann was singing as she washed up dishes. Elizabeth, as Mabel said, had simply no idea how to treat a maid; she was incapable of keeping her own place, and therefore unfit to keep other people in their places.

'Well, Mary Ann, are things looking up?'

'First rate, mem. . . . I had a rare time last nicht.'

Mary Ann beamed, and plunged into the soapy water again.

'Here, give me a dish-clout and I'll dry the dishes. I can't settle to anything this morning.'

'You're looking tired,' said Mary Ann, with affectionate concern. 'Dinna you touch that dish-clout. I should have had thae dishes done lang syne. I'll no' be a minute. And then I'll make you a cuppie o' tea, will I?'

'You think a cuppie o' tea is a cure for everything, Mary Ann.'

'So it is,' said Mary Ann stoutly. 'Gi'e me a cuppie o' tea and I dinna care what happens next.'

Elizabeth sat down on the kitchen table.

'How's the lad getting on?'

'Eh, fine, I tell ye. He's coming on. He gi'ed me a pickle sweeties last nicht. I gi'ed him one on the lug he wasna looking for.'

'Aren't you afraid to hit a policeman, Mary Ann?'

'Me? No' me. A polisman's only a man-body, especially if he's your lad. A bit dirl on the lug's good for them.'

'What did he say?'

'"You're a daft besom," he says, "Mary Ann," he says, "but I like you for it," he says, rubbing awa' at his lug. "Do you ever think about me?" he says, the great soft gomeril. "Whiles," says I, "but no' aye!" That gi'ed him something to think about. "Whiles," says I, "but no' aye!"'

Mary Ann chuckled as she cleared the dishes away. Elizabeth sat lamely on the table, realizing that good-humoured banter can be as efficient a barrier to intimacy as the most discouraging aloofness. She did not know how to begin confiding in Mary Ann.

'Now for the cuppie o' tea.'

Mary Ann bustled to the stove.

'All right, Mary Ann.' Elizabeth slipped off the table. 'Bring it into the drawing-room.'

Her half-conscious wish to talk to somebody became a definite desire to consult Emily Scrymgeour. She felt that she was blindly going round and round in circles and that talking to a third person might clear her vision. Since that unlucky evening of the dinner-party she had not seen Emily, but that active lady had already guessed something of what was happening. Scandal in Calderwick percolates at first by a kind of osmosis from one mind to another long before it becomes current, and various people had remarked Hector's frequent appearances in Mabel's new car and his increasing devotion to the whisky at the Club. In fact, Emily was waiting for her friend's confidences.

'I'm sorry for her, mind you,' she said to the doctor, 'but she's such a queer mixture that she'd shy off if she thought I was trying to poke my nose in too far, even although she thinks the world of me. She's really very reserved – like you.'

That judgment would have amazed Elizabeth.

'She takes the wrong things too seriously,' said the doctor. 'Bound to get hurt.'

'Jim! And you've only seen her once! You *are* a clever wee man, you know. It isn't everybody can get a husband like *you*.'

This complacent reflection was never absent from the background of Emily Scrymgeour's thoughts, and made her tolerant of other wives' difficulties.

Elizabeth did not suspect that she was falling like a seed into a carefully prepared bed when she walked into Emily's drawing-room, apologizing diffidently for her defection of the past week. She did not realize it even when Emily sent Teddy out with Peggy the maid, averring that she had so much sewing piled up in the basket that she could not afford to go out, and that anyway it was better to sew with somebody to keep one company.

'Don't you hate sewing and darning?' said Elizabeth.

'No, I love it. Haven't you ever seen my white embroidery? I like working with my hands and I make all Teddy's clothes myself. Look at the design on this romper. . . .'

'I wish I was some good at sewing,' burst out Elizabeth. 'I can't even knit.'

'Your hands look capable enough,' returned Emily, working busily with her own quick short fingers. 'I hate to see women with helpless-looking hands, but yours aren't like that.'

Elizabeth, thus admitted to the same pinnacle of womanliness as her friend, squirmed there in silence for a minute and then abased herself.

'My hands are all thumbs, Emily, in every way. You don't know what a fool I am.'

Her voice roughened as she said this, for she was executing one of those complicated manœuvres of which the human spirit is strangely capable. Her vanity and her love were hurt, her pride was bewildered, and she had a longing to weep on Emily's shoulder; but at the same time she could not abuse her husband to anybody, and the only alternative was to abuse herself. The savage roughness in her voice was caused by anger, and as she started up to walk about the room her anger increased. She was contemptuously furious with herself.

'A fool!' she kept on saying. 'A damned fool!'

'It's unlikely that you're the only fool in the world,' said Emily, laying her work aside. 'People do quarrel with their husbands, you know.'

She laughed at Elizabeth's startled face and patted the sofa, on which she had expressly seated herself.

'Don't prowl like that, but come and sit down and tell me all about it. I've been married for eight years, Elizabeth.'

'How did you know?'

'It's not difficult to guess, is it? What else could it be?'

'Oh – anything. I'm an ignorant fool, I tell you. I never suspected that I was a half-wit, and it's unpleasant to discover it.'

'Do you think I'm a half-wit too?' said Emily, smiling.

'I think you're the only intelligent woman in Calderwick.'

'Do sit down and be sensible.' Emily was still smiling. 'What you really mean is that you didn't learn at the University how to manage a husband.'

'I haven't learned how to manage *myself*; that's what's bothering me.'

Elizabeth ceased prowling, and looked directly at her friend.

'I feel that myself has let me down. I don't know at any minute what damned silly thing I'll do next. Yes, I have quarrelled with Hector, but that's not the worst of it. The worst of it is that I haven't sense enough to know how to set things right. Emily, I can't speak to him without bursting into silly tears.' This was the most revealing speech that Elizabeth had ever made, even to herself, and for a moment she had the feeling that something within her was struggling into consciousness, some recognition of an incompatibility too fundamental for compromise.

Emily brushed it away.

'You take the wrong things too seriously.'

'Do I?'

'Of course you do. You are turning a simple quarrel into something much too tragic. My dear Elizabeth, I've known you for long enough to see that.'

'Do I?' repeated Elizabeth. Almost absent-mindedly she

sat down beside Emily, and leaned forward, clasping her hands together.

'It's not such a simple quarrel,' she said suddenly. 'I don't think he loves me any more.'

'What makes you think that?' Emily quietly resumed her sewing. To herself she said: Aha! Now we're getting at it.

'Because if he loved me as – as I love him,' Elizabeth's voice faltered, but she went on, 'he couldn't keep things up against me the way he does. Emily, if you love a person you *love* a person, no matter what's said or done. Quarrels are only on the surface —'

'That may be true of women, but men are different. Now, listen to me.' She checked Elizabeth's protest, laying a hand on her arm. 'There's a lot of nonsense being talked about the equality of the sexes, chiefly by mannish women. I'm not a mannish woman; I don't believe in them. Men and women are quite different. I'm going to talk to you very frankly. Hector is the first man you ever slept with, isn't he?'

Elizabeth nodded, blushing.

'But you're not the first woman he ever had.'

Elizabeth's blush deepened.

'Of course you're not. It doesn't mean so much to him as it does to you. It's you who will have the babies. That makes a big difference, don't you see? Every wife has the same handicap in her relation to her husbnad. Marriage for a woman, my dear, is an art – the art of managing a husband – and that means not taking his passing phases too seriously. Strategy is what you need, and tactics —'

'I want to live with Hector without any tactics,' broke in Elizabeth. 'I want to live with him and just be myself.'

'But you can't,' said Emily firmly and decisively.

'Then I'll run away.'

Emily pulled her down again on to the sofa.

'That would be the silliest thing you could do. Where would you go?'

'I can teach,' said Elizabeth stubbornly.

'No school would take in a woman who had run away from her husband.'

'I could take my own name and leave Scotland.'

'I thought you said you loved him?'

Elizabeth hid her face in her hands. There was a long silence.

Waves of self-reproach were rising higher and higher in Elizabeth, and the unspoken thing which had been struggling into consciousness was finally drowned.

'I do love him; I do love him,' she whispered. Without removing her hands she added: 'I've been thinking all the time about his love for me, not about my love for him.'

Emily patted her shoulder and said nothing.

'He's miserable too,' whispered Elizabeth. 'He gets drunk nearly every night.'

After some minutes she sat up, with a bright eye, and looked at her friend:

'I've been a bad wife, Emily. Thank you, very much, for clearing me up.'

'What about some tea?' said Emily briskly.

Elizabeth could not help laughing.

'All crises in women's lives seem to be punctuated by cups of tea,' she said.

Later that evening Emily sat on the rug by her husband's knee and told him about her successful management of Elizabeth: 'Don't you think I was right?'

The doctor in his thin voice said: 'You should have told her to have a baby.'

'So I did, after we had tea. I told her a baby was a wonderful thing for making a man human. Aha!'

She pinched the calf of his leg.

'I suppose,' said the doctor, 'you didn't think of asking her how they got on in bed?'

'She'd have been dreadfully shocked if I had. Besides – I shouldn't think there would be any difficulty there – her husband's a Shand.'

'Their reaction times may be different,' said the doctor.

'Jim,' said his wife, 'what a wee devil you are!'

Elizabeth had yielded herself to the stream of traditional wifehood, and the boat of her soul no longer rocked. She had but one course to follow – to devote herself to her husband, to love him selflessly, exacting nothing and giving much. She had been a bad wife, and now, God helping her, she would be a good wife.

A cynical observer might have remarked that she was now inflating with sentimentality her own image instead of Hector's and setting it up in the role of Noble Wife. Yet these wind-blown puppets of our imagination play more than visionary parts in the drama of the soul, and have the advantage of being able to collapse suddenly when the need for them is over. Elizabeth, hidden within the self-made figure of the Noble Wife, was shielded for the time from social disapproval as effectively as a pneumatic tyre is shielded from the bumps of a hard road. Moreover, she now presented the comforting appearance that Hector expected of her.

She must have known this instinctively, for she first bathed and powdered her face, and then put on her prettiest frock. In Calderwick at that time it was considered slightly improper to powder one's face by day, but Elizabeth excused her daring by reflecting that darkness had already set in, although it was not yet five o'clock. She inspected herself in the glass and added a string of coloured beads, signs of dawning femininity which might have pleased her sister-in-law.

She then put on a hat and coat and left the house with a quick, firm step. She could not wait for Hector; she was going to the office to bring him home. This time she would not burst into tears when she saw him. No wonder he got fed up, she told herself; any man would be fed up with a wife whose nose was always blobby.

The image of the Noble Wife was growing rapidly in size. Unconsciously, without words, Elizabeth was adding to the number of its attributes.

The perfect wife was not only selfless and loving – she was sympathetic, understanding, tactful and, above all, charming. . . . She must always be pretty – no, not pretty, Elizabeth did not aspire to prettiness – she must always look 'nice'. The *frou-frou* of femininity was beginning to rustle round Elizabeth. Here, too, was the cloak of charity which should cover her husband's many sins, while her devoted love sustained and comforted him. . . . Elizabeth was not far from the final dogma that woman exists for the sake of man. She was going beyond her teacher, Emily Scrymgeour, who believed only that woman should pretend to exist for the sake of man.

There is, however, a keen ecstasy in renunciation. We must not pity Elizabeth as she makes her way upstairs to the inner office of John Shand & Sons; she is transfigured by happiness. All the doubts that have vexed her for the past few months appear now as selfish hesitations: she feels that in spite of herself she has been miraculously led from one stepping-stone to another until she has emerged from the fog of uncertainty to find herself safely across the Rubicon in the full sunshine of wifehood.

Some of that sunshine was needed in the inner room where Hector was still sitting at his desk. He was alone: John had been out all day at the farmers' mart, for it was a Friday, the weekly market-day of Calderwick. The outer office was empty, except for Mason, the head clerk, who was nervously hovering about his desk, and peeping every now and then through the glass partition to see if Mr Hector wasn't thinking yet of going home. Mason had never known the junior partner to sit so long in the office.

For hours Hector had been humped over his desk in listless depression, drawing lines and diagrams on a bit of paper. He had put in what he called 'a thick week', and the defiant recklessness that had carried him along was now ebbing away, leaving behind it disgust and staleness. There were heavy black pouches under his eyes, and his mouth was drawn tight as if he were afraid it would fall out of control were he to open it. One could almost see the inchoate sagging outline of the form that might be his at the age of fifty, the ghost of the father, Charlie Shand, horribly incarnate in the flesh of the son.

Whether this illusion of Charlie Shand's presence was the cause or the effect of Hector's thoughts it is impossible to say. His father was haunting him. He was going the same way as the old man, he thought, jabbing furiously at the paper: drink and women, drink and women; and he would end in the same way. Might as well be dead. He saw himself again lying on a bier in a place that looked like a church.

That might be the best thing for all concerned. He was sick of everybody and sick of himself. Might as well *be* dead as feel dead.

He hadn't a dog's chance in Calderwick. The place was too full of his father. . . . He shuddered and shut his mouth more tightly than ever, while he drew aimless little pictures down the side of the paper. Then he set to work drawing a ship, a child's ship, with masts and sails growing out of a rudely sketched hull. He became absorbed in it, and after he had finished the sails he put in a solitary figure in the bows, and then printed a name on the stern, ELSA. Elsa? There was another queer word struggling in the back of his mind, Koben, Kjobben something, and a doubling, a thickening of shadowy images, as if he were retracing some experience he had had before. . . .

His mouth fell open. He had seen the ship *Elsa* in the harbour, with foreign fellows jabbering along her deck, and from that day to this he had not thought of her until his pen had printed the name. The rope curling on the quay beside him. . . . Better to drown in the open sea than in a stagnant dock. . . .

He sat motionless for a while, with a new feeling springing up within him, a feeling faintly like hope. He was superstitious; he believed in omens; and the ominous dream of his own death had oppressed him heavily. This ship, he felt sure, was a sign. A sign of what?

His mind suddenly cleared, and he knew as well as if he

had thought it out that he would take ship for some far-off country, Australia or Brazil or the South Seas. He would sign on as a sailor, a cattle-man, anything: the voyage would take months, months of hard work far from pubs and women; at the other end there would be at least one's pay, and a week or two of glorious rioting in a new country. Somewhere in the South Seas. He had had enough of the North.

Hutcheon's people were shipping agents: young Hutcheon would help him to do it and would keep his mouth shut. He would sign on to work his passage. He still had over two hundred and fifty pounds of his own: that would help to start him in something at the other end: or he could ship again for another voyage somewhere else if there was nothing doing where he landed. Clear out! By God! he would.

He sat staring into vacancy, lost in his dream, voyaging into that unknown which put Calderwick in its right perspective, reducing even John to a fat, foolish puppet whom it was absurd to take seriously. He had been too young, too raw, when he was shot out to Canada; he had not seen how unimportant the family was, how little Calderwick mattered; but this time he would stand on his own feet. He snapped his fingers. The ghost of his father wavered and vanished from his brain.

Hard work, hard physical labour, and then a spree; that was a life he could enjoy. In Calderwick there was opportunity for neither the one thing nor the other: all a fellow could do was to soak himself rotten in the rotten Club, and then addle himself still more on an office stool, or go to church on Sunday like a good little boy and be jawed at by all his family. . . . An uneasiness began to disturb him: he jabbed at the paper again. Well, let them think he was a quitter – a natural, heaven-born quitter: if that was his line he would follow it out. To hell with them all!

A noise outside made him start. He sat up and moistened his dry lips; he became conscious that he wanted a stiff whisky. He looked at his watch; it was past five o'clock. Old Mason must think he'd turned damned industrious. Hardly had the thought shaped itself when he was again startled. Wasn't that Elizabeth's voice?

In the few seconds during which he sat staring at the door before it opened he was, as he would have termed it, in a blue funk. He had avoided thinking about Elizabeth while dismissing her from his life, as he had avoided thinking about Aunt Janet, or even Mabel. By lumping them all together as 'women' and putting them in the same phrase as 'drink' he had escaped the necessity of considering them as individuals. Even now he was unwilling to think of Elizabeth as Elizabeth. His sense of guilt and his resentment at feeling guilty, which combined to produce the blue funk, threw up another impersonal phrase. 'Just like a woman. Just like a woman,' something muttered savagely at the back of his mind as he sat with jaw set and eyes fixed on the door.

It is much easier to dismiss people from one's business than from one's life. The absolute importance of money is impressed on us both directly and indirectly with such force that it seems a final argument to say that So-and-so costs us too much; even So-and-so sees the force of it, although he may resent dismissal. Money, after all, is money. But we do not feel with the same conviction, with the same prospect of general approval, that we are, after all, ourselves, and that if So-and-so costs us too much he must be thrust out of our lives. Civilization, in binding us to one another with a solid wall, turns into ramshackle structures the private dwellings of our spirits; we lean lopsidedly upon each other and hesitate to complain of encroachment, or to refuse support even when the rooftree is cracking under the strain. We rely more and more upon the wall of civilization to stave off collapse, and less and less upon ourselves. In fact, we live so much upon the wall and so little in ourselves that we do not often know what condition our house is in, or whether it needs repairs.

Hector's decision to rid his house of encumbrances and to repair it was so recent, and apparently so spontaneous, that he could not justify himself, and it was natural that the arrival of Elizabeth should put him in a blue funk. She was ushered in by Mason, who was relieved to find that there was a comprehensible reason for Mr Hector's waiting so long in the office. Mason's eye was rather appealing, and Hector, glad of a diversion, answered the unspoken appeal.

'We won't be a minute, Mason,' he cried, hastily rising. 'Get me my coat, will you?'

To Elizabeth he said nothing: he could not think what to say, but stood leaning his hands on the desk. Without noting whether Mason had shut the door again Elizabeth ran towards him. 'My dear love,' she said, 'my dear, dear love.'

Hector, armoured in the conviction that she despised him, had been hard to her. He had returned an equal coldness and silence to hers, and had been infuriated by her tears, which he interpreted as reproaches. But she came towards him now with such tenderness in her eyes and in her voice that he was taken off his guard, and before he could stop her she had her arms round his neck.

'My dear love,' she said again, with a vibration in her voice which he had never heard before. He remembered that her bosom was comforting, his head sank, his arm went round her, and for a long minute they embraced each other. When he tried to lift his head Elizabeth stroked it and whispered: 'I've come to tell you I've been a bad, bad wife, and now I'm going to be a good one. My darling, my darling.'

His eyes blurred and he put out a hand to steady himself against the desk. He was damned tired, he remembered. Elizabeth felt the almost imperceptible droop of his body and for the first time since coming in she looked at his face. His eyelids were wet. She kissed them, but he kept his eyes shut.

'I'm damned tired, Elizabeth,' he said.

She took his coat from Mason, who was coughing in the doorway, found his hat, and led him downstairs. They walked home arm-in-arm, closely pressed together.

Elizabeth did not suspect that the tears in Hector's eyes might have been tears of disappointment. She felt tender and protective towards him, as if he were a baby she must foster and encourage, and the strength of her feeling at the moment excluded any doubt of its necessity. The perfect wife is bound to assume that her husband requires her devotion, that without her he would be 'lost'. This traditional and easy attitude fits loosely over the real problem, the problem of one individual's relationship to another, and conceals its shape exactly as the cloak of charity conceals failings.

But Hector surrendered himself without resistance to his wife's devotion. He had been unconsciously reaching for that cloak of charity ever since his marriage. Time after time he had confessed his sins in Elizabeth's lap as if she were his mother, but he had never got the desired assurance that whatever he did she would still be a mother to him. That assurance was now hovering around him at last as he sat in the arm-chair before a glowing red fire and let Elizabeth put on his warm slippers for him.

And yet he felt miserable. The spark of hope in his breast seemed to have been blown out. He tried to excuse himself.

'I've been thinking all day what a rotter I am. . . . Going the same way as the old man did, Elizabeth. You won't let me come to that, will you?'

Elizabeth sat on the padded arm of the chair and took his head on her bosom. Her face shone with exaltation.

'No, I won't let you. I love you more than anything in the world – more than myself even. I've just discovered that.'

'Keep me off the drink, Elizabeth. . . .'

She kissed him on the forehead.

'I promise.'

He suddenly lifted his head.

'And make me a good boy for ever and ever. Amen.'

His tone was bitter, almost savage. Elizabeth peered into his face.

'What is it?' she said half under her breath.

He buried his face in his hands. Elizabeth knelt beside him and tugged at his wrists.

'What is it, my love? Hector, I want to help you.'

She clasped his wrists and caressed them. Strong arms, she thought, sliding her fingers and the palms of her hands down his arms; strong arms, with their short black hairs, and their sinewy hardness under her soft palms.

'I'll make you happy,' she said. 'As happy as we were at first. . . . Us two against the world, Hector. We'll show them. . . .' She went on caressing his arms, but a strange anxiety was spreading in her heart. Hector's face was still hidden: he made no response to her assurance. She felt as if she were desperately fanning an extinct fire.

'I'll do anything you like, Hector. I tell you I've been a

beast to you, but it's going to be different. . . . I'll give up Emily Scrymgeour. I'll behave like a *perfect* lady, except when we're just together, us two. Us two, Hector. . . . I'll back you up all round. . . .'

'For God's sake, shut up!' said Hector. Then seizing her hands he laid his forehead on them and groaned: 'No, I didn't mean that. I didn't mean that.'

Elizabeth's lips trembled, but she made no sound. She could feel Hector's eyelashes quivering on her fingers, and she pressed her hands closer to his face to stop that fluttering. She bowed her head upon his and, still on her knees, began kissing the back of his neck.

The scent of peat and tobacco smoke from his tweed jacket, the thickness of his black cropped hair, the strength of his neck and shoulders inflamed her senses. After weeks of estrangement they were so near to each other that all this misery seemed to her suddenly an absurd irrelevance. She tried to force her hands from Hector's grip. Laughing, she struggled with him.

But Hector held on to her wrists as if they were straws and he a drowning man. The softness and warmth of her caresses and of her body drew him towards her almost irresistibly, and yet he resisted with all his force. He had the feeling that if he yielded now he would be bound for life to the fate he had escaped in imagination that afternoon.

Elizabeth, still laughing, sank back on her knees. She did not take Hector's resistance seriously.

'Let me go,' she said.

He tightened his grip.

'Listen. . . .'

Elizabeth looked up in alarm. His eyes were black and sombre.

'Let me go,' she said in a sharper voice. 'You're hurting me. Let go!'

Hector set her free at once, and she sat on the rug chafing her wrists.

'Will you let *me* go?' he said, and as if this unequivocal statement had broken a dam his words came rushing out in a whirling flood, tossing at Elizabeth's feet the sediment of his despair.

'Damned, mean, narrow little world, Calderwick,' he finished. 'I'm done for if I stay in it any longer. I've got to clear out. Will you help me? Will you back me up, Elizabeth?'

Elizabeth sat staring at him.

'Go away?' she said. 'Without me?'

She seemed to herself to be shrinking and dwindling to a vanishing point on the hearthrug, her voice was small and forlorn.

The sweat stood on Hector's forehead.

'Don't you see,' he said, 'if I go, I don't know where I might land: I can't risk taking you —'

'But I can risk going!' cried Elizabeth. 'I'd go with you to the end of the world.'

'But I mean to work my passage. . . . I can't afford to take you.'

He bent forward and took her hands again. 'Don't let me down, Elizabeth. Back me up. I'll find something for both of us. . . . If I don't get out —'

He shuddered.

'You must go,' said Elizabeth. 'Of course you must go. Haven't I always wanted us to go to Canada or somewhere? But why can't I come too? I'll work at anything, Hector. I'll wash dishes. I'll scrub floors —'

'A fellow can't let his wife do that.'

Elizabeth sat still for a moment. Then she began to laugh hysterically.

'What's the matter?' said Hector. 'Stop it, Elizabeth: stop it, for God's sake!'

Elizabeth's laughter wavered into a shrill sound and died away.

'I *am* your wife,' she said. 'Am I not? I *am* your wife, Hector. I'll be a good wife. What do you want me to do?'

'I want you to wait for me,' Hector bent and unbent her fingers. 'I don't know where I'm going yet. But when I find a place fit for a woman —'

Elizabeth felt the idiotic laughter bubbling up inside her once more. She clenched her teeth on it. Shut up, she said to herself. I'm not me. I'm a wife, a woman, who has to have places that are fit for her.

'But what am I to do while I'm waiting?' she said aloud.

'I thought – I thought that perhaps you could live with Aunt Janet. . . .'

Hector had a momentary fear that Elizabeth would perceive that he was improvising. He was very grateful to her when she looked up quietly and said: 'I'll wait for you, Hector, as long as you like. I love you, and I shall always love you. But I won't be a burden on anybody! I'll find a teaching job, somewhere. After all, I'm a highly qualified young woman: it would be absurd of me to sponge on Aunt Janet.'

Hector was ashamed.

'I don't like doing it,' he muttered. 'I've two hundred pounds. I'll leave you a hundred. . . .'

'Nonsense! You'll need as much as you can scrape together. Where did you think of? . . .'

'Anywhere. . . . South Africa, Australia, Brazil. Pick up any chances going.'

Hector was surprised to find how reasonable and practical his adventure began to appear when it was looked at steadily. His sense of guilt evaporated.

'After all,' said Elizabeth, 'all this furniture was given us by Aunt Janet, and we can't fling it back in her face without an explanation. We must have it out with her, and with John too.'

'John won't raise any objections if you don't.'

Hector stared at his wife after saying this. A murky corner of his brain seemed to clear up. She was backing him; she was standing by him; and because she was backing him he wouldn't have to sneak away like a coward. She was taking all the moral responsibility off his shoulders.

'By God, Elizabeth,' he said, 'you understand me better than anybody!'

It was a sincere tribute to the impersonation of the Noble Wife. A lump rose in Elizabeth's throat, but she returned his look unwaveringly.

There was one curious consequence of this interchange. Both Hector and Elizabeth felt embarrassed when they kissed each other.

ELEVEN

On the same Friday Ned Murray was sitting over his midday dinner, which, as had become his custom, he devoured alone after his brother and sister had left the room. The manse cat, a large black-and-white creature cherished by Teenie the maid, was sitting on the floor beside him, receiving portions of fish which Ned laid down with his fingers on the carpet.

The meal was usually conducted in silence. Teenie brought in the dishes, set them dumbly on the table, and forced herself to walk back to the kitchen instead of running. On this day, however, when she saw him feeding the cat so kindly she ventured a remark as she set the pudding down.

'Tam's in luck to-day.'

Ned looked at her hastily. There was still a remnant of fish on his plate, which he had intended to give to the cat, but he now crammed it into his own mouth, without a second glance at Teenie who was waiting to remove the plate. Thomas, a wise cat, knew that the piece of fish should have been his, and laid a paw on on Ned's knee with an inquiring mew. Ned flung his knife and fork down with a clatter, pushed the cat away and started to his feet crying: 'Self, self, self! That's all you think about, is it?' Thomas, in amazement, paused for a moment, and then as Ned continued to berate him fled to the kitchen.

Ned turned upon Teenie.

'I might have known it. Another dodge. You're all trying to live off me, the cat and all of you! Get out, do you hear? Get out!'

He pushed the palpitating girl into the kitchen, slammed the door upon her, locked it and put the key in his pocket.

Having staved off aggression from that quarter he made himself finally secure by carrying his pudding up to his own room, where he locked himself in.

Sarah emerged from the sitting-room across the hall when she heard him go upstairs, and made for the kitchen. To find her kitchen door locked against her angered her more than such a trivial incident might warrant, and she rapped upon it loudly, calling: 'Teenie! What's the matter, Teenie? It's me: open the door!'

Her anger increased to fury as she stood there holding the door handle, listening to Teenie's muffled explanations. She felt that the whole economy not only of her household but of her life was in jeopardy. It was with a feeling of 'now or never' that she mounted the stairs, saying to herself: I'll sort him.

She rattled Ned's door, crying: 'Give me the key of the kitchen door at once, do you hear? At once, or I'll bring the police to you.'

Her voice was hard and full of decision: it betrayed no doubt of her ability to enforce her will, and its conviction penetrated to Ned. The door was unlocked and flung open. Ned glared at her, but he retreated a step, although he said: 'Your impudence is beyond bounds. This is *my* room.'

'Give me that key. How dare you intefere with Teenie?'

'How dare she and all of you interfere with me?'

'Hold your tongue!' shouted Sarah. 'Give me that key!'

It was the first time that she had ever shouted at her brother, and her passion seemed to sober him.

'Oh, get out,' he said in an exasperated but normal voice. 'There's your key.'

He flung it on the table and Sarah pounced on it.

'If I find you doing such a thing again I'll – I'll thrash you within an inch of your life! And I'll have you jailed.'

'Get out, get out,' repeated Ned, in a reasonable enough tone, urging her to the door as if she were demented and he in full command of his senses. 'Get out of this; I have some work to do.'

'Kindly give me your pudding-plate.'

'Oh, take it, take it, take it. Is there anything else you want?' inquired Ned ironically.

'No nonsense from you, and don't you forget it, my lad.'

Sarah slammed the door behind her and marched downstairs again. She freed her kitchen door and said to Teenie:

'He won't do that again. Don't you worry; just leave him to me.'

Then she did an unheard-of thing: she invaded the study.

William was finishing a sermon on the text: 'Though He slay me, yet will I trust in Him.' The God of wrath and the God of love were incomprehensibly one and the same; it was not for His children on earth to question His doings. . . .

The Book of Job lay open on the desk befor him; he was sitting with an idle pen, staring at a certain verse.

'I must speak to you, William,' said Sarah.

William's heart contracted. Some fresh trouble?

'Put your pen down and listen to me.'

What had happened to Sarah? William turned round in his chair.

Sarah was sharp and concise. This kind of nonsense could not go on, and she would not allow it to go on. To his astonishment William discovered that his wrestlings for the soul of his brother were included in Sarah's definition of nonsense.

'Either you leave him alone,' she said, 'or you back me up in my treatment of him.'

William began to grow angry. He found it easier nowadays to transform heaviness of heart into anger.

'Do you know what you are talking about, Sarah?' he said sternly.

'I think I'm the only person in this house who has any sense at all of what I'm talking about. You've been preaching to Ned about sin and prayer and the will of God, and the only result is that he's ten times worse than he was. You just drive him past himself, and it's me who has to suffer for it. Arguing with him about sin isn't of the slightest use: what he needs is discipline, not argument. I'm going to discipline him, and I want you to leave him alone.'

'It's my duty,' began William, 'as a minister of God's Church' he was going to say, but instead he turned to the desk again and hid his face in his hands. What was his duty?

Was Ned visited by God's wrath because of some secret sin? Or was the visitation incomprehensible, as in the case of Job? Ned had a lively conviction of other people's sins, but not of his own. All Ned wanted, he said, was security, justice, a right place in the world; and was it his fault that the world conspired to defraud him of that? Logically, William was no match for Ned, who could twist any of his arguments by the tail. He had finally preached contented submission to the will of God, resignation, acceptance without murmuring, but that had only roused Ned to frenzy, so that for a whole day he had done nothing but bang in and out of the study, screaming forth blasphemies againt the God of his brother. . . .'

Sarah relented when she saw the minister hide his face.

'There might be a time for that kind of thing, later,' she conceded, 'but he's in no condition for it just now. What he needs is firm handling, as if he were a bairn. I'm going to make him get up for breakfast, and dress himself decently. And I'm going to cut off the gas at the meter at eleven o'clock every night. A regular way of life —'

She broke off. Her resolution was not sufficient to enable her to finish her sentence. A regular way of life is the first duty of a Christian, she was thinking, but William, she knew, would not agree with her. Men got such queer bees in their bonnets; even the best of them.

William still sat motionless.

'You said before – don't you remember? – that I was quite right in standing up to him.'

Sarah was insensibly taking up the defensive.

The minister roused himself with a sigh.

'Yes, yes: you're right to a certain extent, Sarah. . . . He must learn to live in this world as well as in the other.' He smiled a little wryly. 'But washing one's face and putting on a fresh collar every day is only cleaning the outside of the platter after all.'

'It's at least a beginning,' said Sarah, turning to go. 'And it's the only way that some bairns can be brought up to understand that there must be order in the world.'

The door closed behind her, cutting her off, but leaving the last sentence still hanging in the air.

Order in the world? Did William really believe that there
was perceptible order in the world? What he believed was
that God pervaded the world; but more and more he was
being driven to acknowledge that God's order was beyond
human comprehension, although not beyond human faith.
'Your God allows mean cunning,' Ned had said. 'Your God
allows sheer cruelty. Your God allowed Christ to be
crucified, and still allows it.' Ned was blind to everything
but the evil in the world. . . . There was one remark of his
which persisted at the back of William's mind. 'Your God
allows brute savages like Hector Shand to do things to people
that I wouldn't even think of, and then gives him a job and a
wife and a home. . . .'

He had not known what answer to make, for he too felt
there was evil in Hector Shand.

Strangely enough, although Ned was becoming more and
more exasperating, the minister was now convinced that
there was real innocence in the boy. He was not evil in
himself. He was twisted with fear, but he was not evil. Ned
was a queer tangle of odds and ends, like the reverse of a
pattern which might never be discernible this side of the
grave, but which one felt was there. God's pattern, thought
the minister.

He summoned to his recollection what he could remember
of his brother's life. It was not much. There were six years
between them – a large gap when both were young. He was at
the University when Ned was at school: and he was in orders
when Ned came to the University. But there was one domin-
ant characteristic in all he could remember: Ned's
amiability, gentleness, docility – whatever it was, it was an
almost excessive mildness of temper. Ned had been tied to
his mother's apron-strings until she died. He must have been
about ten at that time.

The minister sighed, and followed in his memory the
phantom of his mother. She had been gentle too; gentle and
frail; uncomplaining under the harsh and somewhat frac-
tious rule of her husband.

An odd thought struck him. Sarah was always like father,
he said to himself in surprise, and Ned and I were like two
different versions of mother. . . .

The more he brooded on this resemblance between himself and his brother the more agitated he became. It was as if he were resisting with all his might the temptation to catch hold of an idea which was struggling for recognition. How could there be a fundamental resemblance between two people whose vision of life was so different? Ned's vision was a nightmare; by an unhappy fatality he saw nothing but evil in the world. It was an impossible nightmare; one could not go on living in it; and yet the minister suddenly comprehended with agony that the nightmare closed round Ned with an immediate certainty that prevented him from questioning its truth. It was as real to him as water closing over his head. But if Ned were like a man weighted down so that his head was just under water, with a little readjustment could he not be as easily cradled on the top of the sea, and would he not then be exactly like his brother?

The minister swerved away from the implications of this admission, and forced his mind back to Ned. When waters are closing over his head a man can think of nothing but himself: he cannot be gentle and amenable; he must insist that his feelings are of the first importance, and that he is suffering; he must be in a state of terror. All that was true of Ned. Nor is a man necessarily a devil because he is drowning and clutches at other people and curses God. An infinitesimal readjustment to bring his head above water will suffice to restore his natural gentleness.

The verse in the Book of Job detached itself once more from the page:

'O that one might plead for a man with God, as a man pleadeth for his neighbour.'

Oh, that one might!

What was this sea that closed over Ned's head and for so many years had cradled himself in security?

The point of the idea had at last pricked the minister's consciousness, and he started. Ned saw nothing but evil around him, and for years he himself had seen nothing but good. He had believed in a consoling dream exactly as Ned was believing in a nightmare. Was the dream as false as the nightmare? Or were they *both* real?

The minister felt as if he were on the verge of a sickening abyss.

When he recoverd himself he said aloud: 'Neither heaven nor hell. Or both heaven and hell?'

He remembered, as if from a far-off world, that he had once guessed at a final state of being where there was neither punishment nor forgiveness, neither good nor evil. . . . But that must be on the other side of death. . . . On this side of it both heaven and hell were real. You could not have one without the other: you could not live without admitting both. That had been forced upon him.

They must be real. They must be real. But God was incomprehensible.

'O that one might plead for a man with God, as a man pleadeth for his neighbour.'

But one might not. Sympathy was unavailing. That, too, he had had to learn.

The minister offered up a prayer to the incomprehensible God he acknowledged, asking that his feeble spirit might be sharpened and hardened to do God's work as a faithful member of His Church.

Later he finished his sermon.

Precipitation

'And my cats?' said Madame Mütze, pausing on the terrace. 'You will be good to them while I am away, Madeleine?'

'Bou Di,' said Madeleine, the tears running down her broad cheeks. 'But I shall fatten them up for the return of Madame. Madame is too good to all the creatures.'

'If it comes very cold leave the little shed open for them.'

Madame looked up the valley towards the col, which was powered with snow. Behind the long low house the hillside rose steeply, thickly grown with thorny scrub, in which sheltered the stray cats who so mysteriously appeared every morning at the back door of the Villa Soleil. The sky was grey. Madame turned slowly round and looked over the sea, marvelling as she still did after three years at the persistent blue of the water in spite of the grey sky above it.

In her childhood she had imagined heaven as a space of luminous blue, behind the bright blue sky of the hymn, and the magic of that infantile heaven still cast a glamour over the Mediterranean; for the sea remains changeful and mysterious even to those who are disillusioned about the sky. Yet although the sense of magic suffused Elizabeth Mütze when she looked at the blue sea her characteristic passion for analysis insisted that a colour so independent of the sky must be caused by minute particles of some kind held in suspension in the water. In another person the analytical passion might have dispelled the sense of magic, but Elizabeth Mütze had preserved them both; and on this dull day she wondered as usual whether it was limestone or salt in the water that made this southern sea so magically blue whenever one looked at it with one's back to the sun.

She turned to Madeleine again.

'Au revoir. Madeleine, I shall return soon; in three weeks,

perhaps two, if I am very frozen in Scotland.'

That Madame should be going to the ends of the earth in the middle of winter! Madeleine's protestations broke out anew, but her mistress laughed and said: 'Be at ease. I shall return long before the snakes come, Madeleine, and that is what you really fear, is it not?'

A broad smile irradiated Madeleine's tears.

'But it is true, that about the snakes! Madame is learned; she does not believe it; but it is true!'

Madeleine's husband, the old Antoine, carried Madame's suitcase to the carriage, in which the young Antoine was already cracking his whip. It was not far down the winding hill-road to the station; Madame's seat was booked, she had nothing to do but to think. Madeleine, craning her neck after the cloud of white dust, said to herself: The poor Madame, she goes away to forget.

Elizabeth Mütze might have said that she was going to remember. The two halves of herself which Karl had held together were now falling apart again. When she first met him, ten years ago, she had told him that she was like an ill-regulated alarm clock; the hour struck at the right time, but the alarm did not go off until days after, when it was too late. The hour was now striking for her departure to Scotland; the mechanism ticked correctly; her luggage, her tickets, her seats, were all booked; the carriage was creaking down to the station; but she felt as if she wre going only a few miles away, and when the alarm did go off, days – or perhaps weeks – later, everything would already be changed and irrevocable.

This time-lag in her feelings had become painfully evident since Karl's death. She thought she had squarely faced the likelihood of his death; she had seen it coming for long enough to be prepared; she had discussed it with him calmly. When he was dead she had closed his eyes and given the necessary orders with a fine fortitude that was the admiration of her friends. All was over, she told herself, and thought that she knew exactly what that meant. But a month later the alarm had begun to go off. A voice within herself cried passionately night and day: You did not tell me it would be like this! And she could only grieve, and found no answer but that she was apparently as blind a fool at thirty-nine as she had been at nineteen.

Yet age made a little difference, she thought, sitting composedly behind the young Antoine. At nineteen Elizabeth the first was at least thrilled by the events into which she so recklessly plunged Elizabeth the second; at thirty-nine Elizabeth the first was *blasée*. She ought to have been excited over her return to Scotland; an absence of twenty years was no trifle; but she felt as if she were only stepping into the train for Monte Carlo. . . .

And yet, as usual, Elizabeth the first had no hesitation. To go back to Scotland was the right thing to do. One should have a standard by which to measure one's growth. In returning to the home of her childhood and stormy girlhood she would perhaps find out where she now stood. Karl had been her measure for so long that without him she was lost. Madame Mütze settled herself in the corner seat and wondered whether everyone had as cold and imperative a monitor as she had within herself.

When she was a little girl Elizabeth the second had been, if anything, a few moments the quicker of the two, and Elizabeth the first was restricted to making sarcastic comments. It was in her teens that the sarcastic devil had taken the lead, and by the time she ran away from Calderwick with Fritz Elizabeth the second was toiling well in the rear, and all her agony had not availed to change events.

Nor did it now avail. Karl was dead and buried, Elizabeth reiterated to her other self. The clear, firm contours of the land she had been living in had made her beliefs sharp and concrete. None of your Celtic twilights, said Elizabeth the first grimly, looking out of the window at the well-defined planes of the landscape and the houses. In the south of France appearance *was* reality. Karl was dead and buried. Life went on. Moreover it was only fools who needed to be reminded of that, she told herself. The one grossly obvious fact about life was that it went on, on and on and on. Life was like roulette; if the stakes were never removed from the encumbered table the game would have to stop. Karl was merely a stake.

You are making phrases again, protested the other voice.

I'm telling you the truth, she answered. . . . This craze of humanity for preserving the last resting-places of its dead is going to have queer results in another half-million years. What will the living do when the cemeteries of the dead are spread over half the habitable globe? Find a new theory, I suppose, about the Day of Resurrection.

However divided one may be, to travel alone in an express train induces a sense of singleness. The multifarious world, so inexorably receding and renewing itself on both sides of the train, compels the lonely spirit by contrast to become aware of its integrity. Long before she reached Saint-Raphael Elizabeth Mütze had ceased to debate with herself, and had given herself up to the impressions which flowed upon her from outside. Like the thrust of a pin helping forward one by one the cogs of a reluctant wheel, each new vista moved her thoughts a little further from her painful obsession with the dead by forcing her to realize the living.

The solitary passenger has a peculiar, almost a god-like, detachment from the lives through which she flashes; then, if at any time, she can contemplate individual destiny *sub specie æternitatis*. She can see without being seen and without responsibility for what she sees. Children stop playing in the dust to wave a hand; startled small animals lift their heads; in one continuous movement she experiences countless disconnected existences, bound to their environment and changing in nature, in occupation, as that changes. Thickly cultivated ground, lonely waste, wayside village and spreading city all spoke to Elizabeth Mütze in their own voices as the train sped on, and by the time that darkness fell she had become a passive listener.

Here I am, she said to herself, walking up and down the platform at Marseilles, and that is the last irreducible fact. Karl was, and is not. All these people simply are. *Why* they are, and *how* they are, is of no conceivable importance; it is sufficiently remarkable that they *are*, that they exist. It is most extraordinary that I exist, that I am here, walking on a platform in a city called Marseilles.

She slept in the train more soundly than she had slept for months. When she awoke the passivity of the night before was faintly irradiated by a more positive feeling, as if to the statement 'Here I am' she had added a hesitating query: 'What next?' The fields and houses running past no longer beat into her consciousness; she sat gazing at them only half-seeingly. Now and then something caught her attention, a receding line of swaying poplars, or the silhouette of a hill, but what she chiefly observed was the gradual thickening of the air, the encroaching clouds that brought the level sky closer to the earth and spread a veil over the sun. It was nearly two years since she had been even so far north as Paris; four years since she had been in London; twenty years since she had been in Scotland. The clear, sharp contours of the land were softening into a blur in the hazy atmosphere; presently it would be raining; but she assured herself that her stark vision of facts would never be dimmed, no matter what happened to the landscape.

Yet she did not now repeat with savage vehemence that Karl was dead. Instead she brooded over the years that they had spent together. What had she brought out of them besides the elemental consciousness of being alive and the determination to face facts? Karl had always told her that she was an extraordinary combination of scepticism and vitality. 'I look for what is true,' he had said in delight, 'and you leap like a tiger upon what is *not* true. So we correct each other.' She had leaped like a tiger on many of his theories. . . . Madame Mütze found herself smiling. Karl invariably looked at facts as if they were hieroglyphs, and his divination in reading the ciphers was sometimes marvellous. A great part of that, at least, he had left behind him, in his seven books. 'Meine sieben Sachen,' he had said, laughing, a fortnight before he died, 'they are literally all I have to show.' He had written them since meeting her and – how characteristic that was! – he had written them in his study surrounded by mountains of reference-books, without once visiting the countries whose ciphers he unriddled. Her vitality, he had said, was all he needed to provide him with vegetative material on which to feed. . . . Women were like grass, he said; they were the fundamental nourishment. . . . Anonymous nourishment, thought Madame Mütze, remembering how she had objected to this description. Karl had always explained her elaborately to herself; but he had explained himself too; he was able to say at any point precisely what influences were affecting him, and she had never subscribed to his explanations. Still, Karl survived in these seven books, and she survived only in herself. She had nothing else to show. Was she, then, mere pasture on which an imaginative man could browse?

I wish I could really *see* myself, she thought, gazing out of the window. I can see other people clearly enough; myself I cannot see. I know nothing about myself, except, simply, that I am here and going to Scotland.

Karl had been amusing about Scotland. 'I have never been in Scotland,' he had said loftily, 'but I know that you cannot be Scottish. No, it is impossible. You have the rational scepticism of a Latin, and the temperament of a Latin. That is why you had the sense to run away from Scotland, my Elise.'

Karl should have written a book about the primitive people of Scotland, she thought with a spurt of amusement. He would have inspected their mythology as if they were Tlinkit Indians. He would have explained their ideology to them. Ideology was a favourite word of his.

What was the ideology of Scotland? Looking back, Elizabeth Mütze strove to revive her memories of the little town in which she had been born and brought up. For years before she ran away she had lived in a state of perpetual resentment, it seemed to her, but there was no bitterness in the recollection. It was like looking through the wrong end of a telescope at something so distant that it became impersonal. Her emotions remained untouched.

Yet why had she written to her brother John? She had regretted the letter as soon as it was posted. It was a capitulation to all that she had run away from. It had seemed to make her marriage vulgar. The people in Scotland would never understand that marriage; she had not attempted to explain it to John; she could barely explain it to herself. At the time she had thought it amusing to end with marriage instead of beginning with marriage; and she and Karl had laughed over it once the argument was settled. She was herself surprised at the curious ferment of feeling it caused in her some days afterwards, a ferment which brought up from the depths of her nature the desire to let John know, and, less excusably, the desire to let Aunt Janet know. It was partly devilment that had prompted the letter, the devilment of a schoolgirl. Madame Mütze was ashamed to remember it.

Karl had also written to his people in Mecklenburg, and he had neither excused nor regretted his letter. My parents love me very much, he had said, and they will continue my allowance to my widow, which they would not have done to my friend. Neither the genuine sentiment nor the equally genuine element of calculation had disturbed Karl; presumably Germans had a different ideology. . . . Or was it merely that Karl was a different kind of individual? As soon as she had posed the question Madame Mütze realized how absurd it was. One could not classify people in that way. Karl was a German, but not a typical German; she was a Scot, but not a typical Scot; had one really explained anything by saying that?

In Scotland, at any rate, she would find out how far she had progressed. She smiled again at her assumption that Calderwick had stood still for all these years while she had been moving swiftly. Could one ever correct the delusion that life decreased in importance and intensity the farther it was removed from one's own immediate neighbourhood? One's very eye fostered such illusive analogies; the fences and telegraph poles next the train appeared to be moving at great speed, while the trees in the middle distance were slower, and those in the farther distance stood still, like Calderwick.

But if Calderwick had also progressed how could she measure against it the changes in herself? There was some conspiracy in the nature of life which would always prevent one from seeing oneself clearly against an unchanging background. That was in itself a kind of proof that nothing stood still, whatever one's illusions.

Madame Mütze was not in the mood to protract her journey by lingering in Paris or in London. One did not dally with the spoon when one took a nauseous draught, less than ever when one had deliberately prescribed it for oneself. She was an excellent traveller, and she conveyed herself ruthlessly from train to steamer, from steamer to train, and,

crossing London by night in a taxicab, settled herself to sleep
in the Scottish express. The comfort of her present journey
was in sharp contrast to her flight to London with Fritz so
many years ago. What a disappointment London had been to
her then in the smoky grey morning after a night spent in a
crowded huddle on a third-class seat! She had expected a city
of palaces, in wide and beautiful streets; and her first vision
had been of dusty litter, grime, and staring advertisements of
Reckitt's Blue. She remembered that pang of disappointment much more clearly than her growing disappointment
with Fritz.

This time there would be no disappointment at the end of
the journey. She had ceased to believe in miracles.

The train attendant spoke to her in a precise Scots accent.
'Two minutes past ten,' he said, in an almost defiant tone,
when she asked the time of their arrival in Calderwick. 'But
you'll have to shift out of the sleeper at Dundee, about eight
o'clock.'

He said that as if it gave him a kind of satisfaction to put
passengers in their place, looking through his spectacles with
a shrewd, defensive glance. Take it or leave it, he seemed to
be saying. Elise Mütze's charming air left him unaffected.
She could not help smiling as she locked the door upon him.
Compared with the young Antoine or the old Antoine he was
an ungracious figure, although probably more efficient than
they were. It was the tone of his voice that did it – a thin, dry,
blighting intonation which suddenly re-created Calderwick
for her.

Br-rr-rr! she said to herself.

But although she lay down with confidence in her ability to
sleep soundly she was disturbed by dreams. Something
within her was uneasy and apprehensive. One of her dreams
woke her up. A voice, a dry Scots voice, was saying: 'You'll
be exactly as you were before, only the inconvenience will be
removed.' It was a surgeon, she realized: an operation had
been performed; something had been cut out of her, and
they were just going to remove the bandages, saying that it
was all healed up now, when she awoke trembling because
she was afraid to see the scar.

Her dreams were rare but vivid, so vivid that it was

difficult to believe them unreal, and for a second she felt her body, thinking that the bandages were after all removed, and yet the scar was not there. The same confusion of categories led her to assume for a moment that she was travelling through France towards Menton, and that Karl would laugh when he heard of her absurd dream. But Karl was dead and she was doomed to travel at great speed backwards through her life, as if she were reversing a spool, until she was shot out again at her starting-point, a resentful girl of nineteen brought back to an angry home.

Through these shifting planes of unreality her mind hurried, looking for solid ground, and came to rest on the consciousness that Karl was indeed dead. The uncertainties of her half-dreaming state resolved themselves into a regular rhythm of the engine beating out: Karl – is dead; Karl – is dead; and Elise Mütze buried her face in the pillow.

She awoke finally when the train jolted into the Waverley Station at Edinburgh. The Scots voices in the corridor and on the platform caught her ear, and she pushed aside the blind and peered out. The morning was still dark, but under the lights she had glimpses of what seemed to her large and brosy faces; while a diminutive boy was calling down the platform a cry she seemed to remember: 'Chawk-olit, Edin-burry rock.'

Forgotten scenes were knocking at the door. I must not miss the Forth Bridge, she said to herself, and became aware that she was excited at the prospect.

The excitement remained, even when the looming spans of the Forth Bridge ceased their recurrent flicker. With every mile the countryside grew more familiar as the day slowly broadened, and she sat gazing at the farm-lands, at the absurdly small grey cottages, without any of the philo-sophical detachment which had immobilized her in France. She paused only once to reflect that it might have been different had she been coming back for good, but that to a visitor everything remembered was delightful.

Before they crossed the Tay Bridge the attendant reminded her that she would have to change, and told her he would get someone to help in carrying her suitcase. He seemed more human. The *blasée* part of her shrugged, and thought: He's expecting his tip. But even as she tipped him, lavishly, she smiled upon him with direct friendliness; the cynical voice of experience was overwhelmed by an assurance that it was she who had altered, and not the man; she had moved from one frame into another, and her judgments were prejudiced in a different direction. She judged the man more truly, she thought, in her present mood than in her past one; her foot was on her native heath, and unconsciously her estimates of human worth had changed.

Yes, it was like moving off one shelf on to another.

Her excitement became painful as the train neared Calderwick. Every inlet of the grey North Sea, every little bridge and clump of trees woke memories. She admitted to herself at last that what had brought her home was her need for John's affection and her conviction that it remained unshaken after all those years. His letters left no room for doubt. John's affection might not enable her to see herself more clearly, but it gave her an immediate sense of her own value. That was what she needed. She was leaning out of the window when the train puffed into the windswept station of Calderwick. For the moment all the various personalities in Elizabeth Mütze were fused into one.

TWO

From the beginning Madame Mütze's appearance in Calderwick produced effects she never guessed at. John was the only one of her circle who was not thrown off balance. As soon as he saw her he knew that his heart had been right; it was impossible that Lizzie should ever be anything but just Lizzie.

'You are exactly the same,' he said as they clasped hands, and he meant it honestly.

Mabel, however, peeping through the drawing-room window to see what she had to expect, was staggered. Arm-in-arm with John the most elegant woman she had ever seen was mounting her front steps. She met her sister-in-law effusively, almost obsequiously; clothes such as hers, worn as she wore them, exacted deference. Mabel capitulated on the spot. But her capitulation meant more than mere homage to superior taste and knowledge. Here was a woman who had committed the unpardonable sin, and instead of being made to repent in a tawdry equivalent for sackcloth and ashes she had prospered, and not only had she prospered, she moved with assurance and distinction, as if no breath of derogation had ever dimmed her lustre. She must have made a brilliant marriage, thought Mabel, observing with one swift glance after another the details of the newcomer's toilette. She sighed with happiness as she promised herself a long, *long* talk with her new sister.

'It seems absurd to call you Lizzie,' she said. 'You don't look in the least like a Lizzie.'

'Most of my friends call me Elise.'

'Elise!' chuckled John. 'I thought it was Mrs Doctor Bonnet, with a bee in it.'

John acquired importance in Mabel's eyes that morning.

Elise (she loved the name Elise) was apparently devoted to him: and although Mabel ran about in her sister-in-law's wake she never quite caught her up; it was John whose company was preferred. But Mabel did her best. She consulted Elise upon every detail of the dinner for the evening.

'Who's coming?' said Elise.

Mabel was apologetic.

'I'm *so* sorry, we asked only Hector and his wife. Aunt Janet's coming for tea. But we'll have a real party for you next week, won't we, John? Let's give a dance for Elise.'

'I'd forgotten about Hector,' said Elizabeth Mütze. 'I didn't realize that I had so many connections, John.'

John's gaiety clouded for a moment.

'Hector's only your half-brother.'

'And Aunt Janet's only my half-aunt. Aunt on the father's side but not on the mother's.'

They looked at each other and laughed.

In spite of the laughter Elizabeth Mütze was determined to allow no claims upon her except John's. As soon as they walked out of the station – for she had insisted on walking – she knew that she had returned to John but not to Calderwick. Calderwick had shrunk incredibly; it was like some clean and quaint Dutch town, she observed; where had it got that smack of the Dutch? Everything seemed to be in miniature: the little market-square of the High Street, the gabled houses, the short, straight little streets running downhill towards the sea. It was all the same, yet not the same, and by labelling it Dutch she kept it at a distance.

'I know what everybody's saying,' she remarked. 'They're saying: "Eh, that's Charlie Shand's wild dochter come back!"'

A faint uneasiness disturbed her. If she allowed it, Calderwick would reduce her too in size until she was merely Charlie Shand's wild daughter again. Within the first ten minutes she had found out what she wanted to know, that the second half of her life was of much more value to her than anything in the first half. Except for John. It was at that point that she slipped her arm into his.

Elizabeth Mütze's determination to keep Calderwick in the proper focus as a *genre* picture which she could inspect with detached interest was perhaps what baffled and fascinated Mabel. It baffled Aunt Janet also, but without fascinating her. Janet Shand came to tea, as a concession to family feeling, but she came amply clothed in the righteousness of disapproval. Her niece's clear, amused eye seemed to strip her naked. Janet felt a little helpless because Mabel had apparently gone over to the enemy, but she returned several times to the attack.

'I'm glad to see you're wearing mourning, at least, Lizzie.'

'Oh, this isn't mourning: I wear black sometimes because I look well in it.'

'That's real lace, Elise, isn't it?' broke in Mabel, who had been eyeing the ruffles at her sister-in-law's neck and wrists.

'Quite real. I'll allow you to call it demi-mourning if you like, Aunt Janet, if it's a comfort to you. Eminently suitable for a demi-mondaine, don't you think?'

She regretted this remark as soon as she made it, but Aunt Janet seemed not to have understood the word.

'What is it they call you now – Mrs Moots, or something like that?'

'Frau Doktor Mütze. I'm really a German now, you know. Karl thought it better for me to take his name rather than my own, for, in German, Shand means disgrace.'

Elizabeth Mütze laughed merrily. But Janet Shand went away trembling with indignation. Lizzie was as heartless and unprincipled as ever. Although she was nearly sixty-four Janet still believed that the good were rewarded and the wicked punished not only in the next world but in this, and Lizzie's apparent immunity from punishment upset her. She also blamed Mabel bitterly for her defection; it was disloyalty to all respectable women to countenance such a creature as Lizzie. Her only consolation was her belief that Lizzie would yet come to a bad end. Lizzie was worse than her father, and despite her strong affection for Charlie Janet acknowledged that he had deservedly come to a bad end.

Mabel marvelled more than ever at her sister-in-law as she watched her fencing with Aunt Janet. Elise seemed to come from a world she could only surmise, a world where morality, as she knew it, was superseded by something else.

'Tell us about all the things you've seen and all the people you know,' she begged. 'You must have met lots of interesting people, Elise.'

There were times, Mabel suddenly realized, when Elise was uncannily like Hector. She was much smaller of course, but she had the same neat hands and feet, the same quick movements, and at this moment she had the same devilry in her eye, although her eyes were a clear grey and Hector's a dark hazel, so dark as to be almost black. Mabel bridled a little in response to the queer smile and the wicked look in her sister-in-law's eye.

'Of course, if you don't *want* to tell me, don't. I suppose you think I'm not able to understand,' she said, like a huffed child.

Elise flickered her eyelashes. 'Nonsense, Mabel. I don't know where to begin, that's all. Besides, although I've met lots of queer people, I've met none queerer than myself.'

Her smile broadened and became frank as she caught her brother's eye. John leaned back in his chair and guffawed. It must be admitted that this constantly recurring situation was trying for Mabel. She controlled herself admirably.

'Begin where you left off, when you came here, Elise. Tell us about your house, for instance.'

'My house? It stands nearly at the top of a hill, and there's a terrace with great brown jars on it, full of geraniums. Not genteel geraniums; masses of them, cascades of them. And from the terrace you look up the valley towards grey craggy mountains, and down the valley towards the sea. . . . Italy is on my left and France on my right, and the Mediterranean is my washpot. . . . And seven stray cats come every morning to my back door.'

John smacked his thigh.

'She could never go down the street without speaking to a cat!' he said.

'It's an interesting question,' went on Elise reflectively, 'this question of the relationship between humans and animals. . . . I can comprehend why I like cats, but why they like me remains a mystery.'

'You feed them, don't you?' asked Mabel.

'That doesn't explain why they all come walking with me

whenever I go up the hill. I never feed them at the top of the hill. They don't go up there by themselves, either; but every time I go up, one after the other joins me until I have the whole cortège frisking beside me. . . . It's the companionship they like. . . . They get it from nobody down there except me. . . . But why should they like it? It must be a give-and-take, but a give-and-take of what?

She had fallen, insensibly, into one of the musing discussions she used to have with Karl.

'There are snakes up on the hillside too,' she added. 'Oh, grass snakes, quite harmless and rather beautiful; as thick as my wrist. They come in the summer – I don't know where they spend the winter. Madeleine, my maid, swears that they all come looping down from the mountains in the early summer, and vanish there again in the autumn. At any rate we had a couple on our land all last summer, and every time Madeleine had to cross the hillside I had to escort her, because she's convinced that snakes follow up women in the hope of sucking milk from their breasts. She has the most gruesome stories of young mothers falling asleep and wakening to find a snake suckling them! Madeleine is nearly fifty, and twice as broad as I am, but she wouldn't go to the wash-trough if I didn't come with a stick to fend off the snakes. She's full of queer superstitions about animals, almost all of them about the peculiar dangers women run. She thinks that men haven't nearly as much to fear. It must be a very old belief, as old as the affinity between Eve and the serpent; but it's not a belief in companionship; it's a sexual fear of some kind, perhaps —' She broke off suddenly.

'But you're not interested in that kind of thing. You must excuse me. . . .' She glanced at them, smiling. John was tugging his beard with a puzzled look in his eye. He was really wondering how Lizzie had managed to remain the same creature as the little girl who had believed in magic and had tended bruised bees in a paste-board hospital, furnished with flower-heads and lumps of sugar: but his puzzled expression misled his sister. Mabel, she divined, was merely bored; the superstitions of maid-servants did not interest her; but John, she thought, was troubled because of her queer ideas. . . . Oh, Karl, Karl! what shall I do without you? the other voice cried suddenly within her.

'My husband had a passion for myths and legends and superstitions. . . . I must have got into the habit of talking about them,' she said, and immediately thought: What a fool I make myself appear, aping the dutiful wife! Is this the effect of Scotland?

'Will you give me a cigarette, John, and a light?' she asked, producing an amber holder from her handbag.

'I suppose everybody smokes on the Riviera?' said Mabel enviously.

'Don't you? Give your wife a cigarette, John. I'm sorry mine are all finished: I must get some more.'

John offered his packet to Mabel, with a half-doubting, half-roguish expression on his face. Mabel laughed, and took one, feeling very daring.

'I know how to smoke all right,' she said, cocking her eye at John as she puffed while he held the match. 'I used to smoke them on the sly behind the bushes at Invercalder. You never knew that, John, did you?'

'Bou Di!' said Elise, sitting up in her arm-chair. 'Is it still very wicked for a woman to smoke a cigarette in Calderwick?'

'Of course it is.' Mabel blew out smoke. 'It's not *done*, my dear Elise.'

'I can only suppose, then, that a cigarette has a suggestive shape and that when a man sees a woman sticking a cigarette into her mouth —'

John looked embarassed: Mabel giggled. But Elise was furious with herself for not having said outright what she meant.

'It's not funny,' she said. 'I didn't mean it to be funny. The idea that it's unchaste for a woman to smoke a cigarette is on a level with Madeleine's superstitions about snakes.'

Mabel as well as John now looked embarrassed. A little leaven may leaven a whole lump, but when it is a moral process the leavening may take a long time. Even although she had decided that it paid to be like Elise, even although she had determined to be like Elise, Mabel felt uncomfortable.

Elise, however, suddenly chuckled and lay back again in her chair.

'Upon my word,' she said, 'here am I glowering in your drawing-room, John, just as I used to glower when I was fifteen. I'll tell you what's the matter, it's Aunt Janet. She's brought it all back to me. She used to put me in a dumb rage from morning till night, Mabel, and I find the old rage rising up again.'

'I don't remember that it was ever a very *dumb* rage,' said John.

'Yes, it was! It seethed inside me for weeks before it boiled over. I remember thinking,' and she laughed, a clear laugh, purged of resentment, 'that for Aunt Janet the world was nothing but one enormous fig-leaf! And I thought of pointing out to her that one is entitled to the fig-leaf only *after* eating the apple from the tree – not before. However I—'

John knew very well what she was hinting at. In picking that German fellow she had picked a sour enough apple from the tree of knowledge of good and evil, and surely she might have the decency to admit that it had set her teeth on edge. The very thought of it had set *his* teeth on edge. He liked Lizzie to be light-hearted and audacious; her audacity thrilled him; but, after all, there was a limit.

Elise observed his uneasiness.

'I've shocked John again,' she said. 'I always did. But you like being shocked: you know you do.'

Of course he liked it. John smiled at her. Yet his uneasiness persisted. Lizzie's freedom of speech was exhilarating, but she had upset him once by showing that it could lead to freedom of conduct, and now he realized that he could never again trust her completely. Lizzie had come back exactly the same Lizzie that she used to be, and in bringing back the old delight to him she had brought back the old problems.

To disapprove, to check Lizzie's exuberance, was as difficult and as necessary as it had ever been. There was a limit; of that John was convinced; a firm line of demarcation ought to be drawn: but how insubstantial, how elusive did that line become when scrutinized closely by the dazzling searchlight of Lizzie's gaiety!

'It's Aunt Janet's fault,' said his sister, 'if I have a passion for tearing off fig-leaves. . . .' To herself she added: That must have been what Karl meant when he said I pounced like a tiger on what was *not* true. Fig-leaves!

An incongruous but relevant memory intruded itself, of a statue she and Karl had chanced upon in the Salzkammergut, a statue representing the Trinity. God the Father, she remembered, had a long beard and a cock eye: God the Son was wearing the dove of the Holy Ghost in place of a fig-leaf. Aunt Janet would like that statue, she thought. . . .

She glanced round inquiringly, and Mabel found an ash-tray for her.

'Thank you. Would you mind very much if I had a bath now and took a rest before dinner?'

'You won't have very long,' said Mabel. 'The Hector Shands will be here in about half-an-hour.'

'I think you'll like your namesake,' John put in. 'I've seen her smoking a cigarette.'

Elizabeth Mütze stood still.

'My namesake?'

'Hector's wife. Her name is Elizabeth. Elizabeth Shand.'

'How dare she?' said Elizabeth Mütze.

THREE

Elizabeth Mütze lay in the bath sniffing at a clear, maroon-coloured piece of soap. It was like John, she thought, to stick to the soap they had always used as children. She had no doubt that the violet-scented soap was Mabel's, and the plain soap John's. So damned healthy. . . . He was just the same. He had always liked her, and yet he would have preferred her to be plain Jane and no nonsense. He was just the same: terribly moral, terribly sensible. . . . She could twist him round her little finger up to a certain point, but beyond that point—Schluss! Beyond that point John was quite impervious to argument. It was queer that he, the brother, should be so bound to the moral code while she, the sister, followed her own line. The sheep and the goats again. . . . The one could never have any but a purely sentimental attachment to the other. . . . Affection plus disapproval was of no bloody good to anybody.

I shall clear out immediately after Christmas, she thought, pitching the maroon piece of soap into the soap-dish. Any attempt of mine to hang on to John is damned silly. Surely I can stand on my own feet?

This assertion of herself was followed by a slight shock as she remembered that she had a namesake in Calderwick. Another Elizabeth Shand in the family seemed an insult, as if an interloper had pushed her out of place. Yet what place had she in the family after all? Why should she care how many provincial nonentities assumed her name and style? Elizabeth Shand! She said it aloud, with exaggerated scorn. Thank God I'm not Elizabeth Shand any longer! she added, climbing out of the bath and towelling herself furiously.

If she stayed long in Scotland she would have to live on the defensive. That was, of course, an admission of weakness.

She had not expected to resent Aunt Janet so much. Damn the woman!

Here I am glowering again, she said, laughing a little as she lay down on her bed. The relaxation of her limbs relaxed the tension in herself and she continued to smile as she shut her eyes. Let them all sit in judgment: there was no gaol to which they could consign prisoner at the bar. Aunt Janet's morality was a fiction; it had no relation to the one important thing in life, the integrity of the spirit. What was it you used to say Karl? *Integritas, consonantia, claritas.*

She rested for a time on these cool words. . . . And yet, she thought, absurd as it is, I find it trying to be treated as a fallen woman.

Her smile became mischievous. She continued her inaudible conversation with Karl:

Aunt Janet despises me as a prostitute. Mabel envies me as a successful prostitute. John worries about me as a prostitute turned respectable, who may lapse again at any moment. Not one of my kin can accept me as I am . . . as you did.

The smile faded from her lips, and she was lying very still on the bed when Mabel herself knocked on the door, crying: 'Aren't you ready yet, Elise? Can I come in?'

Elizabeth Shand, meeting John's kind eyes in the drawing-room, felt guilty. Her courage was screwed up: she was ready to tell John that Hector wanted to go away, and that for his own sake he must be allowed to go away, but Hector had objected to her telling John that evening.

'No, no, damn it,' he had said, 'I want to enjoy myself to-night. Time enough to burst it on him in a day or two.'

The knowledge that he was going to be quit of everybody in a short time exhilarated Hector. He had no consequences to fear: whatever he said or did would be wiped out by the simple act of departure; and he found that he did not care what other people might do or say. He was even prepared to have some fun with his disreputable sister. 'Let's all go on the blind together,' he said to Elizabeth: 'let's make a night of it.'

Elizabeth could not approve of his recklessness, for she was too deeply committed to the responsibility she had assumed. The Noble Wife must help her husband to be his best self, not his worst; she must form him, and that, of course, meant that she must reform him.

Elizabeth's voice was a little sharp as she refused to consider the possibility of making a night of it. It would only make John angry, she said: and it would be bad policy to make John angry.

Hector, knowing instinctively that the greater the sin the more effective is subsequent repentance, waved her argument away. If old John were in a paddy he'd be all the more pleased to get rid of the villain. 'He'll even pay me to clear out if I play my cards well enough.'

Yes, thought Elizabeth tartly, but what about *me*? She did not elaborate the thought; she even stifled it: she must not think of herself, she must remember only that she loved Hector. Yet the look in Hector's eye as he spoke of playing his cards well alienated her; and the boisterous manner in which Hector and Mabel greeted each other alienated her still more. For a moment Elizabeth wished that Hector were already out of the country.

Mabel ran upstairs to summon her sister-in-law and, left alone with John and Hector, Elizabeth felt awkward. With the departure of Mabel, Hector seemed to think that social interest had also departed. He turned over the gramophone records, whistling a tune as if there were nobody but himself in the room. For the first time since coming to Calderwick, instead of wondering whether she was a credit to Hector Elizabeth began to wonder whether he was a credit to her.

A little reflection might have shown Elizabeth what was happening to her, but incipient reflection and dawning doubt alike were caught up and blown into nothingness by the entrance of Elise.

The eye sees what it looks for, and Elizabeth was looking for her other self. Had it been a man whose arrival she was expecting with so much interest she would have been embarrassed by that interest; had it been a man who now came into the room she would have been afraid of her own emotion; but since Elise was a woman Elizabeth did not know that she actually fell in love with her at first sight.

Elise, cool and sparkling, noted that it was Mabel who

showed off Hector, and that it was left to John to bring forward the shy, large, awkward creature who called herself Elizabeth Shand. She examined her namesake with a satirical eye: one of these earnest women who don't know how to do their hair, she decided, and turned to Hector again with unconcealed surprise.

'I should have guessed you were a brother of mine even if I had met you at the bottom of the sea.'

She stared at him frankly.

'What a curious experience it is to meet someone so like oneself!'

'You're not very like each other, really,' put in John.

'Oh, but I think they are,' cried Mabel.

'Well,' said Elise, 'it takes the conceit out of me to find that I am merely a family type instead of an original model.'

But even as she said this she was discovering that Hector's mouth was different from hers: the lips were less finely turned, and opened over slightly irregular teeth: it was a larger mouth, too, a less discriminating mouth, a weaker mouth than hers.

'You're both black Shands,' said John. 'I went through all the family papers and albums when our father died, and I found that it was our father's grandmother on his father's side who was the first of that type in the family. But it's only a general family resemblance.'

'Black Shands?' commented Elise. 'I suppose Black Sheep is what you really mean, John?'

'How did you guess it, Elise? Hector is a double-dyed black sheep.'

Mabel's playful, provocative tone perfectly underlined her meaning, which was further emphasized by the hand she laid on Hector's shoulder. She wanted to let Elise see that she, too, had a way with men. Hector, who was a little taken aback by the elegance of his half-sister, welcomed Mabel's gambit with relief, and followed it up so thoroughly that the room was presently dominated by their brisk exchange of invective, which was kept up even after they were all seated at table.

Elise was half exasperated and half amused. She thought that they were both 'showing off' before her. How was the wife taking it? she wondered, and stole a glance at her.

Elizabeth Shand's eyes were cast down: it was impossible to tell from her face what her feelings were. A real Scottish face, Elise thought, all nose and cheek-bones: the black Shands were certainly of an entirely different type. 'That great-grandmother of ours,' she said to John, 'the first black Shand, was she a Scot, do you know?'

Her eyes were still resting absently on the face of the other Elizabeth, as if it were merely an exhibit in a museum of Scottish faces, but she was startled by the change which flitted over it when she began to speak. The girl lifted her eyes as if with an effort, as if a weight had been holding her eyelids down, and looked straight across the table at her. Elise almost jumped: the eyes were so intensely alive, the expression in them so completely altered the whole face. She felt unexpectedly embarrassed, as if she had been caught prying.

'There was a kind of suggestion, not certain enough to be a tradition,' said John, 'that she was partly a foreigner – an Italian or a Spaniard or something.'

'Ah!' Elise smiled. 'That might explain a lot.'

She deliberately included Elizabeth in her smile, and received another shock. The girl blushed.

Does she never open her mouth? Elise wondered. Is it shyness, or is she indulging her sense of power by keeping out of the conversation?

Aloud she said to John:

'This interests me. Have I inherited more than just the features of my outlandish great-grandmother? Am I to suppose that I'm not a free individual, but a victim of heredity, John?'

John was disconcerted by the question. He was inclined to agree that she was a victim of heredity, and to make excuses for her on that score: but he knew that nothing used to enrage Lizzie so much as having excuses made for her.

'No, no—' he stammered.

'What? You don't think that our great-grandmother, who may have been a wild baggage, is responsible for my being such an unsatisfactory sister?'

'And Hector an unsatisfactory brother,' interposed Mabel.

'Tut!' said John. He was annoyed. 'There's only a general

family resemblance between you and Hector: it means nothing, absolutely nothing.'

He said this with all the more conviction since he was uneasy in his mind: the unpredictable waywardness of his sister was in some respects too like the unreliability of Hector. 'Nothing at all,' he repeated.

'I think it does mean something,' said Elzabeth Shand, in a low, hesitating voice.

'That's no compliment to you,' Hector turned to Elise. 'Elizabeth knows what a bad lot I am. Don't you, Elizabeth?'

'Elizabeth may not know what a bad lot *I* am,' said Elise wickedly, keeping her eye on the embarrassed girl. 'Some are born to be black sheep' – she indicated Hector – 'some achieve it' – she rolled an eye at Mabel – 'and some have it thrust upon them' – she looked at Elizabeth and John – 'but I am the three in one, and the one in three.'

She was so droll that everybody laughed. Like a good player, having secured the attention of her audience, Elise exploited it to the full. Her light, sarcastic self was escaping successfully from the other self within her, which could not believe that Karl was dead. Her mind was alert and cool, pinking its objects neatly, like a rapier. These objects for the most part were human oddities whom she had met in nearly every corner of Europe. Elise was a good mimic and represented their differing accents with spirit.

Mabel was delighted to hear at last the word 'baroness', which Elise used with apparent unconcern.

'So there she was, sitting up in bed; and she had staged herself gorgeously, with a crimson cushion behind her and an enormous parasol spread over her head. "I expect him in two minutes," she said, "my dearest Elise, will you tie this over the light to make it more flattering?" And "this" was a pink silk nightgown. Of course, I tied it over the light for her.'

'Was she a real baroness, Elise?' said Mabel eagerly.

'Well, her husband was a German baron. She herself was a Hungarian. She couldn't speak English at all, and the man in this case was an American who spoke neither French nor German, so that was why I had to interpret. "Tell him," she would say, "that he is a volcano." "Tell her that the volcano

is an extinct one." "Ah, tell him that I know there is a glow
kindling beneath the ashes." "Huh, how kin she tell that?
Kin she tell how far a frog kin jump?"'

'Were you her companion?'

'I? Of course not. I was merely holidaying in the same
hotel.'

So her sister-in-law really hobnobbed on level terms with
baronesses, thought Mabel.

'Women who are convalescent in bed always seem to be
amusing,' went on Elise. 'There was an American woman I
met in Vienna, a huge, jolly creature, with a fist like a ham,
and a voice like a fog-horn. In her clothes she was majestic
and somewhere between fifty and sixty; but in bed with a
pigtail over each shoulder she was just fifteen. I used to take
in cups of tea to her while she was indisposed, and one day
she said to me:

'"Why doesn't the doctor ever come in to see me?" She
meant my – Karl – and I said: "I suppose he's shy of coming
in while you're in bed," and she returned: "Tell him that if
he comes into *my* room he'll be as safe as if he were in God's
pocket."'

Elise laughed and held out her glass to Hector for refilling.

Hector had been filling his own glass very frequently, and
while he replenished Elise's he gave her a confidential leer.

Elizabeth, on the other side of the table, noted that. Of
course he was thinking that his sister was 'hot stuff' and that
they would probably get gloriously tight together. She felt
that this unspoken assumption could not but annoy Elise and
make her withdraw into silence and she wanted Elise to go on
talking, it did not matter about what. She plunged into the
first sentence that occurred to her.

'I suppose you speak German very well, Elise?'

'I do know it pretty well.'

'It's an awful language though, isn't it? I had to get it up a
little to read some notes on texts. They call a girl "it", don't
they?'

Elizabeth stopped breathlessly, for she was overwhelmed
by the conviction that her remarks were banal. Elise,
however, set down her wineglass and took up the subject.

'Yes, a nation must be held guilty of its language. And

they don't call only a girl "it", they call a woman "it". "Das Weib" is a worse offence than "das Madchen", for it hasn't the excuse of being a diminutive. "Das Madchen" can be passed, for, after all, they say "das Bubchen". But to take "Weib" and subject *her* to a grammatical gender is purely pedantic. Is there another language in the world which makes a woman neuter? I could swear there isn't. Latin, French, Italian. . . ? I don't know any others, but I'm sure there isn't. What an indictment! Oh, I must point that out to some of my German friends!'

Elise looked pleased.

'It's the finest example of pedantry that I've ever met. . . . The rule is everything, the fact nothing. . . . As if there shouldn't be exceptions to every rule! . . . As if the right end of a word were more important than the right end of a woman!'

Elizabeth was delighted. How deftly Elise had caught the clumsily thrown ball, and how skilfully was she turning it round!

'So you think the psychology of a nation could be deduced from its language?' she asked.

'Not by me,' said Elise coolly. 'I should suspect myself of merely confirming my own prejudices. I can't track down ideas: I have to wait until they strike me. I knew – someone – who could shut himself up in a room and hunt ideas like big game. But I always suspected him of collecting only the horns and the skins. . . . I distrust any systematic interpretation of everything.'

'But, Elise,' cried Elizabeth, 'everything has a meaning if one looks at it. Everything implies everything else —'

Her mind was in a glow and thoughts were crowding upon her, as if she had pulled the end of a skein which was going to unwind until the whole of life was explained.

A daisy in a field, she was thinking, isn't just a daisy; it's the meeting-point of an infinite number of cross-sections of the universe.

'I dare say,' Elise interrupted her. 'But how do you know it's a true meaning? One of the things I liked best about Ilya, the Hungarian I was telling you about, was that she always said: "Life has no meaning, none at all. But I find it very enjoyable!"'

She gave her brother a smile, and Elizabeth, with a sense of rebuff, realized that Elise had not forgotten the rest of the company, and that she had. She was silent for the rest of the dinner.

They all removed to the drawing-room, and Hector, kicking rugs aside, began to dance extravagantly with Mabel to the gramophone. Elizabeth lingered beside Elise and John, praying for a chance of getting Elise all to herself. She wanted to communicate to the other woman her own fervour, and at the same time to relate it to everything in heaven and on earth. Whenever Elizabeth had a strong feeling she was impelled to give it a cosmic background. Yet, in spite of her excitement, she feared that Elise would find her dull. She had said nothing to interest the newcomer; nothing at all; she had only listened. . . . If she had not been so inexperienced Elizabeth might have known that everything comes to her who listens. She was, indeed, a gifted listener. Elise had already become aware that she was drawing vitality from the silent girl. What Elizabeth had said was negligible, but the warmth that streamed from her had given Elise a curious feeling of trust. One could trust this girl, she thought, without defining more closely in what respect the statement was true. Besides, Elise had once quoted to Karl, 'I am like a match; I must have a box to strike on,' and in Elizabeth, her namesake, she now perceived a very serviceable box.

'Come and sit beside me, Elizabeth – unless you want to dance with John?'

'Don't *you* want to dance with John?'

Elizabeth shyly slipped into the proferred seat. She did not want to dance. She did not want to be reminded that Hector and Mabel, having opened the door, were now glissading into the hall outside, like a pair of children. She wanted to thrust Hector out of her consciousness, but she felt a certain inexplicable anger against him, an anger which extended to Mabel. Elise had opened to her a world of escape from Calderwick, a world sparkling with interest which convinced her that she had been stagnating in mind if not in heart ever since coming to Calderwick, and, without suspecting for a moment that Elise had cut herself to the quick to achieve her apparent detachment, she envied her that detachment and was prepared to regard Hector as an encumbrance. Yet she was angered to see how well he and Mabel danced, and how closely they held each other.

John, too, was angered. His wife was almost flouting him in her disregard for propriety. He tugged at his beard, but he tried to look genial. The fellow, after all, was Elizabeth's husband and his own half-brother. Thank God, he thought, neither Elizabeth nor Elise seemed to take their behaviour amiss; perhaps there was nothing in it, after all.

Elise looked at him with an air of mischief.

'This kind of dancing is too expressionistic for John, isn't it, darling?'

'Too shameless,' growled John.

'But dances are always inspired by love or war,' went on Elise, 'and in either case, you know, a flank attack is the most successful.'

Elizabeth laughed, a clear spontaneous laugh.

Perhaps Elise had been deliberately testing the girl; at any rate when Elizabeth laughed without any undertone of disapproval her sister-in-law joined in the laugh with obvious satisfaction.

As far as Hector was concerned, the evening fizzled out lamentably. He had managed to kiss Mabel twice in the hall, but she was not sporting enough to keep it up, and he had to return in her wake to the family group. Elise, probably discouraged by John's unamiable temper, had not got drunk with him, although she had been friendly enough. Elizabeth had been a bit on her high horse, especially on the way home. And although she had made it up with him, and let him into her bed, there had been a something.

There was indeed a something, which Elizabeth recognized at first as the persistence of the embarrassment that had recently arisen between her and Hector whenever they kissed each other. Her body craved his embraces, but when he was in her bed she felt that a great part of herself withdrew from the physical contact. Her mind, too, was in a ferment, as if her encounter with Elise had roused a long-dormant faculty; scraps of the evening's conversation darted into her head and out again, followed by brilliant and exhaustive supplementary discussions of everything that had been touched upon; ideas branched and grew in all directions; the significance of heredity, of language, what she ought to have said about the meaning implicit in all things, beginning from the daisy in the grass – in short, her conjugal embarrassment was complicated by a bad attack of *esprit d'escalier*. Her mind kept flying away from Hector, and even from herself; it was no longer Elizabeth who put her arm round Hector's neck, it was a wife embracing a husband.

Her mental activity, however, was not the cause of the embarrassment, of this partial withdrawal. Something had been lacking ever since she had agreed to Hector's going away. The glamour had vanished, the deep, passionate excitement that had made her shut her eyes whenever Hector kissed her. And to-night her eyes were far from shutting. She despised her body; it had still turned to Hector although she herself resisted; her arm had snuggled of itself round his neck although she was cold to him. She despised Hector for flirting with Mabel, a shallow, commonplace pretty doll, and when she compared him with Elise he himself seemed shallow and commonplace.

It was the thought of Elise that gave poignancy to this contempt. It was because of Elise that she was ashamed of Hector. It was through Elise's eyes that she now looked at herself and her husband and despised herself for having fallen in love with a man who had neither wit nor brains, a man whose sole social accomplishment, flirtation, was crude both in its technique and in its objects.

Elizabeth disentangled herself from the sleeping Hector and climbed into his vacant bed. Oh, I am a fool, she said to herself, turning over and over between the cold sheets. She could not shut her eyes and sleep; she could not shut her eyes to anything. She was a fool. But how? And why? She took the wrong things too seriously, Emily Scrymgeour had said; and now, contrasting herself with Elise, she found herself stupid, heavy, clumsy and solemn; she wasn't even pretty like Mabel. She fell into an agony of humility.

But if she judged herself so worthless what right had she to despise Hector? What was it in herself that sat up aloft and belittled these two living creatures, herself in one bed and Hector in the next? What was it that tempted her to despise her body? Had she not always found a magical satisfaction in the thought that she was in her own little finger, her toes, her thighs, her belly, and her breasts? She ran her hands over her body. You are me, she said, repeating the statement again and again as if it were an invocation. She had cried out upon William Murray for saying that the body unsanctified by God is evil, and now she had herself fallen into that heresy, the heresy of thinking that the body, when some part of oneself holds aloof from it, is the wrong-doer. . . . Her arm, when it ached to snuggle round Hector's neck, was it in the wrong because something in herself rejected the action? Or was it her arm that was innocent, and her contempt, her withdrawal, her sense of shame, were they not evil? The spirit denounced the body as evil; could not the body also denounce the spirit? She had been despising Hector, envying Elise, abusing Mabel and belittling herself; if *that* was not the sin against the Holy Ghost, what was it?

Elizabeth went on stroking her body, almost mechanically. She herself, body and spirit, was also, like the daisy in the field, the meeting-point of an infinite number of cross-sections of the universe. But, unlike her, the daisy was folded up in a simple unconsciousness of its position. A daisy would never be ashamed of itself. . . .

As she lay quietly alone in bed an image of herself grew before her, hovering in space, an extended, shadowy image, clearly defined at each extremity and thickened into obscurity in the middle. It was an overlapping of vibrations rather than a solid form, and the vibrations extended beyond the farthest stars. One end of this shadowy projection had long, slow, full waves; that was the body and its desires. At the other end were short, quick waves; these represented the mind. And the space in between, she asked herself, the thickened obscurity, what was that? Muddle and confusion of forces, in which she was now involved? She strained to hold the image, waiting for illumination, but it changed; the middle portion condensed into her own shape, but the two ends diffused themselves throughout space, as if her head and her feet had spread into infinity. At the same time Elizabeth felt in her feet that desire to run which she had had so often, ever since childhood.

The firmness of sandy soil, the coolness of short grass on the naked foot-sole, the wet softness of drifting leaves in a ditch, all the sensations her feet had ever experienced, seemed to become a part of her again, and drew her down through her feet until she was the earth and all that grew upon it. Her blood ebbed and flowed with the tides of the month and the tides of the seasons, and she was no longer separate in her own body but a part of all life. And suddenly, as if she had broken through a barrier, in that world she found Hector. She remembered his grace and strength in running, his rejoicing head cleaving the waters of the sea, his quick eye and hand controlling a frightened horse; his neck was a column, his thighs were grand like trees; her body tingled with the remembrance of his body. All that she had not felt when he lay so recently beside her thrilled through her now; the glamour came back; and she knew that she had done wrong to be ashamed of him. She saw with immediate clearness that it was only inside a room, in the world of talk, of articulate expression, that Hector was trivial. Out of doors, with no roof but the sky, he was like an impersonal force. In loving Hector she had loved something transcending both of them.

The life which had streamed out through her feet, as if into a sea out of which all creatures rose like waves, returned upon itself as she lay rigid and flowed up – up, like sap rising, until she felt as if her head were branching. This was the other end of her vision, and she knew what it represented. It was the world that Elise had recalled to her, the world of thought, of ideas, spreading into vast impersonal abstractions which made another infinity.

And that was the world in which Hector had no part. . . . And between the two, stretched as if on the rack, lay the shape of Elizabeth Shand.

FOUR

I

Sarah Murray no less than William was being forced into a fatalism regarding Ned, but for different reasons. It had taken only two days to make a breach in the fortifications of her disciplinary theory. She had discovered that discipline depends eventually on might even more than on right, and within the four walls of the manse it was beginning to look as if might and right were on opposing sides.

On Friday night, as she had threatened, she had cut off the gas at eleven o'clock, after giving Ned fair warning. She ought to have gone to sleep with a quiet conscience, but she found herself lying listening in the darkness to the unceasing prowl of Ned's feet, up and down, up and down. There was something terrifying in the fact that he was not daunted by the darkness, that he had not taken refuge in bed. It suggested to Sarah that the darkness within Ned, to make him capable of disregarding the darkness around him, must be tenfold the blacker of the two.

After a long interval she heard the scrape of a match and the clatter of feet upon the narrow stairs. She half raised herself. Where was he going? Down into the dining-room. What was he doing, prowling about downstairs? But the doors and windows were all locked; the cupboards were shut up: there was nothing he could despoil except a tin of biscuits; and it was hardly likely that he would go out into the streets. She made herself lie down again.

He was walking up and down the dining-room between the table and the door. She could not help hearing him. Monotonous, insistent, his feet sounded first on the carpet and then on the boards. Should she go down after all and order him to bed?

Her disinclination to rise made the first small breach in her system of discipline, for of course it was absurd to have anyone prowling about in the small hours and she ought to have insisted on his going to bed. But she was so tired. Confused dreams ensnared her; the more she swept out corners the thicker she became entangled in cobwebs, and finally an enormous, hairy spider crawled over her shrinking body. She twitched and moaned, but she was asleep, and Ned remained downstairs.

On Saturday morning Sarah felt more irritable. Ned had got at the biscuit tin, and apparently he had been drinking water out of a broken cup; there were burnt matches all over the floor of the dining-room and the kitchen, and it was impossible to surmise at what ungodly hour he had gone to bed. But he must get up for breakfast all the same. . . . Sarah pounded on his door and then marched in.

Ned was lying on the bed in his shirt and trousers. He had kicked off his slippers, and thrown his collar on the floor, but these were all the preparations he had made for sleep. His unshaven chin looked dirty, and even in sleep his mouth was wry as if he had drunk a bitter draught.

Sarah shook him.

'Get up! It's breakfast-time.'

'What the hell!'

'Get up! It's breakfast-time. You're to come downstairs to breakfast like everybody else.'

When she and William were nearly finished breakfasting Ned had burst in upon them, in his socks, shirt and trousers exactly as he had tumbled out of bed, unwashed and unkempt.

'Go and wash yourself and put on a collar and tie before you get your breakfast.'

With a malevolent glance at her, but without a word, Ned had sat down as he was and seized the loaf in his filthy hands. So the issue was joined; the battle of wills begun.

Sarah had not spared herself. She heaped as much abuse upon Ned as he did on her. But she had been weakened by the look of sick distaste on William's face. Much good William was; he only got up and went out of the room. She was angry with William; he ought to have backed her up instead of tacitly agreeing with Ned's reiterated: 'Virago! Virago! Virago!'

The battle had raged all day. At dinner-time Ned was still unwashed, still without his collar and tie; and at tea-time, and at supper-time; and it was to be presumed that he would go to bed again in the same condition. But that was not what disturbed Sarah most. What disturbed her was that she was beginning to fear Ned. His voice had gone on all day like a saw; but towards evening the saw had taken on a sharper edge. He had turned upon her the very threats she uttered the day before. 'I'll thrash you within an inch of your life,' he had said, and 'I'll inform the police of the way you are treating me.' She had never seen him look so ugly. Even in his socks he towered above William, and she knew he was strong. Before he went up to his room Sarah felt that if she were for a second to relax the tension in her backbone he would be at her throat. She had let herself down to his level; and now that his first surprise was over he was emboldened, she felt, to attack her as an equal. For the first time in her life Sarah Murray locked her bedroom door from the inside. On the Saturday night she hardly slept at all, and heard Ned not only descend to the dining-room as before, but come up again towards three in the morning. She heard him say, as he passed her door, 'I want to know the truth, the truth,' and the savage despair in his voice struck to her heart.

Next morning, it being Sunday, she surrendered. She did not waken him at breakfast-time, but fed William and herself in the quiet peacefulness appropriate to the Sabbath. She established another record in her life by absenting herself from morning church, since Ned had not awakened by the time the bells were ringing, and she was afraid to leave him in the house with Teenie.

It had come to that. Sarah was trembling and afraid. There had been a moment on the previous day when Ned had grasped the bread-knife and her knees had knocked together. Ought she to have mentioned it to William? Her anger against William rose again. In his own way he was almost as bad as Ned. She felt resentful even of the fact that he had escaped to church, while she had to stay at home and face it out.

But life must go on, even in a manse on a Sunday. Although at the moment she should by rights have been sitting in the manse pew Sarah could not sit idle in her chair at home. She would help Teenie with her dishes since, of course, she could not sew or darn on the Lord's Day, and the idea of reading the Bible gave her a slight nausea. Without being aware of it, she was really angry with God as well as with William. . . . When Ned was about she had more faith in the police than in God, in the law of earth than in the law of heaven.

The two women were still in the kitchen when a noise on the stairs made them both stiffen.

'He's got up,' said Sarah dryly. 'Make the tea, Teenie.'

She carried a pile of dry plates to the cupboard and set them down on the shelf without a tremor. Yet her heart was fluttering queerly, though her hand was steady. She would not ask Teenie to do anything she was afraid to do herself, and so she could not send Teenie in with his breakfast. Methodically she began to arrange a tray.

The suspense before an expected blow falls is more painful than the blow, and Sarah thought that the time during which she arranged the breakfast-tray and waited to hear Ned slam his way into the dining-room behind her appeared long only because of her suspense. In reality Ned had passed the dining-room and was now at the front door. If he had gone quickly Sarah would not have been in time to prevent his going out, but he was walking slowly, as he had come downstairs, pausing now and then to mutter. Sarah suddenly heard him speaking to himself in the hall and darted from the kitchen through the dining-room without stopping to think.

Ned, in his dirty shirt and trousers, was opening the front door with a slow, abstracted movement, as if he were somnambulizing.

'Where are you going, Ned?' cried Sarah in a voice more anxious than sharp.

'I must go and apologize to Hector Shand.' Ned's voice was reasonable, even mild, but curiously remote. That gave Sarah courage. She sprang to the door and shut it.

'Hector Shand's in church.'

She stood with her back to the door. Ned did not seem to see her.

'I must know the truth, the truth. I must see Hector Shand.'

He began to tug at the door apparently without noticing her.

Sarah turned the key behind her and drew it out of the lock. Her personal fears had vanished, swallowed up by a greater, nameless fear as she looked at his dull remote eyes.

'The door's locked,' she said, trying to keep her voice from shaking. 'And Hector Shand's in church. Wait till the church comes out.'

For a moment it looked as if the mask of remoteness were to be broken up by a violent spasm of anger. Sarah repeated over and over again, 'Wait till the church comes out,' and finally Ned turned in the same meandering, absorbed fashion and drifted into the sitting-room. Sarah sagged against the door, but immediately recovered herself when she saw Ned trying the latch of the window. She opened her mouth to scream, but only a hoarse sound came out:

'Teenie! Teenie!'

An equally hoarse whisper answered her:

'What is it, Miss Murray?'

'Run for the doctor. Quick. And then fetch Mr Murray. Get him out of the church. Get John Shand too, quick. Lock the kitchen door and take the key with you. Quick.'

She followed Ned and spoke to him as if to a small child:

'Never mind the window, Ned. Wait till the church comes out and then you can go by the door. You're too early —'

She repeated these simple statements again and again, although she felt that the wheels racing madly in Ned's brain could not be controlled by anything so pointless as her words. Yet they were the only tools she had. . . .

The cogency of words is at all times mysterious, and perhaps the tone in which they are uttered has a more direct effect upon the hearer than the meaning they convey. A dog, for instance, will wag his tail when he is told in a kindly tone that he is a dirty scoundrel. These overtones or undertones of the spoken word are so potent even in human intercourse that precision in the use of language is almost impossible.

Sarah was right; mere words, however reasonable, however clear, might convey to Ned the exact opposite of their intention, or might convey nothing at all.

But there was something in her voice for which she had not allowed, and which penetrated to Ned. In spite of his size she could not help feeling that he was a bewildered child, and her heart swelled with an unfamiliar emotion when he turned obediently from the window. She remembered what a good child he had been, what a good boy, and it was with real kindness in her voice that she said: 'Besides, it's raining, and you would catch your death of cold like that.'

After a moment's irresolution Ned sat down at the piano and began to play.

II

On that same morning, after her vision of the night, Elizabeth woke with a sense of freedom. Mary Ann in the kitchen, hearing the sounds of romping in the best bedroom, smiled and sang as she laid the breakfast-table. The master and the mistress had made it up thegither, she thought, and the house would be itself again. It was a cold, rainy morning, but the merry skelp of feet on the floor above her head was as good as a blink of sunshine.

How easy it is to be happy, thought Elizabeth. She even particularized the thought, adding: How easy it is to be happy with Hector. It was as easy as in the first days of their courtship and marriage. She gazed with affection at him as he put on his collar; how lovable was the strength of his neck and shoulders! She was happy with that thrilling, apparently unmotivated happiness which, for so long as she could remember, had from time to time irradiated the world for her. It was a condition that arose spontaneously; it seemed to flow in upon her and through her, and had no perceptible connection with daily routine. It transfigured even ordinary objects and events, as moonlight transfigures a landscape, and with the same large carelessness as moonlight obliterated all sense of difficulty, of the incongruous, the impermissible. It fell upon Elizabeth most frequently when she was gazing into the gulf of the sky, or at the sea; but it had surprised her also in the enclosed haven of a summer field as she lay among flowering grasses, watching a minute insect climb a jointed stalk; and there were rare days, as now, when she woke to find it already in her heart. Her vision of the previous night had evoked it, she knew; and she thought, too, that she knew from which of the two infinities it sprang; it was not born of the head.

Her preoccupations of the past weeks sank into triviality. She had found herself again, and she was as happy as in the first days of her love for Hector, but, she told herself, it was a more informed, a better-grounded happiness. She no longer expected him to fill the whole world; he had his own kingdom; and instead of despising him for what he was not she rejoiced in him for what he was.

It must be admitted that Elizabeth remembered only the two extremes of her vision; she ignored the middle region in which was condensed the shape of Elizabeth Shand – the region, it may be presumed, of daily life, within which fluctuate the conventions that seek to form it. Between poetic passion and intellectual passion there lies a difficult and obscure space, in which many people spend their whole lives. . . .

Elizabeth, however, ignoring this middle region in which she was conventionally a wife in a tradition of wifehood – forgetting, that is to say, the burgh of Calderwick and all it stood for – was radiantly happy on this Sunday morning.

Hector announced that he wasn't going to church. In spirit he had already said good-bye to Calderwick, except for a few private qualifications, and refusing to go to church was a symbolic gesture. He would smoke his pipe and read the Sunday papers; he might even toddle down and pull Hutcheon out of bed.

Elizabeth laughed. 'I wouldn't go to church either if I didn't want to see Elise,' she said.

It was almost a point of honour. 'Shall I see you at church?' she had asked eagerly, and Elise, shrugging her shoulders, had answered:

'Church? Oh well, I never miss my cues.'

It would not be fair not to turn up at church after pledging Elise like that. Whether Hector came with her or not didn't matter. Whatever Hector did on the surface of life was now gloriously unimportant. The universe would have to be rent to its foundations before she and Hector were separated. He might leave Calderwick – he should leave Calderwick – but she would go with him, or follow him after a brief, impermanent interval of time. Measured by eternities their absence from each other whether she went to church or Hector to the South Seas was momentary and insignificant.

Under her own umbrella Elizabeth became a drop in the river of bobbing umbrellas that slowly flowed along the pavement of the High Street towards the churches. Elizabeth felt kindly towards the other umbrellas; they were all gong to worship the same God as herself, even although they had a partial and limited idea of the cosmic force which she acknowledged as the Godhead. She wished that people were not divided off into congregations; how much more sincere and moving would be a service if it were shared in by the whole populace of the burgh assembled in a gradiose and shadowy building! In a small church like St James's one was too conscious of the individual members. Elizabeth yearned for a tribal gathering of vast proportions, the vaster the better.

John was guarding the end of the pew, with Elise next to him. Mabel and Aunt Janet were sitting beyond Elise. After a moment's hesitation Elizabeth slipped in between John and his sister.

Elise sat looking round her with interested eyes. What a queer experience it was to be once more in the poky little church where she had suffered so much in childhood! She could even identify some of the people, grown older, but still sitting in the same pews, still clad in decent black. The same ornate chandeliers. The same flat white clock face. The same hideous yellow pine seats, and awful terra-cotta pillars painted behind the pulpit. The only difference was the presence of a small pipe-organ, each pipe decorated with squiggles of gold and terra-cotta, in front of which sat an organist embroidering a slow march with flourishes of his own devising. Elise remembered the old precentor with his tuning-fork; he was better than this.

She had almost forgotten that there was a beadle, who solemnly bore the big Bible up the pulpit steps and then stood at the foot of them awaiting the arrival of the minister from the vestry. It was not the same beadle; old Mr Webster was probably dead. . . . He had a comfortable, motherly wife who kept hens and always had fluffy chickens to show little Lizzie Shand. . . . Dead too, probably – all dead.

Elise began to feel as if she were in a churchyard. Each pew was a memorial to some dead member of the church; the blanks in the seats she remembered were more numerous than the survivors. The manse pew was quite empty. . . . The last minister she had 'sat under' was an unctuous vulgarian whom she had christened 'Pecksniff', and Mrs Pecksniff and all the little Pecksniffs used to fill that pew. How Pecksniff used to strut down to the pulpit, his black robe billowing behind him! And what a sermon he had preached after attending an elder's death-bed! Elise smiled; she would have enjoyed that sermon better now than in her younger days; she had now a more catholic taste in absurdity.

The minister was coming. The organist surpassed himself in a final flourish. The minister's gown hung lank; it did not billow like Pecksniff's. He held it closely round him with one hand; he stooped slightly as he walked. But quite a young man! Why did he walk like an ancient? A young man, and a hungry face. Poor devil, thought Elise. . . .

The rustling of pages began, and the organist pulled out stops. Elise recollected that she had no Bible, and rummaged in the shelf below the reading-board. All the old Bibles seemed to be still there; she examined first one, then another, and finally with a strange exultation drew out her own, dog's-eared and rusty, the very Bible Aunt Janet had given her on her tenth birthday. She opened it and stood up when the others did, but it was not the text of the psalm she was looking at, it was the straggling scrawls covering every blank space at both ends of the book. Her name, Lizzie Shand, and sometimes Elizabeth Shand, was repeated over and over in every kind of writing, sometimes sloping forward, sometimes backhand, with prim letters or curly letters, never twice the same. On one page was boldly written:

Black is the raven,
Black is the rook,
But blacker the Devil,
Who steals this Book.

And under that was drawn a skull and crossbones.

For a moment or two Elise felt not that the long-vanished Lizzie Shand was a ghost, but that she herself was the ghost of that impetuous and resentful small girl. The small girl's emotions touched her again; she was no longer coolly amused at the paltry ugliness of the church, the narrow complacency of the worshippers, she was both furious and miserable at being forced to take part in the service. Her one positive conception of God that He was a miracle worker, an omnipotent magician, had been shattered on the day when she had prayed Him to turn her into a boy and nothing had happened. The God that remained was merely an enforcer of taboos, and a male creature at that, one who had no sympathy for little girls and did nothing for them.

The psalm was finished, and Elise sat down, having travelled in two minutes from one century to another with a glance at John's beard. Elizabeth Shand, Gott sei Dank, was only an uneasy ghost between the boards of her Bible.

But another Elizabeth Shand had grown up meanwhile. Elise turned her head again, this time to look at the girl beside her. She had a vague idea that this Elizabeth Shand had sung heartily every verse of the psalm.

That was somehow out of character. . . . Elise felt, irrationally enough, that the resentments of her own youth should have passed on to the next generation of girls. Young things who did not know themselves were always at a disadvantage, and young girls faced with the traditional doctrines of the Church were at a special disadvantage. They ought to be resentful. And yet this young Elizabeth Shand had apparently accepted the old tradition; and these small children fidgeting on the next seat would in their turn grow up and fill the same pews, and believe in the same old – Or would they? Could such a hocus-pocus of nonsense prevail over human intelligence for ever?

The young Elizabeth Shand caught her eye and smiled, irrepressibly, it seemed, as if she were bursting with happiness. Elise again felt the curious warmth that streamed from her. The girl had vitality, at any rate; perhaps she was not imposed upon after all. She did not look as if she were.

An odd memory darted into her mind. She had found one Sunday two lines in a book of devotional poems she was set to read and had outraged Aunt Janet and delighted John by quoting them gravely at all times. What were they?

To me, to all, Thy bowels move;
Thy nature and Thy name is Love.

She shook with sudden mirth, and took out her handkerchief to stifle it.

John at the end of the seat tried hard not to smile. Lizzie had one of her old giggling fits; she always had them in church, the besom! How little she had changed! He hunted in his pockets for a peppermint; he always used to slide one into her hand when she giggled. She turned imploring eyes upon him above the handkerchief, but he had to shake his head. Not one, in all his pockets.

Elise bit her lip, struggling to control herself, but Lizzie Shand, although bidden to vanish, was a persistent ghost.

The jet bugles in Aunt Janet's bonnet trembled. Her face was very red. She had peppermints in her pocket, but she would have died rather than pass them to Lizzie. Mabel was surprised to see Elise forgetting her dignity. She felt a little superior and also a little nearer to her sister-in-law, less disposed to be snubbed. Elise had her weak points too. And after all, her past was *not* irreproachable although she had been clever in surmounting it. Mabel sat up straighter. Elizabeth the younger smiled openly. . . . The impish ghost of Lizzie Shand had apparently brushed against all of them, in spite of Frau Doktor Mütze.

The giggling fit left Elise as suddenly as it had seized her, but she too was no longer quite the same woman who had entered the church. Not only in memory but in feeling she had identified herself with the life of Calderwick, and in that brief moment, far beneath her consciousness, something had germinated.

But the unease in the Shand pew seemed to have spread

through the congregation. For a shocked second Mabel thought that all heads were turned in their direction. She was immediately reassured, however; it was the beadle everybody was regarding as he made his way on tiptoe down the passage towards the pulpit. The minister had just finished a prayer and was about to read the chapter from the Old Testament, but the beadle mounted the steps, passed him a piece of paper, and tiptoed creakily back.

A wave of expectation rippled through the church. Somebody ill? Somebody dead? A doctor or a relative urgently asked for? The minister looked upset. He sat down for a minute and buried his face in his hands. The congregation stopped rustling and sat in breathless stillness.

William Murray stood up, holding on to the book-board of the pulpit. He spoke in his ordinary voice, not his pulpit voice, and that struck many of his hearers as sacrilegious:

'There will be no further service. . . . I have had bad news; I must go home at once.'

Without another word he shut the Bible and descended the pulpit steps.

An excited buzz in which there was a note of indignation filled the church even before he had disappeared, and many were so busy whispering that they did not observe the beadle coming round to the Shand pew. But when John Shand got up and went out the buzz swelled in volume.

'What a like thing!' said Mary Watson to the people in the pew behind her. 'Not even a benediction. It's not decent.'

Most of the church members were of the same opinion. Nobody wanted to be the first to rise. The congregation had attuned itself to reverence, and its mood had found no communal discharge.

Two events stood out in the general uncertainty. Young Mrs Hector Shand and that sister of John Shand's, that hizzy – ay, she had had the face to come back – rose together and went out with unseemly haste, as if it were not the House of God they were leaving. Almost at the same moment the organist, with the satisfaction of one to whom a great moment has come, moved to the organ and began to play a doxology reserved for special occasions:

Now to Him who loved us, gave us
Every pledge that love could give. . .

Waveringly at first but finally united the congregation sang it through.

FIVE

'Don't distress yourselves,' was John's parting admonition at the vestry door before he caught up on the minister and the manse servant.

A half-apologetic glance at his sister excused himself for having included her in advice that was really intended for the younger Elizabeth. Elizabeth was, indeed, extraordinarily agitated. Elise had marked the girl's agitation as she started to her feet in church, ejaculating something about Ned, and took to her heels. That was partly why she had followed her; partly too because she was both curious to know what had happened and thankful for a pretext to leave the church. Elizabeth had darted round the corner of the street to the little door giving access to the vestry, and all she had said was: 'I'm sure it's Ned. I know it's Ned.'

'What Ned?' asked Elise, but got no answer, for at that moment the two men and the maid appeared, and Elizabeth, disregarding John, flew at the minister with the accusing question:

'What have you been doing to Ned?'

John's intervention had saved what might have become a painful scene, thought Elise, as she drew her sister-in-law away, for the minister's defiant attitude could have been expressed in the Biblical words, 'Am I my brother's keeper?' and Elizabeth seemed to be primed for an explosion. The girl was full of surprises, thought Elise, with a half-smile, as she remembered her dumb shyness of the previous evening.

The wind had veered a point or two towards the north; the grey clouds were breaking up and blowing over a pale, cold blue sky; only the puddles with their ruffled surfaces told of the morning's rain that had driven in from the North Sea. It was towards the shore of the North Sea that the two women now turned as if by consent, although hardly a word was spoken.

Salt spindrift and an occasional fan of sharp sand stung their faces when they came out on the dunes. The sea was choppy and fretted with white caps; no whalebacked billows heaved from the horizon as on that day when Elizabeth had exulted in their power; the water looked cold and ugly, except towards the north where the broadening space of clear sky spread a greenish light over the bay and outlined the headland above it.

'How clear the light is over there!' cried Elise. 'Look, you can see every tree on the skyline.'

'You can see more than trees,' said Elizabeth, with a curious bitterness. 'There are the chimneys of the asylum William Murray is going to send his brother to.'

'Well, why not? Why are you so angry about it?'

'Because I'm sure he's pushed Ned over the edge. Weeks ago he said Ned was in hell, and since then he's been preaching hell fire and the wrath of God and original sin. What nonsense, what damnable nonsense!'

'In that case the brother will probably be better off in the asylum than in the manse.'

'Oh, Elise!' the girl's voice broke. 'Can't you *imagine* what it must be for a sensitive and nervous boy to find himself in an asylum for the insane? If he was bewildered and frightened before he'll be a hundred times more lost and terrified in the asylum. How is he to know that the world isn't cruel if he's kept under retraint? What can he find to believe if it's suggested to him on every side that whatever he thinks and feels is mad? And could he believe anything madder than that God punishes people by putting them in hell? If Ned Muray is to be shut up in an asylum I think William Murray should be shut up too.'

'If all the people who have delusions were to be shut up in an asylum there wouldn't be many left outside.' Elise was quite cheerful. 'Come and walk on the sand; it's too cold to stand still.'

'But why should Ned be singled out then? He's not really insane; he doesn't imagine that he's Napoleon or Alexander the Great or anything like that; he's only afraid that everybody's against him, that people are mocking him and trying to hurt him.'

'Perhaps they are. I've known people who attracted ill-treatment as a horse attracts flies. It sounds to me as if he were the kind of person who asks for insults. He'll be safer in an asylum. I am much more interested to know why you feel so strongly about him.'

'Wouldn't it upset you to hear that a young man you knew was being sent to an asylum?'

'I shouldn't be *angry* about it.'

'I *am* angry,' confessed Elizabeth. 'It's such a shame. It's such a waste of good material. . . . He was one of the best mathematicians at the University.'

'Even that doesn't move me to anger. I am prepared to be sorry for him, and to be sorry too for that poor devil, the minister, whom you were so ready to scratch.'

Elizabeth was silent for a moment. Then, almost in tears, she said:

'Don't laugh at me. I know I'm a muddled creature. But I am angry – I *was* angry, rather, and I don't know why.'

'I have found,' said Elise slowly, as if she were choosing her words, 'that anger – or resentment, which is the same thing – is a symptom of weakness in oneself, a sense of being at a disadvantage. My weakness is usually a susceptibility to public opinion. I try to cure myself by seeing the absurdity of public opinion when it is judged at the bar of my own reason. But I don't see what public opinion has to do with your anger in this case; for you are resenting an action in which you have apparently no part. That's what interests me.'

It was a long time before Elizabeth spoke again.

'I do have a part,' she said in a low voice. 'It's myself I am angry with; you are right.'

Elise made no comment. But Elizabeth could not leave the matter there.

'I have a bad conscience about Ned,' she burst out. 'He was a queer, solitary creature at the University. You know, in a university the effect of a crowd of students is exhilarating, but frightening too. Everything you do is done against a background of people your own age. Especially in a small university like ours. Even walking down the street isn't simply walking down the street; it's more like walking down a stage. You have to harden yourself against the crowd, or pander to it, and enjoy it. I did both. Never mind that. . . . But Ned Murray never pandered. Apparently he didn't harden either, although he might have armed himself in conceit because of his class record. . . . He simply hid. He slinked. He scuttled round corners. . . . And so they ragged him. He had a chest of drawers and a table piled against his door; he was as frightened as that. . . . And they pulled him out. He screamed until they had to gag him. . . . They shaved half his head and nearly drowned him in a fountain. . . . If people did that to me I think I'd want to kill them. And yet I laughed. I knew about it beforehand and I was amused. I heard about it afterwards, and I said: 'Well done!' And now I know what a dreadful, horrible effect it must have had on a nervous boy like Ned Murray, and . . .'

She was crying.

Elise patted her arm.

'I've *helped* to send him to the asylum,' sobbed Elizabeth.

'If you had made a public martyr of yourself and objected beforehand, would the ragging have been prevented?'

'I don't know. . . . I d-don't think so.'

Would Hector have refrained from being the ring-leader if she had objected? Elizabeth could not tell. But somebody else would have led the attack at some other time. . . .

'If a boy insists on being like gunpowder waiting for a spark the spark is bound to come, sooner or later,' said Elise, 'whether from your hand or another's.'

'But one should help other people and not hinder them.'

'In the long run one can never help other people.'

Elizabeth wiped her tear-sodden face and looked up.

'What?'

'People can help themselves only,' affirmed Elise with decision.

'That's what I used to think, that one was separate, but now I know it's not true, Elise! That doesn't go deep enough. We're only separate like waves rising out of the one sea. Last night I saw it and felt it so clearly, the oneness underneath everything – and I knew that religion and poetry and love were all expressions of that oneness. . . .'

Elizabeth had taken Elise eagerly by the arm, as if she would communicate her vision by contact as well as by speech. She poured out her sentences in a rush of words, forgetting herself in the urgency of her gospel.

'That's the oneness beneath us, out of which we rise, and there's another above us to which we grow, the oneness of intellectual truth. . . . It made me so happy; it cleared up something for me that I've always felt and never understood. And this morning I was at peace with the whole world because of it. And now – I can't go back on it. I can't shake off all responsibility for Ned. And that's partly, too, why I was so angry with William Murray; instead of preaching the real religion that strengthens the sense of oneness he was preaching separateness; he was cutting Ned off; he was turning what should have been a source of strength into a bugbear. . . .'

Exaltée, thought Elise, walking on in silence. There's something wrong here. Yet she sees through her own eyes, at least.

'Have you considered,' she said aloud, 'that this missionary zeal of yours would saddle you with the responsibility for every deranged and unhappy person in Calderwick – not to speak of the whole world?'

'No, Elise, that's absurd. I'm not really absurd. I'm concerned only with people I know, with people I meet, with people on whom I have some personal effect.'

'A limited liability company. . . . Well, I don't feel inclined to be a shareholder. Your universal sea out of which we all rise is too featureless for me. If I have risen out of it, which is possible, I'm not going to relapse into it again. The separate wave-top is precisely what I am anxious to keep.'

She looked up at the strong contour of the headland, brooding now in an almost animal solidity against the lucent green sky. Her thoughts were light and clear again; she felt revivified, as if new strength had been given her, and words came to her of their own accord:

'I maintain myself in the teeth of all indeterminate forces. This wave-top, this precariously held point of separateness, this evanescent phenomenon which is *me*, is what I live to assert. . . . And I should like to know why *you* want to drown yourself?'

For drown yourself you will, if you go on like that, she added mentally.

'It's not drowning,' said Elizabeth earnestly. Her tears had stopped. 'It's diving for something. Yes, that's what it is. Life is such a muddle, Elise – at least for me. I haven't your sureness. And the ordinary conventions haven't any meaning for me; I must dive for my own religion, my own meaning. Some day I shall find it. I think I have found some of it.'

She looked into Elise's face and smiled, the same shy smile of the night before.

'Do you know, in spite of what you say, you have helped me a great deal, Elise? You're the only person I've ever met who understands what I'm driving at, even although you don't agree with it.'

Elise too smiled.

'I understand it to some extent because I went through something like it myself. But that was before I was fourteen. Fourteen is the right age for missionary fever. You ought to have got over it long ago.'

All the way home Elise turned over in her mind the thought that something must be wrong between Elizabeth and Hector. One didn't dive into general love for humanity if one had a firm title to the love of one man. Not in her experience.

They were an ill-assorted couple, no doubt. . . . Elizabeth was intelligent, but innocent, whereas Hector! Probably the first man who ever kissed her, thought Elise, with a half-scornful, half-sorrowful smile. It wasn't her business anyhow.

SIX

Teenie the maid had called in at the doctor's house on her way to the church, so Dr Scrymgeour was the first to arrive at the manse. Sarah was in the dining-room, watching the street from the window. Ned was still playing the piano, but his playing had become more vehement, more bizarre, and every now and then she could hear him rise from the piano and walk about the room. She tapped loudly on the window as the doctor emerged from his car, and when he turned to peer at her she waved her hand and ran to the door. This effectively hindered him from ringing the bell.

Sarah opened the door with as little noise as possible.

'Come in,' she whispered. 'Don't let him hear you.'

'A grand clatter he makes on the piano-keys,' said the doctor, sitting down at the dining-room table and drawing off his gloves. 'Now, what is it, Miss Murray? I got a message that you were frightened for your life. . . .'

Sarah hurriedly related the gist of what had been happening in the house for the last few weeks. . . . She hoped that the minister and John Shand wouldn't come in before her recital was finished, for she couldn't resist getting in a few flings at William.

'If I had Ned to myself I think I could manage him, Dr Scrymgeour, but there's Teenie – she's worse frightened than I am – and there's William, and he just drives Ned from bad to worse with his preachings, and, to tell you the truth, I'm fair worn out with it all. I thought I was at the end of my tether this morning when I sent for you, but the laddie hasn't been so bad since then. If he's handled like a bairn he can be managed; it's when William tries to reason with him that he gets past all bounds.'

'But the minister wasn't in when you sent for me, Miss Murray.'

The doctor looked at her keenly.

'No!' admitted Sarah; 'it was a new ploy of Ned's that frightened me. He was trying to get out into the street in his old shirt and slippers, saying he had to apologize to Hector Shand. . . . But I wiled him away and he began to play the piano, and he's been at it ever since.'

'M-m, yes.' Dr Scrymgeour rubbed his chin. 'I can hear him all right.'

Ned broke off short at that moment, and walked up and down the sitting-room arguing something in a high, excited voice. . . . Then as suddenly as he had left off he plumped down on the piano-keys again.

'Apologize to Hector Shand? What else did he say, did you notice?'

'He was roaring in the night, and this morning too, that he wanted to know the truth.'

'Ay, poor lad . . . poor lad. The truth's a kittle business, even for the best of us, Miss Murray. He doesn't sleep well, does he? More or less excited all the time?'

'He dozes off in the early morning and sleeps till twelve o'clock if he's left. But he never stops speaking to himself or roaring at us all the rest of the time. . . . I don't know how he can keep it up. It wears me out just to hear him.'

'Has he ever mentioned Hector Shand before?'

'Not that I can remember. But they were students together, of course.'

'Has he threatened anybody with violence?'

'N-not exactly. . . . I *was* frightened for a minute yester-day. . . . But he wouldn't lift his hand to folk, not really, Dr Scrymgeour. . . . He was always such a gentle laddie. He never used to say "No" to anything or anybody!' Sarah wiped her eyes. She was herself surprised at the excuses she was putting up for Ned.

'Quite so,' said the doctor. 'Quite so. And now he won't say "yes" to anybody or anything. . . .'

'But it canna last, doctor!'

'It may not last for very long. . . . We'll hope not. . . . But human beings are thrawn, Miss Murray.'

'Is it just pure thrawnness?'

'No, no, that's hardly what I meant. Let's say "persistent" instead. We couldn't go on living if we weren't persistent, you know. . . . And this laddie seems to have a lot of strength.'

'But why, doctor, why should he carry on like this? It's not common sense.'

'Not even the most sensible body is all common sense, Miss Murray. There's not much common sense about some of the things we keep in the wee corners of our minds. Eh?'

He darted his 'Eh?' at her with a kind of giggle, and at that moment the front-door bell rang.

Sarah flushed a dull red and went to open the door. It was John Shand and William, of course; she ought to have been looking out for them instead of listening to the doctor. Ned, of course, had heard the bell. He had stopped playing. Would he come out?

'Whisht!' she said sharply, indicating the dining-room door. 'In here.'

She shut the door behind her, and stood against it to keep Ned out should he try to come in. William looked 'raised', thought Sarah, as if he had been quarrelling with somebody. Her eyes rested on John Shand with a certain satisfaction. John Shand had more sense than any of them.

She repeated again her account of Ned's doings that morning, addressing herself more and more exclusively to John.

When his brother's name cropped up John Shand's face darkened.

'What has Hector been doing? Why should there be any mention of *him*?'

'Probably no reason at all,' said the doctor. The confidential manner in which he had spoken to Sarah had vanished; he was now cold and brief.

'Delusions, you think? But why my brother rather than somebody else?'

'The connection may be of the slightest, Mr Shand. The patient's statements can hardly be accepted as facts, although they may provide clues to his mental state – very tangled clues.'

'You think my brother – is insane?' asked the minister in a strangely dry voice.

'It's a difficult word. A border-line case, perhaps. But I think he should be removed for treatment. The sooner he's away from here the better.'

The minister nodded.

Sarah swallowed something. 'It's my fault,' she said, 'for getting frightened this morning. . . . But I'll not be frightened again. Couldn't you give him some medicine, doctor, and leave him here for a while till we see?'

'It'll take a few days in any case, for I see no need of an emergency certificate. . . . But I think, Miss Murray, you would be well advised just to let him go. . . . He's been getting worse instead of better for all these months he's been at home.'

'Do you think *we* are to blame?' asked the minister in the same dry voice.

'There's no question of blaming anybody,' said the doctor, with a hint of surprise. 'This is a case for investigation and treatment, not for blame. . . . Could I see the patient now, do you think?'

Sarah found that this was the moment she had been dreading.

'I'll come with you,' she said.

William Murray remained standing where he was.

'Perhaps I'd better slip away now,' said John. 'I wouldn't have come, you know, Mr Murray, if your sister hadn't sent for me.'

'It was very good of you to come.'

John Shand, feeling more and more embarrassed, picked up his hat and umbrella.

The minister turned round and arrested him with a question:

'If it was *your* brother, Mr Shand, would you send him to an asylum?'

'I should do what the doctor advised. . . . Certainly — What's that?'

There was a scuffle and a woman's shriek from the hall. Still holding his umbrella John rushed out, and saw Ned Murray pushing the doctor by main force to the front door.

'Out of this house! Out you go!' he was repeating in a clipped, harsh voice, apparently exasperated beyond endurance.

'Oh, John!' called Sarah, clinging to Ned.

John dropped his umbrella, seized Ned and held him pinned by the arms. He was the only man there who was physically a match for Ned, gaunt though the boy was, and he had to exert all his strength to keep him prisoner, for Ned kicked and struggled and spat with vindictive fury. Hard kicks on the shinbone are bad for the temper, and John began to twist Ned's arm behind him.

'You bloody coward!' screamed Ned. 'Where's the police? Open that door and bring the police!'

Sarah was now hanging on to John.

'Oh, dinna do that. Dinna hurt him,' she was sobbing.

'Lock him in the sitting-room,' said John, addressing the minister. 'Take the key from the inside and I'll push him in.'

Ned kicked at the locked door until the wall beside it shuddered and a picture fell on the floor with a crash. The minister stood as if paralysed, then wiped some spittle from his face with his handkerchief. John Shand was dusting his trousers violently.

The doctor drew Sarah into the dining-room.

'It's an emergency case, after all. He'd better go this afternoon.'

Sarah braced herself and stopped trembling:

'He'll never go of his own free will. I dinna want an open scandal, doctor.'

'I'll send down two powders as soon as I get home. Put one of them in his dinner, or in anything he'll eat: the whole of it, mind. That'll settle him. I'll send full directions.'

'Yes.'

Sarah followed him. Once in the hall, where Ned's deafening assault on the sitting-room door made it difficult to hear oneself, she seemed suddenly to lose her temper. She flung the door open, and literally hustled out the doctor and John Shand, slamming the heavy door upon them.

Then, without a word, she unlocked the sitting-room door, pushed it open a little way, and stood back.

Instead of rushing out headlong, as she had expected, Ned drew himself up in the doorway. He was panting and dishevelled; his eyes were enraged; but he was more 'on the spot', Sarah said to herself, than he had been earlier in the morning.

'Cowards. Sneaks. Lowest cunning. Brute ignorance. . . .'

Sarah turned abruptly and marched into the kitchen. She neither knew nor cared what William was to do. She could hear Ned's voice rising in pursuit of her:

'My sister. My *sister* turns them on to me.'

John Shand's hat was still on the dining-room table where he had dropped it. With a vicious baff of the hand she sent it flying to the floor.

In the kitchen she locked the communicating door, sat down on a chair and burst into tears, awkwardly comforted by Teenie.

SEVEN

The manse was extraordinarily quiet. Teenie had washed the dinner-dishes and had gone home, as usual on Sunday; the minister had driven off to the asylum with Dr Scrymgeour and Dr Macintyre, following the ambulance, and Sarah was sitting alone in the house. The winter afternoon was closing down; in another hour it would be quite dark. The small fire in the sitting-room grate between its restraining bricks lipped and leapt up the chimney, and the only other sound was the ticking of the marble clock.

The stillness, although it enfolded Sarah, began to oppress her. She did not now need to stretch her ears listening for Ned. Ned had been carried out to the ambulance like a dead log, and she it was who had doctored his food for him. . . . Where would they all have been without her?

Sarah's lower lip trembled and she began to smooth her black skirt over her knees. Ay, she always had the heavy end of the stick. And in spite of all she had done it was her that Ned blamed and would go on blaming: 'My *sister* turns them on to me.' Not a word to William.

It was her that Ned had abused most hatefully all these months . . . all these months. And what had she ever done to the laddie except try to guide him for his good? She had taken up from her dying mother the burden of looking after him and of standing between him and his father. She had darned and mended and cooked and washed and pinched and scraped for all of them – for her father when he was bedridden and ill-tempered; for her brother William in his manse, and for Ned all the time; even when he was away at his classes she had sent him his clean clothes and a cake and scones every week, every single week.

Thankless work. Ay, thankless work. Sarah's lip trembled still more. Not one of them valued what she had done. Ned least of all. And now, at the end, they had forced her to be a Judas. She it was who had called in the doctor and put the powder in Ned's soup.

But she had called in John Shand too, hoping against hope that he at least would be able to manage Ned. . . . And all he had done was to hurt the laddie. . . . Not one of them knew how to do it except herself, and she was tired out. . . . None of these men could stand from Ned the half of what she had stood, for all their size and strength. . . . If it wasn't for the women the world would be in a gey queer state. And the women got little credit for it.

Ay, well, she would do her part, as she had always done, thanks or no thanks. She would have to economize more than ever now, for how was Ned to be paid for in the asylum? Of course they couldn't let him be a pauper patient. . . . Still, he wouldn't be wasting the gas and coal at home.

This return to the more practical side of life comforted even while it challenged Sarah. Ned, after all, had been a burden, and he need not have been a burden; he could have been earning his own living. A certain sympathy for William began to trickle back into her heart; William had had them all to carry on his back. If it hadn't been for William they wouldn't have had a roof over their heads. William was a half-wandered creature himself, and he couldn't help it if he didn't know what was the best way to handle Ned. He was better than John Shand, whom she had held up to herself as a model man. Her sense of humiliation and failure concentrated itself into a rage against John Shand which deepened until it drew off all the overflow of her emotion.

What right had he to look so embarrassed when he came in, as if he thought she had no business to summon him to what was a family affair? He might have remembered that she wasn't the woman to do things for no reason at all, and that there was perhaps something he could help her in. . . . He hadn't thought of her feelings at all. . . . Besides, he was William's leading elder. . . . That was another reason. . . . She had expected something more from the man than brute force. But when it came to the bit that was apparently the only answer he could make. . . .

She was almost glad that Ned had shown so much violence. That had at least given John Shand something to do. She would never call him in again, never. She and William would shoulder their own burdens in future.

Sarah rose to her feet and poked the fire until it blazed, in defiance of all housewifely principles. Her lip no longer trembled. She would be beholden to nobody.

And for a start she would redd up the house. John Shand's hat and umbrella had already been dispatched to him by Teenic. He needn't bother; it would be a long time before she sent for *him* again. . . .

Sunday or no Sunday, she would clean the scuffed paint on that door. She would not be reminded at every turn of what had happened in the morning. If folk could kick paint on a Sunday, folk could clean paint on a Sunday. She fetched a bottle of paraffin and some rags. . . .

When she had done her best with the door she went up to Ned's room with a set face, cleaned out the grate and put into drawers and cupboards every vestige of her brother's recent presence.

She had barely emptied the ash-pail, downstairs, when the bell rang, and to her surprise Dr Scrymgeour came in with William.

'I thought I would just look in and tell you that it's all right, Miss Murray. Your brother'll be well looked after. . . . Dr Eliot out there is a good man, you can depend on him to do everything that can be done. . . .'

The doctor suddenly smiled his nervous little smile, and said: 'Besides, I want to be sure that you're all right. . . . You've had a trying time, and I think that you'll be none the worse of a tonic, Miss Murray – if you don't mind my saying so.'

'Me?' said Sarah. 'A tonic?'

She was 'black affronted', as she said to William afterwards.

The doctor turned to William:

'Your sister's a gallant woman, but she mustn't be allowed to wear herself out. . . .'

This unexpected commendation had a strange effect on Sarah. She began to cry.

'There, there,' said the doctor. 'What did I tell you? A wee bottle of tonic, Miss Murray. I'll write the prescription now. And see that you don't pour it down the sink when you're feeling prideful. Keep it going until I give you leave to stop it. Where's my pen?'

'Come into my study, doctor. You can write it there.'

The doctor's eye rested for a moment on the minister's face and looked away quickly. The doctor's fingers replaced the fountain pen in the pocket where they had discovered it. The doctor's legs carried him towards the study, unwillingly, but obedient to something within the doctor's skull. However nervous one is, one cannot leave a fellow creature to drown in imaginary waters.

'Tell me,' said William Murray in a shaking voice, 'as a medical man, tell me honestly all you know about my brother's derangement.'

'And what good,' countered the doctor sharply, 'would it do you if I did, Mr Murray?'

'I want to know is there a reason for it?' said the minister. 'A medical reason? Something you can put your finger on? Something that's definite, like a microbe —'

'It's not infectious, man, nor hereditary. You gave us all the medical history of the family yourself; you know well enough it's the first case to occur. And, speaking as a medical man, I wouldn't commit myself until he's been thoroughly examined – maybe not even then.'

'But you think it possible that there may be a physical reason for it?'

'There's bound to be ultimately a physical reason for it, as you put it, but whether we know enough to identify it and set it right, Mr Murray, is beyond me to say. A wee bit chemical change somewhere, a lack of balance in internal secretions, an exhaustion of nervous tissue – it may be something that's been going on for years, and it may not. Some idiosyncrasy in an organ the size of a pinhead may be at the bottom of it, Mr Murray. . . . I–I–I think I know what's bothering you – and this is not speaking professionally – you were too anxious this morning to know if you were to blame in any way, Mr

Murray. There's no single individual now living that could have caused or hindered this breakdown in your brother. You needn't reproach yourself.'

William Murray stared haggardly at his comforter.

'But his fears, Dr Scrymgeour, his suspicions, his – his – lack of faith —'

The doctor checked something that was on his tongue, and then said suddenly: 'That persecution mania nearly always accompanies obscure breakdowns. It's one of the symptoms. Considering the long biological history of man, and the fact that herd animals nearly always reject their sick, it's not surprising if an unhappy human being fears that he's to be rejected by his herd. We haven't outgrown our origins, Mr Murray, and I doubt if we ever will. . . . All communities persecute, and in that light persecution mania is reasonable enough.'

'So Ned's fear is a fear of the evil in the human heart?'

'You can put it like that.'

'But all disease doesn't lead to that fear, Dr Scrymgeour.'

'No, I grant you that. But a certain kind of obscure disease leads to it, as I said: cases that we call mental.'

'But it's not a disease of the *mind*, doctor. Ned's mind is acute enough. . . . He's a brilliant mathematician.'

'Um,' said the doctor. 'Well, call it a disease of the ego then. There's not much room for the ego in mathematics. You can't put into a formula a single half-hour of your own life, whether you call it $t1$, or $t2$, or $t3$, or t anything. And from something Miss Murray said I suspect your brother's ego has been ailing for a long time. She told me he never could say "no" to anything or anybody. That's an abnormal timidity, and looks like a constitutional or acquired defect going back to childhood.'

'But he hadn't this fear then!'

'I'm afraid I can't agree with you, Mr Murray. It may have been gathering all these years till it had to burst out. There's maybe more hope for him now that it's come to a head.'

'But, doctor, there have been lifelong invalids who — Don't you see that one couldn't fear evil in others unless there was evil in oneself?'

'Oh ay,' said the doctor. 'We're all human.'

'These dark places in the soul – these are what I should be able to illuminate – these are *my* concern, doctor, as the obscure diseases in the body are yours, and that's where I may have failed my brother . . . that's where I may help him, if I can. . . . I thought you might tell me. . . .'

'Havers, man!' said the doctor firmly. 'Listen to me. I said, and I say it again, there's no single individual now living could have caused or hindered your brother's breakdown. I'll go further, and say that our imperfect civilization may have been partly responsible for your brother's breakdown. We're all reared on fictions from the breast up, and it's more than one man's job to undo the effect of these fictions, especially if they're working on an ego with some possible deficiency in its make-up. You've done all that you can do for your brother in putting him in charge of experienced medical men. You're more than twenty years too late for anything else.'

'You leave no room for God, Dr Scrymgeour.'

The minister said these words almost in a whisper.

The doctor shrugged his shoulders and took out his pen.

'Here's your sister's prescription, Mr Murray,' he said.

EIGHT

There was one shop in Calderwick that kept its doors open on Sundays. Even without that distinction to emphasize its alienation from a Presbyterian community the shop would have been at once picked out as an exotic by the casual visitor, for it was painted in three colours like a Neopolitan ice, and the outlandish name of Domenico Poggi appeared above its doorway. The majority of the citizens – especially the other shopkeepers – regarded the portly Domenico as a son of Belial and spread tales about him that amply justified their disapproval. Domenico indentured his shop assistants and house-servants from his native land and oppressed the poor creatures, it was said, as if they were slaves, giving them no wages but blows, working them twenty hours out of the twenty-four, and keeping them in an unimaginable state of filth. Mrs Poggi was rarely seen, for she was always big with child, but she was often heard screaming in one of the back rooms above the shop, where Domenico was supposed to thrash her black and blue, and on one occasion, it was said, she had tried to poison him. The children, it was reported, hated their father like the very devil, and now that they were growing up he did not dare to abuse his wife so violently as at first, but everybody knew that the whole Poggi family lived in constant strife. In short, had Domenico sold Bibles he would not have escaped calumny in Calderwick, for he was a foreigner, he had not been settled above twenty years in the town, and he was making money. His business, however, was of a kind that lent itself to denunciation by the godly. He pandered to whatever lust for pleasure survived after a hard day's work in the mill hands of both sexes and the plough-men who came in on bicycles from the country districts. As an alternative to the muddy gutters of the High Street

Poggi's gaudy establishment competed successfully with the public-houses, where no social or other intercourse was encouraged between the sexes. Poggi supplied drinks that made up in colour and variety for their presumably non-alcoholic content, ice-cream in cones and wafers, fried fish and chips, liqueur chocolates, cigarettes, billiards (in a back room), dancing (also in a back room) and pornographic postcards (in a remote corner of a back room). An automatic musical instrument liberated gay, tinny snatches of Italian opera, still further exciting senses already stimulated by Poggi's bright lights, red and yellow paper chains and shining mirrors. His clients were not ungrateful; unlike the more respectable citizens they took the alien to their hearts and referred to him affectionately as 'Podge'.

Poggi's children, black-eyed, black-haired, with finely drawn eyebrows and splendid teeth, spoke with the native accent of Calderwick. Some of them resembled their father, looking like Japanese dolls in childhood and growing into lowering and sullen young ruffians; but two or three 'took after' their mother, who was admittedly a 'bonny creature' when she first arrived in Calderwick as Domenico's girl-bride. The eldest daughter, Emilia, now seventeen, was almost beautiful, with cheek-bones, jaws and chin subdued to a pure oval uncommon in Scotland, and was a favourite even with her father, who trusted her alone of his numerous progeny to take charge of the shop in his absence.

On this Sunday morning, Milly Poggi, perched on a stool behind the cigarette and chocolate counter, was opening her heart to two lady friends. Business was always languid on a Sunday morning, and the shop seemed to be still yawning after its late dissipations of the previous night; the floor had not been swept, nor the small tables wiped; it was obvious that Domenico was not yet out of bed and that his slaves knew it. Milly would hardly have been so candid had her father been within earshot.

'Some blinking old Italian I've never set eyes on,' she concluded. 'I'll see him far enough first. I'll rype the till and run awa' wi' Charlie.'

Becky Duncan, her chum, gazed at her with awed eyes.

'I believe you would,' she said.

But her elder sister, Bell, whom she had brought in to see Milly, laughed scornfully:

'Hear the young things blethering! You've a hantle to learn yet, you twa.'

Milly and Becky, who were jealous of Bell's prestige and experience no less than of her real fur coat, turned upon her fiercely:

'We ken as muckle's you do, and as muckle as we *want* to ken.'

'Wha's this Charlie, then? Has he ony siller?'

Bell fingered her pearl brooch as she asked the question. Milly's reply came hot and quick:

'I'm no' the kind o' lassie that takes siller off a man.'

'The mair fool you, then, to make yourself so cheap.'

'I dinna make myself cheap, Miss Duncan, and I'll thank you to remember that this is my father's shop —'

'Haud your tongue, Bell; you're off your eggs and on to chuckie-stanes,' interposed the young Becky. 'Charlie Macpherson's been at Milly for months to run awa' and marry him.'

Bell tossed her head and shrugged her plump shoulders.

'And if he has siller he'll no marry her, and if he has nae siller the mair fool her.'

She shook off her annoyance at being, as it were, bearded by these young and ignorant creatures, and with maternal solicitude added:

'Dinna say I didna warn you. Once a man gets what he wants he flings you off like an old glove. Even if it's been force-wark. Maybe you dinna ken what force-wark is. I said you'd a hantle to learn.'

Milly, whose ambition it was to become Mrs Charles Macpherson of the fish shop, and to push a baby round Calderwick in a perambulator, like any other respectable married woman, began a swift reply, which was suddenly checked by the shadow of a customer darkening the doorway. Bell nipped her young sister's arm and turned away to look at a showcase, muttering:

'Govey Dick, if it's no' Heck Shand!'

Hector Shand, having sat for an hour and a half on Hutcheon's bed while his host shaved, dressed and discussed under oath of secrecy the possibilities of working one's passage on a cargo-boat to South Africa, or even Australia, was sauntering home with one hand nursing a pipe, and the other in a pocket, when the open doorway of Poggi's reminded him that he was nearly out of tobacco. A certain respect for himself as a potential magnate of Calderwick had kept him hitherto from entering Poggi's shop, but on this morning he had no hesitations.

Milly Poggi, he thought, scanning her as he gave his order, was a damned good-looking kid. He had heard a fellow at the Club lamenting her inaccessibility; apparently her father was always just around the corner with a belt. That wouldn't have frightened *him* off when he was younger. One could do a lot across a counter.

He leaned on one arm and cast a roving glance round the notorious establishment, pleasantly titillated by the sense of being in what was, for Calderwick, a den of vice. The same fellow who had spoken of Milly had shown him one of Poggi's celebrated four-leaved-clover postcards. As he looked at the low-hung doorway leading into the back premises, where he had heard these and other aphrodisiacs were distributed, Hector had a faint recurrence of the thrill that the smelling of the corks from his father's whisky bottles had given him as a child. Milly, picking up the half-crown, warm from his trouser-pocket, that he had thrown on the counter, could not keep her eye from sparkling and her mouth from smiling. She knew that Hector Shand had been packed off to Canada four or five years ago because of Bell Duncan, and if Bell herself made no move towards him she would say: 'There's an old friend of yours here, Mr Shand' – if only for the pleasure of seeing Bell disconcerted. Bell wouldn't have turned her back on him like that if she had been sure of a greeting.

But Bell, having settled her hat by the reflection in the glass showcase, faced round with great composure and said:

'You didna expect to see *me*, did you?' holding out her hand at a fashionably high angle.

Hector took the hand and swept off his hat before he recognized the speaker. But when he did recognize her he shook her hand again. It was a warm, plump hand, a hand that snuggled when one held it.

'I didn't know you, Bell, you're such a toff.'

Although Hector rather self-consciously collected his small change without making further advances, Bell felt reassured and confident after that handshake.

'I've just come down for the week-end to see ma mither.'

'Ay,' said Hector. 'You're fine and braw. Better-looking than ever, Bell. What have you been doing with yourself?'

'Oh, I've been getting on AI. I've been a barmaid in Glasgow. Plenty o' siller in Glasgow.'

Bell tossed her head and pulled her fur coat over her bosom. Hector's eyes followed her movements, but he rattled his change in his trouser-pocket and said nothing.

'I hear you've been getting on AI too,' she went on. 'You're in the mill now, aren't you?'

Hector's dark eyes began to glitter.

'No thanks to *you*, Bell,' he said, moving nearer until he almost touched her.

Bell slowly flushed up to the eyes, but she stood her ground.

'We'll let that flee stick to the wa',' she said. 'You were aye a deevil, and ye're just as muckle o' a deevil as you ever were.'

'So you didn't come to Calderwick just to see me?'

'Hear him!' Bell was growing shrill. 'I came to Calderwick, Heck Shand, to say good-bye to ma mither. . . . I'm sailing for Singapore on Friday.'

Hector Shand stared at her without moving, and his eyes no longer glittered. The unaccustomed flush subsided from Bell's cheek.

'Singapore!' he said at last. 'Have you got a lad out there?'

'I wouldna go the length o' my foot for any lad. My eldest brither's out there, and he's started a bar, and he's sent me my passage money, and more forbye.'

She pulled Becky forward.

'This is my young sister and you can ask her if you dinna believe me.'

Becky giggled with embarrassment. Hector picked up his packet of tobacco.

'Sailing from Glasgow?' he asked.

'Ay, Friday.'

'How long are you in Calderwick?'

'I'm going back to Glasgow the morn's morning.'

'Come here a minute, Bell.'

Hector beckoned her to one of the small tables, where Becky and Milly could not overhear what was said.

Bell tossed her head again, with a side-glance at the two flappers, to see that they were properly impressed, and minced her way across the shop.

'Come out and meet me at the old place to-night,' urged Hector.

Bell looked him in the eye.

'I'm no' so green as I used to be.'

'Nor me either.'

Hector smiled upon her.

'You used to like me well enough,' he added.

'I liked you owre weel, Heck Shand, and fine you kenned it, and you were for flinging me awa' like an auld glove, and that's the truth of it. But you'll no' get the chance to do it again.'

'Bell, as sure's death, you'll not be the worse of it if you come out and meet me to-night.'

'It's owre cauld, and wet forbye; this is no' the middle o' summer.'

'Bring an umbrella, and I'll see that you're not cold.'

He was grinning now.

'It would be a lark, Bell, for you and me to have a walk and a crack together.'

'Ach, away with you!' said Bell, thinking with a kind of rueful scorn that she still appreciated the hint of a dimple he showed when he smiled.

'Meet me at eight o'clock, in the old place. I've something to tell you, and something to ask you. Bye-bye!'

His broad shoulders darkened the doorway again, and he was gone.

'He's just as daft about me as ever he was,' said Bell loftily to the two younger ones.

NINE

The church bells began to ring for the evening service, and John Shand hastily stopped the gramophone. Before he could put into words, however, the inquiring look he gave his wife and his sister they both protested, one from either side of the fireplace.

'No church! Oh, no, John, no, John, no!'

'This is the only evening we're likely to have Elise to ourselves; don't let's waste it on church.'

Mabel thought she had put that in rather neatly, in case Elise *should* suspect that one hadn't invited people because – well because one didn't know that Elise was so presentable.

'A nice quiet family evening,' she went on. 'That will be lovely. Put on another record, John.'

'No, the church bells would spoil it.'

Elise swung her feet down and made room on the sofa. John closed his new cabinet gramophone – the only one in Calderwick – and sat down beside her.

'That was Bach, wasn't it?' said Mabel, laying down her magazine.

'No, Beethoven.'

'I'm sure you told me last week it was Bach.'

Mabel was cross. She didn't like to be caught out by John.

'I wonder if the *Ninth Symphony* has been recorded,' interrupted Elise. 'When I lived in Germany I went to hear it every March. The concert season always finished up with the *Ninth*. I must try to get it for you, John, when I go back.'

'It's not listed in this country, so far I know. I've never heard it.'

'Oh, Elise, you mustn't speak about going back. You've only just come.'

'I feel as if I'd been here for months – you've made me so much at home.'

Did the second half of her sentence save the first half? Elise wondered.

It was true. That Sunday afternoon in the Shand drawing-room had given her the illusion of having been there for an eternity. Generations of dead-and-gone Calderwickians were approvingly ranked behind everything that John or Mabel said and did; the *clichés* might have sounded differently in an age of bustles and side-whiskers, but the sentiments, Elise was sure, had been the same. . . . There was nothing so immortal as respectability. . . . All the pre-Mabels must have found something or somebody every day to be 'not quite nice', although they probably used another adjective, and the pre-Johns must have judged everything by its reliability or some equivalent term.

On the whole, John was better than Mabel. He had a real feeling for music, although he was starved of good music in Calderwick but for his gramophone. And he had affections strong enough to puzzle his principles, strong enough to have kept his sister alive in his heart and imagination long after his conscience had cut her off. A queer kind of immortality, thought Elise, a simulacrum of herself that would go on existing even if she were to die to-morrow – a simulacrum that might become a family legend if John had any children.

She looked up, but contented herself with thinking instead of uttering the question: Why haven't you any children? Mabel had a beautiful body; her children should be shapely. John was strong and healthy; his children should be sound. They were the very people who should have children; they were nothing if they were not links in a chain. . . .

'How would you feel, John, if you had a daughter exactly like me?'

The question delighted John – perhaps the supposition delighted him even more.

'Now, how in the world did you get to that from Beethoven's *Ninth Symphony*?'

'It made me think of immortality.'

That was only half a prevarication, for Elise realized that all day the great chorus,

> Seid umschlungen,
> Millionen,

had been singing itself at the back of her mind, even while her thoughts were running on the linkage of one generation with another, and now she found ideas crowding upon her that must have been hiding behind the music.

After translating the words of the chorus she said: 'It's a grand surge of sound, and because it's a surge of human voices it hits you directly on the solar plexus and drowns your separate self and sweeps you away on a broadening tide of anonymous emotion – and that's one way of extending oneself, by losing one's personality in the flood. Then there's another way of extending oneself – by multiplication, by producing children who produce more children, and so on. But there's a risk in that of transmitting family rather than individual characteristics, so that you, for instance, might have a daughter like me. That was how I came to it, I suppose.'

She knitted her brows and went on thinking aloud:

'But neither of these extentions satisfies the conscious part of me, which wants to extend itself for ever lengthways; to be me and to go on being me. Of course, that's why people believe in personal immortality. . . . And yet I can't believe in it. . . . And yet Beethoven still lives in his music, although he's dead, and millions of people now walking about don't live in anything at all—'

She stopped suddenly, for she perceived that she was on the point of telling Mabel and John that they were as good as dead.

'If I didn't believe in personal immortality,' said John gravely, 'if I didn't believe in another world that this, I'd throw up the sponge.'

That's what's wrong with Lizzie, he was thinking; that's why she's so flighty and unreliable; she's got no hold on anything. His heart grew heavy.

'You don't surely think that people should do exactly as they please?' he asked.

'For myself I think so, but not for other people,' said his

sister, smiling. 'Or rather, I think that people should all *think* what they like, and not take their thoughts ready-made from any source whatever.'

John shook his head.

'You would put an end to all authority and tradition.'

'I should *digest* authority and tradition. I should extract the grain of truth from the husk of symbol and digest it.'

John shook his head again.

'But I put more faith in human nature than you do,' insisted Elise. 'The result would be a better and not a worse standard of conduct. I would neither sacrifice myself to others nor others to myself. That's walking on a razor-edge, or course; a kind of balancing trick that needs courage. But better than walking along a chalk-line like a hen, even although it brings one ultimately to the same goal.'

'I think I'll stick to the chalk-line, Lizzie,' said John.

Elise looked at Mabel, who was again hidden behind her magazine. A pert and fresh-coloured girl's face was on the cover. Mabel wasn't listening. Elise permitted herself a dig at John.

'And then, if you bump into me, you can always point to the chalk-line, can't you, as a proof that you're right and I'm wrong?'

'Especially when I bump into you,' amended John.

Elise half turned towards him and said in a low voice:

'Then why did you invite me to Calderwick?'

John did not look at her, but put his hand over hers and squeezed it. They both kept silent for a few minutes. Elise removed her hand at last.

'All the same, John, I wasn't wrong. You mustn't draw lines for me. I could never have stayed in Calderwick. . . .'

John remained silent, watching the fire.

'I realized that clearly in church this morning,' said Elise. 'You know it's much more difficult for a thinking girl to swallow tradition than for a thinking boy. Tradition supports his dignity and undermines hers. I can remember how insulted I was when I was told that woman was made from a rib of man, and that Eve was the first sinner, and that the pains of childbirth are a punishment to women. . . . It took me a long time to get over that. . . . It's damnable the way a girl's self-confidence is slugged on the head from the beginning.'

John chuckled a little at that.

'You used to bully me from morning till night,' he said. 'A boy needs *some* tradition that will back him up where girls are concerned. I know I used to curl up inside every time I had to pass girls giggling in the street.'

'I didn't bully you, John, did I?'

'You didn't suffer from lack of self-confidence, anyhow,' grinned John.

'But I did suffer, all because of superstitions that are long out-of-date and still perpetuated. I *did*. It came over me this morning in church, I tell you, all-of-a-sudden-like.'

'Was that what you were giggling at?'

Elise told him what she had been giggling at, and John was surprised into such mirth that he forgot his concern for his sister's lack of belief in authority.

'Poor Murray,' he said, when his laughter had subsided. 'It's just as well you didn't go to church to trouble him to-night. He's had trouble enough for one day.'

'Elizabeth poured out her heart to me about it. She's a strange girl, John; I think there's a lot to her.'

Mabel looked over her magazine.

'Elizabeth?' she queried. 'She's one of the stodgiest women I know. I can't think what you see in her.'

'I like her too, I must say,' said John, with vigour. 'And she's far too good for Hector. But wasn't it surprising how she attacked poor Murray at the vestry door? I didn't think she would have flown at him like that, and just *then*—'

'What struck me,' put in Elise, 'was that she spoke to him as a human being, not as if he were a figurehead. . . . I bet you nobody else in his congregation does that.'

'Why, she *is* rather like that. A kind of simplicity – very charming.'

'I don't suppose Elizabeth knows it's a gift,' Elise commented.

'It isn't a gift,' said Mabel. 'It's the complete lack of any social sense.'

Elise leaned back on the sofa and thought deliberately: Elizabeth is the most interesting woman I've met for years.

She had just discoverd it, to her own surprise, as if Elizabeth had gone on growing within her since they last met. And she recognized, too, that the chorus from the *Ninth Symphony* which had been haunting her had been released by Elizabeth's words of the morning: we're only separate like waves rising out of the one sea.

    Seid umschlungen,

    Millionen,

hummed Elise to herself. That chorus, she thought, is the nearest I can get to religious feeling, I suppose. And it isn't anything but mass emotion. . . .

Elizabeth gets more out of *hers* than mass emotion, she went on thinking. To her, it isn't merely an indulgence. She hurls herself into it impetuously. . . . But how alive she is! She goes on living in me and excites me to rhapsodizing about choruses before John and Mabel. . . . She's more alive in me than I am in John.

John would embalm me in his affection, she thought, like a fly in amber, immortally preserved in the heart of his immortal respectability. All he asks is that I should make him laugh occasionally – pipe a merry tune in my little cage.

'Some more music?' said John hopefully, preparing to rise. 'I've a very pretty thing of Mozart's you haven't heard.'

Affection plus disapproval, repeated Elise to herself, is of no bloody good to anybody. She regarded John affectionately, none the less, as he wound up his other canary, the gramophone. But her attitude could not have been represented by William Murray's text: 'Though He slay me, yet will I trust in Him' – a text which the minister at that very moment was elucidating with fervour, even with passion, his eyes fixed on the unresponsive white face of the church clock.

TEN

The events of the morning had agitated Elizabeth, and her talk with Elise had only partially allayed her agitation. But for the rest of the day she had no chance to review her feelings and come to terms with them. Hector was too full of his own plans, too restless, too exhilarated: he scrambled over the surface of her attention like an excited child. In most cases of distress surface distraction has its uses, for it may divert the mind from premature interference with the deeper emotions, and if Hector had not distracted her Elizabeth might have had instinctive recourse to one of those games that involve the movement of cards, or pawns, or fragments of words, and hold the attention without disturbing the feelings, or she might have spent the time reading a novel, an occupation which, it is alleged, supplies the same need.

Hector's exhilaration had appeared at the luncheon-table. He came home full of a new project recommended, he said, by Hutcheon: he should make for Singapore and reconnoitre from there. Hutcheon knew somebody who had made money there out of a café-bar. Hector could look round a bit and put his money into anything that would pay.

Neither Hector nor Elizabeth had much knowledge of Singapore, but their ignorance did not hinder them from crossing and recrossing it on imaginary tracks until a map of their mental meanderings would have looked like a piece of cross-hatching. Conversations which take the place of dominoes or patience can be as intricate as any game, and demand ingenuity rather than knowledge. They were both confident in their ignorance, Hector because he was genuinely reckless, and Elizabeth because she did not expect the universe to go bankrupt and dishonour the promissory note she had drawn on it. Had she known, however, that Hector was proposing to himself a departure to Singapore on the Friday of that week, in four days' time, her confidence might have wavered. To Elizabeth a month or six weeks seemed a long time, just as two hundred pounds seemed a large sum of money, but her courage might have contracted in proportion had the month on which she reckoned been reduced to four days. Perhaps that was why Hector refrained from reducing it. What she didn't know, he thought, wouldn't hurt her.

While running riot hand-in-hand with Hector over the Straits Settlements Elizabeth had glanced now and then at her own plans. She would, of course, find a job in an English school. On the very next day she would consult the advertisements in the English newspapers at the Public Library. Strangely enough, the prospect of teaching in a school for young ladies in an unknown country exhilarated her, and she thought that she understood Hector's exhilaration because she shared in it.

After supper, however, Hector vanished immediately, saying he must discuss the project further with Hutcheon, and Elizabeth was left to herself. Her mood darkened at once, as a landscape darkens when the sun is veiled, and her thoughts flew back to Ned Murray and William.

Ned Murray was in the asylum. Coming home with Elise she had met John Shand, hatless and perturbed, and what he had to tell distressed her now even more than it had distresed her then. Her imagination credited Ned with the despair of a young child torn from his familiar nursery and thrust into a blind cell with no one to hear his cries. A vague feeling of guilt oppressed her, as if she ought to have done something, and could have done something, to prevent it.

Yet, in spite of her self-accusation in the matter of Ned's ragging at the University, her feeling of guilt remained vague and would not attach itself to a definite act of omission. She could not fix on anything that she might have done or said. Why, then, did she feel so guilty? Elise, for instance, had been very cool and sensible about it. . . . But then Elise had not been mixed up in it. . . .

In thus admitting to herself that she was mixed up in it Elizabeth was brought up short. If she were involved at all it could only be through her relationship to the minister. She was assuming, in fact, that she was so intimate with William Murray that her actions might have affected his. . . .

Elizabeth's ears began to burn. She recollected that once or twice during that week when she had walked so often with the minister she had fancied — but no; it was impossible. He liked her and she liked him, that was all. She shrank from imputing to William Muray an inclination to fall in love with her as if it were the imputation of a crime, so strongly was she influenced by the code in which she had been brought up. And she shrank with equal dismay from the suggestion that she might have encouraged him by her unreserve. Elizabeth was far from being an emancipated young woman. She remembered her own horror at Aunt Janet's insinuations. It was vulgar to think such things. It was vile. William Murray wasn't that kind of man. . . . They had got on very well together, that was all, until he began to say such dreadful things about the body being unsanctified. . . .

Elizabeth's hair almost crisped on her head as she realized how well William Murray's sudden denunciation of the body fitted in with the theory she was trying to discard. If he *had* found himself falling in love with her he was bound to experience a revulsion from physical passion. He must have struggled against it. She remembered that cold flash of his eye from the pulpit. . . .

There was shame on every side, however she tried to evade it. If she were mistaken, if he had not fallen in love with her, he might have misinterpreted her kindness to him exactly as she was now misinterpreting his kindness to her. . . . Perhaps some of the malicious gossip had even been retailed to him, and that was why he had looked at her like that. . . .

The blood in Elizabeth's head rushed back to her heart; she felt cold and faintly sick. It is extraordinary how the mere hint of a sexual relationship can distort the image of one's fellow-creatures. But for her gratuitous sense of shame Elizabeth would have perceived, as she had once done, that William Murray's character contained no conventional malice, and that even if he had been told that Mrs Hector was setting her cap at him he would have scouted the suggestion.

Elizabeth's fear that she had been unwomanly may, indeed, have sprung from something in herself she did not suspect. The crimes one imputes to others are usually crimes of which one has secret and often unsuspected knowledge, and it is permissible to infer that Elizabeth was secretly attracted to William Murray. That would partly explain her unaccountable feeling of guilt. It would explain, too, why she suddenly rebutted with fierceness the very idea of flirting with a minister. A man who despised his body! A man who could preach hell fire! With this denunciation her sense of guilt vanished, and was replaced by scorn. In merely entertaining the possibility of such romantic, if not vulgar, nonsense she was letting herself down to the level of Calderwick.

For perhaps five minutes Elizabeth looked steadily at Calderwick, seeing it with the depressing, prosaic bleakness of a winter noon under grey skies. Life was terrible when the transfiguring glow vanished from it. Whatever she did in Calderwick would look ugly in that bleak grey light. . . . Thank God, she was going to leave the town!

Almost as Elise might have done she shrugged her shoulders. Calderwick was to blame, not she. She had done her best. Elise was right; she should not take the fate of the Murrays so much to heart; it was their own concern.

With the thought of Elise an infiltration of colour, of warmth, irradiated the landscape again. It did not occur to Elizabeth that her attachment to Elise could infringe upon her loyalty to Hector, and so in considering Elise her vision was not distorted by shame. One can surmise that for that reason alone Elizabeth would always be more at her ease with women than with men, unless she were to outgrow the half-conscious taboos of her youth.

Her sense of guilt had vanished, at any rate. But she was left with a new problem. Was Elise right, then, in her other contentions? Was it not only undesirable but impossible to love one's fellow-creatures, to identify oneself with them? Was that oneness of which she had dreamed – that oneness of the earth-life, that ecstatic communion with all living things – nothing but a lie? Was she fooling herself? Was Calderwick, in fine, a fair sample of the world?

It was a pertinent question, but she did not put it fairly. To her the choice seemed to lie between a world transfigured by the warm glow of feeling and a bleak grey world in which isolated objects harshly repelled each other. She was young and warm-hearted; there could be no question on which side her choice would fall.

She began to walk up and down as her imagination kindled again. She caught at her love for Hector and concentrated on that as one concentrates rays with a magnifying-glass, until the flame rose up and once more the grandiose images she lived by illuminated her mind. She was linked mystically to her husband by nothing less than a universal force. Their love was like the sea, the mountains, the rushing wind and the evening stars. It was drawn from the source of life itself, and would bear them up through every vicissitude. On a billow so enormous they could both ride out of Calderwick without any risk of not being eventually cast up together on some more fortunate shore. . . .

'The lunatick, the lover and the poet . . .' It is to be feared that it was the light of the moon in its full splendour that was now intoxicating Elizabeth.

ELEVEN

By Monday morning the clear space of sky in the north-east had spread southward far beyond Calderwick, and looked as if it were to maintain itself, promising days of light frost and sunshine, nights of hard frost and brilliant stars. A delicate rime picked out with white crystals every blade of grass in John Shand's garden, and each twig, each branch, each stiff leaf on the evergreen bushes, was similarly outlined by pale, unemphatic but crystalline sunlight.

'I had forgotten that you had light of this quality in Scotland.' Elise turned from the window to the breakfast-table. 'It's hard light, like the light in the South, and it shows up the shape of things.'

Did it reveal the fact that the edges of her thoughts were becoming blurred? She felt curiously soft and impression-able that morning.

'What are you thinking of doing today, Lizzie?'

'I've no idea. What's the programme, Mabel?'

Even while she politely included her sister-in-law Elise, trying to sharpen herself, commented inwardly that Mabel expected and actually liked to be pointedly included in a conversation.

Of course, said Mabel, she had no plans; of course they would do whatever dear Elise preferred.

'I thought that perhaps you would like to come and see over the mill this morning?'

Elise cocked a laughing eye at her brother.

'With all my heart! I know you want to show it off.'

John cleared his throat.

'Mabel thinks the mill a messy place. . . . You won't mind, my dear, if Lizzie leaves you and comes with me?'

Mabel, it appeared, would mind; she had never said the

mill was messy; naturally she would like to accompany Elise. . . . But, of course, if Elise would rather go alone . . .

An hour later, as she sat waiting in the drawing-room for her sister-in-law, Elise permitted herself further sarcastic observations. Women like Mabel were the very devil. This simple visit to the mill was now turned into a kind of social function, a diversion provided for a guest by a thoughtful hostess, and the hostess was busy, no doubt, dressing the part. She doesn't even know she's acting, thought Elise, recalling her own excellent but always conscious performances on the social stage, and recognizing that it was years since she had last done that kind of thing. Like other insincerities social hypocrisy had faded so imperceptibly out of her life with Karl that she had hardly realized its departure. . . .

Her thoughts were softening again. It was a queer world they had lived in together, she and Karl. Elise bent closer to the fire as if in the hope that its glowing heat would scorch her eyeballs dry. For with a sudden rush of tears, as if congealed and frozen feelings had thawed, the flat line-drawings of memory, which she had thought were all that was left to her, took on flesh and blood, and in an instant were corporeally real. She did not *remember* sitting in the same room as Karl, she *was* in the same room as Karl. That moment was real to her as a dream is real to the dreamer: the very richness of its content showed her the emptiness of mere memory, and how much she had lost of which she had barely been aware. . . .

It passed as suddenly as it had come, long before Mabel opened the door. Elise sat alone again, shaken and weeping, in a palpable fog of sentiment, a fog in which every shape was blurred, a fog peopled by ghosts that had inexplicably drunk blood, a fog that she made no effort to dispel, even after she had calmed herself.

Mabel had indeed dressed herself for the part with extreme care; she had even pinned a red chrysanthemum in the collar of her coat; and she looked so youthfully pretty that Elise was touched. After all, she thought, dressing-up and make-believe are a comfort to bairns – especially in a dead-alive hole like this. Her moment of transfiguration had left Calderwick more drab than ever, and she was sorry for those who were doomed to live in it. Yet before they had walked a hundred yards the keen air began to blow away her depression, while at the same time she found herself stepping carefully over the well-earthed joins between the irregular grey-blue slabs of paving-stone, exactly as she had done in her childhood, and was both disturbed and amused by the discovery. She sniffed the salt tang in the air.

'There's always a sea-wind blowing in Calderwick.'

'It takes the curl out of my hair,' complained Mabel. 'I have to be always washing out the stickiness. You'll find that too, if you've forgotten.'

'I have forgotten a great deal. . . . *Br-rr-rr*, that's a seeking wind!'

They were glad to whip round into the shelter of the mill-yard, where some carters were beating their arms across their bodies like flails. Mabel picked her way among the round cobbles, holding her skirt high, without a glance to right or left, but she knew how many men were in the yard, and if she did not peer up at the office windows it was because she divined at least one pair of eyes behind them.

As they paused inside the doorway of the shadowy main building Hector came clattering downstairs in high feather.

'Here we are, ladies! Come up into the office.'

Hector's exhilaration was probably caused by the weather: like the children in the streets he ran faster and shouted louder because of the frost and the sunlight, thought Elise, touched for the second time that morning by the youthfulness of her relations. Yet, as she went round the mill beside John, she observed that there was more in Hector's exhilaration than mere youthful well-being. His quick eye was less guarded, and he was openly, even shamelessly, flirting with Mabel, who grew every minute pinker and more girlish. Following John up a wooden ladder leading into a loft Elise cast a backward look at the other two, and for the life of her could not avoid giving a smile of comradely appreciation as she caught Hector's eye. With excessive pantomime he blew her a silent kiss to which she returned a wave of the hand. It was not until a few minutes later that she remembered with rueful dismay that the couple whose flirtation she had encouraged were John's wife and Elizabeth's husband.

Emboldened, perhaps, by her obvious appreciation Hector and Mabel had removed themselves on tiptoe from the foot of the ladder, and Elise found herself alone in the loft with John. With some idea of covering their escape and also, inconsistently, of comforting John, she launched into warm praise of all that she had seen in the mill.

'You've made it twice what it was in father's time. I can see that, John.'

'The business is as sound as a rock now, although trade's bad in general. I've been offered the chance of capitalizing it on a bigger scale, as a limited company. . . . Of course, if I did that, I should be the chief shareholder: I should keep it in the family, Lizzie.'

His dream was coming true. He had his sister beside him in the citadel of his achievements, and in the fostering warmth of her admiration John blossomed until he opened out into vainglory:

'It's been an uphill fight, Lizzie, I can tell you. For years it was touch and go—'

But at that height John stopped, suddenly conscious of danger. It would never do to draw Lizzie's attention to the difficulties he had had. . . . What on earth was he thinking of? He felt confused by his own carelessness, and would not allow his mind even to formulate the fear that Lizzie would mention her supposed share in the mill.

Elise, however, desiring only to tease him a little now that he was boasting, rushed full upon the subject: 'Capitalizing, did you say? You'll have a fat tummy before you know where you are, and you'll be grinding the faces of the poor as well as corn! I'll have to keep an eye on you. Shall I be entitled to a seat on the Board?'

Human spirits have a mysterious faculty of communicating even unformed thoughts, and perhaps Elise's question was not so fortuitous as it seemed, perhaps she was beginning to read the thought that was arrested by fear in the bottom of John's mind. He could not hustle it away quickly enough, and had such a guilty expression on his face that Elise laughed. 'Oh, John! You look as if you had been caught cheating. Have you been pocketing some of my income all these years?'

The flush of distress deepened on John's brow, but he struggled to smile. Before he could say anything, however, the unconscious process of transmission was completed and Elise had read off the message.

'John!' she said, seizing him by the arm. John tried to meet her eyes frankly. 'You've been paying me money out of your own pocket all this time.'

John succeeded in smiling.

'Well, why not?'

Elise stood looking at him without a word. Then she laid her cheek on his arm and said softly: 'My dear, dear John. My dear, dear John.'

It was, after all, one of the most exquisite moments John had ever experienced.

'Do you mean to tell me,' said Elise after a while, 'that at the same time as you disowned me you began to support me?'

'I didn't see what else I could do, Lizzie.' They were sitting side by side on a couple of sacks. 'I didn't know but what you might be in Queer Street.'

'In Queer Street I should have been many a time if it hadn't been for my quarterly cheque.'

She relapsed into silence, while John patted her hand.

'I *did* wonder a little,' she brought out at last slowly, 'why I should suddenly have an income I had known nothing about, and why it should be paid before I was twenty-one, but Tom Mitchell was so positive about it that it was easier not to wonder. . . . I knew you had just taken over the management, and I thought perhaps my share had been allotted at the same time. . . . Oh, I think I must have shut my eyes wilfully! . . . There can't have been any money to spare at that time, John?'

John refused to speak. Elise leant over and kissed him.

'Don't say anything to Mabel,' he said presently. 'She doesn't – nobody knows except Tom Mitchell.'

'I wouldn't have believed you could be so close about anything! Your face gives you away completely, John, when you have a secret.'

'Only to you, Lizzie. There's nobody else knows me so well as you do.'

'I verily believe that's true. Isn't it queer?'

'It's only natural.'

But Elise did not reciprocate by telling him that nobody knew her so well as he did. She looked absent, as if she were still digesting what she had learned.

'I won't offer to pay you back, John,' she said suddenly. 'There's no need of that between you and me. But I won't take any more, indeed I won't. I've got more than enough money. Karl's people are rich, and I have a very adequate allowance from them, besides the royalties on his books. And there's something else; something you won't approve of, I'm afraid. Two years ago I made a grand haul at Monte Carlo – and I still have most of it.'

'Gambling?'

'Gambling on the wicked green tables, John. I had phenomenal luck. I think it was fifteen hundred I made.'

John gasped.

'I never knew anybody like you, Lizzie. Never.'

They both laughed, Elise first and then John, louder and louder, and as they laughed the tension of the last half-hour slackened off, the bitterness of John's twenty years' regret vanished, and Elise felt in her heart a native warmth that had been for months unfamiliar to it.

Their laughter became almost hysterical. In the middle of it a hallo came up the ladder and Hector's head appeared:

'Aren't you ever coming down, you two stick-in-the-muds?'

He gaped when he saw them, and shouted to Mabel at the foot of the ladder: 'Gone dotty up here, both of them.' But as he looked at Elise he said to himself: 'She's a sport. I've a good mind to tip her the wink about everything.'

Hector had divined a new mother-confessor in his new sister.

TWELVE

At about five o'clock on the same day Elise, attending to Mabel's guests at tea, watched them as if the drawing-room were a tank of air in which samples of humanity had been enclosed for her inspection to help her in solving the riddle of existence. For if Karl's death had impaired the visible structure of her life John's few words in the upper loft of the mill that morning had brought it about her ears. On the platform at Marseilles she had rejected as irrelevant the question: To what end does one live? – contenting herself with what appeared the irreducible minimum: the fact that one lived and would go on living; but that apparently irreducible minimum, that stark assertion of herself, had enclosed an element of pride, the pride of the independent creator who looked at her own work and found it good. During the afternoon before the tea-party guests arrived that pride had been squeezed out of Elise to the last drop. The house of which she was so proud had been built only in the hollow of John's hand. It was as much by the grace of John as by its own qualities that it had maintained its equilibrium. Elise felt as if she stood now on the bare ground of existence, uncertain whether she could claim anything as her own achievement.

To what end, then, to what end? Was the question perhaps less irrelevant than she had decided?

Any valid answer to the question, What is the end of human life? must be true for everybody, Elise reflected. The lowest common measure of any assortment of people might provide an answer – the lowest common measure, for instance, of Mrs Mackenzie, Mrs Gove, Mrs Melville and Miss Pettigrew. . . .

As if her fate depended on the result of her observations she watched the ladies in Mabel's drawing-room. Like herself these women were economic parasites, absolved from struggling for the means of life and presumably free to follow its ends. What did they live for?

Elise smiled, for at the moment the chief end of life for these ladies seemed to consist in being 'upsides with each other', and in effacing the impression made by Mrs Smith who had been boasting of her success in breeding Cairn terriers. Against the Cairn terriers Mrs Mackenzie set her son, who was to be a civil engineer; Mrs Gove extolled her own dog, a Shetland collie, who was as intelligent as a child; Mrs Melville described two Chinese jars she had recently inherited, and Miss Pettigrew mentioned the part she was to play in a forthcoming production of *The Mikado*.

Elise listened and watched. No; she had not misjudged them. Not one of the topics – neither the education of sons nor the nature of animals nor Chinese art nor light opera – was taken up; there was no exchange of information; any objective interest that the ladies might have in these subjects was not allowed to appear. They were absorbed in upholding their status as successful people, with power over children, dogs, objects of art and rival competitors. Personalities spreading like trees, thought Elise, measuring their importance by the size of the shadow they cast. . . .

And why not? It was the nature of life to push and grow, to rise out of the jungle undergrowth, to overshadow rivals. Even knowledge served that end at times, or else one would not speak of 'mastering' it. . . . Mrs Melville, in spite of her reticence, might conceivably know something about '*famille verte*' and '*famille rose*' – and what did it matter whether she did or not, if the end of Chinese civilization was to provide her with a pair of fine jars for her mantelpiece?

To put it that way was of course absurd. Teleology led to queer conclusions. Had canine and human life evolved merely to enable Mrs Smith to breed Cairn terriers?

Elise shelved the intruding reflection that canine life – perhaps all life – was extraordinarily accommodating in allowing itself to be bred to a pattern.

To what end, she repeated – looking round the drawing-room – to what end the pains and persistence of countless anonymous generations, the faith, the philosophy, the sci-

ence of countless civilizations? To produce in this year of
grace in a room in Calderwick Mrs Melville, Miss Pettigrew
and myself?

The absurdity of the answer made it at least probable that
the question itself was absurd. . . .

No, she said aloud, replying to Mrs Mackenzie, she was
never sea-sick when crossing the Channel. No, it was not
because of any specific nostrum.

'My boy went over to Paris this last summer, and he was
terribly sick in the boat. He wasn't even able to take any
refreshment when he reached his destination. . . .'

Motherhood? queried Elise. The physical capacity for
motherhood was a common measure, perhaps the lowest
common measure, of all present. But like the urge for power
it was an attribute, not an explanation, of individual life.
From the racial standpoint, of course, it could be argued that
the individual existed to continue the race, that Mrs Mackenzie lived to produce her son: and from the standpoint of
Mrs Mackenzie's son that was doubtless an all-sufficient
reason. Any individual must feel that in producing *him* his
parents had amply justified their existence. . . . Teleology
was plausible when one looked backwards . . .

That's it, said Elise to herself. I believe I've hit it. Teleology works backwards but not forwards. . . . To look forward from the Chinese artist making his jars and to see at the
end of the vista Mrs Melville's mantelpiece is preposterous,
but to begin with the mantelpiece and trace events back to
the production of the jars is exciting.

'Do let us have some of your amusing stories,' interrupted
Mrs Melville. 'Mrs Shand tells me you have met so *many*
interesting people.'

Mabel and the other ladies looked expectant. Elise isn't in
form at all, Mabel was thinking; what on earth is the matter
with her? Is she going to let me down?

As she spoke, Mrs Melville exhibited her social smile –
that is to say, she narrowed her eyes, thrust out her chin,
bent her head sideways towards her left shoulder and
uncovered all her front teeth. Elise, pursuing problems in
teleology, passed no judgment upon Mrs Melville's smile,
yet an irrelevant breeze of fury rippled through her,

breaking up the dead calm in which she had been tranced. As if she were hanging on to a sail that threatened to belly out and carry her through the walls of the room Elise tightened her fists and knitted her brows, then rose quickly to her feet, saying: 'I have a headache. I'm afraid I must be excused.' For a second she regarded the company with an unseeing look, then she made a queer little foreign bow and walked to the door. Mabel tried to detain her with offers of aspirin, but Elise said briefly 'I have everything I want' and ran upstairs.

Once she had shut and locked the door the breeze of fury became a hurricane and Elise let it blow through her. In the body she was pacing only up and down the room, but in the spirit she was rushing furiously through space – or was it time?

'Anything is better,' she found herself crying, 'than that soft strangling.'

What soft strangling? Where did that phrase come from, and to what did it refer? 'I'm damned if I know!' she said, coming to a stop in the middle of the floor. Was it the fingers of teleology that had been loosened from her throat, or the fingers of Calderwick? 'I'm damned if I know!' she reiterated, and in that moment of consciousness she caught sight of herself in the long mirror.

One cannot look at oneself and remain angry; contrariwise, if one insists on remaining angry one cannot go on looking at oneself. Elise stared; the mirror was like a fog enclosing a ghostly image; gradually the image grew clearer, took shape, and Elise, breaking into a smile, said: 'Hello, Lizzie Shand! Where have *you* been all these years?'

The impetuous, resentful small girl who had hovered in the church and stepped with Elise over the paving stones of Calderwick had come back, and with her had come a passionate sense of individuality that required no teleological argument to sustain it. On the Marseilles platform it had been Karl's widow who tried to adjust herself, in the mill-loft it was John's sister, but the woman who now looked at herself knew that she was more than widow or sister or daughter. She had already caught up on the last week; she had perhaps caught up on the last twenty years as well. The

time-lag that had troubled Elizabeth Mütze was beginning
to shorten.

She was not to be explained away. She would have been
herself even if she had had to sing in the streets for a living.
The assurance that in essentials she had neither been planned by fate nor deflected by circumstance invigorated her.

Forty years, she thought, nearly forty years it's taken me
to find that out. A long and obstinate adolescence. . . . She
had been running away from things all her life. She had run
away from Calderwick – from Fritz – from Fritz's anarchist
friends in Brussels – from one city to another, from one
clique to another, from one job to another. I was never more
than a year in any town, she thought, until Karl cornered
me. And how she had run away from Karl!

During all these years she had struggled to keep herself
untouched by sentiment, fastidiously shaking herself free of
entanglements, pruning her own emotions and ruthlessly
lopping with the knife of reason every tendril that sought to
fasten upon her. That was the reason why her marriage was
put off and put off; she had feared for what she called her
independence; and now she realized, with a scorn of her
fears, that if Karl had not been dying she might never have
married him. . . . For years she had been strangling herself.

Her scorn, her aversion from her past cowardice, moved
her again to anger; again she paced the room; but there was a
queer gladness beneath the anger, and finally she said:
'Well! Now I've run away from a tea-party, and most
extraordinarily have cornered myself.'

When she went downstairs the guests had gone and Mabel
was petulant. Elise smoothed her sister-in-law's ruffled feathers and entertained the dinner-table with zest. Before the
fish came in she had already plunged into reminiscence: 'I
once knew a Professor of Demonology in Brussels—'

John laughed and was happy: his misgivings about Lizzie
had vanished, like smoke, in the fire of their mutual
affection.

But next day Elise surprised both John and Mabel by a
desire to spend the morning alone.

'I want just to potter today,' she said. 'I want to wander all
over Calderwick, down the High Street, round the harbour,

and into every hole and corner where I used to play.' Lizzie
Shand, who had never picked up stitches in her life, was
going to do nothing but pick up dropped stitches for three
mortal hours. . . . She almost ran down the front steps.

THIRTEEN

The bright frost still held, and Calderwick was beginning to look parched as if in a summer drought; in the dried-up roads the ruts were sharp and iron-hard; the depressions where once puddles of water had stood were now covered by thin brittle shells of white-bubbled ice beneath which no trace of water remained. Young Mrs Hector Shand's inner world, although still bright, was also beginning to look parched. For, now that she was prepared to be supremely happy beside Hector, it was becoming increasingly difficult to find herself beside him at all. On Monday evening, after office hours, he had vanished soundlessly from the house, and did not return until midnight. On Tuesday morning he dressed himself in his sports tweeds, announced that he was going with some fellows to have a pop at a rabbit or two and wouldn't be back till after dark, and, to use his own terms, *did a bunk* immediately breakfast was over. Elizabeth, with a cheerful air, set about buying small Christmas presents, but she was perhaps unduly ruffled by a remark of Mary Watson's. 'An' hoo's your man?' said that stern woman, looking incongruous behind an array of Christmas 'fancy goods'. 'He's like a' the men, I warrant; he needs a guid eye kept on him.' Elizabeth thought she heard somebody giggle in the crowded shop and went out with a hot face. To restore her equanimity she walked down to the seashore, and after aimlessly wandering over the crust of frozen sand began little by little to quicken her steps as her imagination caught fire again. It was so much easier to make contact with the present Hector of her imagination than with the elusive Hector of actuality.

When he came back, however, bringing with him a faint chill from outdoors, a suggestion of withered bracken and beech-leaves, Elizabeth rubbed her soft cheek against the stubble of his jaw, pushing upwards so that she felt the prickles, and pressing hard so that they hurt. She sat on his knee, contentedly sniffing the scent of peat and tobacco on his old jacket. His strong body, glowing after exercise, fascinated her; she punched and tickled him and finally kissed him on the neck inside his collar. But after five minutes Hector put her off his knee, lit his pipe, and began to fidget up and down the room. He declined to be entertained by a sing-song at the piano, and when Elizabeth proposed the cinema he said, although kindly: 'Don't feel like anything tonight, girlie.' Then, knocking out his pipe, he added: 'Think I'll take a turn down to the Club.'

It is arguable that the excessive omission of the first personal pronoun in conversation betrays an excessive consciousness of its importance. Elizabeth stifled a dawning resentment that might have brought her to this conclusion, and with a slight effort maintained her cheerfulness. But as she sat by the fireside she felt that the whole day had somehow been wasted. . . . She had not even seen Elise.

That night she was still more demonstrative towards Hector, and Hector, marvelling, commented privately that all women were hot stuff once they knew the ropes. She whispered in the dark that his hair was like grass, his shoulders, she said, running her hands over them, were mountain ridges; she clung to him until they were both stilled in sleep, folded in perfect conjugal amity. The invisible current flowed apparently unbroken around them.

Yet next day Hector proved as elusive as ever.

'No, I'm not going to the office,' he said, as he dressed. 'Told you I wasn't going back.'

'What'll John say?'

'He'll give me the sack, I hope and believe.'

He looked neither defiant nor apprehensive, and Elizabeth had to return his smile.

'Well, must you be sacked just before Christmas?'

'I can't stand being preached at, that's all, and I'm not going to give John the chance of preaching; he can sack me instead. Oh, I know *you* think he'll give me his blessing if I go on my knees to him—'

'I do believe if you went frankly to him he'd help you out—'

'Yes, with his foot.'

Hector's cheerful recklessness made his wife laugh.

'Let John give me the sack: that makes it all the easier for me to clear out.'

'But,' said Elizabeth, and stopped in perplexity. It *would* make things easier for Hector. But would it not make things more difficult for her?

Hector did not give her time to think it out. 'Ba-ba-ba-ba!' he said, whirling her round. 'You leave your Uncle Hector's cards where he likes to keep them – up his sleeve. Besides, who wants to go to an office on a fine day like this? I'm going to take all I can while I have the chance.'

'Chance is a fine thing,' quoted Elizabeth from Mary Ann's stock of sentiments. Yet she was uneasy. This new stroke of Hector's would cut the knot effectively; it was a bold stroke, a reckless stroke, and she could not but admire the recklessness of a man who deliberately and in cold blood gets himself sacked. Yet she was uneasy, as if she surmised that in cutting the knot of diplomacy Hector was severing himself from all other ties, including his tie to her.

After breakfast she ran into the kitchen to ask a trifling question or two, but Mary Ann prolonged the interview for nearly half-an-hour. Smiling, Elizabeth strolled back to smoke a cigarette with Hector and found that he had disappeared. He was neither upstairs nor downstairs.

Her uneasiness increased to apprehension, and she was disturbed by the sick, crawly feeling usually termed a sinking of the heart. But the doubts and fears stirring within her were like subaqueous creatures that could not push their heads through a mat of surface vegetation, so compact and impenetrable was the texture of her belief in the love between herself and Hector. She now stood by the window weaving new strands into that belief, designed to make it even more impervious, and the crawling fears gradually subsided.

Meanwhile Hector, with a pair of skates under his arm, was entering the garage off the High Street where Mabel's new two-seater was kept. He did not want to have Elizabeth hanging round. She was being damned decent to him, but he wanted to keep out of her way – just as he wanted to avoid Aunt Janet. Isn't it like women, he thought, to begin hanging round your neck as soon as you try to shake them off? All that he desired, for the two days he was to remain in Calderwick, was the sense of utter relaxation, of letting go, that was his conception of freedom; and, whether they knew it or not, both Elizabeth and Aunt Janet were always screwing him up to something. Women couldn't help it, he supposed. Mabel, in her own way, was just as bad, thinking she had an 'influence' over him. Unlike Elizabeth and Aunt Janet, however, Mabel need not be taken seriously. . . . She was just a skirt, and he rather enjoyed playing her up. Not a bad little skirt, either, if it wasn't for her ideas of being a somebody in Calderwick. He wanted to borrow her car, anyhow, and he wouldn't mind borrowing her company as well. If he turned up all ready at her front door she wouldn't be able to resist the prospect of skating on the Dish at Invercalder. Frosts in Calderwick never lasted for long, and if they didn't take this chance, he would tell her, they might never get another. She wouldn't know how true that was.

So on that Wednesday morning, about half-an-hour after John's punctual departure to the mill, a loud honking from the kerb drew Mabel and Elise to the window, where they perceived Hector clambering out of a car. He flourished a pair of skates and grinned. Mabel almost collided in the hall with her maid, to the maid's surprise, for Mrs John Shand did not usually answer the door herself.

Hector coaxed and argued, waving the skates; Mabel demurred and hesitated, with appeals to Elise; Elise smiled and shrugged her shoulders.

'And why aren't you at the mill? John was furious with you last night.'

'He'll be twice as mad tonight, then, for I'm going to skate on the Dish whether you come or not.'

'Do you like skating, Mabel?' Elise was driven at length to ask, amused by Mabel's determination to make her a party to the affair.

'I simply love it.'

'Well, then,' and Elise shrugged her shoulders again.

For the next few minutes Mabel pressed Elise for an assurance that she did not object to being left alone, and that she would not think it rude if Mabel deserted her. Elise stood the fire calmly, and in a few minutes more the last shot was discharged. Mabel went upstairs to dress.

'I think I'll go up to the High Street and ask Elizabeth to come for a walk,' said Elise, not without mischief, for she wondered how Hector would take her reference to his wife. 'Is she busy?'

But she was surprised by his enthusiastic assent. The very thing, he said; it would do Elizabeth good. Besides, there was something they wanted to consult Elise about. He meant to say, he himself was in a bit of a hole and would love to talk it over with Elise. The fact was, they were both thinking of clearing out. Leaving Calderwick. At least he was, and Elizabeth thought she was too. But he would spit it all out to Elise if she would meet him next day, say at the Pagoda Tearooms at eleven in the morning? There was a quiet corner there and over coffee he would tell her everything.

What woman could deny herself the pleasure of being told everything by a young man? The Elise who had first come to Calderwick might have done so, but not Elise in her present mood. Moreover she had not yet enjoyed the honour of being Hector's confessor: if it had been the third or fourth time of asking she might not have been so complaisant.

'Not a word to Mabel – or to John.' Hector put his finger to his lips, as Mabel's heels came click-clacking merrily down the stairs.

'Shall I mention it to Elizabeth?'

'Of course,' returned Hector. Her second probe, it seemed, had also failed to make him wince. Apparently the utmost confidence existed between Hector and Elizabeth. Or else he's quite indifferent to her, thought Elise, watching the two-seater drive away.

FOURTEEN

I

Elise's present mood, the mood that made her amenable to Hector's advances, was unprecedented in her experience. She had no resentment left. . . . It began on the morning when she pottered alone about the streets of Calderwick, giving herself up to caprice; loitering in odd little back lanes; staring into the small windows of shops that sold home-made brown candy, halfpenny boxes of sherbet and lucky-bags; peering between the planks of the jetty at the restless green water lifting and dropping the fans of seaweed that grew on every wooden prop; and even standing for a while in the shelter of a ruined sea-wall with a vacant eye on some shawled and scarfed children who were playing there with flat, wave-worn bits of glass and red brick. These clean little streets, that looked shallow because the houses on either side were so low, recovered something of what they had once held for her in the days when there were chickens or rabbits, it seemed, in every back-yard and slices of bread-and-jam at every back door. She was no longer detached from Calderwick and no longer contemptuous of it. She sat down for a few minutes on an ancient wooden seat that fronted a leprous blank wall, and remembered that the ugly wall provided an excellent surface for the rebounding of soft rubber balls, and that neither she nor her schoolfellows had ever seen that it was ugly. Children never co-ordinate what they see, she thought: every bit of a landscape or a town or a house front is as important to them as every other bit. . . .

That night she dreamed that she was sitting on a bank of shingle before a stretch of sand; far out the sea crawled sluggishly among sandbanks and children were trotting with mothers and nurses to be dipped in the shallow pools. A long, distant, menacing roar reverberated from the horizon, and Elise had time only to remember that heavy rollers were reported on the Atlantic – without surprise she realized that it was the Atlantic she was fronting – before an enormous, endless billow came blotting out the sky and broke over her head. With a start she awoke, confusedly thinking of the helpless children, still hearing the roar of a second billow mounting behind the first, and with fear leaping in her bosom. As she awoke to fuller consciousness the fear ebbed away, leaving her in a queerly lucid and calm impregnability. She did not open her eyes; she was aware of herself as one is aware of a steady light in darkness; she was an unassailable point within the compass of her body, the centre, as it were, of a dimly perceived circle. This central point, she felt, was beyond the reach of accident and passion; it could not be touched through injury to the body around it. Unmoved, assured, it could look fearlessly at anything.

In the morning the calm acceptance, the tranquillity, of that inmost self still remained with her. There was no resentment left.

Her new attitude combined incompatibilities, as if the lion and the lamb had lain down together. She saw Mabel's faults, for instance, none the less clearly, but she was tolerant of them; she could still make sarcastic private comments at Hector's expense, but she could not take sides against him; she did not like her family any better, but she felt no desire to fend off any of them, not even Aunt Janet. That was the most surprising consequence; she saw that Aunt Janet was a weak-minded, prejudiced old woman, and yet she did not resent Aunt Janet. The centre of one's being, apparently, was both tranquil and inclusive. It was only on the circumference that people stood shoulder to shoulder and rubbed each other up the wrong way. Those who lived in the centre of themselves could treat neighbours with all the courtesy traditionally accorded by one ruling sovereign to another.

But surely I shall begin to resent things again sooner or later, she thought, as she walked briskly towards the High Street after seeing Mabel and Hector disappear. Was it possible to go on living in the centre of oneself? Nobody could tell, she decided; for that clear-eyed, tranquil *something* in the core of personality might be a comparatively recent human development, unpredictable and unforeseen. What *it* would do if Mabel or John or Hector or Elizabeth asked for partisan sympathy she did not know, but she surmised that *it* would not be partisan. To that new self all triangles must be equilateral triangles. . . .

Elizabeth, although crammed with unasked questions seeking an answer, was shy and silent as they climbed the ridge to the south of the town on top of which lay a moor that blazed red in August and purple in September but was now merely bare scrub on black peat, pitted with pot-holes of water, black, too, with ice.

'Look at that crow.' Elise pointed to a large bird sitting solitary in a tree. 'How monstrously disproportionate he seems! All birds look much bigger when the trees are bare.'

'I never noticed that before,' said Elizabeth.

'No?'

Elise did not turn her head but went on gazing at the prospect before them. They were on the edge of the moor, facing north, on the rim of an enormous pie-dish of which one end was broken clean off where it met the sea. In the hollow beneath them lay Calderwick, with its spires and chimneys pricking up through a faint haze of smoke, and behind it the plough-land, cut into rectangles, tilted upwards towards the rim of hills. The masts of fishing-smacks could be seen lying along the jetty; the little river flowed invisibly along the foot of the ridge on which they were standing. It was a spacious and peaceful landscape, filled with light.

Elise, as she looked at it, was divesting it of civilization, restoring its forests, its swamps, its naked moors and sandhills. Unpredictable and unforeseen, she was saying to herself, thinking alike of the new self she had discovered and of the new character that humanity had impressed on the landscape before her during the past two thousand – four thousand – she did not know how many – years.

Elizabeth stood silent, gradually surrendering to the impersonal peace and beauty of the scene. To her, however, it was not impersonal, for she was peculiarly susceptible to the pathetic fallacy, and the quietness of earth and sky, their unassertive air of being there for all time, reassured and confirmed her faith in the permanence of human love and aspiration.

But neither speculation nor reverie could long outface the wind that blew upon them as cold and pure as if it came straight from the Pole. They stepped down from their hummock of peat and struck across the moor. Elise paused beside a bog-hole and said: 'How black that ice is!' Then, hacking on it with her heel: 'And how thick!' These idle words unbarred some limbo in her mind to which she had regulated everything unconnected with her recent speculations – or, indeed, they may have been scouts sent out by the temporarily forgotten prisoners.

'How stupid of me to forget!' she cried. 'I met Hector before I came up for you and he told me that you were both thinking of leaving Calderwick. . . .'

At a bound Elizabeth's shyness turned itself inside out and was revealed as loquacious confidence. The more she told Elise the more she found to tell. In the most innocent-looking streams of memory she discovered unexpected opinions, hard little judgments, as hard and clear as crystal, and she exhibited their facets with increasing enthusiasm. 'People become what they are expected to be, and Calderwick *expects* Hector to go to the bad.' That was one of them. 'In Calderwick I feel like a threshing-machine that gets only a little chaff to thresh.' That was another.

Elise, listening, discovered that Elizabeth's ideal of living was a perpetual intoxication by what she called the 'earth-life', that power which she had fantasied as coming out of the earth and spreading to the stars. According to Elizabeth this power, whatever its source, inspired all poetry, all love, all religion, and was markedly absent from Calderwick, or, at least, unacknowledged there. Elizabeth spoke as if it were the water of life, in the absence of which Calderwick was a desert of sand fit only for ostrich-like inhabitants to thrust their heads into. She conjured Elise to tell her that elsewhere the world was not like Calderwick, so arid, so desiccated into conventions, so removed from all that was spontaneous and natural.

When she was moved Elizabeth could be eloquent, and

her eloquence delighted Elise. It did more; it challenged Elise, as if she saw a vast force of water running to waste for lack of a channel. Her newly discovered, central self all at once found something to do besides contemplating its own impartial tranquility.

'Unpredictable and unforeseen' Elise had called it, and it now justified these epithets by exhibiting a desire to educate the young, or, at least, to inform the young that one need not be completely submerged even by billows rising from the sea.

Her opportunity came when Elizabeth, carried away by her own words, translated the 'earth-life' into cosmic terms, confounding God and Nature in one terrific rush through the universe.

Elise interrupted her by remarking that Nature was sufficiently condemned if it were true that one touch of it made the whole world kin. In any case, Nature was an anachronism in the present stage of human development, which had gone far beyond anything either planned or foreseen by Nature. Nature envisaged nothing but birth, survival and reproduction, and was no guide to mankind beyond these simple limits.

While we must struggle to live, said Elise, we have no uncertainty about what to do. But when we have once secured the means of living, when we have established ourselves and grown strong – when we have done, that is to say, what Nature expects us to do – then we are plunged into horrid uncertainty, then we have to grope, tentatively; we grope into absurd blind alleys, sometimes; we take up hobbies: we collect stamps, for instance, or breed Cairn terriers; but too often, having no further obstacles to overcome, we merely fabricate new obstacles to keep ourselves busy, because an immediate obstacle makes life look easy. . . .

Mankind, said Elise, groping like this in the dark, helped only by the infernal adaptability of Nature, had created the arts and the sciences out of a void. The adaptability of Nature was itself an argument against following Nature; Nature was fool enough to follow anything. One should ask only: Is this intelligent? and never: Is this natural? People who urged intelligent men and woman to go 'back to Nature' were merely imbecile, in Elise's opinion. It was no use trying to drive either oneself or Calderwick back to Nature; if one wanted to drive anywhere it should be towards a more enlightened understanding. . . .

In short, civilized mankind was what it was, good or bad, mainly through its own efforts, and might develop in the most unexpected directions if it were encouraged to trust its intelligence and to outwit Nature wherever it could.

Elizabeth, startled, provoked and stimulated, convinced as she was that in any argument one need only go 'deep' enough to find fundamental agreement, protested against the use of the expression 'to outwit Nature'. Could one not rather say 'to transcend Nature'?

No, Elise insisted on outwitting Nature, saying with a laugh that that was how she felt about it. Nature was too strong, too cunning; one had to filch from her the energy for one's own purposes. Especially if one was a woman. It was not for nothing that old superstitions credited Nature with being more dangerous to women than to men.

Elise had suddenly remembered her maid-servant Madeleine and the snakes. . . . She had to tell Elizabeth about the snakes, and about Madeleine's fears, and about the possible symbolic meaning of those fears, and about the special difficulties that hampered women from girlhood. Conversation seemed inexhaustible. And in the heat of discussion Elizabeth quite forgot to ask where Hector was going when Elise met him. Nor did it occur to Elise to mention that Hector had gone with Mabel to skate at Invercalder.

'Marriages that need children to hold them together are merely copulations,' she was saying instead. 'The innocent child that reconciles his father and mother is made into one of Nature's panders; he's only asking for more brothers and sisters, the little brat.'

Elise was enjoying herself wholeheartedly; she was 'having her fling'. The apparent resentment which actuated her gibes was only apparent: she felt no bitterness. And in a pause of the argument she said, without premeditation: 'You and I, Elizabeth, would make one damned fine woman between us.'

II

Mabel and Hector did not return until four o'clock. This protracted absence, whether foreseen by Nature or not, had certainly not been foreseen by them. It had come about so 'naturally', however, that Nature might well have had a hand in it.

The Dish was a small, deep lake in a fold of the hills behind the village of Invercalder, some five miles from Calderwick. It was much in use for curling, for it lay high enough to ensure ice in a cold spell and it was so still, being sheltered by larches at its open end, that its ice was like glass.

Hector's strong and supple body adjusted itself with apparent effortlessness to every kind of rapid movement; he was swift and graceful on skates as he was in the sea or on the football field. Mabel, although a practised skater in the best Invercalder style, had never attempted to dance on skates as she was now required to do, and in every sense was swept off her feet by her partner. In vain she tried to attribute her admiration of him to the fact that he looked so much more of a gentleman than anyone else on the lake; the touch of his fingers, the strength of his arm, the recklessness in his eye all excited her as no lady should ever be excited.

Naturally, therefore, when they called at the Mains of Invercalder to see her father before going home and found that brosy man just sitting down to his midday dinner, Mabel was not unwilling to join him and put off for a while the inevitable return to decorum.

'Hoots,' said Mains, 'the broth's just coming in, and there's plenty o' a'thing. Bring twa chairs inowre, Nell.'

Mains, Mabel's father, was a large, long-limbed man, with a red face, a slow voice and no regard for the proprieties. He was a widower of long standing, and a succession of housekeepers came to the farm and went again, usually with alimony. The present incumbent, Nell, as Mains informed Hector with a jerk of the thumb and a slow wink, after she had discreetly removed herself, was 'the grieve's dochter frae Nether Calder. A fine lassie. But she's like the lave o' them: I doubt she'll no' be muckle use

to me in a whilie. God kens how *you* manage to get awa' wi'
it, Mabel; twa years married an' no sign o' a bairn yet.'

'Wheesht, father,' said Mabel calmly, unfolding her
napkin. Perhaps the most admirable trait in Mabel's character was the calmness with which she accepted her father.
There was a firm affection between them. Her mother she
barely remembered: a pretty young creature, to judge from
her wedding photograph in a stiffly bunched dress with a
rose at her bosom and incredibly innocent eyes. Mabel had
created a legend of refinement around her mother's
photograph, and, supported by that, met her father's
frankness with equanimity.

The Mains of Invercalder was a prosperous, well-stocked
steading. The farm-house was a tall, white-harled building
with a gable-end at right angles to the main structure, and
an ample carriage-sweep. Behind it stretched an array of
byres, barns and stables. Mains was a noted breeder of
cattle and horses as well as a successful grower of wheat.
From so much engendering of animal life a strongly sensual
atmosphere hung over the farm, an atmosphere which the
conversation of its master did not dispel; and after a
generous dinner followed by whisky and an inspection of
Mains' young horses both Hector and Mabel were kissing-
ripe.

Mains, clapping his hat on his head, departed finally to a
remote part of the farm, leaving them alone together in the
darkness of the empty stable where the little Singer was
garaged. It was only natural for Hector to clasp Mabel
tightly in the most alarming embrace she had ever experienced in reality or in imagination. They were both moved
by a craving as immediate and apparently as simple as
hunger or thirst.

Its apparent simplicity was, of course, profoundly
treacherous. The sexual instinct has such complicated emotional effects on men and women that its masquerade as a
simple appetite ought not to be condoned. Mankind has an
inkling of this fact, and much ingenuity is applied to
shielding the young and inexperienced from the bewildering
effects of sex. It is thus of some interest to know what
particular consideration saved Mabel from the technical

surrender of her virtue. It was not her marriage vows, as one might think, nor a conviction that sexual indulgence was wicked in itself: it was the sudden recollection that she had people coming to tea and whist.

But she could not really forgive Hector. Whether she could not forgive him for his attack on her or whether, as Elise suspected when Mabel tearfully confided in her, it was his abandonment of the attack she could not forgive, it would be difficult to determine.

FIFTEEN

Elizabeth, happy and hungry after her walk, was not disturbed by Hector's absence as she might have been had she known what he was about. Her faith in the natural, the spontaneous, the unrestrained, was still bubbling up like a fountain, and the force that made it play was the force that had brought her and Hector together, and would keep them side by side, she thought, until the end of time, for it was inexhaustible. One could not measure it and draw it off for irrigation, as Elise insisted. No, no, Elise; one did not measure and calculate one's life. One did not cut and prune oneself; one simply grew. One grew and took one's chances.

That sounded reckless enough, but Elizabeth was not genuinely reckless. She thought herself daring, as she thought herself broad-minded, whereas her courage and her broad-mindedness were ideal rather than actual, the outlines of an imaginary structure not yet filled in by experience. In following what Elise called Nature Elizabeth was following what she conceived to be God, consequently in taking her chances she was taking what she conceived to be ultimate certainties. The seed has the same faith when it is in the ground and begins to grow; even if it finds itself growing in a cellar it does not abandon its faith without a struggle; and should it be tough enough in its kind, as a bush or a tree, it will break its prison by virtue of its faith. That instinctive faith governed Elizabeth, and although it cannot be called recklessness – for genuine recklessness can be found only in the human consciousness, while Elizabeth's faith is common to all plants and animals – it inspires actions that usually pass for reckless.

Elizabeth, however, being more than plant or animal, was fated to have her faith disciplined. She could not, as she imagined, escape pruning. There are people like Elise who prefer to do their own pruning; there are many who submit to pruning by others; there are a few, like Elizabeth, who do not know that pruning is inevitable and do not foresee that their eager growth will be broken off by circumstance – pruned raggedly, that is to say, instead of cleanly, by the apparent cruelty of chance instead of by design; a bruising and breaking of shoots that inflicts more pain than the quick cut of a knife; although, if the tree survives, the fruit that is formed may be none the worse.

In marrying Hector Elizabeth had entered upon a discipline that was to bruise her much as the discipline of the Church had bruised the minister. In either case a wide, formless, ecstatic feeling was being forced in an unforeseen direction by what one may call hard facts.

On this afternoon, however, Elizabeth, being not yet so hard pressed as William Murray, sat dreaming beside the fire. Her mind no longer leapt up to meet Elise's sallies; she was brooding instead on the charm of Elise herself. That a woman could be so lovable and so wrong-headed! When Dr Scrymgeour said he had no poetry in him she was sure that he belied himself, and she was equally sure that Elise belied herself in railing at Nature.

Elizabeth now felt a warm, protective tenderness for the wrong-headed creature. In spite of her years and her undeniable dignity Elise was so small, so vivacious and so impertinent! And she had run away from Calderwick with a married man. . . . And now she said that Nature was an anachronism. The besom! said Elizabeth, with a slow smile of appreciation.

Gradually she ceased to say to herself: Elise is charming; or: Elise is a besom; she merely thought: Elise is here, in Calderwick; and as she thought it her smile grew drowsy and contented. When Emily Scrymgeour came bustling in upon her she felt exactly as if she had been caught in private drug-taking.

'All alone in the dark?' said Emily. 'I've only looked in for a minute or two. . . .'

Elizabeth lit the gas, for it was dusk although only three o'clock, and disentangled her visitor's fingers from the corkscrewed strings of half-a-dozen small parcels.

'I never knew anybody like you for wee boxes and wee parcels, Emily.'

'Christmas presents – or they're going to be when I'm done with them. My dear, I've simply had to *fight* my way out of Mary Watson's. The shop's clucking like a hen-house; half the town's in there. I've had a whole half-hour of intensive scandal.'

'What about?'

'Now, just fancy anybody asking that! About the Murrays, of course. The Reverend William shouldn't have walked out of his pulpit without any formalities; he may have to walk out of it for good. Do you know what Mary Watson says? "Flying in the face of the congregation as well as in the face of God." She's got her hackles up properly. She says Ned's madness is a judgment on the minister. If he has the nerve to show his nose at the sale of work on Saturday I pity him.'

'But that's abominable!'

Elizabeth started up in anger. Calderwick and its damned prejudices! What else could the minister have done but leave the pulpit? He was too upset to be anything but natural.

'I heard that you were there,' Emily's tone was sly. 'I heard that you and your new sister bounced out of the church like two rubber balls. But Mary Watson doesn't lay the blame on *you*; she's willing to put it all on Miss Shand.'

'Aunt Janet? What's she got to do with it?'

'No, no; your sister-in-law. Isn't she a Miss Shand?'

'My dear Emily, she's a Frau Doktor. A widow.'

'A widow! Did she marry the man then?'

Elizabeth began to grow red.

'She married a famous scholar recently.'

'Aha! Now, that's what I call a clever woman. So that's why she came back, is it?'

Emily Scrymgeour, although she was also small, vivacious and impertinent, suddenly appeared so much inferior to Elise as to be insignificant. From that moment Elizabeth would have sacrificed Emily Scrymgeour, together with the whole of Calderwick, as a show-offering, if not a burnt-offering, before Elise. But what she said was: 'Oh, nonsense,

Emily; don't be silly. Elise isn't that kind of woman at all. I admire her immensely. I like her *very* much.'

O sancta simplicitas! one might have said to Elizabeth. *That isn't the way to allay one woman's jealousy of another!*

'I'm sure she's all you think her. . . . Of course she's ever so much more interesting than us old-fashioned housewives in Calderwick,' said Emily. For two pins, she was thinking, for two pins she would get Elizabeth off her high horse by just telling her—

What could she have told her? An important addition to the volume of scandal, some information about the movements of a certain Bell Duncan. . . .

It was unfortunate that William Murray had dismissed his congregation so prematurely, thus letting loose upon the High Street three-quarters of an hour before their usual time a body of experienced scouts whose eyes had raked Poggi's shop through its ever-open door.

But Elizabeth of her own accord climbed down from her high horse, and the information was not passed on. Emily did not want to forfeit any advantage she had in Elizabeth's regard. She reverted to the safer topic of the minister.

'Jim said to me yesterday that he wouldn't wonder if he had William Murray on his hands as well as the brother. He said they were both – now what was it? – "over-valued neuropaths". Isn't he a little terror, Jim?'

When she got home she appealed for approval to the little terror.

'You do think, don't you, that I was right in not telling Elizabeth what they were saying about her husband?'

'Let ilka herring hang by its ain tail,' was the doctor's comment.

'I've just had Murray at me again,' he added. 'He's trying to torment me as well as himself. . . . "Man," I said to him, "considering your profession, there's only two alternatives before you, and you'd better swallow one of them and be done with it."'

'What were the alternatives, Jim?'

'Ah, I didn't tell him that.'

'But you can tell *me*?'

'Well . . . he's bound to swallow one of the God plusses.'

'What on earth—?'

Emily's eyes danced, and she laid down her sewing.

'He's asking himself two questions about his brother's condition: first, could God have prevented it? Now, that can be answered in the positive or in the negative: God plus, you see, or God minus; second, could human agency, including himself and the poor laddie, have prevented it? Man plus, we'll say, or Man minus. But that's two gey awkward questions to put side by side, for being a minister he's bound to say "God plus" to the first and that brings him hard up against it whichever way he turns. . . . It's a fine problem. . . . But he's one of your born God plussers and there's nothing that can be done with *them*,' said the doctor.

SIXTEEN

I

Three confessions in twenty-four hours, thought Elise, looking gravely at Hector. Yesterday morning, Elizabeth; in the evening, Mabel; and now Hector.

She had looked at him with grave attention ever since he began talking; she did not appear shocked or angry, but neither did she seem to be sorry for him. Hector was a little nonplussed.

He drank off another cup of coffee. His head needed clearing. He had had a good few drinks the night before, after being turned down by Mabel. . . . He wished to God that Elise would say something.

It was absolution, of course, that Hector wanted, not a judicial summing-up; and Elise, who knew that, kept her observations to herself. She was also wondering why this spate of confessions had broken over her. Three confessions in twenty-four hours. . . . Was it a consequence of her own *Aufklärung*? Did the dispassionate, central self attract confessions?

Hector's confession had begun as a compound of excuse and self-accusation, but the excuses had tailed away and the self-accusation had mounted in enormity under the grave eyes of his listener. He had spent his whole life, she discovered, either in lifting women's skirts or in hiding behind them, and the one habit accused the other. He should confine himself to the first, she thought. Probably that was what he *would* do after leaving Calderwick.

'Well,' said Hector, making an effort, 'what do you think about it?'

Elise's hand moved towards her handbag and drew back again.

'What do you think about it yourself?'

'Calderwick's a damned rotten hole, and the sooner I'm out of it the better.'

'I think you're right in going,' said Elise quietly.

Hector snatched eagerly at this morsel of approbation.

'I knew you'd understand. Damn it all, Elise, *you* didn't regret leaving Calderwick, did you?'

'No,' said Elise, adding, with a smile: 'I mean to do it again.'

'Elizabeth,' said Hector, and stopped. That was the snag; yes, that was the snag. 'She's going too,' he said, and stopped again. Then he plucked up courage. 'John damned well *ought* to support Elizabeth until she gets a job; he's done the dirty on me often enough.'

'Don't you worry about Elizabeth,' said Elise. 'I'm going to look after her.'

This resolve, which had sprung fully armed from her head on the previous evening, still surprised Elise, as the appearance of Minerva must have surprised the Father of the Gods, and, like Minerva, it was helmed and weaponed to resist attack.

It was Mabel's confession that had evoked it, and in especial her half-angry, half-ashamed indictment of Hector as the kind of man who couldn't stick to any woman. Yes, Elise agreed; he was probably the kind of man who needed a wife to run away from. 'But it's more exciting to be married to a man like that than to John,' wailed Mabel, luxuriating in her self-sacrifice. If only Hector had been the senior partner, or had some money! She frankly called John an old stick and Elizabeth a great lump. Her one consolation was the probability, to which she returned, that Hector could never stick to one woman, not even to a pretty woman.

A 'transient', said to Elise to herself, suddenly remembering her early twenties. In Brussels she had studied the tenets of the Saint-Simonians, amongst others, and had accepted Enfantin's classification of temperaments. 'Permanents' and 'Transients' they had called them in Brussels . . . in those days when one believed in categories. . . . Elise smiled at the recollection; she had begun as a 'transient' herself, and ended up as a 'permanent'. But there was not much likelihood that Hector would ever follow her example; he was a natural 'transient'.

And Elizabeth—?

Again Elise felt compassionate towards Elizabeth's youth and ignorance. She did not know what she was heading for. Her vision of life was almost sublime in its credulity. . . . One ought to do something about it.

Mabel's sobs grew more infrequent; she wiped her eyes and sat up. 'I never want to see him again,' she said. 'He's not worth it. I want to get away from him. . . . Oh, Elise, couldn't you take me back with you when you go?'

It was at that moment that Minerva, fully armed, astonished Elise. She found that she had decided to take Elizabeth back with her. . . . And to make things fair all round she would give Hector some money.

This resolve withstood attack, and it withstood what was more disturbing, the aloofness of her isolated, central self. . . . Within its citadel that self refused to approve or disapprove. She might be doing a magnanimous thing, or she might be simply stealing the girl. In supplementing Hector's two hundred pounds, which Elizabeth had mentioned with such pride, she might be paying back part of her debt to John, or she might simply be buying Hector off. . . . The central self was not moved by such arguments as: 'Freely ye have received, freely give.' Inclusive and impartial, it refused to decide which of the two interpretations was right – foster-mother or kidnapper, generous philanthropist or payer of hush-money.

'Why, child, you would be bored to death in my house,' she said to Mabel. 'I don't keep rich young men on tap. . . . You had much better get John to take you south.'

Mabel's troubles weren't worth bothering about. They would solve themselves once Hector was gone. But that was just when Elizabeth's troubles would begin. . . .

'Don't you worry about Elizabeth. I'm going to look after her,' said Elise.

Hector was loud with surprise and gratitude.

'That was the one snag,' he said. 'That was really what I wanted to sound you about. Although, mind you, I think

I've managed to get the sack from John, and he'll probably feel responsible for Elizabeth.'

'Have you got the sack?'

'Haven't been to find out yet. I expect it's waiting for me in the office.' Hector grinned. He was beginning to feel reassured.

'Did Mabel?' He cocked an eyebrow at Elise.

'No, she hasn't told John. I don't think she will. But the next time John abuses you she won't contradict him.'

'They can blacken me as much as they like; I don't give *that* for them now.' He snapped his fingers.

As he sat there exulting in his freedom – for he had shelved all his responsibilities – Hector was a sample of genuine human recklessness. Elise recognized the quality; she had it herself. It was a readiness to throw up everything, to break all ties and disappear into the unknown, trusting neither in chance nor in Providence. . . . In her present mood she stigmatized it as cowardice, but she recognized it with a certain sympathy. The two black Shands were not unlike in some respects.

This reflection made it easier for her to open her handbag and produce the cheque. That cheque had worried her. . . . She could not afford to shower upon Hector and Elizabeth all the money she had received from John during twenty years. . . . After some hesitation she had compromised on three hundred pounds for Hector, with the reservation that he might have some more later. . . . But she wouldn't tell him that.

'It'll take perhaps a fortnight to cash,' she was explaining. 'You must not tell anyone about it, not even Elizabeth.'

Elizabeth would be off to Singapore too if she knew there was so much money. . . . Elise could not entirely stifle a sense of guilt.

Hector stared at the cheque as if it were a warrant for his death. He did not touch it. Without looking at Elise he said between his teeth: 'I'm going to-morrow. I've booked my passage. I'm going with that girl I told you about – Bell Duncan.'

Elise clasped her hands tightly.

'Does Elizabeth know?'

'No.'

Elise leaned forward a little. As she moved Hector looked up.

'Yes,' he said. 'I'm a cad.'

'Don't be melodramatic,' said Elise coolly. 'How queer!' she was commenting. 'Nature is definitely melodramatic – like this.'

'I'm leaving Calderwick to-night,' insisted Hector. 'I'm sailing third-class with Bell Duncan.'

Elise unclasped her hands and leaned back. She saw that there were beads of sweat on Hector's brow. How irrelevant it all was. . . . What did it matter whether he went now or later, with this girl or with another?

The central self was faintly bored by such peripheral matters. It was also rather bored by sex. . . . If all people were to live in the centre of themselves, Elise suddenly realized, the human race would soon die out.

With that her last resistance to the transaction vanished. Her sense of guilt had already vanished. All she had to do was to get rid of Hector as quickly as possible.

'Pick up that cheque,' she said. . . .

II

At about twelve o'clock Hector Shand came out of the Pagoda Tearooms with a cheque for three hundred pounds in his pocket and an urgent desire for a drink. The sky was darkening with clouds; the wind had shifted a point to the east; the frost was slackening, and the air was raw. There might be snow before nightfall. Hector turned up his collar and made for a bar.

When he came home for lunch he was effusive, almost maudlin; but he was sober enough to remember that he had vowed to conceal the cheque from Elizabeth, and to have her informed that he was booked for Singapore next day.

'I shall stop the cheque at once if I find that you have broken your promise,' Elise had said, shaking back the white ruffles from her wrist as she lit a cigarette.

But one couldn't just cough it up over the luncheon-table, ducky. . . . Poor Elizabeth. Poor lil Elizabeth; a no-good husband; a rotten husband. Do you still love your Uncle Hector?

Elizabeth tried to laugh him off, and when that failed, to scold him off. He had some food and sobered up a little; but his melancholy deepened as he grew sober, and after lunch he flung himself on his knees with his face in her lap.

'I'll never be any good, never.'

Stroking his hair, Elizabeth passionately denied that mistakes were irretrievable or failings ineradicable.

'You'll forget all about me when I'm gone, and serve me right,' he mumbled.

Never, oh, never! How could he even *think* that? The tears started to Elizabeth's eyes. She forced his head up and saw that his eyes were also wet.

'Here we are,' said Elizabeth. 'You and I, under this roof, and it might be any roof in the whole wide world and we should be just the same to each other. . . .'

Hector raised himself and buried his face in her breast, holding her tightly.

'Oh, Elizabeth!' he muttered. 'Oh, Elizabeth!' Had it not been for some malice, some dirty trick of Fate, he felt, how happy they might have been.

Outside, the first flakes of snow, so light and small that one could hardly call them flakes, were thickening the air and driving almost invisibly past the window.

Hector kept his face hidden.

'I've something to tell you. . . .'

'What is it?'

She could feel him draw a shuddering breath, and she laid her hand on his shoulder.

'I'm booked to go to Singapore to-morrow, and I have to leave Calderwick to-night.'

'To-night! Oh, Hector!'

SEVENTEEN

I

A vacant body – that is to say, an idle body – often denotes an active mind, and there are people who hold the reverse to be true. Of these Elizabeth was probably one, for she helped to pack Hector's effects with a fury of activity that must have been designed to prevent thought. As he rejected one thing after another which her solicitous hand had tucked into corners Hector wondered how he had ever imagined that he could slip out of the house unobserved, or, on the pretext of a mere week-end in Dundee, carry off the two large suitcases which he had prescribed for himself.

It may have been because the snow was now falling thick and fast that he tried to dissuade Elizabeth from coming with him to the station. But if he was afraid that she would embarrass him by weeping on his bosom, as some return for the tears he had shed on hers, he must have been pleased by the propriety of her demeanour on the platform, especially as Hutcheon was also present.

Elizabeth was cordial to Hutcheon. Perhaps she had been suspecting him as a Mrs Harris to Hector's Sairey Gamp; his presence, certainly, relieved her mind of something she could not quite define. His awkwardness did not surprise her; he had always been ill at ease while talking to her; she could not imagine why.

On this occasion, however, Hutcheon's awkwardness was the dissimulation of something like panic. He exchanged a quick glance with Hector and almost imperceptibly jerked his thumb towards another part of the platform. There were few people travelling by so late a train, and these were mostly huddled in the shelter of the newspaper kiosk, for the platform, though roofed, was open at both ends, so that the

station was a funnel for the blizzard. The light, too, was dim.
But Hector's keen eye descried the cause of Hutcheon's
panic, a slim young girl in a mackintosh carrying what
appeared to be a pasteboard box tied up with string. Shortly
afterwards he walked Elizabeth down to the far end of the
platform and there slipped his arm around her and gave her a
kiss. When they came back Hutcheon was holding the
pasteboard box.

Elizabeth saw it. But even if she had questioned it she
would have answered herself that Hutcheon had retrieved it
from one of the seats where he had left it lying, and that it
probably enclosed some foolish parting gift for Hector.

Becky Duncan, having given up the package and watched
it go into Hector's compartment, ran home to report that
Heck Shand's wife was actually down at the station, and that
Jim Hutcheon had 'snickit' the box out of her hand before
she could say Jack Robinson. Mrs Duncan pursed up her
mouth and said: 'Ay. Ay. Imphm. Just that. Oh ay!' –
remarks which were highly non-committal, and could scarcely have provided a foundation for the rumour that was to
run through Calderwick that very evening. Her next-door
neighbour, who was in the kitchen sharing a fly cuppie of tea
with her when young Becky returned, nodded her head more
but said even less, except when she asked: 'What was in the
boxie?'

And although Mrs Duncan gave an inventory of all she
had put in it – item, a shortbread, item, a Scotch bun, item a
pound of black buckies – a local sweetmeat – and several
fal-lals my lady had left behind her – it is not easy to see how
that list of innocent Christmas comforts sent by a mother to
her daughter could possibly justify the positive statement
retailed within two hours all over the town that Heck Shand
was off to Singapore with Bell Duncan. One can explain it
only by admitting that the Scots are a highly intelligent
people.

Jim Hutcheon, however, left alone on the dark platform
with Elizabeth when the train had thundered away, showed
little of his native intelligence. He was tongue-tied and he
looked stupid. In reality, he was both sorry to lose Hector
and envious of his luck. To him, as to Hector and to most

men of that age, any place east of Suez spelt enchantment. The Singapore of Hutcheon's imagination was constructed on the same principles, and ministered to the same needs, as Domenico Poggi's gaudy establishment in the sober High Street of Calderwick.

But he could not enlarge on it to a respectable married woman, least of all to one whose husband had set off in questionable company for that delectable land. He was a nice lad, young Hutcheon, and he was tongue-tied beside Elizabeth. With her he could not pursue those never-ending speculations that had kept him and Hector awake for hours, such as: is it true that a woman never forgets the first man she sleeps with? or: is it true that a stallion or a gelding can swim for hours if need be, while a mare must inevitably fill up with water and founder? . . . He could not even ask Mrs Shand to come and have a drink.

Elizabeth was melancholy, Hutcheon tongue-tied, and so these two children of a romantic age walked out of the station on either side of a wall of silence. At the mouth of the entry leading up to her house Elizabeth said mechanically: 'Good-night, Mr Hutcheon.' Then, with one of her abrupt and disconcerting movements, she thrust out her hand and shook his. 'You'll miss him too,' she said and, turning away, ran up the 'close' to her own front door.

If she had not run away Jim Hutcheon might have said something. As it was he went off into the snow thinking that it was really a bit thick of Hector. . . . What would she feel like when she found out?

There is an undercurrent of kindly sentiment that runs strong and full beneath many Scots characters, a sort of family feeling for mankind which is expressed by the saying: 'We're all John Tamson's bairns'; and it was perhaps a touch of that sentiment which made Hutcheon sympathetic to Elizabeth in spite of his prejudices as a man and a friend. It is a vaguely egalitarian sentiment, and it enables the Scot to handle all sorts of people as if they were his blood relations. Consequently in Scotland there is a social order of rigid severity, for if people did not hold each other off who knows what might happen? The so-called individualism of the Scots is merely an attempt on the part of every Scot to keep

every other Scot from exercising the privileges of a brother.
We should misunderstand Calderwick as completely as
Elizabeth did if we did not recognize the sentiment underlying its jealous distinctions, its acrimonious criticisms and
its awkward silences.

One must admit that a stranger would find it difficult to
recognize. He would observe that Mrs Duncan of the Fisherrow could not aspire to official acquaintance with old Mrs
Macpherson of the fish-shop in the High Street, and that Mrs
Macpherson in her turn was ignored by Mrs Mackenzie the
fish-merchant's wife, but he could not know that each of
these ladies took as much personal interest in the others'
doings as if they were sisters. Mrs Mackenzie sails past Mrs
Duncan in the street, but she has just spent an hour discuss-
ing Bell Duncan over a tea-table, and has finished up by
saying: 'I'm sorry for Mrs Duncan; she seems a decent
body.' There is nothing that concerns young Charlie Macpherson that the other two mothers do not know, and if they
were to meet on a desert island or in an English town they
would fall upon each other's necks. The acrimonious tone of
Mary Watson's voice, which offends the outsider, is exactly
what she employs in speaking to her sister Ann, and John
Shand treats his brother Hector as he would treat any of his
men. The whole of Calderwick is bound together by invisible
links of sympathy. . . . It is not everyone who can live
without embarrassment in a Scots community.

So Elizabeth, shutting her front door behind her, thought
herself alone in her castle, but if she was alone anywhere it
was in a castle in Spain. From kitchen to kitchen shawled
wives were running with the news that Heck Shand had gone
off by the six-o'clock train on his way to Singapore with Bell
Duncan, and one after the other they said: 'Isn't it terrible
for his wife, poor lassie?' By eight o'clock in Elizabeth's own
kitchen Mary Ann Lamond was listening to her mother, who
had arrived out of breath and covered with snow, saying:
'They tell me . . .'

'I dinna believe it!' cried Mary Ann. 'And you can tell
them that from me. The mistress hersel' was down at the
station. "It's very sudden, Mary Ann," she says, says she,
"but we've had it in mind a long time," she says.'

'Aweel,' returned her mother, 'I had it from Mrs Ritchie, and she had it from Mrs Beattie, and she had it from Mrs Kinnear, and she had it from Mrs Pert, that bides next door to the Duncans. And you ken yoursel' that Bell and him were seen thegither on the Sunday.'

No messenger ever proved his credentials more thoroughly. Mary Ann laid her head down on the kitchen table and blubbered.

She assumed at once, as everybody did, that her mistress was betrayed, and with the heroic spirit of a Mrs Partington keeping the Atlantic at bay with a mop she set herself to isolate Elizabeth from the rumour.

'You'll no' be going out today?' she said next morning, setting down the breakfast teapot. 'A body canna see an inch in front of their nose, the snow's that thick. Just you bide by the fire, and if there's anything you want tell me and I'll run out for it.'

Elizabeth propped up a book against the milk-jug. It was like a return to student days, she thought, and there was something pleasant in being on one's own again. . . . She had fifty pounds, more money than she had ever possessed at once. . . . There were three vacancies in English schools that she had already applied for. . . . And Hector would make a fortune for both of them. . . .

Her eyes suddenly overflowed. But though one or two tears rolled down her cheeks and her mouth twitched a little Elizabeth went on reading. She had 'had her cry out' during the night and was determined to be sensible. It was only her silly eyes that wept a little now and then because Hector had not let her go with him to Singapore.

Silly fool, said Elizabeth in a rough voice, and turned another page. She had nothing to cry about and plenty to do. She must interview John – that would be easy – and Aunt Janet – that would be difficult. In the three or four weeks remaining to her she must settle up the house and come to some arrangement with Aunt Janet about the furniture. Worst of all, she must explain the whole affair to her parents, who had never approved her marriage to Hector because he was not, as they said, a godly man.

It was a strange thing that Elizabeth, who was willing to

explain herself by the hour to Elise, had always shrunk with impatient irritation from explaining herself for even five minutes to her father and mother. She scowled a little as she thought of it.

The snow was indeed as thick as Mary Ann had said, and it was driving before gusts that sounded eerie in their violence. As she looked out of the window Elizabeth felt isolated from the whole world, secluded behind thick veils of snow. But it was not unpleasant. . . . She remembered all at once that this was a Friday, a market day, and that John would be up in the farmers' mart. She could not go there looking for him. . . . Put it off, said a voice, put it all off, keep today for yourself.

When she was a small girl it had often amazed her parents that Elizabeth could shut herself off with a book so completely that even shouting failed to arouse her attention. She sat down now by the fire with *Pride and Prejudice*, and in ten minutes was utterly absorbed.

II

Meanwhile rumour had begun to percolate from kitchens to drawing-rooms, and the news that Hector had gone off arrived at number seven Balfour Terrace together with the day's bread. Mrs John Shand was both dismayed and flattered when she heard it: dismayed because Hector had gone off with such a common girl and flattered because she thought he had done it for her sake. It was just the kind of thing that would happen in one of her favourite stories, when the villain with the heart of gold sacrifices himself to save the heroine's honour. . . .

Frau Doktor Mütze was less pleased.

'It is all over the town already?' she asked, with some tartness. 'This might be the African jungle, the way news travels.'

Yet she was relieved. She could now be open and aboveboard with Elizabeth. She could now say, in effect: Hector is a worthless creature; forget him, and come with me. Salutary medicine for Elizabeth – but bitter, bitter as death, Elise suddenly realized, remembering all that Elizabeth had said to her. . . . Elizabeth's feelings struck their roots deep; they were no hardy annuals like Mabel's. . . .

Elise looked at the falling snow, then went quietly upstairs and put on stout shoes and a thick travelling cloak. The sooner the better, she said to herself, feeling as if she ought to take a small black bag with her, like a physician.

She arrived at Elizabeth's door fifteen minutes after Emily Scrymgeour. Mary Ann, barring the door with a brawny arm and a firm statement that Mrs Shand was not at home to anybody, had been no match for the agile little wife of the doctor. She jinked round me as if I was a lamp-post, thought the discomfited guardian, sitting in the kitchen and stretching her ears to listen if the mistress was greeting. But when the door-bell rang again she made no effort to keep out the newcomer. This visitor was one of 'the family'; and although Mary Ann, a true daughter of Calderwick, had never heard the phrase 'it's not my place to do so-and-so' she knew that it would be exceeding her powers to turn away 'the family'.

The mistress was not greeting; she was even smiling. More and more disconcerted, Mary Ann closed the drawing-room door and retired to her kitchen in bewilderment.

But Elizabeth too was bewildered. Emily's commiseration was so very excessive. Emily was so incredulous when she was told that Hector's departure was a planned affair, approved and abetted by Elizabeth. 'I took him to the station myself,' Elizabeth was saying when Elise appeared. She was beginning to feel impatient; why should Emily Scrymgeour insist on her sitting in sackcloth and ashes, so to speak? She hailed Elise with joy and proudly presented her to Mrs Scrymgeour. 'My next-door neighbour, who is almost angry with me because I'm not in tears. . . . I suppose you've heard too that Hector went away last night? When I told you about it on Wednesday I didn't expect him to go *quite* so soon.'

Something in Elise's cool glance might have offended Emily, or perhaps she was only jealous because she had not enjoyed Elizabeth's confidence while the other had. At any rate she looked as sharp and dangerous as her favourite weapon, a needle.

'Well, thank goodness there are some things *I'm* too old-fashioned to countenance,' she said, looking first at Elise and then at Elizabeth.

Elizabeth straightened herself.

'What do you mean, Emily?'

Elise turned her back and drummed on the window-pane. Emily Scrymgeour's short nervous fingers worked over each other as if they itched.

'You know very well what I mean. I mean that I don't approve of married men running off with girls. And if their *wives* encourage them to do it I say it's a disgrace to womanhood. You should be ashamed of yourself, Elizabeth Shand.'

Elizabeth bounded from her seat with a dark flush on her brow and set herself between Emily and the door.

'You don't get out of this room until you take that back,' she cried. 'What do you mean by your vile insinuations? What the hell do you mean?'

Elise turned round:

'Let her go, Elizabeth. Let her go, I tell you. There's more behind this than you imagine.'

She walked forward slowly until she stood before Emily Scrymgeour, her face grave and quiet.

'I think you'd better go,' she said. 'Please.'

Then she continued towards the door and, throwing it open, stood waiting.

Emily Scrymgeour went.

Elise shut the door and looked at Elizabeth.

'Hector,' she began. Then her compassion for Elizabeth obscured her judgment.

'There's a rumour in Calderwick that Hector has gone to Singapore with a girl called Bell Duncan,' she said.

'But that's absurd,' returned Elizabeth, in the same quiet toner. 'That's just the kind of thing they *would* invent in Calderwick.'

'I think there's no doubt that the girl is on the same boat.'

'How do you know?'

Elizabeth's tone was still quiet, but she began to shiver and caught at a chair.

Elise said nothing.

'Elise! For God's sake, tell me the truth! I must know exactly.'

'Her mother says so.'

'That's no evidence,' said Elizabeth, her teeth chattering. 'That's no evidence at all. I must get at the truth of this. I must get at the t-truth. Can't you *see*, Elise, I must get at the truth. She may have followed him. I know all about her. She may have gone after him deliberately. Even if she is on the boat I don't believe Hector knew. . . .'

Elise sighed, and said what she had been trying to escape saying:

'He did know, for he told me yesterday morning that he was going with her.'

'He – he told you?'

'Yes.'

'And you d-didn't tell me?'

'No.'

'My God, why not? I could have stopped him. Why not? Why didn't you tell me? I can't help my teeth chattering, Elise, but I'm quite calm: I'm not going to make a fool of myself—'

With that Elizabeth pitched in a dead faint on the floor.

EIGHTEEN

A mere fall of snow could not keep Sarah Murray indoors, for the sale of work was to be opened next day and she had to spend the morning and afternoon in the mission hall of St James's supervising the reception and arrangement of goods. It needed someone in authority to keep the stallholders from poaching each other's show pieces. Sarah had tried to organize the sale in what she called 'a business-like manner', but although she had put up labels identifying Mrs Gove's stall as Fancywork and Mrs Mackenzie's as Woollens she knew that, left to themselves, these ladies would soon make the labels look silly. The consciousness of being the supreme judiciary, the manse delegate, gave Sarah an added firmness and impartiality; she was a good administrator and she enjoyed her day's hard work.

When she came back towards five o'clock she found the minister's lunch still untasted on its tray.

'Has he never stirred, Teenie?'

'No, Miss Murray.'

Sarah clicked her tongue on the roof of her mouth. 'He should never have gone out there yesterday,' she said. 'But he wouldna be advised.'

All day William Murray had sat at his desk with his head bowed on his hands. The minutes slipped past him irrevocably; one by one they slipped away, and, once gone, he knew that they were irretrievable. Outside, the snowflakes slipped past the window, and the minutes were light and unnoticeable in their passage like the snowflakes, but each one of them was a doom, and the sum of them was a man's destiny. That was the mystery. Time, so fleeting that one could never arrest it, was weighted with eternal consequences.

Last Sunday he had committed Ned to the asylum, and, whatever happened, that Sunday could never return, that deed could never be undone. Lord, forgive me, he cried, for I knew not what I did!

Thursday was visiting day at the asylum, and he had insisted upon seeing his brother. If Ned had received him with curses he could have borne it, but with a young beard on his thin face, weeping and wistful, he had plucked at his sleeve and begged to be taken home. 'Out of the question,' said Dr Eliot firmly; 'quite out of the question.'. . . What is done can never be undone. One by one the irrevocable minutes pass. . . .

And what was to keep a man from making a false step? How could he know if it was God or the Devil that prompted him? How discriminate between righteous anger, for instance, and unrighteous? There was no answer to that, save the conviction, now pressing heavily upon the minister, that both kinds of anger were of the Devil: a conviction for which his own feelings were the last authority. Since allowing anger to invade him under the pretext of driving out evil he had known the calm of determination but not the peace of holiness. . . . And yet God was a God of wrath as well as a God of love.

The minister agonized with himself until, weary and famished, he sat in a kind of stupor, holding his heavy head in his hands. Once or twice he muttered: 'The Lord's will be done.' He desired to sleep and to forget.

Sarah went into the study and touched him on the shoulder. He did not move. She shook him gently.

'Come to your tea, Willie.'

It was many long years since she had called him that. The minister stared at her and then pushed his hair back confusedly.

'I think I've been alseep,' he said.

He staggered as he got up, for his legs were stiff. How long had he been sitting there? And what strange dream had he fallen into? A yellow river, as broad as the eye could compass; turbulent water yellow with fine mud; and he careering down the middle of the stream on something resembling a large wooden tea-tray, perfectly round, with a hollow in the middle on which he had to balance himself. . . . One false step, and he knew he would be lost in one of the dimpling whirlpools around him. And all he had to steady himself by was a straight short pole. . . . The shape of his curious vessel made it impossible to steer in any direction; he had to follow the current as best he could. He had an idea that the river was in China, but that, at the same time, it was the river of the will of God. . . .

He had never been in China, but he was certain, in that moment, that the yellow river he had seen was a real river.

He washed and brushed before he sat down to the tea-table, and he looked almost cheerful as he took his cup from Sarah. The dream was a kind of answer. . . . There was nothing to be done but resign himself, as many greater than he had done, to the will of God. An Oriental philosophy, no doubt.

William Murray set his cup on the saucer and stared at Sarah.

'I've had such a queer dream,' he said, 'about China and a tea-tray—'

'You would be dreaming about your tea,' said Sarah, 'and no wonder.'

The minister smiled, shook his head, and said nothing more. When he was finished with the meal he asked for his outdoor shoes.

'Where are you going in all this snow?'

'This is my night for visiting old Johnny Pert.'

'Johnny Pert's not dying yet, and he can do without you to-night. You're not fit to go outside the door.'

'I must do my duty by the folk in my charge,' said William in a mild voice, 'so long as I'm their minister, Sarah. It wouldn't be kind to disappoint the old man.'

'Kind!' Sarah exploded. There were folk one should be kind to, and there were folk one shouldn't be kind to, for they just took advantage, like that Johnny Pert, and, indeed, all the Perts, who hung on to the minister merely for Church coal and Church poor-box funds, and were always making a poor mouth about themselves—

'And who is to judge them, Sarah? Not I, not I. . . . I can't even guide myself, far less others.'

'And you'll not let yourself be guided,' snapped Sarah.

'I'm learning,' said the minister, putting on his coat.

The blast whirled right into his face when he opened the door; it was blowing straight in off the sea with such a drive of snow that one could hardly see the next lamp-post in the street. The minister bent his head forward and plodded into the heart of it. Old Johnny Pert lived in one of the tenements in the Fisherrow, the nearest approach to a slum that Calderwick could show. It lay round the corner from the harbour; one had to go straight down Dock Street and then bear to the right. . . .

The flurry of snow and wind made the town strange and ghostly; the force of the elements reminded the minister of the torrent force in the yellow water of his dream; but this time he was striving against the current, not carried away by it. When one had an objective one could guide oneself. What was God's objective? To what strange purpose did He hurry His children along the stream of Time? The minister did not know. . . . All he could say with certainty to his congregation was that one should not wreck one's neighbours in the river. . . . Little children, love one another. . . . And even that had not availed with Ned.

He braced himself against the stronger gale that shrieked from the estuary and met him with full force in Dock Street. The darkness of the river-mouth, like an encroaching hand, here seized upon the town, blotting out the whirling battalions of snowflakes. Now that he could no longer see them the minister felt more acutely how the snowflakes pelted into his eyes, and he screwed his face up till his eyelashes met. He wished he had taken a walking-stick. He could have used it, like the pole in his dream, to keep his course even. A queer, queer dream. . . . Hurried on, irresistibly, on the tide of God's will to what unknown sea? . . . The Pacific, of course, thought the minister, almost smiling in the darkness. The sea of God's peace. . . . He stumbled, staggered, and then stumbled again.

NINETEEN

The postman left a flat basket of snowdrops that Mabel had ordered from Dundee for her stall at the sale of work.

'Aren't they lovely!' she said. 'I wonder where they come from.'

The snowdrops were tied in tight little bunches, with a ring of dark ivy leaves around each boss of flower-heads. Elise bent over the basket and picked out four bunches.

'I'll buy these from you now.'

'Oh, take as many as you like, Elise; never mind the money, it's only for Foreign Missions or something. . . . There's the telephone!'

Mabel's voice sharpened as if in fear:

'What, John?' she said. 'What? What? Oh, my God!'

She turned to Elise.

'John says Mr Murray's been found drowned in the dock. They think he missed his way in the storm last night.'

Two startled faces looked at each other.

'Poor devil,' said Elise.

'There won't be any sale of work,' said Mabel. Her lip began to tremble. She sat down and cried into her handkerchief.

'I'm – I'm frightened,' she sobbed. . . . 'I hate anybody I know to die. It makes me so frightened.'

'Poor, poor devil,' said Elise, thinking of the young minister's thin, hungry look. She walked to the window and looked at the round blobs of snow capping the evergreens. The hungry sheep look up and are not fed, she said to herself.

Mabel mopped her wet cheeks. 'I don't see why people need to die before they're old. It's – it's so *mean*.'

So meaningless, thought Elise, still looking out of the window. Even if one has found a central self, to have it blown out like a candle in the dark. Not even burned down to the butt.

'What will poor Sarah Murray do?' said Mabel. 'She won't have a penny.'

Elise made a little impatient movement. Life was too short for that kind of thing. Elizabeth – yes; Sarah Murray – no. She didn't want to hear about Sarah Murray's sorrows.

'She hasn't anybody in the world but her brother Ned, and he's in the asylum.'

Mabel's voice was awe-stricken.

Elise turned abruptly and picked up her snowdrops: 'I'm going to see Elizabeth.'

Elizabeth – yes, because that's my caprice, she thought, walking rapidly up the street. And Sarah Murray – no; because that's my caprice too. . . . I decline to pad my actions out with reasons. I can find myself a dozen reasons on either side, and I decline to do so. . . . That's what it has come down to. It's more honourable to strip one's actions bare, to say: 'Yes, I want to do that; no, I don't want to do the other, and any motives I might allege for either action are probably spurious, so I shall leave them out.'

'How is your mistress, Mary Ann?'

'She's just aye sitting on the sofa, mem. She'll no' gang to her bed. She's had a cuppie o' tea, but she'll no' eat a bite.'

Elizabeth was sitting staring at the floor with her hands clasped between her knees. When Elise came in she looked up, and pressed her finger-nails into her knuckles: but she sat there dry-eyed and mute, as she had done the day before; the only difference was that she was more white-faced.

It's time to shock her out of it, thought Elise.

'William Murray was found drowned this morning,' she said quietly, standing before Elizabeth with the snowdrops in her hand. 'In the dock.'

A long and difficult tremor shook Elizabeth; she looked desperately at Elise and then flung herself round with her face to the wall and sobbed.

Elise sat down and caressed her.

'That's better,' she said. 'That's better. Cry, my dear; cry.'

'Oh – oh,' moaned Elizabeth.

Elise began to stroke her gently, rhythmically; and after some time the sobs ceased to be vehement. Elizabeth caught Elise's hand and pressed it to her face without lifting her head from the sofa-cushion.

'You're so good to me,' she muttered. 'And I was a brute to you yesterday. I couldn't help it, Elise; I – I couldn't help it.'

'You *were* rather a brute. I felt quite worn out by the time I got home.'

'But what's the use? I can't feel that there's any use in anything. I might as well be dead. . . . The minister is in luck,' whispered Elizabeth. She began to cry again. 'Is he dead? Is he dead?'

'He missed his way in the storm last night and fell into the dock.'

'That too,' muttered Elizabeth. 'Why not? Why not?'

'Why not what?'

'I fainted yesterday,' said Elizabeth, her face still turned to the wall. 'I never fainted before. I felt a queer something rising up, and I said – *I* – that I wouldn't make a fool of myself, and my own body, that I have lived in all my life, that I have trusted as myself, let me down. . . . I loved Hector. I trusted him as myself, and he let me down. . . . I believed that there was a God somewhere, and that He was in the stars and in myself and in Hector's love for me' – she began to sob again – 'and He has let me down; and if the sea in Calderwick harbour, in his own town, can deceive and drown William Murray, why not? Why not?'

In a minute or two she began again, in the same harsh, quick voice: 'I've been sitting here since yesterday, seeing it all, over all the world. Everything we trust in lets us down. . . . People build their houses on a green hillside, and laugh in the sun and praise God, and the hillside opens between the hearthstone and the door and swallows them up. Why not? . . . The ox shelters under a thick, tall tree that it has known in the home field since it was a calf, and the lightning splits the tree and the ox together. Why not? . . . I've seen all that – and worse – since yesterday, sitting here. Everything dies, everything *can* die, and why should William Murray not be drowned?'

'Amen,' said Elise. 'You wouldn't listen to me yesterday, but you must listen to me now. Who are you that you should *not* be let down, as you call it, by the chances and accidents of life? Who are you that you should *not* be let down by your feelings and your blood and your nerves and your reasoning, like any other human being? The marvel is not that we are fallible and foolish, but that we have the wit to see it and to go on in spite of it. We are burdened with error and prejudice, like a rich field covered with stones, and the marvel is not that we stub our toes against the stones, but that we have sense enough to clear them away – even if we clear only the little patch that is ourselves. And even then, I have realized, we clear it not only for ourselves, but for the toes of other people who come after us. . . . I don't know whether there is a God or not, but I do know that there is humanity, that there is a rich field, and that there are tons of stones to be cleared away. . . . And I think,' concluded Elise, 'that you should regard Hector as something that had to be cleared out of your patch. Of course you loved him; of course he loved you; but it was only nature, it wasn't anything more. . . . You fell in love with his body and pretended to love his mind, or his spirit, or whatever you call it. On the whole, that's better than falling in love with a man's mind and pretending to love his body. . . . I did that once. . . . Some day I'll tell you the story of Fritz. . . . But you can't expect, brought up as you have been, to find that the first man who attracts you is your mate for life. You were too hungry when you met him, that was all. That's nothing to be ashamed of. . . . And I think that you are ashamed to admit to yourself that you hung your dreams round the neck of a man who didn't want them.'

'No!' cried Elizabeth, her face still buried in the pillow. 'That's not it,' she said, lifting herself a little. 'I failed him and myself too. I let myself despise him and scorn him. . . . Something in me hit out at him, and I let it. And then I knew that I had done wrong, but it was too late. . . .'

'Well, that may happen to anybody,' said Elise coolly. 'You have learned something. You can't live with a man you don't respect.'

'Oh, Elise—'

Elizabeth sat up and looked at her friend.

'That's the worst of it . . . I can. Even though I *know* he's gone off with – that girl – and she had him before I did – my arms are aching for him now.'

She burst into tears again, but this time, thought Elise, they were healing tears.

She rose and took off her hat and cloak.

'I'm going to put these snowdrops in water,' she said.

TWENTY

Fifteen days later an express train from Paris to Ventimiglia carried two women passengers travelling together. At first glance they were remarkably unlike: the elder and smaller of the two was elegant and assured, with a cool eye and a humorous mouth; the younger was a tall, awkward, shy creature who shrank into herself when she thought anyone looked at her. But the face was strong, thought a fellow-passenger as he looked again, although of an uncompromising gravity – only a woman so young could look so serious – and in time would be better worth modelling than the other. A good face for a sculptor in another few years. . . . Were they Russians? he wondered, and was extremely surprised to hear them exchange a remark in English.

They did not exchange many remarks, for they were alike in being silent. Elise was contrasting her present journey through France with her last, and her infrequent glances at Elizabeth contained surprise as well as satisfaction. Here she was, returning with a brand-new daughter, or sister, or wife, or whatever it was, having carried her off like a second Lochinvar. She had not anticipated that when she went up to Calderwick. . . .

At least I kept my head to some extent, thought Elise; I actually left Mabel and Sarah Murray behind!

She mused over the difference betwen Calderwick as she had found it and as she had left it. Was it entirely a subjective difference, a measure of the difference in herself? In Calderwick she had knitted together the two halves of her life, and the town as well as herself appeared to have a new harmony, a new humanity; but was it not essentially the same that it had always been? . . . Perhaps. . . . She remembered Mary

Watson's face on the day of William Murray's funeral. . . .
Even when Elise first ran away from Calderwick Mary
Watson had been a grim character. But on William Murray's
funeral day the tears lay on her cheek as she said, humbly: 'I
think we all trauchle ourselves and other people ower
muckle.'

Perhaps the difference was not merely subjective. . . .
Life was unpredictable and full of surprising changes.

Had Aunt Janet changed? Elise recalled how she had last
seen her aunt straying aimlessly around the house, picking
up trifling articles which she carried absently from one room
to another and hid behind cushions. Had she not always tried
to hide things behind cushions? . . . People said that Hector's last escapade had 'broken' her; but was she really
changed?

Mabel had been shaken up, but would go on much the
same. John too. He was sound and sweet at the core, thought
Elise; she would not have him change. . . . That hard-faced
spinster, Sarah Murray, seemed to have a grudge against
him, even although he had installed her as Aunt Janet's
companion, and John bore it with amazing patience. . . .

Well, *I* have changed, thought Elise, giving Elizabeth
another quizzical glance. Perhaps it was only tart, unripe
characters that changed as they mellowed. I have a lot of
mellowing to do yet, she decided, with a sudden chuckle.

What was to happen next she simply did not know. When
she rediscovered Lizzie Shand she had thought that a final
revelation, but almost immediately she had gone on to
discover Calderwick, and then she had found her central,
dispassionate, impregnable self, and then she had found that
the presumably final impregnable self tended to become a
little inhuman, and that if one listened exclusively to its voice
one remained perched on a high fence without any incentive
to descend on either side of it. . . . But she had descended,
flouting the impartial self, and somewhat petulantly had
declared that in the end one acted on caprice, on naked and
unaccountable caprice, and that it was dishonest to pretend
otherwise . . . and, presto! within half-an-hour she had
burst into surprising eloquence about stones that had to be
cleared away from the toes of future generations. . . . And

she meant it too. There was something in it. She had not thought it out yet, but she felt it might be her *Gebiet* to clear away stones of prejudice and superstition so that other girls might grow up in a more kindly soil. And Elizabeth would help her . . . until she fell in love with somebody the exact antithesis of Hector. . . . But that might take years.

Elise looked out of the window. Her eye fell full on a square white house with a roof of thick tiles, thick and curved, as if they were halved flowerpots, fitting loosely one upon the other, tiles that had once been red and were now bleached in parts to a calcareous whiteness, thick, casual-looking, familiar tiles. . . .

'Elizabeth!' she said, leaning forward. 'This is the Midi!'

'What are those twisted little stumpy dwarf trees?' said Elizabeth, pointing to them.

'Vines,' replied Elise, with great content.

Vines! thought Elizabeth. She had never imagined that vines looked like that. . . . She had imagined something more lush . . . not this dry, bright landscape with those gnarled little trees, that looked as if they had been maimed and tortured. . . . Crippled, like herself.

'This is the South,' said Elise, smiling.

A good many miles nearer to Hector. . . . Elizabeth turned her face aside again; her mouth trembled, and her eyes overflowed.

A step paused at the door of the compartment, and a fresh, jolly voice cried: 'Jesus, Maria, Joseph! Du, Elise?'

'Ilya!' said Elise. 'What are *you* doing here?'

Ilya came in, with loud vociferations of pleasure. She had curly yellow hair, Elizabeth saw, and bright little blue eyes, twinkling above powder and rouge. . . .

'Does she understand German?' asked Ilya, indicating Elizabeth. 'No? Well, my dear Elise, you have run away with her, you say? Have you then given up men?'

With every word Madame Mütze felt Calderwick receding farther and farther, for Ilya's conversation travelled even faster than the train. . . .

CANONGATE CLASSICS
A NEW PERSPECTIVE FOR
SCOTTISH LITERATURE